VALTERIAN

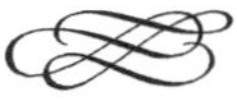

KAYDRIE TOLBERT

❀ Created with Vellum

To Nash, for inspiring me to be the best version of myself and showing me the power and joy of being a mother. I love you, my darling boy.

CHAPTER 1

$\mathcal{I}$ was facing Killian once again. His mischievous, inexorable smile stirred the fear that was prominent in my gut. He had an invasive power over me that made me feel utterly hopeless. Despite my best efforts, he knew the effect he had on me, and it only fueled his cruelty. He stripped away any happiness I ever felt, finding pure pleasure in my misery.

We were on the battlefield once again. The rain pounded the ground in anger, pelting the bodies that surrounded us. Aleron was helpless, barely able to hold his body weight as he kneeled in surrender to his brother. I looked down at my trembling hands, stained in my own blood. As I pleaded with Killian, I had never felt such disgust and resentment for anyone before. I still felt myself shiver as he spoke, the echo and familiarity of Killian's voice to Aleron's making my head spin as it always did. It abused Aleron's innocence, being associated with such a despicable, sadistic person, and my heart felt conflicted each time.

I could hardly hear the panic in my voice as Killian reached for the hilt of his sword, his hesitation unwavering despite my desperate attempts of negotiation and understanding. Before I could scream the cries I could feel ready to explode, a violent shaking overcame me.

"Allene! Allene! Ugh, please wake up Allene!"

I slowly managed to lift my heavy eyelids, surprised to no longer be confronted with the bone-chilling face of Killian but rather a bewildered Risa.

Instant relief overcame her as she realized her attempt to wake me had succeeded. *If only I could feel the same ease.* My body still trembled, my stomach nauseated as she reached an arm underneath my shoulders, pulling me up to her embrace. My cries had escaped my lips and filled my quiet room. Risa was patient as she tried to soothe me. The warmth that radiated from her quickly made the sobbing subside, and unflattering sniffles took their place. *It was just a dream Allene, it wasn't real.*

I felt Risa's hand smooth back a piece of my sticky, tear-soaked hair, pulling it from my burning cheek, her gesture comforting.

"It happened again, didn't it?" Risa asked, the sadness in her voice weighing heavily in the air. I nodded in reply, then let my head hang low to my chest — my neck unwilling to bear the strain of my emotions.

"Allene, you have hardly slept since your return. Your body isn't going to be able to keep up much longer if you don't get proper rest." She stated the obvious but provided no solution to fix it.

"I will get plenty of rest once this is all sorted out," I insisted, my stubbornness taking over the need for sleep.

"You can't keep doing this. I know you feel a responsibility to make things right, but there is only so much you can do at the moment. You have done everything you can; that needs to be enough," Risa pleaded with me.

"It's not enough; nothing has changed," I hissed impatiently. "It has been weeks, and we have made no progress."

The weight of reality made me *almost* wish I was dreaming again. Still, Killian's face crept into my memory, reminding me that reality was only slightly better.

Hassan, Aleron, and I had arrived back in Valteria five weeks ago. The journey home was difficult, but it was incredibly short-lived. Search parties had been ongoing since my capture on the battlefield. We had only been walking for half a day when a soldier had stumbled upon us.

I shuddered at the reminder of the awkward silence that we exchanged on our way back to Valteria, hardly any words being passed between the three of us. To add to the bleak atmosphere, the soldier had informed us of the heavy loss we suffered in the battle. Fortunately, the Praserian's retreated soon after my capture. However, it still left an astounding number of injured soldiers and many more among the dead.

None of us could quite find the words to address what

had happened, and handling anything else before that seemed inappropriate. Aleron was dispirited, Hassan was cumbersome, and I was indignant. We were dealing with a flurry of emotions and all for different reasons. I had never felt so overwhelmed. *So much death, so many innocent people fighting our battles — and for what grand purpose?* It wasn't justified, it wasn't necessary, and worst of all, I stood by and watched it unfold, unable to stop it. My worst fear was maybe I could have done something different to avoid all of it. If I had escaped Praseria when I had the chance, how different could have things been? If I hadn't let my emotions for Aleron take precedence over my duty to Valteria, what would have changed? There wouldn't be mothers and fathers without their sons and widows grieving their husbands or children praying for their father to return. I knew how that felt. I wouldn't wish it upon anyone, especially my own people.

The reality of what had happened, knowing it was likely my decisions that had catapulted the ill-will between our two kingdoms, plagued me deeply. I only felt some relief from the guilt if I tortured myself for it.

Upon our arrival, Aleron was quickly ushered into the palace, my mother trying to avoid a scene. I wasn't sure what I thought would happen once we got to Valteria. Still, I definitely wasn't planning on the immediate separation from Aleron. My mother was still unwilling to indulge in our relationship. She wanted time to know how to best approach the *"unfortunate"* situation.

I immediately regretted the lack of communication I

could have had with Aleron earlier. I mulled over all the opportunities I had missed to explain who I was and, to be honest. I regretted how long I had waited to tell him the truth and my ridiculous assumption that waiting until the last possible moment would somehow still turn out okay. *How different would our time have been if I had told him? Would it have been better or worse? Would he still be in Praseria right now if I had told him my identity sooner? Would the relationships of our families still remain intact if we had had more time?* The unknown of it all ate me away inside. Aleron was now locked away in a room on the bottom floor, far from my reach, and I could hardly bear not knowing how he was coping. If I felt this awful, I could only imagine how the situation was affecting him.

I had been burdened with nightmares every night since my return, a tiny shred of the self-torture I subconsciously was inflicting upon myself. Killian was the dreadful focus of each one, his primal sneer perpetually haunting me. The amount of sleep I managed to receive was close to none. The lack of rest had made me consistently woozy and irritable. I tried drinking tea before bed, stretching, exerting all my energy, and many other useless tactics to exhaust me into a submission of sleep. I held out hope that the nightmares would miraculously disappear. As a last resort, I asked Risa to stay with me, hoping her cheery presence would help — none of the attempted remedies seemed to be effective.

Up to this time, I had missed my father dearly, but the *need* for him had never felt so pressing. It hurt me knowing he couldn't help me in the most challenging situation I had been faced with. I knew he would be on my side, I knew he would've found a solution, and I knew he could've made it better. *What I wouldn't give for a chance to speak with him, even just for a moment.*

My mother had refused to see me until she felt she could be unbiased in her decision going forward. Damien, along with the other soldiers, were working overtime, trying to prepare for whatever Praseria and their new prince, Killian, may send our way. Hassan had requested to go home for a little while. His mother and sister had been worried about him, considering the news of him being captured as well. With Hassan gone, it left me with only Risa to turn to.

Risa pulled back my attention, caressing my forehead. "Allene, it pains me to see you this way. I have never seen you like this. . . you are even more upset than —," she hesitated, "than when father passed."

We were silent. My lips creased together, my teeth bit my cheek as I suppressed the tears that wanted to burst inside me for the hundredth time since our return. Risa was soft as she spoke again. "There must be something I can do."

Risa's voice was full of defeat. My heart sank as I noticed the dark circles that surrounded Risa's eyes from the sleepless nights she had willingly endured with me. I felt guilty for dragging her through the same hopeless feelings I had been battling. She didn't deserve it — I deserved it, I deserved to feel helpless and hollow, but she didn't deserve it, and I wanted her to feel her efforts were worthwhile.

"Risa, I appreciate your unwavering determination to see that I get better, but I would be lying if I said I had the slightest idea of anything you could do." I felt my shoulders shrug, too tired to pretend for anyone's sake, even Risa's.

Risa pulled together her abnormal amount of positivity with one final effort to make me happy. "I'm sure mother will come to a decision soon, and you will be able to speak with Aleron. Until then, Hassan returns to the castle tomorrow. Maybe he can offer some insight into what you are feeling," she suggested, hoping the news would lift my spirits.

I hadn't told Risa about the recent development of complicated feelings between Hassan and me; there was already too much going on. I hadn't shown it, but I was secretly grateful he had decided to go home. It had spared me from an awkward conversation and feelings I wasn't ready to address. I knew Risa was coming from an innocent place, so I faked an excited smile, wanting her to feel somewhat triumphant.

"You might be right, Risa." I felt my cheeks hurt from the lack of energy that I somehow forced into my grin.

I pulled my legs to my chest, replaying the dream in my mind again to distract my thoughts from Hassan. I remained quiet, and Risa remained patient. Slowly, I noticed Risa's cheer fading away as her eyelashes fluttered up and down from her need to sleep. I watched her head gently touch her shoulder — her eyes immediately becoming alert from the sudden touch.

"Why don't you go to your room for the rest of the night?" I encouraged her — the tiredness in her face adding to my worry and guilt.

Her eyes brightened for a moment. "If you really wish for me to leave, I will go," she tried to say subtly, but she couldn't conceal how appealing the offer was to sleep in her own bed. Her exhaustion must've been equal to mine, given how submissive she was toward the suggestion.

"I mean it, Risa, go." I nudged her shoulder, pushing her off my bed.

Risa sighed, relieved to finally be getting some sleep. "Get some rest and sleep in if you can, Allene. Sweet dreams." Risa had squeezed my hand as she gracefully stood from my bed and left the room.

I tossed and turned; the pressure of how late it was, the knowledge that the sun would be up too soon, made the challenge of sleep seem even more impossible. I twisted in the direction of my window, rolling onto my side, the tranquil stars mocking me, tormenting me, as they found solace among the surrounding darkness of the night. They took comfort in it, found peace in its abyss, and I never imagined I would ever envy the stars. At that moment, I wanted nothing more than to be an inanimate flame in the shadows of the sky.

I stopped counting the minutes when an hour had passed. My thoughts kept me awake, consuming me with one after the other. Risa's reminder crossed my thoughts. *Hassan will be here tomorrow.* I was disappointed that the realization didn't lend any comfort. The way we left things in Praseria was unfinished. Hassan leaving so suddenly upon our return to Valteria only managed to evade the needed discussion of our relationship. Now that so much time had passed, I didn't know where to even begin. The conversation we needed to have would require a lot of speaking, a lot of thought, and a lot of delicateness, more than I was able or capable of giving. Imagining different scenarios that I may face tomorrow, I tried to find a sliver of fortitude from the idea that I could mentally prepare myself for what was to come. It didn't matter how many I invented, they all were unwieldy, and I dreaded each one.

I watched as the moon crawled its way across the darkened sky, its movements slow and captivating. I shut my eyes tightly, trying to shake away the worries of Hassan. Instead, my mind found its way to another hurtful place — Aleron.

I felt my chest tighten as I imagined his face — his flawless, stunning face. I wondered if he was having nightmares too. I wondered if they were treating him well. I knew he was in a room similar to my own, but the idea that he had no one here or in Praseria made my heart ache.

Aleron was adored by everyone that knew him: his family, friends, and his people. In a single day, it was all taken away from him. He lost everything. I could relate to the feeling, having gone through a similar experience when I arrived in Praseria. However, I was relieved to get away from Valteria when that happened, and the choice to stay in Praseria was entirely my own. Aleron was abandoned by the people he thought loved him and would be loyal to him constantly. I couldn't imagine the anguish he must've been feeling. It was a different kind of loss that no one could comprehend. It was a betrayal. Ruthless, stinging, unkind betrayal.

I tried to picture him only a few floors below me, wondering if he was thinking about me too. I could almost feel my arms wrap around his waist as we would hold each other in comforting silence, knowing at least we had each other. Then it hit me. *Do we have each other?*

We still hadn't had a proper conversation regarding where we stood in one another's lives. *Because the complications in our relationship were attributed to Killian, did that mean Aleron and I would go back to how things were before the war? Was it right of me to disregard the conversations I had with Hassan and the feelings it had evoked? They weren't the same feelings I had for Aleron, but maybe that was a sign?* I wasn't sure how to interpret it if it was a sign, and that realization alone terrified me.

~

I did precisely as Risa instructed. When the sun rose, I made my body believe it was a mistake — it wasn't time to get up. I closed my eyes the majority of the morning, attempting to fall asleep but knowing I couldn't with the sun's glorious brightness kissing every corner of my room.

I eventually gave up once my stomach interrupted

with its growl of hunger and a timid knock at my door. I groaned as I used every bit of energy I had left to heave my body off my sunken bed. I wasn't startled by the knock, I knew exactly who it was, and I was almost grateful for the company after my long night in solitude.

I fumbled with the door handle and opened it to find my handmaid, Sonora, standing patiently for my invitation to enter. She graciously broke the barrier between us, her soft smile a joy to see.

Risa had begged me to allow a handmaid to help me with daily tasks, realizing I wasn't doing an excellent job at taking care of myself as of late. At first, I didn't want to listen. I had always been independent here, and I didn't want to seem weak by accepting the extra help. Risa understood I was too prideful and forced it upon me, saying it was by her instructions. I was thankful to her for sparing me any additional humiliation.

Sonora was slightly taller than me. Her short blonde hair was situated neatly under her cap, her uniform pressed to the point that I didn't think a wrinkle could ever appear. She had glistening olive eyes that were not afraid to look at yours directly. She was bold yet subtle, and I began to enjoy her presence more than I thought I would. I didn't know much about her yet, but I could tell that we were becoming close friends.

"Another sleepless night, your majesty?" she asked, concerned, aware of my inability to sleep but too kind to ask why.

"It's that obvious, is it?" I tried to giggle, but a short sigh was all that could be heard.

"Princess Risa informed me of your guest that will be arriving soon. We will finally be getting you ready today to actually be seen! I can have you cleaned up in no time, and I will make sure you don't display even a speck of exhaustion." She gave a firm nod, confident in her abilities to hide the sleepiness plastered onto my face.

I felt uneasy at the mention of Hassan again, but I ignored the comment and let her get to work. Sonora was purely elegant as she managed to twist my hair into a low bun and place additional curls to perfectly frame my face. She moved quickly and effortlessly, her movements and ease a talent in and of itself. She hummed a song as she applied my makeup, bragging about the new make-up's magical abilities to make any infirmity disappear. I would need to ask her one day where she got it. I had a feeling I would need a lot of it if my sleeping patterns didn't improve soon.

Sonora patted my shoulders, softly nudging me to my feet as she slipped me into a long gown that was light-weight and airy. It was cream in color and feathered on the short sleeves. After pulling on some heeled boots, she let out a long, content sigh. She clapped her hands quickly in anticipation for me to see the final product of her hard work.

I leaned forward, letting the mirror in front of me catch the rays of light in my room to illuminate her masterpiece. Just as she promised, my face appeared completely rested and alive. She somehow hid the puffy dark bags that had hung underneath my eyes and even managed to make my eyes look bigger. My cheeks were rosy rather than drained of color, and my cracked lips were smoothed over in a beautiful shade of pink. With my hair being so neatly done, I appeared put together. It was a miraculous façade that I hoped I could pull off.

"You are incredibly talented, Sonora. I could never have done this myself," I complimented her, utterly sure of my statement.

Sonora shrugged off my praise. "You make my work easy, your majesty; I hardly had to do a thing. However, I am delighted that you approve." She was beaming as we both stared in the mirror at my image.

Sonora looked upon me like I meant the world to her. I couldn't recall a time when one of my people admired me the way she did. It was refreshing and, all at the same time, confusing. I wasn't sure how to respond to her kindness, a kindness I knew I didn't deserve right now. I felt ashamed that even knowing I didn't deserve it, I was still desperate to accept it.

At first, I thought Sonora's kindness was an act. As I had spent more time with her every day, I realized how genuine she was towards me. It was a relief to have someone display kindness to me despite all that had happened.

I turned and faced Sonora, holding one of her hands in mine. "I want to thank you for always being pleasant towards me. I can't recall being treated this way by anyone in the castle, aside from my sister and Damien. I don't know what makes you treat me differently. Still, I am grateful for it," I whispered my appreciation, hoping she could understand how much it really meant to me.

Sonora's eyes seemed astonished and sad as she swiftly responded. "Princess Allene, you deserve respect and adoration."

"I don't, I really don't."

Sonora sighed, her mouth turning down into a frown. "I can hardly imagine the things you have gone through, especially recently. It is wrong for anyone to judge you — even yourself."

"I've been judged for a long time, Sonora. I finally see what all of Valteria has seen in me for so many years. After what has happened, I have turned into the one thing they feared the most — the enemy in their midst." The words hung in my mouth, their sharpness practically cutting my lips.

Sonora hesitated, her head bowing in shame, her shoulders cowering as she looked down at the ground. "I won't deny that was a fear many Valterian's had at one point in time," her eyes shifted up now, bright once again. "But I can honestly tell you there has been a change since the war."

My brows furrowed in confusion. "What do you mean, a change?"

Sonora clasped her hands together, eager to reassure me. "All that fear towards you has dissipated. Rumors of your sacrifice for Aleron on the battlefield circulated —"

"Wait, it didn't make the people hate me more?"

"Hate you? No!" Sonora waved her hands quickly, trying to hurry her following words. "Your selflessness for the people you love has become obvious to everyone. People are sensing a new hope for Valteria — I know I have. After your father's passing, not everyone held the confidence in your mother to lead us on her own. I'm confident that the new hope we are all sensing is coming from you."

I blinked, stunned. "Why?" was the only word I managed to say.

Sonora smiled. "Because if you can love the enemy in such an altruistic way, imagine the proclivity and actions you would take for your own people."

I felt my eyes fluttering in shock. I could feel my face begin to blush as Sonora told me words I only dreamed I would one day hear. The people were genuinely having a change of heart? And my choice, my decision to choose Aleron, actually gained the favor of my people?

It felt impossible to believe; it was something I never imagined would be possible. The reaction of my family and my few friends had been anything but accepting; they had offered no reactions of hope or praise. Was it even possible that my reputation as a failure was coming to an end? To bring a reign of a new beginning? That I could achieve what my father dreamed of — of peace between our two kingdoms, peace to our two peoples.

I had been searching for a place to feel like home, and I found that in Praseria. Could it be possible that I could now finally make my true home, home? Was this a chance to change my past and build a better future? Despite all the heartache and confusion, could it actually change?

"It is difficult for me to comprehend anyone having a change of heart towards me, but I really do hope your words ring true," I assured her.

"You have been hiding away in this room ever since you've returned. I promise, once you venture outside these walls, you will see the difference," Sonora whispered, patting my shoulder.

"Thank you," I said, not knowing any other words that could convey my gratitude.

"My pleasure. I support you; a lot of us do. We want to see you pull through this to bring Valteria peace once again," she said softly.

I could feel a spark of hope as well, a hope that things would be better. Sonora's words had given me the shred of confidence I needed these last five weeks. I found a new determination kindled inside of me as I pictured the idea of what could be my new future — be Valteria's new future. I wanted to be that princess the people were now seeing. I wanted to be someone they could rely on, to be their advocate. I wanted to be what my father had hoped for — a new era of peace, love, and acceptance.

I was finished having nightmares. I was finished being the victim and the traitor. I was finished being scared and wallowing in my own self-pity. I was finished having to be taken care of. I was finished caring so much about what others thought that I harbor my own potential. I was finished having people manipulate me, control me, doubt me, especially my mother.

For the first time in my life, I realized the word princess before my name actually meant something. I have been Allene, and I have been Amelia, but I have never embraced the title of princess. It gave me power, a power that few could ever have. I felt foolish realizing it took me this long to take that title seriously, to wield it to my advantage. I had to hit my absolute low before I actually would do something about it. I was the only thing that had been holding me back, and now I was going to make sure that didn't happen. Not ever again.

CHAPTER 2

Sonora escorted me to the study. As we walked the halls, arm in arm, I noticed a change. Soldiers, maids, butlers, chefs, everyone was taking the time to acknowledge me with a curtsy or a bow. These interactions felt incredibly strange and, at first, made me more uncomfortable than flattered.

As it happened more, I began to feel a sense of pride take control, almost fueling my determination to see the change. In return, I responded with a smile and nod, hoping that would be an appropriate reaction to their gestures.

The palace hadn't changed while I was gone. Since my return, I hadn't roamed any farther than the floor my bedroom was on. I did this primarily out of spite, and slightly out of fear of running into my mother. I was stubborn and exhausted. The thought of unwelcoming stares deterred me from venturing out of my comfort zone. If I'd known this was the response I would receive, I would have left my room much sooner.

We arrived at the large cherry wood doors that led into my father's old study. I took a deep breath as I observed a scuff mark near the right hinge. The memory of Risa and I running through the palace with one of the chef's carts played through my mind. We'd managed to run into the corner of the door, knocking Risa off the cart and flat to the floor. I remember Risa instantly crying, afraid our father would be upset. Father had been sitting in his study at the time of the incident. He skeptically observed the new accessory we had created for the door. As he pushed our cart inside the study, we prepared for the worst. He took us by surprise, throwing Risa on the cart's top shelf, me on the bottom, and pushing us around his study.

I remember being amazed that he hadn't displayed any anger towards ourchildish shenanigans. Like any good parent should, he cared more about our wellbeing and happiness than his perfectly crafted door. I couldn't recall a single memory of my father that ever made me feel anything less than loved and extraordinary. I missed him dearly.

I pushed back the tears that had come to my eyes. Sonora could tell I needed a moment to myself, and as always, was very tactful in how she handled the situation.

"I will see you before dinner, your majesty," she spoke very softly, trying to be inconspicuous.

I gave Sonora a soft nod in reply. She curtseyed and walked away in the opposite direction.

I had requested to meet Hassan in the study, hoping it would give me the necessary comfort and knowledge that my father always provided. What if he was still angry at me for the choice I made in Praseria? We hadn't discussed anything since then, and the anticipation of our conversation was making me practically sick.

Remember, princess. Not Amelia, not Allene, be a princess. I tried to clear my foggy thoughts from my lack of sleep as I opened the door to the study. I caught Hassan fiddling mindlessly with one of the father's old dictionaries, opening and closing the cover. I couldn't help but wonder if it was from boredom or nerves. *I can at least relate to one of those at the moment.*

Hassan stopped, his eyes struggling to get only a glance at me as he slowly put the book down. I chuckled at his efforts not to stare, trying to ignore his awed expression.

Hassan looked very different since I last saw him. I could smell him from across the room. Being primarily in unhygienic circumstances with one another, I assumed he only smelled of dirt, sweat, and grim. I realized he was probably thinking the same thing about me.

The cleaned-up version of Hassan was entrancing, bringing back the initial attraction I felt towards him at the Gala festival. Even being many feet apart, I could smell his cedarwood scent, the pleasantness of it making me want to move closer. Hassan's hair had been neatly trimmed to weigh more heavily on the top as it spilled over the sides of his head, while his eyes held a lighter tint of brown. His eyelashes seemed to have grown, and his skin had been kissed by the sun, giving him a warm glow. After only five weeks, he no longer showed any signs of bruising or injury.

He stood a little taller as he gave me a swift wink. I was captivated by this new poise and courage that seemed to surge through him. I could feel myself getting lost in him, and a princess shouldn't let that happen. I took control of the situation as soon as I could.

"Hassan, it's a pleasure to see you are well. I am surprised you came back to the palace," I stated, trying to hide the flurry of emotions I could feel brewing in my stomach.

Hassan took a step around the desk, casually leaning back on his hands and propping his right leg against the desk for support, acting like he had been in this room on a hundred different occasions. Where was this coming from?

"Why are you surprised? Did you honestly think I would leave something so important to me behind?" He gave me a half-smile, appearing to joke for amusement, but I knew his comment contained the slightest amount of seriousness to see what I would say. His flirting was more than what my exhausted mind could handle, but I made an effort nonetheless.

"I didn't realize you had anything to leave," I played along, curious to see where his new confidence would take the conversation.

Hassan gawked at my remark. "I am no coward, nor am I a fool. I sensed you were hurting. I wanted to stay and be here for you, but I know you prefer being alone in situations like this."

He stared into my eyes, holding me there until I acknowledged his selfless observance of my character when I was feeling low.

He was right; I did tend to sulk if I was depressed, and I preferred to be alone until I could escape it. It was exhausting enough being upset, having to pretend to be happy or a better version of myself when I was low for the sake of other people; it only made me feel worse. It was easier for me to be left alone in moments like that, saving me from putting on a show.

I gave him a tender smile. "How keen of you. However, I have a difficult time believing that I am the only reason that you left," I challenged him, folding my arms as we stared at each other from across the room.

Hassan chuckled, holding his hands up in defense, his hair swaying to the side as he moved. "Don't get me wrong, I did it for you, but I also did it for my family. I had been gone far too long. And. . ." he hesitated.

"And?" I pressed for him to finish.

"I thought a little separation might be good for us. I hoped that, maybe, you'd even miss me." Hassan had grown shy towards the end of his sentence, the innocence in his voice flattering me beyond what I thought he could.

"Did you miss me?" I fired back, amused by our little game. It was invigorating talking to someone other than Sonora or Risa. I almost forgot how much I enjoyed Hassan's company. It made me remember why he caught my eye the night of the Gala festival, and more importantly, why he made my love life seem so unclear at times.

Hassan chuckled, taking a few steps forward until he was standing a foot away. His scent was even more vital now, and I was quickly reminded how training to be a soldier had graciously toned his chest and arms. Stop it, Allene, pull it together. It's just Hassan. You are simply tired. Aleron is just a few floors beneath your very feet.

"I did miss you. Very much." Hassan swept one of my curls behind my ear, the sheer touch of his fingertips electrifying my delicate skin.

I knew I held affection for Hassan, but it wasn't the same affection for Aleron. I wasn't sure the reason for this newly discovered excitement I was feeling, but I was certain it didn't mean anything. I swallowed hard, suppressing any emotion that was trying to take over my princess moment.

"I can certainly say I missed you more than I realized," I replied. That was the truth. I didn't realize that I had missed Hassan the way I did, but I also didn't think it was the way he was hoping it was.

I instantly regretted those short words as I had let my guard down. I didn't want Hassan to misinterpret me. So much for my strong princess moment.

Hassan's eyes were dancing as he seemed to memorize my face, delighted to hear my honest thoughts.

"Allene, pardon my bluntness; but I would be ashamed if I did not confess how alluring you are today," Hassan whispered in a deep tone, sending chills up my neck that

I was hoping he wouldn't notice. He did, his laughter confirming that he was well aware of his effect on me.

I rolled my shoulders, shaking off the goosebumps. I held a severe face, refusing to amuse him any longer. "You look rather put together yourself. The difference of a good washing can be alarming," I snickered, discounting the intention he had for a flirtatious comment as I walked past him to take a seat at my father's chair. I knew there I could feel comfortable and in control.

Hassan slightly cringed at my reply. "I wasn't stating that you looked clean, Allene. I mean, you do, but that is not what I was implying. I was trying to convey that you look stunning." He willingly gave me another compliment, waiting for me to crack under the pressure of his flattery.

"Thank you, Hassan," I said abruptly, hoping the back and forth would come to an end. Gratefully, it worked.

"Allene, one day. . ." Hassan shook his head as he held back a laugh. I felt my eyebrows furrow, suddenly taken back by his lack of disappointment that our gander had ended.

"One day what?" I pressed, leaning forward in my father's chair.

He paused and held a smug smirk, clearly not eager to share. "A conversation for another time, perhaps. I wanted to address more pressing matters."

I could tell Hassan wasn't one to budge. It was no use trying to lure out an explanation or lose the chance to shift the discussion in a safer direction.

"What is so pressing?" I inquired.

Hassan didn't hesitate this time, as he spoke in a genuine voice. "How are you?" he asked.

I sat up a little taller in my chair, my eyes level with him as his face grew concerned. I tried not to falter in my confidence at the sudden, surprisingly personal question.

"I am well; no reason to be concerned about me. Are you doing all right?" I asked, trying to take the spotlight off myself.

Hassan shook his head, disappointment showing on his face. "I know you want to put up a strong front, but you don't have to with me. Damien mentioned he hadn't seen much of you since our return. Rumor has it I am one of the first people you've talked to," he said, confirming that he did more digging than I was aware of, alluding to me that I couldn't hide.

I bit my cheek. "I recognize I have been a little. . . distant," I admitted.

Hassan moved closer, sitting on the edge of the desk to be closer. "I'm listening," he replied.

"I don't think they are things you'd like to hear, Hassan," I told him honestly. The topics didn't seem appropriate to discuss with anyone, aside from Risa. These topics, my feelings, were especially inappropriate to confess to Hassan.

"Anything that is bothering you, I want to hear," he assured me.

I sighed, not wanting to talk about my feelings or hurt Hassan's. However, as I looked into Hassan's confident olive eyes, I knew he was sincere. I knew not telling him my thoughts, not letting him in, would hurt him even more than if I was honest with him. If he wanted to know, I would tell him. It was the least I could do after everything that happened in Praseria.

I cleared my throat as I prepared to be vulnerable to a new listening ear for the first time in weeks. "I'm exhausted. I am emotionally, physically, and mentally drained." I admitted.

Hassan nodded. "You're worried about Valteria," he read my thoughts.

I sighed. "Valteria, my family, Damien, you —"

"And you're worried about Aleron." Hassan shifted calmly, his face composed.

I faltered, taken back by his comment. "No —" I started, but Hassan cut me off.

"It's okay, Allene, it doesn't bother me. I want to know," he assured me again.

I took a deep breath. Hassan was right; I was worried. I hadn't had the opportunity to see Aleron. I had no idea how he was doing, and I was being haunted in my sleep by his brother. I wasn't okay with any of it.

I offered Hassan a small smile. Despite his assurance that he wanted me to be open and honest, I wasn't jumping to say it out loud. I nodded silently in reply, diverting my eyes to study the wall.

Hassan accepted my unspoken feelings without a tinge of envy, his poise being another characteristic to admire. Or maybe it was the deliberate kiss he was able to achieve five weeks ago that took away his envy. I tried not to blush at the sudden thought.

Hassan nodded like he understood what I was going

through, leaving me to process how to acknowledge his sympathy.

Hassan took the time to collect his thoughts. He pushed his weight off the desk and walked to the nearest bookshelf. He didn't make eye contact as he gave his soft reply.

"I may not be on the best terms with Aleron, but I recognize what he has lost. That day of the battle keeps replaying in my head. I regret the moments that I could have done things differently, possibly changed the outcomes for everyone's sake." Hassan had begun talking to himself, sharing his thoughts out loud for me to hear. Understanding he hadn't acknowledged my problem, he continued. "Have you spoken to Aleron?" Hassan asked, trying not to seem bothered by it.

I didn't respond; I didn't need to — he knew the answer to the question.

Hassan strode closer, his confident voice returning. "Why not? Isn't he here? Fortunately for you, you could solve your problems by descending a few flights of stairs. What's stopping you?" he asked, dumbfounded by my lack of authority in my own home.

I became slightly offended, shifting my elbows to rest on the desk, leaning in his direction. "My mother has strict instructions not to let me speak to him until she decides how to approach the situation further. I plan to discuss it with her this evening to straighten things out," I confirmed, proud of my progress.

Hassan let out his beautiful laugh, making me automatically feel a little happier.

"You've broken almost all the rules the last few months; why do you think you need your mother's permission now?" Hassan was amused by his own comment, and my happiness quickly faded. I was baffled at his insistence for me to see Aleron. Was he not just helplessly flirting with me a few minutes ago? Why would he encourage such a thing?

I addressed the observation immediately. "What is your objective here? You are incredibly flirtatious one moment and practically pushing me into another man's arms the next," I accused, not necessarily bothered but bemused.

Hassan shook his head back and forth, approaching the desk and slightly sitting on the edge with ease once again. He gracefully placed his hand on mine, that electric feeling pulsing between us once again.

"By no means am I pushing. I am playing fair. If you were to compare this to a game, then I currently have the upper hand. I am free to roam the palace, to interact with you; he is confined to a room and hasn't spoken to you since our return to Valteria. I only find it equitable for us to be honest with each other. We can't move forward if you still have feelings to work out with Aleron. I have come to accept that as I have been away," he pointed out, saying each word courteously.

I could feel the color drain from my face as Hassan spoke, the nerves almost restraining my mouth from moving. I stared down at his hands that were now holding mine. His skin was immensely soft, and his touch was warm. He was making me dizzy. I tried to pretend the wobbly sensation was from being overly exhausted; to my dismay, I knew the cause was something much more frightening altogether.

"Hassan, I have to stop you. If I have given you any indication that —"

Hassan immediately interrupted me, not acknowledging his negligent manners and his continuous bold statements.

"That's just it; you haven't given me anything: one dance, one kiss, and a few conversations. I can't speak for you, but the few moments we have spent together are some of the best moments I've had in a long time. You haven't given me proper consideration, and you are not bound to Aleron. You still have opportunities for your life to take another direction. I am one of those opportunities," Hassan paused, his optimism advancing through his tender smile. "Allene, if given an equal chance, I am confident you will see what I see. I refuse to waste any more of our time together. If I want to prove that we have something — something as real as you think you have with Aleron — I want to do it right. You may have feelings for both of us, and that's all right for now; there will only be one of us in the end." Hassan gave a short smile. "Go talk with him. I will see you at dinner," he said with certainty.

"Dinner?" I asked, perplexed.

Hassan's eyes danced with amusement. "You didn't hear? I have been invited by the Queen herself," Hassan replied.

Why would my mother invite Hassan to dinner?

Before I could fumble over a reply, Hassan kissed my hand lightly and turned towards the door, not allowing a single word to escape my lips.

The door shut quickly. The opportunity to discuss the oddness of what had just occurred was sent to a halt.

Hassan's little speech had left me stunned. I had no idea how to respond to his words of affirmation — which, the more I thought about it, I believed was his objective. He had taken me off guard; my attempt at preparation for our discussion had been useless. I had wanted to ask about his mother and sister, how he was handling everything, what he planned to do now that he had returned, but all those questions somehow got swept away and would need to be addressed later. Dinner was apparently going to be that opportunity.

I quietly choked back a half-hearted laugh. I couldn't wrap my exasperated brain around a few of Hassan's statements or the way they had made me feel. Did I actually have feelings for both of them, or was that just Hassan assuming things? Would I consider him — us — as a possibility? What if he was someone I could be happy with but hadn't given him a chance?

I immediately felt ashamed for even considering it. What would Aleron say? I couldn't disrupt anything between us right now, not when everything was so delicate. I knew my feelings for Aleron with absolute surety, and I saw no value in exploring anything else. I had already tried denying my feelings for him once and knew how difficult it had been. The news of Killian being the actual target to spew my hatred towards alleviated any contempt I had for Aleron, the knowledge resolving my feelings back to where they had been before the war.

I was the only thing that stayed consistent as his life had turned upside down. I may not have communicated with him since our return to Valteria, but he needed me now more than ever. Aleron had been my constant support when I needed it, and now it was my turn to be that for him. I was ashamed it took Hassan's meddling to ignite my determination to see Aleron. I was a coward to avoid him, to grovel to my mother. If the roles had been reversed, I am sure Aleron would have found a way to see me immediately. Swallowing more of my regret, I decided to follow Hassan's suggestion. I needed to talk to Aleron.

~

I had to be fast. Dinner was approaching rapidly, and I was pressed for time — or so I was telling myself that was why I was in a hurry to get to Aleron's room.

The real reason, *the possibility of considering that I had feelings for Hassan, and the risk of if I thought about it one moment longer, that I may believe it,* I was completely ignoring. By trying to control my tempted thoughts, I had overlooked the problem I would soon face — getting to Aleron.

I rounded one last corner to find myself at the end of the corridor that led to Aleron's room. As I had hoped, one guard stood alone, protecting the entry to his room.

To my relief, I noticed it was Marshal. *It couldn't be more perfect.*

I approached him slowly, his delayed reaction to my footsteps quite amusing. He regained his posture and seemed a little taller. Rather than seeming bored from his work, his eyes had developed an instant façade of concentration.

"Princess Allene." He bowed deeply, still trying to convince me of his earnest attitude.

I chuckled to myself, breaking the tension. "Marshal, lovely to see you."

Marshal had done a sweep of the area to ensure we were alone. His eyes grew shy and his voice a mere whisper as he approached a subject I wasn't expecting.

"Princess, I had meant to apologize to you for the scene that you witnessed before we left the castle. I am deeply humiliated to have been seen under such private circumstances that were highly inappropriate. I want to assure you I am abiding by the utmost standards of being a perfect gentleman and have distanced myself from Princess Risa." I could hear the restlessness in his voice as he spoke. He was only trying to be comforting, and I appreciated that he was unsettled at the idea of offending me by being with my sister.

I graciously placed a hand on his shoulder, staring into his caramel eyes as I tried to suppress a laugh. "I am not the least bit worried about what is going on between you two. I have never seen Risa so giddy. She is an impeccable judge of character, and I would not doubt the goodness of any man she deems worthy of being with her. All

I ask is that you spend time with her. To hear that you avoided her because of our incident makes me sad. She has been working incredibly hard to make me happy these last few weeks; please do the same for her," I pleaded, acknowledging my acceptance in every way I could.

Marshal hung onto each word I said, his smile growing between each sentence. I stepped away, being proud of the joy I was able to bring to him. He was kind and extremely handsome; I hoped Risa could genuinely find love with Marshal. She would be with a courageous knight, someone who could always protect her purity and decency. I could not ask for her to be in better hands.

"I promise you have my full support and my secrecy," I whispered the last words.

"I am in your debt, Princess Allene," he said softly. *Here is my opportunity.*

"I may ask for that debt to be paid sooner rather than later." I bit my lip, the guiltiness exposing my intentions. Marshal raised an eyebrow, uncertain of what he had just promised. I proceeded before he could take back his offer.

"I came to, *secretly,* see Aleron. I do not doubt that he is being well taken care of; however, I have many things I need to discuss with him. Would you let me in to see him for a few minutes?" I tried to muster distraught in my voice, stressing how much it meant to me.

I could see Marshal's hesitation, trying to figure how to handle the situation best. He wiped his palms on his pants after rushing his fingers through his hair to distract himself from his new nerves. Part of me felt bad for placing him in the situation, but the other part of me knew it was necessary.

Marshal's wide eyes darted around the hallway before settling on my face. "Ten minutes. That's the most I can give you. Supper will be coming soon, and I cannot risk you being seen by one of the maids," he whispered, trying to be discreet.

I nodded my head, a smile instantly coming to my face. "Marshal, you cannot comprehend how much this means to me; thank you. Ten minutes is all I need," I assured him, making my way to the door.

I could sense Marshal's nerves as he staggered to find the key to open the three-inch-thick door, the only remaining barrier keeping me from Aleron. Each second that went by felt like an eternity. I could hear my pulse as it echoed in my ears, my heartbeat racing fast. As the knob turned, a streak of light cracked through the small opening. Without a moment to stall, Marshal ushered me in, locking the door behind me, the reality that I couldn't turn back now hitting me in a rush. I wished I had given more thought to what to say when I got the chance to see Aleron. I was beginning to regret my last-minute decision for not preparing mentally the way I had when I expected to see Hassan. *Not that the preparation with Hassan had helped me anyways.*

Then I noted the difference between the two men. I hadn't prepared because with Aleron, I didn't need to. A sudden new feeling flooded my gut — not anticipation, not fear, not uncertainty. I knew the feeling instantly. It was the comforting warmth that I felt when I was near Aleron.

My excitement grew as my eyes fell upon an elegant figure in the corner of the room. Aleron sat on a chair; his right leg held close to his body as his chin rested neatly on his knee. His startled expression melted into one of longing as his deep blue eyes captured mine. I searched every inch of him, noticing the extended length in his hair, the beard on his face that was thick and full, and the flawless complexion that was masked behind it all.

I couldn't find a mark or a scratch on his body. I noticed his muscular arms, exposed from wearing only his undershirt, were flexed just slightly from the position they were in, and I could feel my heart sink just a little more. To add to it all, he had to show off his remarkable smile, the stark whiteness of his teeth dazzling me. How could I — even for a second —think that I could have feelings for someone else? All I needed was to see Aleron to know what we had.

Right when I thought it couldn't become more of a dream, I was placed into a state of pure fantasy. Aleron only needed to say a few words in his velvet, smooth voice with his enticing lips to make me question my grip on reality.

"Hello, my angel."

I couldn't restrain myself any longer. Before I could say a single word, I defenselessly rushed to Aleron, holding him as tightly as I could. His arms encircled my lower back, cradling me closely as he narrowed the space between us as much as possible. I could feel tears of joy wanting to escape me, but I replaced them with an enormous smile.

I pulled back just enough, so our noses were touching, discovering that his smile was matching mine, his dimple hidden underneath his beard.

"Tell me I'm not asleep; tell me this is real," Aleron whispered, the heat of his breath sending shivers down my back. I immediately obeyed his command, trying to convince myself of the same thing.

"It is real; otherwise, we are both certifiably unstable," I said. Aleron gave a quiet laugh as the vibrations found their way to my bones, making me ache for more. "It is music to my ears to hear your laugh. I have been longing to hear you, see you, and be *near* you for weeks. I am in complete awe that I am here right now," I confessed my thoughts that I had intended to hideaway.

I wanted to keep a strong front, to create a barrier between us while we navigated what I thought would be a complicated moment, but Aleron had successfully brought my guard down, an effect he still seemed to have on me.

The last Aleron and I had spoken was when he found me in the Praserian prison. Under the circumstances, it wasn't the most romantic moment to reunite, especially since, at the time, I had mistakenly assumed he was a conniving, merciless brute.

Although I knew that every wrong shown to me in Praseria was because of Killian, I still had difficulty letting it go. I struggled not to associate the memories with Aleron. At the time, and sometimes even still, I found myself holding a grudge over what had happened. Part of me knew this was why I hadn't made an effort to visit him sooner, as awful as it sounded. I wanted to protect myself; I didn't want to let Aleron in that quickly, but I found my efforts wasted. I was amazed at how untroubling it was to let myself feel for him again. It was dangerous in its own soothing way.

Aleron gently held my face in his hands; his lips pressed to my forehead as he spoke.

"You have been in my every thought, every minute, every day since we left Praseria. Each morning, I hoped that day would be the day you'd walk through the door and into my arms." Aleron took a deep breath and exhaled. "The waiting has nearly killed me, Lia."

His words made me want to hide away in shame, in guilt. It had been five weeks. I shouldn't have listened to my mother; I should have come to see him right away, no matter the consequences, no matter my reservations, no matter my fears.

"I am sorry it took me this long," I apologized with the most pitiful simplicity.

Aleron smiled, his lips moving to my temple as he kissed my skin lightly. "You are here now; that's all that matters."

Aleron's hand cradled my neck as he pulled back to look at me — *really* look at me — his eyes intently studying my face. "You are so beautiful, Lia. Absolutely, breathtakingly beautiful." Aleron's thumb grazed across my cheekbone, his hand settling on my cheek. I could feel my heart racing under his stare and hoped it wasn't loud enough for him to hear.

There were so many things I wanted to say, things I wanted to address, but I couldn't find the words to discuss them. It was short and straightforward, but the following words out of my mouth were at the forefront of my mind.

"I've missed you." My words were merely a whisper, their vulnerability pulling my body closer to his as I inhaled the scent of his skin, my nose resting against his neck.

Aleron bit his lip, holding it back from trembling, his words, however still shaky. "I'd be lying if I said that wasn't a relief to hear. I was starting to worry that you had changed your mind about me."

I felt my body clench at Aleron's reply. "I hate that I made you worry; I should have come sooner. I should —"

Aleron sighed, and with a slight smile, he placed a finger against my lips, quieting me into silence as I stared into his deep blue eyes, his long lashes framing them perfectly.

"Don't apologize. You are *here,* and I am completely elated, Lia. You tend to have that effect on me." Aleron began rubbing his other hand on my back, the movement adding to the solace I was already experiencing.

I closed my eyes, trying to absorb every fragment of the moment. I almost forgot that Marshal only allotted me ten minutes. My mind was trying to regain focus.

"You affect me in more ways than I can number," I whispered, biting my lip at the end to prevent me from saying more. Aleron read the action as an invitation, the bridge between our noses collapsing.

His lips had gently pressed into mine, his arms tensing around me. I felt our scents mingling between each kiss, the intensity growing stronger with every second that passed. Without recognizing it, my hands had moved behind his neck, my fingertips gripping his smooth skin that hid safely underneath his long curls as I tried to pull him closer. I felt a rumble vibrate through my chest, quickly realizing it wasn't my own; it was coming from Aleron. The kisses turned into a sense of belonging, a mutual frenzy beginning to unfold.

Aleron scooped me into his arms and made his way

towards the bed, gently setting me down without breaking away from our kiss. He leaned back on the bed until our bodies were parallel to one another. One hand had found its way to my waist, pulling me in, while the other had buried itself into my neatly pinned hair, unraveling it into a contained mess, but I didn't care. I placed a hand on his chest and another on his arm, becoming lightheaded at every perfect fiber of his being. I could feel his muscles tense as I had accidentally bit his lip, the hunger for one another erupting between us.

I could hardly create a thought that didn't involve Aleron; no rational form of thinking was finding its way into my mind. Somehow my subconsciousness found its way into a corner of my thoughts, telling me I knew this desire needed to stop. My heart protested, saying something different.

Before I could make the decision to separate myself from his enticing captivation, Aleron became rigid as he abruptly pushed my body away and made his way to his feet.

I was immediately hit with a slew of new emotions — embarrassment, rejection, doubt. Each one caused me to freeze in place, horrified that I had done something wrong, that I had misinterpreted what I thought Aleron had wanted — what *I* had wanted.

I somehow mustered the courage to keep a calm face, trying not to let the gesture offend me, no matter how much it hurt. Aleron could see I was disappointed with the separation but still euphoric from the moment we had just shared.

I held my breath, trying to clear my foggy thoughts as I studied his perplexed expression. I was hoping he would speak first, that he would break this tension, that he would tell me what I did wrong, but Aleron became fixated on the door, his only escape from this room, and his only escape from me. My heart sank.

"Are you all right?" I whispered. It was a vague question, but I knew it was the most appropriate. It allowed him to go in any direction — to tell me whatever he wanted.

Aleron was clenching his jaw, the muscles flexing as his stare became complex and impenetrable. I immediately felt a stir in my gut, my senses recognizing that our moment was quickly taking a dreary, unanticipated turn. I still hadn't taken a proper breath; the air constricted in my lungs as I waited for his reply.

Aleron shook his head, his hands combing through his hair nervously. "I let my emotions get the best of me; I apologize. It wasn't my intention to lose control," he said meekly, not returning my gaze as he stared now at the stone wall.

I finally took a breath, his words lifting the weight in my chest. *If that was his definition of losing control, then I needed to be reprimanded, not him.* I sat up, trying to get his attention. I reached for his hand, attempting to free the guilt he was feeling from the moment I selfishly let escalate, but he moved out of my reach. I ignored the anger and pain his reaction had caused inside of me, trying to maintain my focus on alleviating Aleron's culpability.

"If you are embarrassed or ashamed that it got out of

hand, it was as much my doing as yours. I won't let myself get carried away again," I vowed, hoping it would bring some relief to Aleron's concentrated face.

Aleron firmly shook his head, no words following for what seemed like a lifetime.

"I'm not worried about it happening again," he whispered. "It was selfish of me to instigate this when I knew it was coming to an end."

Aleron's words took me many moments to register. The grimness in his voice, his stiff demeanor, evading any eye contact, acting as a polar opposite of the Aleron I had just witnessed seconds ago.

I could feel my heart rate rising and my breath struggling to stay steady, trying to comprehend what it all meant. I was in denial, but I allowed myself to be oblivious for as long as I could, hoping that ignorance could spare me from the mistake I may have just made.

"I am not positive where this is all coming from, but I can assure you that I don't find you selfish, and I don't see this as an *end*. You seem upset, and you have every reason to feel conflicted about many things. However, I have taken comfort that amidst all this chaos, we have *each other*." I tried to justify and explain what I thought he was feeling, trying to fill the tense air with fast-paced words. I wanted to help, to set things right between us, but I knew he wasn't accepting of it.

Aleron kept his distance, biting his cheek as if to hold back from speaking what was on his mind. "I thought I could say what I needed to say, but as soon as I saw you, I lost all resolve. I am so sorry, Lia; I am a horrible person. This isn't how it was supposed to unfold."

My throat became dry as my mind processed what Aleron was implying. I swallowed and nearly croaked out my best reply. "This is all probably coming from a troubled place. . ."

"I *am* in a troubled place." Aleron squinted his eyes in frustration. "I have had weeks to contemplate how to proceed with the situation at hand, and more so, I have had weeks to reflect upon myself — my circumstances. I am not worthy of you anymore." His words were heavy as he revealed his fears. Aleron held his jaw in his hand as he appeared in deep thought.

I reacted immediately, pulling myself off the bed and coming to his side.

"Stop it, please don't speak that way; you know none of that is true."

"It is true. I have been reduced to nothing, Lia. I can offer nothing to you."

"N-no, don't say that. You are *everything* to me. You are the same man you were in Praseria; you are the same man to me. You will always be that man, no matter what has happened," I did my best to reassure him. However, I was beginning to panic; my anxiety began to rise as I tried to remain focused on convincing him of his notability, of convincing him to believe it, if not for himself, at least for me.

Aleron let out a silent laugh, his shoulders stiff as he exhaled. "I have been overthrown, betrayed, and exiled from my kingdom. I am *not* the same man as I was in Praseria. Everything I was has been taken from me."

"Aleron, I refuse to stand by and watch you destroy yourself. You are more than this." I said in desperation, reaching for him.

Aleron caught me by surprise, gripping my arms as his eyes frantically searched mine for understanding. They were filled with torment, the muscles in his face taught from frustration. "No, Lia, this is reality. It would be cruel of me to allow either of us to have hope for such unrealistic expectations. My future is filled with uncertainty. I have been stripped of my title, my legacy — I don't know where that leaves me, Lia. Until I know what I am again, I'm a risk to you and your future." Aleron's grip relaxed, his hands moving to my shoulders, using them for support as his head slumped to his chest. I could feel his body quivering as he refused to meet my eyes. "I need to put you first, Lia. It's the only thing I can control right now, and I will not — cannot — fail you, more than I already have. It will kill me."

I gripped his arms now, desperately clinging to them, doing my best to push back the frustration I could feel raging through me. "Then put me first. Putting me first would be making me happy. I find true happiness when I am with *you*. I found a sense of myself in Praseria, and I attribute that to *you*. You may be exiled, but you still have the potential for a home. You are not abandoned. I am here for you, right here, and I am not going anywhere," I expressed with sincerity, trying to bring Aleron the comfort he needed, praying it would bring him the clarity to see that what he was saying, what he was doing, was entirely wrong.

He held his lips in a straight line, uncertain how to reply. I struggled with encouraging speeches, but I did my best to channel both Risa and my father, hoping to inspire Aleron in some way to bring him to his senses.

"P-please, don't feel lost. We can view all of this as a discovery. This could be a new part of your legacy. Your status, your name, none of it defines Aleron Hadway. Your actions are who you are — they are what define you. That is what I admire about you," I exclaimed, sympathy flooding my voice.

Aleron's eyes finally met my gaze, irritation taking over as he rolled his eyes at my words and dropped his arms to his sides. "*Admire?* My family has been nothing but malicious towards you, your family, your kingdom, and you think I deserve compassion? Respect? I'd be doing you a dishonor by letting you love me as you have," he said the words sharply and unapologetically.

"That is not a decision for you to decide," I spat back. I would not let him give up that easily; we had already been through so much.

"Is it yours? Now you're *forcing* me to love you?" His words pierced my heart, the abrupt feeling of resentment making me numb.

My head was beginning to spin. It completely took me off guard. How is this the same Aleron I was devoting my lips to only mere minutes ago? How was this conversation being exchanged with someone I undoubtedly cared deeply for? I knew how he felt — how *we* felt. This was all a nightmare. Indefinitely worse than the nightmares that most recently had been plaguing my dreams.

"Are you saying you don't love me?" The words hardly escaped my dry mouth, struck by fear of what he would say.

I could hear my heartbeat as it ravaged in my eardrums, my fingers shaking. The silence, the delay in his response, didn't make his words any easier to hear; if anything, it made them sting more.

"As I said, it would be dishonorable if I did," he whispered, once again escaping my gaze.

I bit my cheek, my anger taking over. "That wasn't my question. Aleron, do you *love* me?" I asked the question with all the courage I had left, trying to hide my despair for the words I was hoping to hear. Anything — a nod, a yes, even a maybe, would have been something I could handle, but I wasn't prepared to face what would come next.

"Don't make me say it, Lia." Aleron locked his eyes with mine, their soft, dark blue hue becoming dim with tears. I was astonished that a moment full of passion could so quickly turn to a moment of intense resentment. I was indignant, and Aleron quickly noticed, attempting to trap me with my own emotions.

"Hold onto that anger. If you hate me, it'll be easier to let me go," Aleron confirmed softly. Now I was in a full-blown rage.

"You're incredulous! Don't pretend to be this. . . this person! You're acting like abandoning what we have is going to help us. You can try to push me away, to pretend you don't feel the same, but I know you love me. I understand you are trying to protect me in your own way, but this isn't it. I *need* you, Aleron, the *real* you," I demanded, the princess inside me trying to take over the situation.

I reached for his arm in desperation to snap him out of his daze — out of his absurdity. Aleron seemed in pain, pulling his arm away from me as his hands came to my shoulders, softly shaking me.

"I don't know who the real me is anymore! I have been stripped of everything that defines me!" he bellowed. *That one stung.*

How could he say that? I had found so much purpose, so much of myself when I found him. His love, our connection, had been a defining point for me. What had it meant to him? *Not enough, it seemed.*

I felt my lips quiver as I choked back tears. My mind was racing as fast as my heart, my thoughts nearly incoherent. I couldn't string together enough words to express how deeply I was hurting. Only three words managed to escape the myriad of my thoughts.

"You're a coward," my voice cracked on the last word.

Aleron shrugged as if the comment didn't bother him and folded his arms to create a barrier between us. "Call me a coward, call me selfish — all I need to know is that I am not causing you any more pain. You have suffered enough grief. I will not allow you to continue this path with me; my path is leading to tragedy, and I won't let you be a part of it," he replied solemnly.

He had no right to take away my agency, not to let me choose what was best for my life. The beauty in what we had was how strong we were *together*. This shouldn't be a unilateral conversation, and it shouldn't have been a battle. I didn't expect our relationship to be easy, but I hardly expected to see the man I loved so willingly give up on me, to give up on *us*. I could taste the salt of my tears in my mouth, and I felt nauseated, only letting Aleron continue to hold my shoulders to prevent me from crippling over in distress.

Aleron sighed as he desperately looked into my eyes. "Amelia, I do love you. I love you too much to let you be with someone like me — I need you to understand that."

I do love you. Those words of affirmation that I longed to hear from him every day before now. How could words that once left me encouraged, left me feeling safe, suddenly leave me shattered? The devastation of his intentions flooded inside me.

I stood still, the pressure of Aleron's hands on my shoulders being the only sensation I could feel as shock led me to a state of stupefaction. As if Aleron's assumptions hadn't cut me deep enough, he had to drive his point even further. "Lia, the night we left Praseria, you told me not to let you feel like a fool again. I'm abiding by your request. You would be an absolute fool to allow yourself to continue loving me."

I had finally lost any ounce of patience that had been holding me together. I felt rash for losing control earlier, for letting my guard down, for not being more suspicious, letting my emotions sweep me away into a new kind of heartbreak, and for not being what a princess should be. I was allowing an egotistical man to get the better of me, and I was determined to make sure he knew he wouldn't escape torment that easily.

I shook my shoulders free from his grasp and made my way to the door as the silence surrounded us. My steps felt as heavy as my heart — but I tried to make them appear lighter. If I wanted to be a triumphant leader, a courageous individual, I would need to start acting like one; weakness was not a quality I could possess.

I turned to face Aleron one last time, letting the moment burn in the back of my mind and leave it in the past, accepting what I was leaving behind.

Aleron was trying to read my expression, to anticipate what I would do next. I couldn't tell if he wanted me to object again, fight him until he gave in, or if he genuinely wanted me to let him go. The only clear decision I could make was that I wouldn't allow my heart to suffer any longer.

I buried the feelings that surged within me as I watched Aleron's blue eyes. My eyes shifted to his stagnant lips. *His eyes that peered into my heart and his lips that made empty promises. I should have guarded myself; I shouldn't have let him in so easily.* He had made me unafraid. He had made me *weak*.

I somehow mustered enough strength to tear my eyes away from his, knowing that if I caught even an ounce of pain or regret in his eyes, that I would falter in my words. I took a deep breath, my lips pressed into a frown. I was ready to bring our gut-wrenching argument to an end.

"If this is what you assume is best for us, then you're right — I am a fool; I'm a fool to have believed in you, and

I was an even greater fool to believe in us." I tried to hold back any hint of sorrow that I could feel, trying to abscond into my voice, holding back the sick feeling in my stomach that made me want to vomit.

I knocked lightly at the door to signal I was finished with the conversation. I could feel Marshal's key rattling underneath my grasp as I gripped tightly to the door handle, eager for it to signal my freedom.

Once the lock gave way, I knew there was one more matter to be addressed, one that would take away the excruciating reminder of what Aleron and I had. I spoke to Aleron, but I didn't let myself turn to see his face; I wanted to be as flat and stern as possible, my message clear.

"In the future, you will address me properly. I am not Amelia. My name is Allene. Allene Amena, *Princess* of Valteria."

Without looking back, I stepped through the door, surrendering to Marshal to tend to the broken man I used to love and the crumbling fantasy I had just left behind.

CHAPTER 4

$\mathcal{I}$ tried to hold back the tears I felt pushing to escape me as I sought refuge in my room. Sonora was nowhere to be found, and I was grateful for the moment alone to allow myself to face my towering, all-consuming, emotional disarray. I also knew Sonora would not be happy to see the destruction of her earlier masterpiece.

I tried to process the encounter with Aleron. Each time I came close to understanding his point of view, it would slip away. As hard as it was to understand his feelings, trying not to feel like an imbecile for letting my guard down was even more difficult.

I had no explanation for Aleron's abrupt change of heart. My own heart was unable to keep up with the sudden realization that I no longer had Aleron. The one person I assumed would bring me solace in this time of confusion had made my state of uncertainty grow deeper.

Aleron was my safe place; he was my constant. How was I supposed to pretend it didn't hurt? How was I to act like he meant nothing to me? How could I erase the moments? How was I to change my heart's direction so suddenly? How could I rid myself of the pain that was on the brink of being intolerable? I felt like I was being torn apart, split in two, completely maimed.

Hassan's words had come back to me, inching their way into my heart, leaving me with a small glimpse of hope. *You are not bound to Aleron; you still have opportunities for your life to take another direction; I am one of those opportunities.* I wanted more than ever to believe those words.

My mind was bearing too much to cling to Hassan's proposition just yet, but it at least left me with reassurance. It brought me a tinge of peace. If everything was changing for the better, maybe this was some unseen step that needed to be taken. *It could turn out to be a blessing in disguise.* I could almost hear my father's voice as he would repeat that phrase whenever my circumstances were grim. He had such faith, such devotion that I longed to replicate.

I wanted to be a daughter that he would be proud of. I wanted to be the princess he always hoped I would become. My father never felt pity for himself. He never expected others to apologize for doing him wrong. He held respect for himself because he did what was right, no matter how he was treated. It was my turn to bring that ambition, selflessness, and kindness back to Valteria.

I knew at that moment exactly how I would overcome

this seemingly impossible obstacle. I would work diligently to be worthy of the title given to me. To be Valteria's princess — it would take every piece of me and all of my effort to do it right.

~

*D*inner arrived sooner than I expected. Hassan had seemed adamant about seeing me at dinner, and the anxiety of facing him again made me lose what little appetite I had. To add to the quenching nerves, it would be the first anyone had seen me at dinner since my return. Risa had dinner in my room on occasion, but otherwise, Sonora and I ate at the foot of my bed. After five weeks, I had finally gained and committed the courage to face my mother. It seemed today that I was being forced to meet all my fears.

Hassan or Risa must have spoken to my mother because she formally requested my presence for a *"meal to honor our esteemed guest."* I truly hoped she wasn't referring to Hassan; I was afraid it may have been her way of wry mockery.

Sonora assisted me in freshening up my disheveled appearance. I appreciated that she hadn't pressed me with questions, despite the disapproving look she threw at me as she repinned and redesigned my dismantled hair. She helped me into a crimson velvet dress that followed the contours of my body. Despite the high neckline and the long sleeves, it felt slightly revealing. To add to the discomfort, the train was much longer than I was used to, forcing me to lift the heavy fabric at the hem as I walked. Sonora could tell I was uncertain of the new style that I was presented with.

"It is the newest design for gowns this season. I think you look lovely, your majesty."

I could see Sonora truly meant her compliment, and I tried to embrace this elevated version of myself. I attempted to view the dress from a new perspective. I saw how effortlessly it hugged my body, revealing all the curves of my slim figure. I felt powerful. Growing up with the image of our enemy made it difficult for me to appreciate my appearance. For the first time in a long while, I felt confident in my skin. It was a feeling I never wanted to lose.

I lifted my shoulders a little taller, forcing myself into a good posture to complete my renewed conviction.

"It is time to leave for the dining hall, your majesty." Sonora had just finished placing the last pin on my head, my thick curtain of hair cascading to my right side in voluminous waves.

"Thank you, Sonora." I caught her glance in the mirror, a smile emerging on her face.

"Enjoy your evening." Sonora had opened my bedroom door, holding it patiently until the last of my dress had made its way out of the room.

It required immense effort to find my way to the dining hall without tripping on the fabric that battled me with every step I took. I eventually folded the fabric and draped it over my arm in order to walk with dignity.

As I approached the dining hall, a guard caught sight of me. Try as he may, his eyes couldn't seem to stop analyzing my invigorating dress. I could see his cheeks flush with embarrassment as I held his gaze — acknowledging his stare. The guard brought his eyes forward, extending his hand to open the door without glancing my way this time.

I held back a laugh as I entered the quiet dining room. The extended table that usually only occupied my mother had been filled with numerous faces, all their eyes settling on me. To my relief, I recognized most of them.

My mother sat at the head of a table, a mysterious smile firmly in place on her engaging face. She looked different. I could see a few wisps of gray weaving through her hair, age slowly taking its toll. My mother was not one to appear friendly — but at the moment, she was delighted. She seemed less on her guard. I decided not to question it; I was grateful for the rare occurrence.

Risa sat to the right of my mother, wearing a dress that was similar to mine. Hers was a delicate pink, making her lips and cheeks more noticeable as they managed to match the coloring of her dress perfectly. Her golden locks were pinned tightly on top of her head, making her appear about five years older.

Sitting next to Risa was Damien, hardly able to acknowledge me as he cowered over the mouthwatering feast that taunted him. I noticed that his face had become less round, and his stance was a little stronger. His training and hard work were evident as he gradually was making the transition to manhood.

My heart ached for the days of Damien and me. We were happy and carefree; we had no one to impress and found joy in having a true friend. I had missed being around him. He brought back all our beautiful memories with one of his go-lucky grins that he threw my way, making me cling to the brief happiness it left in my heart.

Hassan sat directly next to his brother. He was smiling from ear to ear, a small dimple showing on his left cheek. I hadn't taken the time to notice that detail, and it made me realize I may have been missing much more of him. I could see him trying to mouth words to me. I had never been good at lip-reading. I think he said *"beautiful,"* but I wasn't sure, so I returned the secret compliment with a gracious smile.

Finally, my gaze fell upon two men that I did not recognize. Mother's invitation wasn't just about Hassan; we were entertaining guests.

The first was a scrawny middle-aged man who had more freckles on his face than hair on his head. The bits of brown hair that he did have were randomly placed, seemingly uncontrollable and curling in different directions. His teeth overlapped, his profile appeared protruded. His small nose and beady eyes made him possibly the hardest person to look upon without a hesitating stare. I tried to maintain my composure as I swallowed the fear to look at the other mysterious guest that I would be sitting next to.

The second man must have been approaching his late thirties. His chestnut hair was combed back as it left a curl at the base of his neck. Even seated, he carried himself with an undeniable confidence as his green eyes seemed to read mine, his sharp features making him intimidating at first glance. He was oddly beautiful. His snow-white skin quietly suggested his lack of exposure to the elements, leaving a new sense of mystery to be discovered. He was much different from the first man, and I was curious how two seemingly opposite people were associated with one another. More importantly, what these new faces were doing at our dining room table.

I made my way to the vacant chair that the second man had swiftly pulled away from the table, gesturing with his hand for me to take a seat. I tucked my dress as best I could underneath me as the man slid the chair to hug the table, leaving no room between me and the piercing wood now invading my rib cage.

I saw Hassan snicker as he noticed my discomfort. I threw him a quick glare as he tried to contain his smirk. In no time, my mother quickly stole my attention, breaking the silence that fell over the room.

"Allene, this is King Nycolas Ulric from the kingdom of Gelva, and his assistant, Quinton." My mother spoke to me like it was a typical day, not acting like we were having any issues at all; she didn't seem to mind that she and I hadn't spoken in weeks.

Quinton instantly smirked at the sound of his name, his teeth resembling that of a rat, making me shiver at the sight. King Ulric, however, did not break his steady gaze as his eyes fixated on me.

I knew very little of the kingdom of Gelva. It was a

small kingdom south of Valteria. It took many days across treacherous terrain to get there through the rocky mountains that separated our lands. Due to the dangerous conditions accompanying the journey, trading between our kingdoms had never been discussed or been an option. We had peace with the Gelvans, and I didn't think they had any problem with any neighboring kingdoms. This left them as wildcards in my book. I wouldn't consider them as friends, allies, or foes; we were simply distant acquaintances.

My suspicion of the reason for their visit grew, but I was still uncertain why we were eating with people we had never associated with in the past.

"Good evening, Princess Allene; I am pleased to meet your acquaintance." Nycolas voice easily held my attention, taking me off guard by his overbearing presence.

"Likewise," I politely replied as I brought my gaze to meet Risa's, trying to get a sense of what this dinner was about, but Risa withheld any knowledge she had, or maybe she was just as in the dark as I was.

Damien shifted uncomfortably in his chair, patiently waiting to get permission to begin eating. I protested against my stomach as it tried to release a grumble, the hunger pangs growing from the smell of fresh potatoes in front of me.

Laerina looked all of us over, acknowledging the food. "Please, eat," she said kindly. She had pulled her napkin away from her plate and shook it lightly, letting it fan over her lap to protect her dark green dress. Everyone responded to her gesture by doing the same.

Moments passed and everyone quietly ate, the only sound that could be heard was Damien and Quinton chewing as they ripped chicken with their teeth. I tried not to cringe at the sound. Soon, it made me lose my appetite. I placed my slice of bread on my plate, slowly pushing it away as I leaned back in my chair. That was when I caught Hassan glancing down at his plate and then immediately looking at me. When he noticed me staring back, he hid a small smile.

I turned my attention back to my plate, hoping no one would notice our interaction. After the drawn-out moment of silence as we ate, my mother finally spoke.

"While you are all enjoying your meal, I would like to discuss why I have asked you all here," Laerina spoke confidently, capturing everyone's attention. Her sudden words even halted Damien and Quinton's chewing. *What a relief.*

"King Ulric has made me aware of a highly distressing matter — one that I thought our trusted friends, Hassan and Damien, could help with," Laerina said admiringly. Damien grew shy at her compliment, and Hassan seemed suspicious. My face reflected a mutual expression, uneasy about the authenticness my mother was trying to conceive. *Friends? That isn't how she felt five weeks ago. She detested the bad influence she claimed Damien and Hassan had been on me. What is mother hiding now?*

"What is the matter you discussed with my mother, King Ulric?" I asked bluntly.

Nycolas cleared his throat at my sudden question, taking a composed sip of his wine before he answered my question. He looked directly at me, ignoring my uncomfortable stare.

"The Red Crows. Have you heard of them?" Nycolas gave a firm reply, seeming to be a straight shot. If he was trying to use that as a way to gain my trust, it wasn't working.

Risa half-heartedly laughed, trying to hold back the food she had just swallowed.

"Like, the birds?" she asked innocently, surprised by his answer.

I looked at Hassan, who held a grave expression. Damien had stopped eating and gave his full attention to Nycolas at the sudden mention. It seemed everyone else understood the significance in his reply aside from myself and Risa.

Hassan shook his head. "Not the birds; it's a group inspired by them," Hassan said starkly, looking my way with a worried stare.

"Intelligent, adaptable, mischievous — it's an insignia that fits them perfectly," Nycolas said, confirming Hassan's statement.

"I've never heard of them," I claimed. I was uncertain where the fear in Damien's eyes was coming from, but it left me slightly shaken.

"You wouldn't have unless they wanted you to," Damien whispered. His words left a chill in the air while Risa and I tried to grasp the seriousness of the situation.

"Your friend is right; this is why I have brought them to Valteria's attention," Nycolas said calmly. He picked at his food, the only one still with a visible appetite.

"I thought the group had dissipated," Hassan spoke directly to Nycolas.

Nycolas let a moment of silence fall upon the room as he slowly chewed on a piece of food — entirely swallowing before responding to Hassan. "Dissipated? No, they disappeared from the watch of the public eye, but their operations haven't ceased," he assured Hassan.

I looked at my mother, who had a straight face, showing no emotion. I couldn't tell if she was as nervous as I was or if she was abnormally calm. I was doing my best to master my own collected and relaxed expression, but Risa looked utterly distressed. She kept rubbing her hands together, a habit she had when she was nervous. Damien was looking at Hassan, the little brother in him shining through as he looked to his older brother for a reply. Hassan and Nycolas had locked eyes, the conversation now exclusive to the two of them.

"How do you know this?" Hassan asked.

Nycolas didn't bat an eye as he replied. "I have had spies in their group since the beginning of its formation."

"For what reason? They are only in Granville and Selvet, not Gelva," Hassan informed Nycolas.

Nycolas paused as he slicked back his hair, taking a very calm approach to Hassan's eager tone. "You think they only infiltrated Valteria's little towns? Son, their reach is as far as Cenan," Nycolas explained.

Cenan was another kingdom that was close to Gelva. It was a three days journey from Valteria by horseback, while Gelva was a four-day journey. Cenan was another kingdom I hadn't had a chance to visit. It was notorious for being cold, wet, and full of strong, penetrating winds. Gelva, known for its mountain landscape and terrains, was also infamous for its snowstorms. Between the two kingdoms, their unappealing weather conditions left them with very few visitors.

Those two kingdoms mainly kept to themselves. They limited trading, which required them to be more self-sufficient. Valteria mostly traded with my mother's cousin and her kingdom, Veruje. Praseria traded with Lokali and Gree. Gelva and Cenan were the odd men out when it came to economics.

"That's. . ." Hassan's voice trailed off as he looked at Damien, unable to finish his sentence as he processed Nycloas's words. They both looked concerned.

Quinton nodded quickly, wanting to apply himself in the conversation. "Dangerous," Quinton filled Hassan's gap. "They are adding to their numbers very quickly," Quinton spoke with a lisp through his crooked teeth, salvia dancing at the corners of his mouth with each word.

"Hassan, how do you know about the Red Crows?" I asked. I pushed my plate aside, catching Quinton tearing at another chicken breast. I was officially done eating.

Hassan took a deep breath, his light olive eyes glistening as he looked at me from across the table. "They have approached me in the past," Hassan admitted, seeming to be ashamed by the confession. I looked at Nycolas, who had a slight grin on his face.

"I asked Laerina if she had anyone in the castle from

Selvet. I'm sure the Red Crows found great value in both you and Sir Damien, considering your positions here," Nycolas suggested. Damien shivered, not bringing his gaze up from the table.

Hassan held his ground, his jaw going slack at Nycolas's comment. "We turned them down," Hassan assured him. Hassan was looking at me again, worry filling his eyes.

"I'm sure you did; neither of you seems like traitors," Nycolas implied.

I sat up a little taller in my seat. "Hassan and Damien would never. I don't know any other people more loyal to Valteria," I said with conviction as I looked at Hassan and Damien. I tried to reassure them with my eyes. Hassan nodded, a small smile lighting upon his face. Damien finally looked up from the table, less nervous now.

"Who are they?" Risa squeaked quietly as she still rubbed her palms together.

"They are a rebel group," Damien replied to her.

"Led by who?" Risa's voice was now a little louder than before.

"That is a question we all want answered. The group has leaders, but the actual mastermind behind it all stays unseen and unknown," Nycolas said.

"Hassan and I were approached by one of the main leaders in Selvet a long time ago. He claimed the mission of the Red Crows was to represent the oppressed in order to achieve justice," Damien said.

Nycolas nodded. "'Revolutionaries' is the term they

use," Nycolas scoffed at his comment, obviously unimpressed with them.

"*Revolutionaries*, a fancy word for reckless criminals who see their crimes as necessary for their cause," Quinton tisked through his lisp.

"What is their cause?" I asked, still uncertain how this group had gained enough importance to strike fear in those that spoke of them. This time my mother chimed in, finally adding to the conversation.

"Freedom, my dear — freedom for democracy. Freedom from royals." Laerina acted like she had a bad taste in her mouth, her lips twisting in a sour manner. Hassan and Damien held still as the room seemed to slow down as I processed this new information.

"They want to overthrow us?" I questioned.

Rumors of overthrowing Valteria had come and gone as years rolled by. These types of dissenting groups and people would leave their riots and protests behind as quickly as they arose. There were always disgruntled citizens that believed they could fix Valteria's current problems. My father warned there would be power-hungry, greedy, and self-righteous people, but if we stayed humble, put the people first and their needs before our own, attempts to overthrow would not prevail.

"They don't plan to overthrow Valteria; they plan to overthrow every kingdom in this vicinity — Gelva included," Laerina explained. The purpose of King Ulric's visit was becoming abundantly more apparent.

I shook my head, still not wanting to believe what

they were saying. "These Red Crows, they started in Valteria?" I asked.

Hassan took the liberty to reply, his soft gaze trying to comfort me. "Yes, in Selvet."

"When did you first hear of them?" I asked Hassan.

I saw his fist clench as he replied. "Four months before I arrived at the castle."

"That was almost a year ago. A year and we haven't heard about them until now?"

"The Red Crows operate with acute secrecy; you don't talk about them unless you want an excuse to disappear," Hassan cringed on his last word as if a memory had played through his mind that made him sick. The entire room could sense the intensity of his words, and I did not take them lightly.

"They sound like an extreme, radical brotherhood," I whispered as I looked at my mother and Risa. It was difficult to believe we hadn't heard about the Red Crows until now. If they struck this much fear in our people, how could we have let them go unnoticed? Why hadn't Hassan or Damien mentioned them to me?

"They view themselves as the sequestered politicians of society," Damien confirmed.

"Their intent is not to cause a scene of commotion; that is how they have kept themselves unknown. That is why I thought their group was no longer operational," Hassan said.

"Why would they be recruiting as far as Cenan?" I asked. The situation was still very perplexing to me.

Hassan seemed to think about the question as well, both of us waiting for an answer.

"Isn't it obvious? They need the numbers. The more support, the greater chance of defeating more kingdoms," Nycolas stepped in, trying to insinuate that we should already understand the situation.

"They haven't been a threat to us before; why would they be one to us now?" I asked.

"Valteria hasn't been weak until now," Nycolas stated bluntly.

My father had done an exceptional job of keeping any rebel groups under control. Since my father's passing, Valteria had been on unsteady terms within our own kingdom, and news of it seemed to catch the eyes of others. I knew part of that was my own doing, which made the reality that much more challenging. As much as it hurt to hear Nycolas's words, I knew they were true.

"Valteria is not weak," I tried to bluff with conviction. I saw Risa's face hesitate at my attempt.

Nycolas turned towards me now, his forearm brushing against my sleeve. The intensity of his stare left chills running up my spine. I hoped my eyes didn't expose how nervous he made me. I stayed firm in my seat, not shifting my eyes as he spoke directly to me.

"Valteria endured the kidnapping of both their princesses in a matter of months. Valteria lost the majority of its army in its battle against Praseria. Valteria suffered a surprise attack. Valteria's king died of illness, with no king to succeed him. Valteria is graciously housing their enemy. Valteria, in the eyes of the Red

Crows, is coming apart at the seams," Nycolas unapologetically declared.

Silence fell over the room, and I felt the blood rush to my head as I battled against Nycolas's insults.

"We have lost credibility; we are no longer viewed as the kingdom of power we once were," Laerina confirmed. My mother's reply only made my head hurt more.

"Which is why our alliance will serve as a way to mend that credibility," Nycolas added. He weaved his hands through his hair again, slicking it closer to his neck as he turned away from me now to face the rest of the group. Leaning back in his chair, he seemed more relaxed than before.

"Alliance? Do you intend to fight against the Red Crows?" Hassan asked directly. Nycolas and Quinton exchanged glances as they then turned their attention to my mother. She held her ground, sitting up a little taller in her chair.

"Yes, and any other kingdom that supports their cause," Laerina proclaimed her plan.

"If the Red Crows intend to rid all the nearby kingdoms of their monarchies, why would any kingdom lend their support?" Risa queried. We all waited for Laerina's response. Instead, she avoided giving one and nodded towards Nycolas, who was still sitting far too comfortably for the tense conversation.

"Simple; to aid in their preservation. It is much easier for a kingdom to unite forces with a rebel group in an attempt to garner their own safety while simultaneously cutting their enemies down in the process. Kingdoms do what is required to survive." Nycolas spoke so softly that it sent chills up my arms, down my back, and to my toes. His voice was sadistically sweet, and it left me uneasy.

"King Ulric's spies have confirmed that the Red Crow's first target is Valteria. They have profitably formed an alliance to achieve their goal."

"Which kingdom has allied with them?" Hassan questioned.

My stomach dropped. Killian's face flashed through my mind; the disconcerting feeling he continuously jarred within me came plunging back. We all knew the answer.

"Praseria," Quinton concluded, his saliva visually spewing from his mouth to land on his plate. I had almost forgotten he was still in the room. He was munching on the food in front of him, disengaged from the conversation once again to give his undivided attention to the remainder of his chicken.

Praseria. Part of me was disappointed that I had come to expect my problems to be tied to Praseria, to Aleron. The other part of me was relieved. The more problems Praseria caused me, the easier it was to evade my heartache by filling it with disdain for Praseria and everyone associated with it — including Aleron.

"King Ulric has gallantly offered to add his support to Valteria by sending his army to join our own," Laerina said.

My eyes shifted to Risa, who seemed even more unsettled than before. I could feel both Damien and Hassan staring at me, waiting to see if I would be the first to reply to the proposition. As princess of Valteria, it was my duty to have the courage to say when something wasn't right. This situation, this dinner, didn't feel right. The new Allene had a responsibility to address it.

"Forgive me for being skeptical, King Ulric, but you said it yourself; we are weak; we have lost credibility. Why would you want to aid us in such a circumstance? Gelva and Valteria have not been friends in the past." I gave my honest, raw reaction to the situation.

Risa's eyes went wide; Hassan tried to hide a slight smirk and a twinkle in his eye while my mother tried to hold back her anger. Quinton and Damien seemed to be frozen from the tension in the room, but Nycolas didn't seem irritated by my question. My mother quickly interjected before Nycolas could reply.

"King Ulric, I apologize; I am sure my daughter did not intend to be impolite. As you know, we are truly indebted to your gratitude and support," Laerina attempted to reassure him.

Nycolas allowed for a long pause between responses, letting everyone hold their breath as he captured everyone's stares. He nodded his head as he looked at his hands, seeming amused. "No need to apologize; it's refreshing to speak to a royal who is forthright." Nycolas narrowed his eyes, staring at me in fascination.

"And ill-mannered," Quinton chimed in.

Nycolas brought up his hand, signaling for Quinton to be quiet. Quinton, like an ashamed puppy, pouted as he looked down at his lap.

"To answer your question, princess Allene, I want

Gelva to be acknowledged as a valuable, substantial kingdom. Valteria was once one of the most revered kingdoms there ever was. Right now, Valteira appears fragile. Combining and uniting the forces of our two kingdoms will aid in returning Valteria's reputation and strength. When you rise in power once again, Gelva will be able to accept part of that renewed credibility and recognition. That is our gain from this arrangement." Nycolas answered with what seemed to be the truth, but I still had my doubts.

My gaze flickered to Hassan to catch his reaction to King Ulric's response, but he wasn't giving away any indication of how he was feeling. Hassan held a smooth face that seemed intentive on the conversation. I still felt like Nycolas was using his supposed honesty as a way to hide something; I just couldn't figure out what it was or what truly was behind his motives.

"You want to use us for your own gain." I rephrased his fancy way of saying just that.

Nycolas smiled. "That is what alliances are for, princess Allene. Mutual benefits, mutual interests, and mutual gains." Nycolas was now leaning forward in his chair, shifting his weight into his arms to inch closer to me. Nycolas's green eyes were sharp and keen. My own eyes tried to retract from his stare, but his gaze held mine firmly, bringing our conversation to a halt.

Laerina stepped in, trying to take control, to break the barrier Nycloas had managed to create. "King Ulric has proposed a plan that will benefit us both. If Praseria is working with the Red Crows while maintaining their alliance with Lokali and Gree, we are left outnumbered, even with Gelva's army. We need to find a way to stall, a way to initiate attacks on each kingdom, if we want to stand a chance against Praseria," Laerina said, trying to drive the conversation in a new direction.

"How do you plan to do that? Even attacking the kingdoms individually would require our entire army. That would leave Valteria unprotected and vulnerable to Praseria; we would be susceptible to attacks if the army is taken away," Risa stated.

Nycolas gave a wicked grin as if he was expecting someone to state such a fact.

"Indeed — which is why we will have reliable sources telling the Red Crows another plan, a plan that Valteria is planning to attack Praseria unexpectedly." Nycolas beamed with pride, obviously satisfied with his proposal.

"Wouldn't that make Praseria even more eager to send an attack upon us?" Risa questioned.

An almost sinister laugh escaped Nycloas's lips, his head shaking back and forth as if Risa had just made a joke that only he was capable of understanding.

"Praseria will be thrilled that they have the home advantage and wouldn't take the risk of leaving to pursue an attack on Valteria if they think they could spoil Valteria's own ruse. It's too tempting of a thought! Our sources will send rumors of a specific date that the attack will happen. We will attack sooner than what the sources inform them, ensuring the smaller kingdoms of Lokali and Gree are not in Praseria yet to offer their support. We leave after attacking Lokali and Gree. Praseria will quickly notice their absence of support, see that they have been fooled, and bring their armies to Valteria — right where we want them to be. Without Lokali and Gree, we can trounce them. We will have taken care of three kingdoms in a matter of days. The Red Crows, if any remain, will see that Valteria and Gelva are not kingdoms to consider threatening anymore. This plan — it's your way to redemption." Nycolas was nearly standing as he explained his plan, his self-gratification making my stomach churn.

It wasn't a terrible plan, but it seemed too put together and unrealistic. I had seen firsthand Praseria's forces in battle, and I didn't like the idea of leaving Valteria unprotected, even if it was for just a few days. I knew what could happen in such a short amount of time.

"You seem to have all the answers, King Ulric," I spoke frankly.

"I have been anticipating this moment for a long time," Nycolas assured me.

"So you're a visionary man."

"No, I'm a proactive one."

The room was silent again. Nycolas was calculated, cunning. I didn't like him.

"It seems that way. Do you intend for us to trust your spies to deliver this false information to the Red Crows?" I questioned their reliability and loyalty, but more so, I questioned him.

"Of course not. I trust both our spies to deliver it." Nycolas stared down at his nails, apparently bored by the turn in our conversation.

"We don't have any spies among the Red Crows," Damien stated, ignoring Nycolas's silent dismissal.

"Yes, I know. You and your brother will be the first." Nycolas now gave a sly grin of satisfaction, like he was happy to finally deliver that news.

My heart immediately began to race as panic swept over me. We had just made it back. It had barely been a month, and my mother and Nycolas were already eager to instigate another war. A war that those I cared about most would fight for. A war that those in charge would not attempt to avoid. A war that didn't seem necessary. A war that was being called for by a man I had just met. This would be a war that would result in more bloodshed, more casualties, more conflict, and more contention.

War wasn't the answer. It was never the answer, but it seemed to be all that cowardly, power-hungry royals could ever agree upon. A disease that built each of their kingdoms, sustained their rule, and dominated their decisions.

For a moment, I could understand what the Red Crows stood for, the motivation behind their movement. I wished to be free from my mother and Nycolas's decision — why would the people feel any different? Seeing their rulers repeatedly risk their own families and people to fight unnecessary battles instigated by rash decision-making over generations and generations.

I watched as Hassan kept his face composed. Damien struggled to do the same. I could tell the proposition unsettled him. I shot imploring eyes at my mother. I couldn't take it anymore. No more deceit, no more lies, no more of those I loved being put in danger. *When would this finally stop?*

Before I could even begin to protest the suggestion, Hassan looked directly at Nycolas.

"When do we start?"

CHAPTER 5

onora had left a bowl of porridge on my writing desk for breakfast, but I couldn't bring myself to eat. I couldn't get yesterday's dinner out of my head. Each time I replayed the conversation, I felt sick, eliminating any chance of an appetite.

King Ulric was overjoyed that Hassan and Damien so willingly offered their services to be spies for Valteria. Nycolas asked Hassan and Damien if they could get in touch with the members of the Red Crows that initially reached out to them; they were confident they could.

Nycolas emphasized that time was of the essence and that we needed to reach out to the Red Crows immediately for his plan to work. The urgency of the situation was another factor that made the plan not feel right. The conversation at dinner felt premeditated. If the problem was as urgent as he conveyed, I thought the plan would have been less structured and calculated.

After Nycolas had made his request to recruit Hassan and Damien, he asked to retire to his room for the night. The conversation would continue the morning after next. He wanted to speak with Hassan and Damien alone this evening before discussing the plan with my sister and mother.

A soft knock came at my door. "Come in," I invited loudly, stirring my bowl of porridge as I watched the grains ripple around the bowl. I heard Sonora huff.

"Is the porridge not to your liking, your majesty?" she asked, concerned.

I shook my head, letting the spoon drop back into the bowl. "The porridge is lovely. I'm just not feeling well this morning. I apologize for letting it go to waste."

Sonora rushed to my side, placing the bowl on a platter to whisk away. "Should I fetch the doctor for you?" she asked innocently.

"I don't think it's something the doctor can fix. Have you seen Sir Damien?" Since our return from Praseria, Damien had been given the honor of knighthood upon turning the age of eighteen and was officially titled, Sir. He adored hearing his new title, and it made me smile just at the thought of seeing his face light up each time he heard it.

"Yes, your majesty, Sir Damien and a few other knights were having wrestling matches out in the practice fields this morning."

I rolled my eyes. That was another thing Damien had developed since becoming an official knight; he was becoming more reckless.

"Would you mind grabbing my coat?" I asked Sonora. She politely nodded and placed the platter down on the desk. She scurried to my wardrobe to pull out my brown coat and quickly came to my side, placing it over my arms.

"Shall I plan on having lunch ready for when you return?" Sonora asked.

I shook my head. "That won't be necessary. If I'm hungry, I will grab a snack from the kitchen. Actually, Sonora, why don't you take the next few days off? I have some things I need to work on, and I think it would be better if I were alone with fewer distractions," I said honestly.

Sonora seemed to hesitate as she debated whether or not to pry. She pursed her lips and gave a firm, fast nod. "If you insist, your majesty." Sonora graciously accepted my nod in response as she picked up the tray of porridge and exited my room.

~

I made my way outside, following the paths to the practice fields. I focused on each step, ensuring I didn't trip on any of the large stones in the path. My hair blew violently in the wind, obscuring my vision. I did my best to pull it to one side, outside of the direction of the wind, but my efforts were wasted as strands of hair found their way into my eyelashes.

It was slightly overcast, and the wind had been strong all morning from the north canyon's opening. The air was cold, and the sky seemed to threaten rain. The practice fields were on the opposite side of the castle, where I expected the wind to be blocked by the castle walls — or so I hoped.

After a brief walk and my body officially shaking from the chill of the wind, I finally made it to the practice fields. Rows of armor and weaponry lined a large shack. I heard blacksmiths grunting as they worked on crafting weapons behind the walls of the armory. Amidst their grunts, I could hear loud laughter and chants ahead.

Passing the armory, I found myself on the outskirts of the wide-open practice field. The wind had died down, and the sun was beginning to peek through the clouds. A group of about twenty men had formed a circle, all of them focused on the people they attempted to corral. The men behaved rambunctiously, each of them was unaware of my presence, still honed in on the match in front of them.

"Come on, Thomas, get in on his knee!"

"Let's go, Damien, fast on your feet!"

"Stalling! Stalling! Get to work, boys!"

"Take him down!"

I kept a distance of about two feet back from the outer men, afraid their excitement would result in one of them running into me. I tried to peer over the tall shoulders, catching glimpses of the wrestling match inside.

I saw Damien's light brown hair bounce up and down as he was in a crouched stance. The base of his scalp was covered in sweat, weighing down his hair to make it flat. Damien was comfortably shirtless, his lean muscles showing off his strength. Damien shuffled side to side, trying to distract his significantly larger opponent.

The man, whom I assumed was Thomas from the men shouting his name, had slight undertones of red in his short curly hair. He was shirtless as well, but he didn't have Damien's lean body type. He was less muscular and larger overall. Damien may have been smaller, but with it came the advantage of speed.

Damien circled Thomas as if he had a surplus of energy. Thomas seemed tired, turning slower and slower each time Damien made his way around. Within a few seconds, Damien made an attempt on Thomas's knee from behind, pushing his body weight forward as Thomas tumbled into the ground. Damien had a firm hold on Thomas's arms, pinning them behind his back as Damien sat on top of him like a horse, gripping tightly to avoid his sweaty hands from slipping on his hold. Thomas was irritated, obviously wearing down in his determination to continue the struggle.

"Say it! Say it, Thomas!" Damien yelled, exhilarated by his progress. Thomas groaned as Damien pushed up on Thomas's arms in the wrong direction, testing the man's endurance. Thomas still tried to throw Damien off by moving his body side to side, attempting to get some leverage, but his efforts were futile, his body nearly limp from exhaustion. Even still, Thomas's resistance only fueled Damien's persistence, Damien pushing against Thomas's arms once again.

"All right, all right! I tap out!" Thomas yelled, his breathing labored.

Damien displayed a glorious grin that went ear to ear. He pushed down on Thomas as he made his way up to standing, pumping his arms in the air as he flaunted his victory to the other men.

"That is how it is done, boys! Three for three! Who wants to challenge me next?" he bellowed, eyeing each of the men in the circle with courage. The men were muttering and commenting on Damien's third victory, each of them avoiding taking him on.

"I will," I offered loudly as I held back a smile, accepting Damien's challenge.

The men seemed to go rigid at the sound of my voice. Each of them slowly turned to face me, straightened their stance, and immediately became quiet upon seeing who had spoken. Thomas was still on the ground, recovering from his defeat. He had a sudden renewal of energy as he scurried to the outer circle where his shirt lay on the grass. Thomas shoved it over his head haphazardly, doing his best to go unnoticed. His face was now as red as his hair as he stood perfectly still, trying to hide behind the other men.

A middle-aged man in the front, with a balding hairline and scruffy beard, held his chin up high as he responded to my unexpected presence on behalf of the group.

"Your majesty, our apologies, we did not see you there," he said in a bashful tone. Damien rolled his eyes as he pushed through the men to greet me, unfazed and unashamed of his shirtless state.

"If you knew your princess, men, you'd know she hates to be treated like one," Damien announced.

I glared at him. That was our secret — but it was true. The men hesitated as they looked at one another; their stances became less like statues as they tried to trust his words. They watched as Damien picked up his shirt and flung it over his shoulder, not giving me any special treatment. The men still seemed suspicious as they gave small bows and dispersed, acting like they had other things to do.

Damien looked around, waiting until they were all out of earshot, and immediately turned his gaze back to me.

"Allene, you stole my moment," Damien complained, the dramatic best friend of mine returning.

"I think I made it better," I pushed back.

Damien had a pout on his face, not convinced by my attempts to justify ruining his glory.

"Nice try. Now people aren't going to invite me to wrestling tournaments out of fear of the princess showing up," he grumbled.

I held back a laugh. "I'm sorry, Damien, I wanted to watch. I don't understand why you want to participate in such an event," I confessed.

Damien stopped in his tracks, giving me an astonished look. "I'm an official knight now, a real man. Men fight, men test each other, men have things to prove. I'm not a kid anymore, Allene," Damien pointed out, his chest puffing up with his last sentence.

His claim briefly saddened my heart. Underneath his newly obtained muscular physique, his increased height, and his accomplished masculine squabbles, I knew he was still that over-the-top, sensitive best friend of mine.

"I know," I said quietly, reassuring him I had seen a change. Damien could see his statement had made me dismal. He folded his arms as he peered down on me. He really had grown.

"I'm still the same Damien you know and love. Just a larger, stronger, more *attractive,* and accomplished version of him." Damien had pulled me in for a hug, squeezing me tightly to his bare, sticky chest. I patted his back, letting him know I appreciated his actions.

"I know that too." I smiled as I held back a laugh at his self-praise.

Damien let me go, casually throwing his sweaty arm around me as he started to walk in the direction of the castle. Despite how gross it was that I could smell his awful body odor, it was still a sweet gesture that always made me feel safe and protected. He may have been younger than me, but Damien did feel like my older brother. I knew he would always be a safe place, the most recent events in Praseria proving the durability of our friendship. We may have had some unsteady moments, but ultimately, we would always be there for each other. After yesterday, it was a comforting reminder.

"I assume you had an important reason for interrupting my tournament," he stated.

"And if I don't?" I questioned.

"Then I guess you would be my next opponent. It would be only fair considering you scared off all the others," he joked.

"Challenge accepted," I said firmly, turning to let him know I was serious.

Damien rolled his eyes again. "Not a chance."

"Are you scared to lose?" I mocked.

Damien's eyes became slits, glaring at me. "I'm only scared of losing my new title. I'm supposed to be a gentleman, remember? Gentlemen do not fight women, especially a princess — even if you are like a sister to me." He playfully shoved me to the side as we walked.

"So it has nothing to do with pride. . . such as losing to a girl?"

Damien scoffed at my remarks. "Definitely not! I wouldn't lose to you in a fight. I'm sparing you from embarrassment, Allene, not the other way around."

I took a moment to ponder his words. I laughed out loud.

"Okay, maybe I would lose in a fight, but you know what I wouldn't lose? A race." I pushed Damien backward as I started sprinting in the direction of the castle, not looking back as I heard him grunt at my shove.

"Hey! That's not fair!" he shouted, close behind me now.

He was right on my heels. He had the advantage of longer legs, but it was worth the attempt to beat him at something; someone had to take him off his high horse.

I pushed my legs as hard as I could, finding twisted relief in the pain I could feel as I ran faster. My heavy breathing drowned out Damien's, my chest becoming tight after a minute of giving it my all. I came to a halt once we approached a large oak tree, skidding on my heels. Damien continued past me, slowing down as he realized I was officially stopping.

He placed his hands on his knees, breathing lightly as he squinted from the sun and his shirt crumbled in his hand. He stood up, shaking the shirt out and putting it on, blocking the sun's rays by meeting me underneath the shady tree.

I sat down on the grass, letting myself catch my breath. Damien took his place next to me, crossing his arms around his legs to bring them close to his chest. I could see the sweat on his forehead and the slight sunburn starting to form on his cheeks.

"I won," he declared, slightly out of breath.

I chuckled and shook my head. "No, I did. The finish line was this tree." I winked.

Damien smirked at my reply. "Sure it was," he said, not protesting my claim.

We were silent for a moment as we both gathered our composure and came down from our rushes of adrenaline. I looked at Damien, ready to take on the real reason I had come to him in the first place, but decided to wait. We hardly had a chance to speak to one another since our return, and I missed our casual, open conversations.

"I've missed you, Damien," I said quietly.

"I haven't gone anywhere," he gave a faint smile.

I rolled my eyes. "You know what I mean."

Damien's eyes became almost solemn, his face grave as he looked at the rolling practice fields in our view. "I do," he confirmed, his lips pursed into a firm line as he tried to hold back his emotions.

Damien always had an emotionally driven personality, his feelings facile to discern, but it seemed like overnight he learned to suppress his show of emotion, to hide it away. He seemed braver, which I am sure was his goal, but it also made him appear more distant. I didn't mind Damien putting on a strong facade in front of the other soldiers; after all, he was now looked up to as a leader; he needed to be reliable. But when it was just the two of us, I wanted *my* Damien. The sensitive, exaggerated Damien.

We hadn't spoken much since Praseria. It's not that I didn't want to, I just didn't know what to say, and Damien had been busy training. It was clear that more effort was required of us to check in on each other, to spend time together than in the past. We were growing up, but I didn't want that to mean we were growing apart.

Damien cleared his throat and sighed. "Things have changed," he stated.

"But we haven't. You are still my best friend," I assured him.

Damien grinned, his mood lifting right away. "Well, *obviously*. That isn't allowed to change, not ever. You're stuck with me, princess." Damien nudged my elbow, his lighter spirit taking over. *That's my Damien. I really have missed him.*

I chuckled. "I'm not complaining."

"You might when we are old, ornery, and each other's only remaining friend." Damien was pointing and slowly waving his pointer finger at me. "When that day comes, I want you to remember this moment."

My eyes crinkled with humor. "Why would we have scared away our other friends?"

Damien threw his hands up dramatically, acting like he was shocked I wasn't following. "Because we are ornery. . . remember? No one wants an ornery friend. We can only handle each other because we are both equally terrible old people."

I bit my lip to suppress the laughter that wanted to escape my throat. "What a charming future you envision for us," I chimed.

Damien shrugged. "Just setting our expectations. You can never say I wasn't honest."

"You're right. You have always been honest with me, no matter how painful it might be." The last sentence came out without me even realizing it. I instantly felt my teeth clench as I waited for the atmosphere between us to change. Thankfully, Damien still managed to keep the mood somewhat upbeat, even with the accidental trap I had sent us into.

Damien's brown eyes were now looking at the ground, his legs crossed in front of his chest, his hands casually placed on his knees. "Speaking of painful . . . are we going to talk about it?" Damien's question held a tone of sincere concern.

I set my eyes on the field. "About what?" I tried to ask casually.

I could see out of the corner of my eye Damien shudder just once. "The long list of awkward things we should talk about that we haven't yet."

"Such as?" I inquired again.

Damien lifted his head, his eyes staring at my face that was still facing the field.

I didn't want him to see the nerves he was already causing me. I knew what he meant, and he knew that I knew. I didn't want him to know how much I wanted to talk about it all, to talk with my best friend about the matters that had been devouring my mind and emotions. But I also didn't want to burden Damien with my problems. I had put him through so much the last few weeks. I felt as if I didn't deserve his kindness, his sympathy, or his comfort.

"You're going to make me say it?" Damien cleared his throat again, swallowing his nerves on approaching the conversation. "To start, do you want to talk about what happened while you were imprisoned in Praseria?"

I shook my head. "No, thank you."

"Your nightmares?"

I felt my heart jump. "How did you —" I stopped myself. *Risa.* I swallowed. "Nothing to discuss," I lied.

Damien still prodded, not skipping a beat on his list of topics we hadn't discussed. "Okay, how about Aleron?"

My jaw went slack at the mention of his name. "Definitely not."

"Whatever weird thing is going on between you and your mother?"

I rolled out my shoulders, trying to release the tension Damien was causing with each passing question. "I'd rather not get into that," I replied.

Damien's tone was now exasperated, clearly defeated but still hopeful. "Hassan?"

My eyes widened. "We are never discussing that."

Damien let out a long breath. "Allene, I just want to make sure you're okay."

My eyes fell shut, my lips twisted into a frown. "I know. I'm just — I'm not ready to talk about any of it yet."

I couldn't see Damien, but I could feel his body move as he nodded in understanding. "Well, when you are ready to discuss it, you know I am here for you, right?"

"I do. Thank you, Damien." I sighed and tried to change the focus of the conversation as I now looked at Damien. "What about you? Are you all right?" I asked.

Damien smiled. "Never been better. Truly. The changes these last few weeks have been nothing less than exciting."

"I am delighted to hear that." I shifted my body weight to lean back onto my hands and gripped the soft grass that brushed against my fingertips. "However, there is one change I could have done without," I added, trying to bring up what I had come to Damien for in the first place.

"Your new makeup?" Damien mocked without even a second of hesitation.

I felt my breath catch in my throat, the surprise overtaking me as my face turned a shade of pink. "Okay, I'm going to pretend you didn't just say that." I shot him a stern glare.

Damien flashed a wide grin, his hand covering his mouth to hold back his laughter. "I'm sorry, we both know you set yourself up for that. I'm just poking fun. You look beautiful, Allene," he reassured me.

"You think I'm beautiful?" I asked for confirmation.

Damien's grin faded, his face now changing a shade in color. I pulled on Damien's arm, hugging it tightly. "Damien, that is one of the sweetest things you've ever said to me."

Damien shook his head, patting my hand away. "All right, all right, don't get all sentimental on me now. Back to what we were talking about. What change were you referring to?" Damien was quickly back to being serious.

I let out a silent laugh, impressed with how rapidly he would change the subject, but I took the bait. I held my hands in my lap, staring at my nerve-bitten fingernails.

"Nycolas." His name almost tasted bitter as I said it. I looked at Damien before continuing. "I don't like him," I admitted out loud. I knew it sounded harsh and wrong to disdain someone so quickly, for not very good reasons, but it was the truth. There was something about the perfectly composed and calculated Nycolas that left me uneasy and distrusting.

Damien's eyes widened in surprise, but he nodded his head, acting like he expected such a statement. "I don't either," he claimed.

I put my head in my hands, holding it up as I looked at Damien. "He's shady," I stated.

"He's many things — shady is just one of them," Damien confirmed.

"So you agree we can't trust him?" I asked.

Damien nodded. "Absolutely. Hassan and I both have unsettling feelings about him."

My ears perked up at the mention of Hassan. I tried to

pretend his name didn't make my stomach churn just ever so slightly.

"Really? Hassan seemed pretty eager to work with him as a spy for Valteria," I reminded Damien of yesterday.

Damien laughed. "You mean eager to spy on *him*. Hassan is smart. He knew the best way to reveal Nycolas's true intentions was by having more time with him. It all comes down to gaining Nycolas's trust."

My heart grew a little less heavy at the news. Hassan was intelligent, but more than that, he was proving to be strategic. He always seemed one step ahead of everyone else.

"I see, so the meeting he requested with Hassan and you for today —"

"Will be very informative." Damien grinned.

I gave a brief smile at Damien's interruption. He knew me well enough to know what I was going to ask.

"Will you tell me how it goes tonight after your meeting? I have a feeling he is going to try and use the conversation between you and Hassan as a way to dominate our meeting in the morning. My mother is overly trusting of him, and Risa seems to fear him. I want to be prepared if no one else will be."

Damien nodded, understanding my anxiety. "I will get information to you before lights out," he promised.

I sighed, taking comfort that I had the support of someone I cared about. I found relief knowing I wasn't alone in my thoughts and opinions.

I laid my head on Damien's shoulder, embracing the coolness of the shade and the slight breeze that still found its way over the castle walls. I wrapped my arms around his, leaning into him. He pressed his cheek against the top of my head, letting out a long sigh. I closed my eyes, listening to his every breath, letting the movement and sound soothe my worries.

"Damien, you're one of my favorite people," I told him.

"I know." He nudged me gently, mimicking my comments from earlier.

We were quiet for a long while, both of us studying the beating sun, enjoying the silence. I was grateful for a friendship that had withstood so much — thankful for some serenity before the storm.

CHAPTER 6

*D*inner had come and gone. I tried to approach the topic of Nycolas with my mother and Risa, but my mother insisted we wait to speak about anything until tomorrow morning. I gave up on the matter quickly; I was not in the mood to argue with her. Risa hated contention and disagreements, so I didn't want to push the conversation — partially for her sake and partially for mine. Besides, I knew my mother probably wouldn't listen to my concerns.

Risa had tried to stir the conversation to the turning of the Fall weather. When my mother, nor myself, had much to add, we ate in silence. I had initially planned to discuss Aleron's situation with my mother just yesterday, but after our surprising interaction, advocating on his behalf had fallen to the bottom of my priority list. As weary as Nycolas had made me, he also brought a distraction from my heartache.

I wanted to pull Risa aside and speak to her after dinner about Nycolas, but she had made arrangements to spend time with Marshal. I knew Hassan and Damien were talking with Nycolas at that very moment, and I wanted to keep my mind occupied while I waited for Damien's visit.

I found myself walking back to my room alone and decided to wander the castle a bit longer to avoid the solitary confinement my room had become in the last few weeks.

My mind wandered as quickly as my feet, the pace of my steps meeting the strides of my rapid thoughts. As I mindlessly rushed through the vast, long hallways, I admired the various artwork and tapestries that hung so proudly on the castle walls. Despite its captivating decor, the castle still felt hollow and cold — nothing like I felt when I first walked through the halls of Praseria's castle.

The simple memory of Praseria's castle brought a rush feeling of warmth and safety as I reflected on my earliest moments in my father's first home. So many awful things had happened in Praseria. It would have made more sense to focus my memories on the most recent events, but somehow my heart had shoved them aside. I realized the need to focus on happier memories to be more robust — to be needed.

I lost track of the time just as quickly as I had lost myself in my thoughts. Memories flashed through my mind of Ezra and of Noni, a smile appearing on my lips as I could almost feel Ezra's weathered hand in mine and Noni's warm embrace. Each memory welcomed bursts of one feeling — pure, unbridled joy. It was a feeling I'd been devoid of for weeks. And to my surprise, the subsequent feeling of joy came from the place I expected it least at that moment. *Aleron.*

My heart began racing as I pictured our first encounter, our first kiss, our first 'I love you'. It was so perfect — *he was perfect.* How had the one thing I had felt so sure about been so wrong?

My feet suddenly stopped as I became nauseated at the thought. I pressed my shoulder against the bare stone wall, leaning into its strength for support as I closed my eyes to steady the lightheadedness that quickly washed over me. I could feel my chest tighten as the brief moment of paradise began to implode. Yesterday's encounter with Aleron briskly took over my mind, corrupting any feelings of happiness I had found.

I heard footsteps walking my way, the noise pulling me back to my senses just enough to let out a shaky breath. I searched around for the echoing steps and placed them to a soldier approaching me from down the hall. I felt my breath become short once again as I realized it was Marshal.

I frantically looked to my surroundings, my eyes settling on the same door I had come to yesterday. The same door I had walked out of — defeated and torn apart. Amid my aimless stroll, I managed to subconsciously find my way to Aleron — the exact place I had tried to convince myself I *didn't* want to be.

I contemplated running. I wondered what was worse, Marshal believing I was crazy, or Aleron discovering I came back to him within a day? *Definitely the latter.*

I tried to remain calm as Marshal approached me, his eyes concerned as he observed me still clinging to the wall for support. I offered him a shaky smile as he stopped in front of Aleron's door, his hands holding a tray of food.

"Princess Allene, is everything all right?"

My body temperature was rising as I fumbled over my words. "Y-yes, yes, everything is fine."

"Are you looking for Risa? I just escorted her back to her room," Marshal said, pointing his shoulder in the opposite direction.

I gave a weak smile. "What great timing; I meant to speak with her. I hope you had a lovely evening." I cleared my throat, ready to escape the trap I had set for myself until Marshal blocked my attempted footsteps.

Marshal looked around, just as he had yesterday, his eyes searching for something, or someone, and finding nothing. I could see the tension in his shoulders release as he confirmed we were alone. He leaned his body in closer as he exchanged words in a whisper. "Are you here to see Aleron?"

I tried to contain the shock and nerves flooding my expression. I knew what I wanted to say, but I also knew it was what I *couldn't* say. My mind was screaming one thing, and yet my mouth muttered another.

"No."

I could hardly process that the word had escaped from my throat. I fought back the urge to correct myself, fought back the strong desire to say yes. I knew it would confuse Marshal, who already seemed worried enough by my unexpected visit.

His brows furrowed as he looked back and forth between me, the tray of food, and the door. He stood still as he looked at me, afraid to make any movements.

"Are you certain? I can give you a few minutes. However, I do need to go in first to let him know you are here. At this hour, he's usually . . ." Marshal hesitated as he debated on his next choice of words. "Indecent."

My cheeks became hot, my mind flustered. I pushed myself away from the wall and rolled back my shoulders to stand tall, trying to convince Marshal and myself that I had some dignity and poise left. "Thank you; I will come back another time." The words were like fire, making my heart race as I declined Marshal's offer.

Marshal pondered my response for only a moment and decided to take my request without protest. Marshal nodded and began reaching for the door.

"And Marshal?" Marshal paused with his hand on the door handle, keenly waiting for my words of caution. "Please, do not mention that I was here." I tried not to sound desperate, not to sound like I was begging, but I was mortified to consider Aleron learning about my surprise visit — the visit that had even been a surprise to myself. How weak I would have seemed.

How weak am I? I almost gave in! I almost said yes when Marshal asked if I was here to see Aleron. Where is my pride? Where is my head? I am not thinking clearly. This would have been a terrible mistake.

The conversation with Aleron yesterday rang in my head. I had to stand by my words. I needed to rely on myself. Coming to Aleron first — and coming to Aleron at all — would neglect my self-respect. I would not back down, and I would not break.

Marshal gave a firm nod in reply, his hand still balanced on the door handle. "Understood, your majesty. I won't speak a word of it," he promised me.

"Thank you. I apologize for disturbing your post at such a late hour. Goodnight." I offered a quick smile and turned in the direction of my room, hoping to put today, yesterday, and the last few weeks officially behind me.

~

I found myself alone in my room, lying on my bed, attempting to write in my journal. My thoughts were scattered, making it difficult to find what I wanted to write. My mind was being pulled in so many directions. I found myself writing about everyone I missed: my father, Noni, Ezra, and Aleron.

As I wrote, my thoughts shifted to the pressures of more war, more lives in danger, more things sacrificed. Then my thoughts turned to Killian. That thought alone made me shiver. I thought about my nightmares of him and that I finally went one night without him terrorizing my dreams. I knew it involved my fight with Aleron; it made Killian feel like less of a threat to me.

I thought about my new friendship with Sonora and my continued friendship with Damien. I thought about

Hassan and our more *complicated* friendship. I thought about King Ulric. I thought about my new ambition to be a better princess, be a better version of myself, and be what Valteria needed.

My eyes became heavy, and my hand tired as my journal entry stretched on for many pages. It had been a long time since I had written in my journal, and things I wanted to vent about seemed innumerable. I needed to keep myself awake, keep writing. I needed to stay up and wait for Damien. I needed answers for the troubles I had just written about — for the problems that evaded solutions.

⁓

I found myself running, racing. I fixated on the tree ahead, joyfully laughing as I approached it. I could hear a voice behind me, cheering me on. Expecting to see Damien behind me, I noticed black hair out of the corner of my eye. Realizing it wasn't Damien, panic began to set inside of me.

I reached the tree and turned, ready to defend myself until I understood who it was. Aleron approached me and pushed me against the tree that we had both run to. He was so beautiful. His hand found its way to mine, squeezing it gently. I felt myself calm down, taking it in. *You came back.*

Aleron seemed to hear my thoughts. His dimpled smile appeared briefly, just for a moment, until it turned malicious in its intent.

"Of course I came back, Allene. I have to finish what my brother started." Suddenly, Aleron's clothes morphed into those of Killian's on the battlefield — his gold armor was covered in blood. I screamed, trying to push him away, but Killian's grasp on my hand pulled me closer to him. He placed my hand on his sword, and I was prepared for the worst. I found myself sobbing, pleading with him. I heard a voice, one I could only assume was an angel. "I'm here Allene, don't be afraid." I closed my eyes, ready to fight from the voice of courage that I could hear beside me.

I jolted up, my eyelids flinging open. My room was dark, and I could feel the paper from my journal had left an indent on my face. I had fallen asleep; it was another nightmare. My body was still shaking with adrenaline that I barely noticed the warm hand placed on my shoulder.

Panicking, I moved back, hugging the corner of my bed.

"I didn't mean to startle you." The same voice of the angel in my dream. It was the voice of Hassan. My breathing began to slow down, realizing I was not in any danger.

My curtains had been left open from my accidental slumber, the moon giving the faintest amount of light to illuminate half of Hassan's face. His honey hair stood out, gleaming in the moonlight, as his dark clothing attempted to camouflage the rest of him.

"Hassan! Why would you scare me like that?" I accused him as I came out from the protection of my corner.

"I knocked, but I could hear crying. I thought you were hurt, so I let myself in. I was trying to help." He defended his innocent actions. It wasn't his fault that I couldn't go more than a day without having a nightmare about Killian. *So much for thinking I was finally past this.*

"I was having a nightmare," I defended the reason for my state of embarrassing distress. Hassan seemed uneasy as his eyes intently focused on mine.

"Does that happen a lot?" he asked.

I wasn't sure how I wanted to respond. *Did I want to tell Hassan the truth that Killian had been haunting my dreams ever since our return?* I decided it wasn't a topic I wanted to dive into. The memories that came with it were not where I wanted my focus to be.

"Now and then," I replied vaguely.

Hassan seemed to sense my apprehension regarding the conversation. He respectfully moved on. "Damien said you wanted to be informed about our meeting with King Ulric before sunrise. He sent me to tell you about it," Hassan explained his purpose for arriving at my chambers so late at night.

I nodded. "Is Damien all right?" I asked with concern. I didn't understand why Damien wouldn't tell me himself.

"He's fine. King Ulric sent him to make contact with the Red Crows."

My eyes widened. "He could be putting Damien in danger. He is not supposed to make any decisions before speaking with us in the morning. We need to stop him." I began to get out of my bed, ready to expose Nycolas's questionable trustworthiness. Hassan shot out his arm, catching my wrist as he pulled me back on the bed, landing me a place on his knee as he held me back gently. I tried not to be distracted as the moon made his light eyes sparkle and his smooth skin shine.

"No, we don't. This needs to happen. It is the first thing Nycolas has done that allows us to doubt his character. We need that, so we wait," Hassan demanded.

"But Damien —" I tried to interject, but Hassan cut me off.

"The Red Crows reached out to him originally. He handled the situation once, and he can handle it again."

I rolled my eyes. "You Durands have a habit of being one step ahead of my thoughts. Am I that predictable?"

Hassan laughed, vibrating my body as he tried to contain the unexpected humor I seemed to present to him. "I only wish you were more predictable. It would make my life a lot easier."

I felt my eyes narrow. "Should I be apologizing?" I questioned.

"Of course not, because it also makes my life more exciting," he teased, gently squeezing my wrist that he still held onto.

I smiled at his playfulness. I was still uncertain how I should take his flirtations. I did the one thing I knew would make me comfortable again — I changed the subject.

"What all happened tonight?" I asked, shifting my weight, so I fell off Hassan's knee to sit on the bed, facing him. He released my wrist, letting me hold my hands as I fidgeted with my ruby ring while I waited for his response. Hassan leaned back on his arms, calm as ever.

"King Ulric wanted to discuss who approached us from the Red Crows."

I put up a hand to stop Hassan this time. I had a question I was anxiously waiting to be answered. "Who did approach you about them?"

Hassan hesitated at my request for the information, but he had always been honest with me; I knew he wouldn't stop now.

"Fen, a childhood friend of ours. He has helped run my father's farm as long as I have. Until he joined them. . ." Hassan trailed off. I could see the pain in his eyes reflecting on his dear friend, who had chosen a rather saddening path. This time, I reached out to Hassan, squeezing his hand. A small smile appeared at my gesture and he intertwined our fingers.

"I'm sorry, Hassan," I expressed my sincerest apology. I understood what it felt like to be betrayed — to be blindsided. If anyone could imagine what he was feeling, it was me. He held a half-smile as he looked at me, his hair sweeping across his forehead as his other hand pushed it back.

"Fen was never given great opportunities to embrace his strengths. He was always ambitious. He has always had the characteristics of a leader. He felt limited in Selvet. The life he was given was not one of prestige, and he was passionate about equality. He would be an easy recruit for a group like the Red Crows. That is their intention, to prey on those that feel disadvantaged.

Damien and I were aware that he had joined them. We hoped his dedication to their cause would pass in a matter of weeks. We didn't realize the extent and rank he had achieved in such a short amount of time would dig his heart even deeper into their cause," Hassan spoke softly, trying not to hear his own words.

"Did you ever feel the same way as Fen, feeling disadvantaged being raised in Selvet?" I almost didn't dare ask the question, but I wanted to know and understand.

Hassan stared out my window for a long time before replying. He took a deep breath, the sudden chill of air making me shiver. "Sometimes," he admitted.

His response broke my heart. Hassan was such an admirable man; he deserved much more than he had. The fact that he felt inferior because he wasn't raised in prestigious circumstances made me feel guilty. I had been given so much, and I still didn't fully appreciate my privilege.

"Why did you turn them down?" It was a sincere question. If I had been in their situation, I could see the appeal of the offer.

He displayed a soft smile, squeezing my hand. "Because of you," he confessed. I was slightly taken back by his words. He was approached two months before the Gala festival — he hadn't met me yet. I chuckled, realizing he was probably just trying to find another opportunity to tease me.

"Hassan, you didn't know me then."

He shrugged, pulling back his hand as he crossed his arms that were bulging as he subconsciously flexed from his nerves. He quickly reminded me how handsome he was, making my thoughts shift back to our time in the prison. The memory of his shirtless appearance made me blush all over again.

"I knew about Damien's plan to introduce us at the Gala in just a few weeks. That was enough to dissuade me from even entertaining the idea of joining the Red Crows. That was the difference between Fen and me — opportunity," he concluded.

His sentiment made my heart swell. I was having a hard time forming words to reply. Hassan was genuine. He was real. He was good. I felt my instinct take over as I leaned forward, giving Hassan a tight hug.

Hassan didn't hesitate at my motion. He swiftly wrapped his extended arms around me, firmly holding me to his chest. I let him keep me there for many moments, appreciating his warmth and solitude. I didn't want to move, and I was pretty confident Hassan didn't want me to move either. He effectively took away my stress and anxiety and replaced it with the tender appreciation of knowing there were people who stood by me. I let him carry my weight as I placed my head on his shoulder, staring into the corner of my room.

"And Damien? What was his reason?"

Hassan chuckled, his rumble vibrating through my chest.

"Damien had plenty. He values your friendship, and he has faith in Valteria. More importantly, Damien has been working hard to earn his station as a knight. He wanted to receive prestige the honorable way by making sacrifices, displaying loyalty — as do I. We both knew there was more than one way to earn our version of freedom. Fen wanted to try a different path." His response completely embodied Damien. I was beyond proud of the man he had become, the man I was able to call my best friend.

My cheek had become warm. I finally lifted my head and pulled away from our long embrace. "I'm grateful you are here, Hassan." I wanted to be open about my thoughts. Hassan had never held back his feelings when he was with me, and it was the least I could do in return. His hands had made their way to my shoulders, holding them softly.

"There is no place I would rather be," he said candidly. I knew he was truthful when he said those words. His display of sentiment made me timid. I impulsively pulled away, creating distance between us once again. Our conversations always had a way of turning our moments into feelings of endearment. It felt natural. I would be lying to myself if I said I didn't know why I pushed so hard to stop it. Nonetheless, it was easier to ignore the reason entirely. I had brought back my defenses.

"Should I be worried about the Red Crows?" I asked. Hassan took a moment to think about the question before giving me an answer. His pause made me nervous.

"I wasn't worried before. That is why I never told you of their existence. However, if the Red Crows are as far as Cenan — if they have formed an alliance with Praseria, then I would be worried. But something tells me Nycolas isn't truthful. It is an audacious claim — one I don't think he will be able to prove."

I was perplexed by the situation. Nycolas displayed a level of fearlessness that I believed resulted from his confidence, which came from what I assumed was his ability to prove he was right.

"You truly believe his claims will lose their merit over time?" I asked. Hassan nodded, taking another relaxed position as he was now laying down next to me, getting comfortable on my bed.

"Absolutely. One thing I learned about Nycolas tonight is that he *loves* to talk. He may be bold, but it also makes him rash. I can see him being hot-headed, eager to prove a point for the sake of his pride, even if he doesn't have substantial proof to back it up," Hassan declared.

"His obsession with being right can be to our advantage," I confirmed.

"Exactly. Damien and I will play out his plan. We will infiltrate the Red Crows as spies, and I am certain we will find their reach is not as exaggerated as Nycolas makes it seem. I believe he is trying to gain an alliance with Valteria for another reason. Whatever it is, I promise Damien and I will figure it out," he assured me.

I knew Hassan and Damien volunteering to be spies for Valteria while being part of the Red Crows was dangerous. I also knew if I protested, it wouldn't change their minds. I had already tried to stop them from fighting in the war against Praseria. Rather than lecturing and worrying, I decided this time I would take a different approach — an approach that the brave princess inside of me would take — being supportive. I appreciated Hassan's dedication to finding answers. My mother and sister may not have been able to see the peculiarity of the situation, but I was thankful that Hassan and Damien could.

"I am certain that you will. If I can help in any way, just say the words." I extended the offer. Hassan seemed surprised by my reply. He must've been expecting a protest from me as well. He didn't dither at the offer, immediately asking a question.

"Did you speak to Aleron yesterday?" His face stayed composed as he mentioned Aleron's name. He took me off guard, my face successfully showing no signs of anxiety, no matter how much I felt like spiraling at the question. I thought I had successfully shifted our conversation away from feelings and the past. Hassan seemed insistent to talk about it, but I did not understand its relevance in this circumstance.

"I did," I curtly replied.

"You need to speak to him again," he insisted. I shook my head, the anger fueling inside me as I thought back to yesterday. I made it very clear to Aleron that I would not be coming back. I was still trying to process my emotions from it all. Diving back into another conversation with him would set me back to the start.

I stood up from the bed, shaking from my rage. *Well, so much for hiding my panic.* I made my way to the window, looking out at the stars as I tried to regain my poise. I didn't turn to Hassan, even though I heard him stand up to be right behind me.

"There is nothing left to speak with him about. We discussed our feelings, and I am moving on from it," I persisted. Nothing could get me to talk to Aleron again. Hassan had asked me to speak to him to get closure, which I achieved.

I heard Hassan sigh. He placed a firm hand on my shoulder, letting me know he was there. My shaking started to subside at his touch.

"Allene, Damien, and I think he could have some helpful information about Nycolas. He is claiming that the Red Crows allied with Praseria, remember? He might know something that could help us," he whispered, afraid to raise his voice any higher than necessary to hear his words. He acted like I was fragile, speaking to me like an animal who might spook if he spoke too loud.

"He won't; he doesn't know anything," I tried to convince myself.

"How can you be sure?" Hassan asked.

I knew he was right. *How could I be sure?* Every time I thought I knew who he was, I would be surprised. Maybe he did know Nycolas. Maybe he had been working with the Red Crows. Maybe he did have something that could help us solve this predicament sooner. Or maybe he would lie to me again. Maybe he would give me false information. *There was no way for me to know anymore.*

I turned to Hassan, his arm falling off my shoulder. I took a deep breath, collecting my thoughts. I offered to help in whatever way I could. Hassan and Damien were taking their own risks; making their own sacrifices. It wasn't fair for me to refuse a conversation. It wasn't about me; it was about Valteria.

"I will talk to him," I spit out the words quickly so I couldn't take them back or stop myself.

Hassan furrowed his brow. "I won't ask you to do something you're not comfortable with," Hassan assured me.

"This isn't about my comfort — this is about the responsibility to my kingdom. I will talk to Aleron," I promised.

Hassan paused, taking time to analyze me. My anxiety fell away, allowing me to approach Hassan with more confidence to support my statement.

"It's late, Hassan; we should get to sleep." I made my way to the bed, trying to put an end to the conversation. I laid down, staring at Hassan, who stood still, not moving.

"I will be back," he said, quickly turning and leaving the room. He obviously wasn't getting my hints. He gave me no option to object or question his whereabouts. I looked at the closed door, confused by his sudden disappearance and slightly hopeful he wouldn't deliver on his promise of coming back. I was sincere in my suggestion of getting some sleep.

About twenty minutes passed, and my eyes were starting to grow heavy again. I was ready to give in to the temptation of sleep. Right before I could, Hassan opened the door and quietly closed it behind him. He made his way over to me and sat on my bed, permitting himself to lay down next to me.

He let himself get comfortable. His head was on my

pillow, our eyes staring at one another, our bodies inches apart. He pretended to close his eyes like he was sleeping. I chuckled nervously.

"What are you doing?"

"I'm staying," Hassan said.

I hesitated. I was unsure if Hassan was getting the wrong idea.

"In case you have another nightmare," he explained quickly, his intentions being pure.

I considered his offer. Hassan staying in my bed, even without suggestive intentions, was inappropriate. If we got caught, I couldn't even imagine the trouble we'd be in. But I trusted him. Risa was no longer here while I slept, and it was kind that Hassan would even suggest such a thing. My only fear would be if someone caught Hassan in my room. However, I had given Sonora the next few days off. She wouldn't be coming in the morning, and I never had other visitors. The chance of him being seen was practically nonexistent. *What could one night hurt? With what might come my way tomorrow, a good night's rest is essential.*

I smiled, seeing his eyes peek open as he looked at me again. I was willing to try anything to avoid another nightmare. Maybe Hassan's presence could be that solution.

"Goodnight, Hassan," I said, snuggling deeper into my pillow.

"Sweet dreams, Allene."

CHAPTER 7

$\mathcal{I}$could feel the sun shining through my window, as my eyelids sensed the light streaming into my room. I didn't have another nightmare. I had managed another decent night's sleep.

I sighed and smiled, realizing Hassan's idea had worked. I heard Hassan clear his throat, obviously noticing that I was awake. I fluttered my eyes open to see Hassan's arm wrapped around my waist, his neck coddling my head. I pulled away gently, taking in all of his features.

His pink lips were slightly parted as he breathed heavily, his cheeks rosy from the heat that had formed between us. His shirt was slightly damp and clung to his broad chest. His hair was somewhat messy, and his eyes were closed, still sleeping. *Wait, he was still sleeping. But I heard him as if he was awake...*

I felt myself cautiously turn as I noticed a figure in the

corner of my room. My heart practically jumped into my throat as I saw Aleron's galled expression. He was sheepishly rubbing his arm, unable to make eye contact with me.

Aleron looked tired. Dark circles were underneath his eyes. His curls were shiny, almost like they were wet from bathing. He was in a pair of fresh clothes. His eyelashes covered his piercing eyes that I was grateful weren't looking at me right now — but I knew they had been, and I was uncertain how long he had been standing there.

I nudged Hassan as I sat up. Hassan didn't immediately respond to my movement. I nudged him again. I was at a loss for words, and I was hoping Hassan could break the silence.

Hassan groaned, stretching his arms over his head, coming up to a sitting position without moving his gaze to the corner of the room. He rolled out of bed, smiling at me sweetly, still oblivious to Aleron's presence.

"Good morning, beautiful. I could get used to this," Hassan said proudly. I held back a blush. I stayed silent, looking down at my hands.

"I'm sure you could," Aleron spoke softly.

I looked up at Hassan's face, waiting to see his reaction. Hassan grinned amusingly; he didn't seem one bit bothered by hearing Aleron's voice. I wish I could have behaved the same.

"You got my invitation," Hassan replied, turning to face Aleron. Aleron was still looking at the ground, standing tall. Even being as tired as he looked, he was still beautiful.

"I should have assumed it was from you," Aleron admitted, shaking his head that he didn't realize it sooner.

Confused, I stood up, holding myself steady behind Hassan.

"What invitation?" My question was more of a demand for an answer.

Hassan continued to keep his composure, showing he could hold a level head.

"An invitation supposedly from Allene saying she wanted to speak with me early this morning. It had instructions to sneak into your room to talk," Aleron huffed, partially referring to me in the third person so he wouldn't have to speak to me directly.

Hassan held back a slight smirk, confirming Aleron's statement. "I sent it last night, courtesy of Marshal." Hassan turned to me, a glimmer of pride in his eyes.

I couldn't decide what I was feeling. Anger? Fear? Was it towards Hassan, myself, or Aleron? I did tell Hassan I would speak to Aleron; I just assumed he would let it be on my terms. I waited a moment longer to hear if he had anything else to say before I made a judgment. Hassan accepted the invitation to plead his case.

"I could see you were worried about speaking with him. I thought you would be more comfortable if you didn't have to speak with him alone," Hassan said, showing his thoughtfulness.

My heart softened slightly at his reasoning. I sighed, finally gaining the courage to look at Aleron directly.

I wasn't going to allow myself to be angry at Hassan. *Not long from now, I will be confronted with Nycolas. I* needed as many answers as I could before then. There was no time to waste.

I pushed aside the twisted feelings of Aleron seeing me with Hassan in a more relaxed and unsuitable manner, getting straight to the point.

"Aleron, what do you know about Nycolas Ulric, King of Gelva?" I asked, stepping in front of Hassan. I made my way to the center of the room, standing in the middle of them.

Aleron squinted as if he couldn't see what was in front of him. He shook his head, pursing his cracked lips as he stroked his beard.

"This is why you wanted to talk?" Aleron questioned in disbelief. He finally looked up at me, his blue eyes full of despair.

I nodded, holding my tongue.

"Lia —, I mean Allene," Aleron caught himself. "I was hoping we could talk in private," Aleron said quietly, eyeing Hassan out of the corner of his eye.

I gawked. "I was hoping we wouldn't have to speak at all; it looks like we both won't get what we hoped for," I spat back. I knew my comment was rude, but I couldn't help myself. Just hearing Aleron even make a request made my blood boil. I was angry with how he treated me, and I had made the point that it would be no more.

Hassan snickered behind me. I couldn't see it, but I

could hear his smile as he held back an even louder laugh. *At least he was trying to be polite — sort of.*

"I'm sorry you feel that way. I will go now." Aleron held back what I assumed was tears as he made his way to the door. I ran over to prevent him from leaving, placing my hand on the door. He stopped, his chest barely touching my outstretched arm.

"Not before you answer my question," I demanded.

Aleron analyzed my expression, trying to see if I was serious. I was.

"You heard the princess. Have a seat, let's talk," Hassan chimed in, crossing his arms to showcase his bulky figure.

Aleron stood his ground for a moment; it didn't take long to give in. He walked over to my writing desk, placing his hand on the smooth surface. He slowly lowered himself into the chair and situated next to it. pulled up next to it.

I took my place next to Hassan again, giving Aleron a disapproving look. We waited in silence. Aleron knew my question, and I wasn't going to repeat it.

Aleron sighed, looking out the window as he spoke. "I don't know much about Gelva, and I don't know anything about King Ulric — only that he keeps to himself."

"You have never interacted with him?" I asked.

Aleron shook his head, still staring out the window. I could sense he wouldn't say more without me prodding.

"King Ulric says the Red Crows have allied with Praseria to strip Valteria of our kingdom — of my home,"

I choked back the last words, hardly able to say them out loud. I was afraid they might come true.

Aleron immediately stood up, his face looking urgent and surprised by my comment. "Did you say the Red Crows?" Aleron pressed, looking at me frantically. I exchanged a glance with Hassan, seeing we finally got his attention.

"Yes," I said.

"How do you know this?" Aleron inquired.

"King Ulric claims to have spies in the organization. Their spies have informed him of their plan."

Aleron shook his head as he paced back and forth now. He was obviously caught off guard from our mention of the Red Crows. Aleron seemed to be deep in thought — something I didn't have time for.

"Why are you surprised?" I asked.

Aleron stilled; his face looked grave. "There is not even the *slightest* possibility that Praseria is working with the Red Crows."

"Why do you say that?" Hassan replied.

"Because we have been trying to stop them from overthrowing our own kingdom," Aleron said plainly.

Aleron's information brought a whole new wave of confusion to the story unfolding before us. Praseria was also trying to defeat the Red Crows?

"You never mentioned it before," I pointed out.

"I didn't want to put you in any danger," Aleron answered.

Great, this group is dangerous enough that Damien, Hassan, and Aleron have left information about them undis-

closed to protect me. The room had become silent again, and the air felt heavy. I wanted to understand his reasoning, but the anger that carried over from yesterday's conversation still made it difficult to hear him objectively.

"The conversation you had with your father in the kitchen about him bringing back Killian. . ." I said quietly, putting the pieces together. Aleron's father wasn't just upset about him choosing to be with me — he was upset by what effect it would have on Praseria in a moment of tension. If the Red Crows were threatening them as well, he probably was afraid to look weak by having his son fraternize with what he assumed was a commoner, and once they knew my identity, the gossip would spread of his son's deep involvement and affection for their enemy. Aleron nodded, acknowledging my conclusion. "The Red Crows have been threatening all of us — Praseria, Lokali, and Gree. That was partly why we formed an alliance in the first place," Aleron explained.

"Praseria has always wanted to see Valteria fall. By joining forces with the Red Crows, Lokali, and Gree, they could do just that. Is that not motive enough for Praseria to align with them?" Hassan encouraged another viewpoint, analyzing the situation from all sides.

Aleron took the question seriously, giving heavy consideration to the thought. "I can't imagine them doing any such thing. Charles, an advisor from Lokali, encouraged us to attack Valteria to show the Red Crows our strength by fighting back after you burned our crops and pillaged our surrounding towns. The point was to intimidate the Red Crows by going against our greatest enemy. I am certain no one would agree to an alliance with the Red Crows, especially my father," Aleron voiced his opinion.

"You don't think it's something even Killian would do?" I pressed. I had no doubt the man that haunted my dreams up until today would do such a thing.

Aleron clenched his jaw at my comment, obviously hurt at the mention of his name.

"Killian is many things, but he is strategic. Aligning with the Red Crows isn't that. He wouldn't encourage it either. Aligning with them would be the equivalency of surrender. That would require being humble — which we both know is not in my brother's character." Aleron was soft-spoken this time, retreating to the window.

I took a moment to process what Aleron had said. I was beginning to put together some similarities between all the stories.

The Praserians strategy for handling the Red Crows matched the same strategy Nycolas had proposed to us. But the Praserians were approached by a Lokali advisor, Charles. It was ironic that we would be advised from smaller kingdoms — that we would be approached at all. Then the words seem to repeat in my head. *We both were given these ideas from outside sources— outside kingdoms. That's it — that's the missing piece.*

I turned to Hassan, excitement and worry filling my eyes all at once.

"What time is it?" I asked.

"Probably near 8 o'clock," Hassan guessed.

"We have to hurry then," I said. Before Hassan could reply, I approached Aleron, grabbing his arm urgently. He seemed surprised by my touch, as did Hassan.

"Aleron, I need you to come with me." I gently pulled on him without a second thought. I ran to the door, flinging it open, motioning for them to follow. I was going to get answers.

Hassan and Aleron hesitated, holding back as they eyed me suspiciously.

"What do you need him for?" Hassan spat as he gave Aleron a mean glare to show his disapproval of my request.

"I need Aleron to confirm who Nycolas is," I replied, surprised they weren't keeping up.

"I've never met him before, Allene," Aleron said plainly, his feet not moving.

"That's exactly what he would want you to think." I motioned once more for them to follow suit. I knew why Nycolas was here, and I was finally going to get us some straight answers.

CHAPTER 8

"Allene, this is not a good idea! We need to talk about this before jumping into anything!" Hassan protested behind me. I ignored his pleas, treading on.

"We don't have time, Hassan. The meeting with King Ulric will begin soon. Aleron needs to see him," I explained.

"Aleron *snuck* into your room, remember? He is not supposed to be seen!" Hassan continued, stopping in front of me, halting my tracks.

I looked up at the massive shadow of Hassan that towered over me. Aleron was slinking behind, cautiously observing his surroundings regarding Hassan's statement.

"The staff will be focused on breakfast or preparations for the meeting with King Ulric this morning. I doubt Aleron will be seen if we take some of the less-traveled routes in the castle," I proclaimed. By less traveled, I meant longer routes, none of the shortcuts — which is precisely why we needed to keep moving.

"Not that it may hold any significance, but I agree with Hassan. He forgot to mention that both of you look disorderly as well." Aleron had caught up to us, joining in the conversation.

I paused, reviewing my appearance in a nearby window.

I was in the same dress as yesterday, and sleeping in it had made it wrinkled. My braid had fallen out, wisps of hair escaping what once used to be a clean, kept look. I had dark circles under my eyes. I could smell a slight odor coming from my dress, probably perspiration attributed to Hassan's hot body temperature last night.

Hassan looked a little better than me, but not by a lot. We did both just get out of bed, so I don't know what I expected. I shook my head. I had to follow through with my plan.

"We will stay out of sight. I just need Aleron to get a glance at Nycolas. We will go after that," I promised, trying to find a solution.

Aleron and Hassan both looked at me. I wasn't worried about Aleron's approval, but I was concerned about Hassan's. His eyes softened. He trusted me.

"Hurry," he said, taking my hand as he pulled me with him. Aleron followed behind.

Deja-vu of walking the halls with the two of them in Praseria came flooding back. It was unsettling how quickly the roles they played in my life seemed to reverse.

We approached the sunroom, no servants passing us by as we took the less-traveled hallways. We stopped behind a large pillar, gathered near one another. Hassan had a putrid look on his face, his nose shriveling.

"Allene, you need a bath," he mocked, trying to lighten the mood.

I shoved him lightly. "Don't blame me; I think it's your sweat," I opposed.

"Right. Never mind, I love it." Hassan grinned.

Aleron's face looked sick once again, not happy to hear about the night we spent together. Although nothing significant or physical happened between Hassan and me, it brought me twisted joy to know it bothered Aleron.

"Aleron, the meeting is taking place in that sunroom. Go over to the far window, look inside and see if you recognize King Ulric," I said, getting back to the reason we were here.

"How will I know which one is King Ulric?" Aleron asked.

"He is the one that doesn't resemble a rat," Hassan laughed at his joke.

I nodded, agreeing with his statement. "There should only be two men. Quinton, his assistant, and King Ulric. It shouldn't be hard to discern between them," I confirmed.

Aleron took a deep breath. "I can't believe I agreed to this. If I get caught, your mother could have my head for spying, for escaping my room. But at this point, I don't have anything else to lose," Aleron said dolefully, staring at me like I had taken everything away from him.

His statement weighed heavily on my heart. I wanted to grieve for him, but I knew he was partly responsible for his sorrows. Hassan shrugged, not concerned one bit by Aleron's claim.

Aleron crouched down, shuffling quietly to the nearest window. He peaked over the frame, observing the scene inside. He stayed there for a few seconds, each one that passed making me more anxious. He finally sunk back down as he made his way back.

Instead of stopping, he passed by, now running at a hurried pace. We followed behind him, trying to catch up without raising attention to ourselves by making noise. Aleron turned the corner and saw the door to my father's study. He motioned to it, opening and shutting the door behind him once we gathered inside.

Aleron looked like he had seen a ghost. His blue eyes were overtaken with concern.

"Allene, you need to remove that man from the castle immediately," he said.

"You know him?" I asked, my hypothesis being proven true.

Aleron nodded, pacing back and forth again, a habit he had when he was nervous. "That's not King Ulric — that's Charles," Aleron confirmed.

"Something tells me that neither of those are his real name," Hassan stated.

"You're right; they're probably not. Any chance either of you knows the name of the leader of the Red Crows?" I boldly asked. Hassan and Aleron exchanged looks. They were both frozen, processing the truth that we had just discovered.

"It makes complete sense," Aleron agreed with my accusation.

"He's pinning kingdoms against each other," I shared my thoughts out loud.

"He's manipulating our downfalls without getting his hands dirty."

"It's genius. It's vindictive. It's cruel," the words felt sour in my mouth.

"And it's already been proven to work," Aleron said coldly, realizing that Praseria had been manipulated in their decision to attack Valteria.

"We have to stop him. If he has already managed to infiltrate Valteria and Praseria, I can't imagine what he has accomplished in the smaller kingdoms," Hassan said worriedly, standing up tall at his proclamation to take on Nycolas — or whatever his name was.

Aleron shook his head, clenching his fists. "There is another problem," he whispered.

"What?" I exclaimed, nervous to hear his reply.

His cold eyes lost some of their light as he proceeded to tell us the news. "He saw me." Aleron barely got the words out, ashamed to admit it.

I closed my eyes tightly, taking in a deep breath, holding my hands over my eyes as I tapped my heels.

I felt my frustration growing internally, wanting to spill over. I couldn't take it anymore. Why was every situation I was involved with so confusing? I wanted things to be simple again. Ever since my father passed, everything had fallen apart. It never happened when he was here, not to this extent. *Oh, how badly I wished he were here.*

"You're certain he saw you? Do you think he recognized you?" Hassan asked.

"The only other person with blue eyes and black hair in Valteria is Allene, so unless he thought I was her. . ."

"Don't forget your noticeable curly hair," I practically hissed.

Aleron was silent. We all knew Nycolas would recognize him.

"Was he alone?" I asked Aleron, my eyes still closed. I was unable to ask the question if I was looking at him.

"He was with your mother and Quinton."

Good. That could give us some time. Nycolas would have to form a smooth excuse to dismiss himself from that meeting. He may not even realize Aleron was reporting to us. He may stick around long enough to have the meeting and then leave. Either way, there was no time to spare.

I turned to Hassan, determination in my eyes. We would not be fooled any longer. We would not be taken as weak. I would fix this — just like my father would have.

"I will go to my mother and stall Nycolas. Hassan, tell Ajax I demand a complete lockdown of the castle and send guards to the sunroom. *Now.*"

Hassan didn't hesitate at my command. He opened the door and took off in a sprint, leaving me alone with Aleron.

"Allene, I'm sorry, I didn't think he could see me; I

thought I was low enough to be out of sight," he defended himself.

I held up my hand, not wanting to hear another word from him. "As angry as I am, about this, about everything, I recognize that you did me a favor. I wouldn't have been able to confirm his identity without you," I begrudgingly admitted.

Aleron sighed with relief, approaching me slowly. I detected the familiar scent of cloves at his closeness. I felt my stomach drop as he grasped my arm, lightly running his fingers up and down my skin. *What is he doing?* I pushed the chills aside, daring myself to look into his enticing eyes. I backed away.

"Don't. Don't manipulate me. Do not construe that recognition as forgiveness. We are far from that," I declared, setting my boundaries.

Aleron held his hands up, squirming back in defense. "I wasn't trying to manipulate you. It was. . ." he trailed off, cowering from me in shame.

"Instinct?" I guessed his absence of word choice firmly. Isn't *that ironic? If it was instinct to comfort me, protect me, and love me, why would he push me away? Why would he have let me go?*

Aleron didn't seem to know what to say. His eyes were empty as he held tension in his jaw, holding back any words. Even if he did have a response, there was no time to waste. There were more important things to handle right now than my discontent for Aleron.

"I'm going to find my mother. It would be best if you head back before the guards are sent for Nycolas. I can only imagine the uproar it would bring if they see you." I didn't wait for his reply. I turned on my heels and ran to the sunroom.

No one was in the hall, meaning the word hadn't gotten out yet to the guards. The sunroom was only a few strides away from my father's study, not giving much time for Nycolas to escape. I pushed my nerves away as I shoved the door open to the sunroom.

I eagerly searched the room, waiting for my eyes to settle on the leader of the Red Crows. The only face I found was my mother. Her eyes widened in shock. I didn't know if it was from my loud entry or my appearance. Either way, she was mortified.

"Where did they go?" I asked hurriedly.

Laerina stood up from the window seat, rushing towards me. "Allene, what are you doing? You cannot be seen like this! Have some dignity, child." She tried shooing me away, ignoring my frenzy.

"Where is King Ulric and Quinton!" I yelled this time, demanding her attention. Her eyes became like fire, anger filling every part of her as she realized how I had spoken to her.

"He has taken ill," Laerina hissed quietly, her anger hardly cooling down, her glances ensuring no one could hear us as she tried to maintain his privacy.

"It is imperative we find King Ulric; we cannot let him escape," I informed her of our task, ignoring her frustration and turning back to the door. I was going to stop him, no matter what it took.

Laerina gawked behind me as I made my pursuit

towards King Ulric's room. Down the hall, I could spot Hassan and a group of guards making their way towards me. I held up a hand, signaling him to stop.

"He's not in the sunroom!" I yelled to Hassan. Hassan held out his arms to push back the men. He took a brief pause, hesitating for a moment while he issued a new plan. I couldn't understand what he was saying, but groups of men hurriedly dispersed in every direction.

Hassan and I ran toward each other. I found myself out of breath while Hassan was hardly making a fuss at the physical exertion. I was slightly ashamed considering how little I had run, whereas Hassan had run from one end of the castle to the other in hardly any time at all.

"Damien is leading a group of guards to the entrance of the castle. I doubt Nycolas knows his way around Valteria well enough to try and leave by any other route," Hassan said.

"You forget this man is the leader of the Red Crows. The knowledge he has access to I think would surprise us both," I pointed out.

Hassan clenched his jaw, obviously sick from the reminder. Under our noses this entire time, the leader of the Red Crows — turning kingdoms against each other, using us as pawns. My mother would not take that information with grace. She couldn't stand manipulation unless she was the manipulator.

"I should go." Hassan's eyes diverted past me, causing me to turn around to see my mother and sister watching a group of guards run past the sunroom.

Risa must have barely arrived for the meeting. She

was wearing a beautiful violet gown that amplified her confidence and glamour. Realizing my appearance at the moment, I felt more suited to catch up with the guards than with my family.

"You don't want my help searching for Nycolas?" I asked. I was slightly offended, considering I was the one to figure out his identity in the first place.

Hassan shook his head quickly, not giving it a moment of thought. "Leave that to us. He won't get far. Go take a bath," he managed to make a sour face to once again poke fun at how I smelled, "have some breakfast, and before you're done, I'm sure Nycolas will be safely locked away in the prison and ready for you to interrogate."

I laughed half-heartedly as I looked up at Hassan. "Be careful," I said softly.

It was hard to imagine what danger Nycolas could cause. I tried to take comfort in Hassan's point of view. As Nycolas was the outsider here, we had the advantage. But it still felt appropriate to extend a word of caution.

"No promises," he chuckled at his honest reply as he jogged away, leaving me with the worst job of all — telling my mother.

CHAPTER 9

"I don't know Allene, that seems difficult to believe." Risa sighed, confusion sweeping over her face as she mindlessly stirred her cup of tea with a spoon by the window. My mother sat directly across from me in the sunroom. Her eyes burned more profoundly as she held her tea tightly in her hand, rigid as can be. I didn't let myself shrink from her disapproving stare. I kept myself composed as I waited patiently for them to accept the news of my discovery.

"I know you haven't been fond of King Ulric and his suggestions, but insinuating he is part of the Red Crows, their *leader* nonetheless, without a confession *or* proof is audacious," Laerina spat disappointingly.

"We don't even know if he is King Ulric," I said softly, trying to prove my point.

"You think he is impersonating King Ulric?" Risa chimed in, sipping her tea now.

"Do you hear how silly you both sound?" Laerina said back, her frustration still hot. Risa put her tea down on the window sill and came to sit next to me. She reached out and took my hand, grasping it lightly for encouragement.

"It may sound unlikely, but you can't deny that it connects everything together," I replied, letting her comment roll off seamlessly.

"You mean connecting the attacks Praseria has made on Valteria?" Laerina questioned.

I nodded. "And the attacks they thought Valteria carried out on their villages and crops. We know we had no involvement, but they were convinced otherwise. So if it wasn't us, who would have done such a thing? Why would they impersonate us? We were at peace. That confusion, whoever caused it, it is what ignited all the attacks and the war," I concurred.

"You said yourself that the connection was an assumption, not fact." As I explained the connection between Nycolas and Praseria, I had to omit that Aleron had confirmed his identity. He was the reason I could make such a claim, but not saying such left me without validity or credibility. I sighed in frustration.

Maybe I should just tell them the entire story — it was probably the only way they would believe me. I hesitated. I didn't want to get Hassan or Marshal in trouble for helping me release Aleron to ascertain the truth. Even if I had told them the truth, I feared I would be wasting time defending Hassan, Marshal, myself, and Aleron — when the real attention should be on Nycolas. I needed to be patient. Once Nycolas was found, he would provide all the proof I needed.

Risa could sense my frustration and graciously intervened on my behalf. "Once we find King Ulric, I am sure we will get some answers," Risa encouraged us both, trying to diffuse the conversation.

We all fell silent after her comment. None of us touched our tea, the steam coming off the cups eventually dissipating into the air. Every minute that passed made my anticipation grow. I was anxious for a guard to burst through the sunroom with news of King Ulric's capture. The castle became eerily quiet as most of the guards made their way outside to continue the search.

The longer we waited, the more my theory was silently being proven. An innocent man wouldn't suddenly be difficult to apprehend. Although my mother wouldn't admit it, I could sense the shadow of doubt looming over her. It brought me ill-suited joy to know for an undeniable fact that I was right in this situation and that my mother would soon learn that too.

Risa broke the room's stillness by approaching the window once again, leaning against the stone wall as she peered out the window and stretched her arms and legs. Seeing her move reminded me how numb my own legs were beginning to feel as we sat and waited. *How long have the guards been searching?* I was oblivious to the effects of time as my thoughts internally consumed me. It seemed like an hour had already come and gone.

Risa squinted her eyes and brought herself closer to the window, observing something in the distance.

"What is it?" I asked her, despite being nervous for her reply.

She shook her head back and forth, acting like her eyes were being deceived. "It looks like the guards have taken an interest in the alfalfa fields. I wonder if they found King Ulric," she proposed. Her words brought me the energy I needed, my attention now shifting to the window.

My mother and I got up quietly and made our way to Risa. I tried to suppress my eagerness, reminding myself that answers would be ours soon enough.

My eyes fell in the direction of the fields on the east side of the castle. The alfalfa fields were quite far in the distance, but the large gathering of guards made it easily stand out. Observing the situation from afar, it was hard to understand what the circumstances were. The guards had seemed to form a defensive line, staying still as they all faced the same direction. The alfalfa fields had orchards on each side, masking and blending whatever it was they were seeing. My eyes searched for what or who they found, the anticipation inside of me stirring.

Our attention shifted as we heard soft echoes in the castle. We could hear the sound of men running in our direction. I was torn, not knowing whether my eyes should remain on the scene outside the window or the scene of approaching soldiers to the sunroom. I was just hoping they came with the good news I needed.

My mother and sister had already turned to the front of the room as Ajax entered with six guards behind him. The men seemed to be catching their breath as they waited for their leader to deliver his message. Ajax did not waste a moment.

"Your majesty, we have found the prisoner in the orchards and have him surrounded. How would you like us to proceed?" he asked firmly.

"King Ulric is not a prisoner until he has a proven reason to be. I want you to escort him back into the castle at once," Laerina commanded, unwavering from her faith in our new enemy.

"Not King Ulric, your majesty; we are still searching for him. We found Prince Aleron," Ajax said, his tone taking on the sound of embarrassment at the confession. My mother's eyes widened in surprise, mirroring my own.

Idiot. I told him to go back to his room before the guards caught him. I was left with two options — pretend I didn't know what was going on or intervene on his behalf.

Despite my anger towards him, I knew I couldn't allow him to suffer for helping me. I addressed Ajax before my mother could, taking control of the situation as quickly as possible.

"Fetch me a horse and tell the guards to fall back — I will go talk to him," I declared, walking towards the guards to make my way to the field.

"My lady, it is not a wise decision for you to approach a prisoner. We will apprehend him." Ajax took a step forward, attempting to block my way.

I sighed in frustration at his protest. "It's not what you think it is," I objected.

"When is it ever?" Laerina muttered under her breath.

I ignored my mother's comment. "Let me be the one to speak to him; your guards can follow behind me at a distance."

Ajax didn't waiver as he gazed to the queen for permission. Risa and Laerina exchanged glances, Risa attempting to soften mother with her sweet smile. Laerina huffed and gave an irritated nod.

"As you wish, your majesty." Ajax turned out of the room.

My mother gave me an undiscerning stare and spoke so quietly it sent shivers down my spine. "I expect an honest and *full* explanation upon your return," Laerina whispered, yet somehow it felt as loud as a shout.

"I understand," I replied.

She put up her hand, indicating she wasn't finished. "*With* Aleron — and whoever else you have been plotting with," she demanded.

I'd been caught. *I was not surprised; secrets don't last very long in my life, it seems.*

I replied with a soft nod and proceeded after Ajax. I wanted to escape the disappointment I could feel strongly from my mother as quickly as possible.

Upon exiting the castle, a grey horse was waiting for me. A few guards stood nearby, one being kind enough to help me mount the beautiful beast. Adjusting my already dirty dress, I headed in the direction of the field.

Ajax and his men trod closely behind me. The ride was silent; we all focused on the speck in the distance that was Aleron "hiding" behind a tree. As I came to the large group of soldiers, Ajax signaled, and they seamlessly made an opening in their barricade to let me pass.

I didn't acknowledge any of the men. I knew they were suspicious of the situation and my sudden involvement. I also couldn't dismiss the fact that I was embarrassed by my disheveled appearance. I would have preferred to be invisible at that moment, but I held my head high, attempting to falsify my confidence. It's what my father would have done.

At that moment, the sound of my horse walking was all that could be heard. With each step that put me closer to Aleron, I expected him to turn, yet he sat still. His back was towards me, his chin in his chest as he seemed to be looking at his hands. I stopped my horse, waiting patiently for Aleron to make eye contact with me. Nothing. I made a slight cough to try to gain his attention — silence.

I could feel the guards staring into me as they watched the odd scene unfold. I had the sense that my mother and sister would be watching too. *I told them I could handle this.* I wouldn't be made a fool again by Aleron. I would force his attention and cooperation, one way or another.

Taking matters into my own hands, I dismounted the horse, landing gracefully to the ground as my feet crunched the alfalfa underneath me. I steadily made my way behind him, speaking as low as possible to avoid the guards overhearing more than they needed to.

"So much for going back to your room," I said quietly, folding my arms in disapproval at his attempt to escape.

Aleron seemed to perk up slightly from the sound of my voice, but he still wouldn't turn to face me. I could hear him sigh as he remained silent in reply.

I was becoming frustrated. Every second that passed, I was being judged by onlookers that expected me to handle the situation at hand. The longer he took to reply or acknowledge me, the longer he was considered escaped and dangerous, and that was something I could not afford. If passive-aggressive comments wouldn't work, maybe sympathy would. *Whatever it takes to get him back.*

"People have the wrong idea of what's going on. Come back with me, and we will get it all sorted out." This time, I stepped closer to Aleron and placed my hand on his shoulder, tugging for his attention. I could feel his body relax and heard a small smile come to his lips.

Aleron kept his head down as he gently moved his hand to touch my own, grasping it softly. "He took such comfort in you; if only I could say the same."

The chilling familiarity of his voice left me frozen. My mind was processing that the words seemed to come from Aleron, yet a sense inside of me knew it wasn't. My hand tensed, my illusion of confidence having lost any chance of survival. Without realizing it, his name escaped my thoughts and left my lips.

"Killian." His name immediately brought panic to my body, terror being my automatic response.

My eyes widened as I peered above him, noticing the patches of fresh blood that stained his coat. It was diffi-cult to see against his coat's maroon color, but the blood on his brow was enough of a stand-out to expose the rest of it. The blood triggered the unwelcome reminder of the war. The war in which he *captured* me, *imprisoned* me, and *hurt* me. I was having a hard time catching my breath as I became enslaved to the memory.

Killian still held my hand in his as he slowly stood to his feet and faced me. His confident posture and elegant poise were equally beautiful and terrifying. His piercing blue eyes demanded my attention, while his gleaming sneer begged to be a tempting distraction. His sharp jawline became more distinct as he tilted his head to the side, his black hair framing his precise features as if by command. His eyes trailed a fire of pain across my skin that left me involuntarily shivering as he methodically studied every inch of my face.

He stroked my hand delicately, each stroke leaving my body cold and repulsed, the urge to shudder and run barely being suppressed. I felt nauseated as I saw Killian's sneer turn to a smile of joy — clearly infatuated with the power of fear he had over me — my reaction aiding his overconfidence.

Killian leaned in closer, his blood-stained cheek lightly grazed against mine, and the nausea worsened. I could feel his smile grow as his lips approached my ear to speak once again, his voice so soft that we both knew only I could hear.

"You don't need to be afraid, Allene," he whispered. The deepness of his voice and the warmth of his breath against my skin left me paralyzed and hollow. My mind was screaming at me to move or speak, to display any sign of mediocre courage, but my body felt tethered in place, and my tongue was numb. It felt like my mind was processing the situation in slow motion — whether from fear, shock, or denial, I couldn't tell. All I knew was I felt petrified, and the amount of shame that was pulsating through my veins, realizing Killian had bettered me once again, left me wanting to cry.

Killian peeled my hand off his shoulder, clasping my hand in both of his as he pulled back just enough to meet my eyes. "I appreciate your hospitality. It's just as you said, we can get this all *sorted out*," he insisted, the sinister undertones that laced his voice piercing through me.

I stared back at him; the light blue hue of his eyes was almost transparent, creating a void of nothingness. Killian stood still amidst my returning stare, his eyes set on evoking intimidation.

The glimpses of Killian from afar made his similarity to Aleron seem nearly identical. Being this close to Killian, for the first time since I learned of his existence, I could make out notable differences between him and Aleron.

Aside from their personalities being absolute opposites, Killian's features were more acute and defined. His shoulders, jaw, cheekbones, nose, and even his temples were fierce and honed. Not a divot, crease, or dimple could be seen, his skin smooth and sharp. His eyes may have been equally blue, but they were glacial — as if they were devoid of color and only reflected vibrancy if they stole it from the sky above.

Killian's lips were fuller than Aleron's, their light pink

hue accentuated by his smooth olive skin. His black curls were heavier, the weight of his hair fighting against its instinct to curl, compromising with loose waves.

From a distance, I wouldn't have thought Killian was taller than Aleron, but his additional inch or so of height made it feel like he towered above me, his broad shoulders casting a shadow over my face.

His voice, another element I once thought was the same, also became more distinct as I heard him speak. Killian's voice was deeper, more methodical, and his tone was more clear. He communicated powerfully with his intense eyes, the same power mirroring in his voice. How I had ever thought they were the same physically, with only personalities to differentiate them, was beyond me. It was apparent to me now in every aspect how different they were.

Killian sighed, his collected stare turning into frustration as if something more important had suddenly plagued his mind, putting his gambit objectives aside for a brief moment. "Generally, I am flattered by rendering someone speechless — I revel in it actually. However, I have had a *very* terrible day, and my patience is growing short, so may I propose two choices. You can be the one to hand me over to the queen, or you can fetch my brother. I dislike both options equally, so why don't you surprise me," Killian proposed cynically.

My greatest fear that I had been battling subconsciously was here in my reality. I had thought about my path crossing with Killian's in the future, and it had never ended well. I wasn't prepared to face him. Not now, not today, but I truly didn't have a choice in the matter.

The thought of my mother seeing me cower to my greatest enemy was not one I would accept. Whatever caused the blood on his body and clothes proved the ability to discountenance a man I considered unshakeable. His comment was exactly the nudge I needed to snap back to reality and regain the courage that he attempted to bury.

The pressure of the guards, my mother, and the kingdom, all seemed to fall away. My eyes fixated on the tree behind Killian, trying to displace him and his unnerving captivation far from my attention.

I took a deep breath, trying to contain any lingering nerves that threatened my illusion of confidence. Gaining my composure, I narrowed my eyes to stare into Killian's, trying not to be shaken by his jeering stare. This man had intimidated me almost beyond comprehension, but I had to believe no man was impenetrable.

Swallowing my fears, I grasped his hand tightly, halting the caressing motion he had tried to start once again. His eyes widened in surprise at the sudden movement. He was taken off guard by my reaction, precisely what I was hoping for.

I placed my other hand on his shoulder and pulled him closer to me, the smell of dirt, blood, and sweat emulating off his body. I shriveled my nose in defense and hovered my lips near his ear as I took back control with a mere whisper.

"You neglected the third option — one that is much

worse than dealing with my mother or your brother," I implied my meaning without having to say the word.

Killian scoffed. "You? I've dealt with you before, dear. Don't be offended when I say that statement doesn't leave me trembling," Killian attempted to mock.

His insult ricocheted, my determination to win this battle of the minds stronger than any words he hoped would debilitate me.

I let out a quiet laugh, surprising myself as an undaunted smile spread across my lips. "You dealt with me in Praseria. You're in my kingdom now, Killian. We will do things *my* way." I pulled back, ready to soak in the shock on his face.

If Killian was surprised, he contained it. The smile disappeared from his face, his lips resting with the softest curve at their corners.

Killian didn't appear angry or offended, but rather as if he was contemplating, fascinated — a look I hadn't expected and hadn't experienced until that moment. Killian's eyes, full of intrigue and curiosity, were almost more terrifying than when his eyes were filled with contempt and malice.

I wasn't going to be a spectacle any longer for him to enjoy and pester. I lifted a hand in the air, motioning to the soldiers on my right, my eyes fixated on Killian's face, searching for any sign of fear as I yelled my command to apprehend him.

"Seize him!"

The soldiers didn't hesitate at my words, immediately charging past me. Four men circled Killian, grabbing his arms and shoulders and forcing his hands behind his back as they shoved him forward.

Through the entire spectacle, Killian didn't flinch or protest — his chiseled face an unreadable canvas. He acted as if the men roughly pushing him past me and towards the castle weren't even there. His gaze was fixated on me, studying me, for as long as he could manage to keep his head turned in my direction.

The further away the soldiers dragged Killian, the more the nausea, the panic, and the stupefaction diminished. It was comforting realizing they were feelings I could conquer; they were moments I could shake.

But the one thing that seemed to linger longer than anything was the fleeting feeling of exhilaration I felt when Killian looked at me with a sense of marvel. I felt sick as I found myself admitting such a feeling had even existed. It had to have been a different emotion — I was confused, I was in shock. I buried the feeling — I buried the thought; I let it die and promised myself it was just a mistake of my imagination.

~

*U*pon returning to the castle, I immediately retreated to my room. I didn't want people seeing me in my current state of slovenliness any longer. With my offer of giving Sonora a few days off — a decision I already had come to regret — it left me to fend for myself.

I hurriedly removed my dress and placed it over my

bed for a maid to grab later. I rustled through my wardrobe as I attempted to find an outfit that wasn't much of a fuss to put on. I frowned. Nothing seemed convenient to put on without assistance, aside from my nightgowns. Sonora had recently replaced most of my gowns with the new trend of high necklines and long trains, which also had many buttons and ties that I am sure I would miss.

My eyes scanned the dresses a little longer, finally settling on a light green tea-gown with only a few buttons to do up near the lower back. The neck scooped, and the sleeves were short; it seemed the most promising.

After putting on the dress, I tackled my hair. Grabbing my silver comb tightly, I mercilessly brushed out the disorder of tangles that had formed through the night and the windy horse ride. The truculent method of brushing left my regularly silky black locks to be frizzy and dry. I didn't have time to oil my hair properly or to take a bath. I had questions for Killian, and I did not want to be left out of anything my mother may throw his way.

I began to separate my hair into strands and swiftly weaved them together to form a loose braid that cleaved to my right side. A bowl of water and towels had been placed on my vanity. I drenched the top towel and patted my face. The towel removed any shine of sweat, and the cold water left my cheeks rosy.

I reached for my pallet of stained oils to give my pale lips a falsified vision of life, painting them red. A few dabs of a new type of powder that Sonora had been begging me to try and a splash of my peony perfume; I was ready to get back to the madness awaiting me downstairs.

I took a brief look in my mirror, pleasantly surprised with my achievement of looking decently put together. I took a deep breath, trying to calm down any nerves I may have been ignoring through the chaos. A short moment of peace was exactly what I needed before carrying on.

Suddenly, everything felt quiet. Even with all the commotion that the morning had brought, everything seemed calm. The sun was shining as bright as it could, the summer breeze was swaying the trees slightly — branches tapping my window. It was beautiful. Valteria was beautiful. I sighed and let out any remaining stress I carried.

Killian's arrival at Valteria was a complete shock. The reason for his arrival, and the fashion of it, was confounding. I felt as if confusion followed me. It seemed with every answer I would receive, two more questions would appear in their place. For once, I wanted to be a step ahead.

My father believed in God. He would probably tell me to pray. Given how disorderly my life had recently proven to be, I thought I would take his advice.

I briefly closed my eyes and muttered a few words to God, to father, or anyone that may be listening. I pleaded for strength. I pleaded for guidance. I pleaded for courage. I pleaded for control.

Nothing significant happened after the small prayer, but a small amount of amity seemed to return, knowing I was doing something that father did every day, doing something he honestly had faith in.

I shook out my shoulders, feeling my dress tugging in complaint at the movement. The moment had arrived.

It was time to face my mother, Aleron, and worst of all — Killian.

CHAPTER 10

"Who would like to start?" Laerina asked stiffly.

My mother had arranged a private meeting in the library. Initially, walking into the room, I could feel the tension immediately. Laerina and Risa sat side by side on a couch in the south end of the room. One spot was left on the right of my mother, the spot intended for me.

Hassan and Marshal framed Aleron, who was sitting in a chair on the south side of the room. An additional chair was set nearby for Killian, who was being guarded by Damien and Ajax. Seeing the two brothers side by side, it was impossible to ignore how Aleron and Killian resembled each other, even with Aleron's brash beard covering up most of his face.

I took a moment to meet Damien's gaze. He had a twinkle in his eyes as if the situation Aleron and Killian were caught up in brought him an immense amount of joy. I moved on past Ajax's hardened face to Marshal's soft expression — a stark contrast. Finally, I settled my gaze on Hassan, his pale olive eyes searching mine.

A sweet smile appeared on his face when he caught me staring at him. He was bulkier and taller than any of the other guards that lined the walls of the large room. He stood out among them all, collected and prepared.

My attention shifted to the Praserians in the room. Aleron seemed irritated as he looked to his left, ignoring the barrier of men that separated him from his brother. Killian seemed indifferent to his surroundings, disregarding his brother's palpable glare. Killian ponderously glanced around the room, now and then displaying a slight grin when he looked at me. I had to focus on not letting my body shiver, no matter how much it made my skin crawl to receive any notice from him.

The room was growing silent to Laerina's question. I wanted to know what Killian was doing here, but I knew it would be better to start at the beginning. My mother wanted to know what involvement Aleron had in all of this. I knew, regretfully, that I had to start the discussion. I began to clear my throat when Killian instantaneously began to speak.

"Queen Laerina, I would like to remind you of the sincere generosity that Praseria displayed towards Risa and Allene in our kingdom when they were prisoners. I would anticipate your kindness to be equal in stride. With that being said, would it be too much to ask for some refreshments? Or a possible change of clothes?" Killian looked down at his coat, dried with blood.

Risa and I scoffed. *Generosity?* He sure had a way with words. My mother did not hesitate at his pitiful attempt at food and water. I almost felt sorry for him — I don't think he realized what such a request would bring.

"Do not barge with me, Prince Hadway. Your attempts to exploit me are useless. Don't you think I have seen this before? I know who you are. I know *what* you are. I know the games you like to play. I have seen it far too many times, men just like you, valuing so highly their own wit. Valuing it so much that they think women of a kingdom would be too dense to follow. It is your flaw — a flaw that men never learn from. You are only invited to this gathering by my good graces to provide me answers to what is going on. I will have you dismissed immediately if you choose not to cooperate."

Killian scowled at Laerina; she had drenched his fire, and the shame of it was enough to scare him into silence.

Laerina didn't take a moment to pause. She looked directly at Damien, addressing him next. "Sir Damien, something tells me the story that needs to be shared will be skewed if I hear it from the mouth of my daughter or our prisoner," she said, nodding her head to Aleron. "Would you like to explain the events of this morning?"

Damien swallowed, his nervousness slightly coming through. "Of course, your majesty." Damien nodded his head, briefly giving me an apologetic stare before continuing. "My brother, myself, and Princess Allene, we were suspicious of King Ulric. In our private meeting with him regarding the Red Crows, something did not feel right. Princess Allene noticed the suggestions and plans that

King Ulric had made for Valteria were vastly similar to the plan and suggestions that Charles had inspired for Praseria."

"And who is Charles?" Laerina interrupted, now directing her question to Aleron.

Aleron seemed tired as he shifted in his seat and obediently replied to her question. "He was an advisor, supposedly from Lokali. He incited the attacks on Valteria."

"What do you mean *supposedly* from Lokali?" Risa now chimed in. The conversation seemed to allow any interjections now. It was my turn to step in.

"The summary of it is, we took Aleron to spy on King Ulric in the sunroom, and Aleron confirmed that King Ulric was Charles. None of us have ever met King Ulric, and it would be mind-numbingly simple to impersonate him. It is a capital offense fit for an experienced criminal — such as the leader of the Red Crows himself," I implied. I spoke as quickly as I could so no one could get a word in before I was finished speaking.

If Laerina was surprised, she did an excellent job at concealing it. Laerina grasped the situation quickly and spoke to Ajax.

"You have no leads on King Ulric?" she asked with a disappointed tone.

Ajax's jaw went slack as he stood a little taller, trying to be unswayed in front of his soldiers that all waited for his answer. "We have men looking for him in every direction. He shouldn't get far, and he wouldn't have been prepared to flee. I am sure we will catch him before sundown," Ajax assured her. Laerina curtly nodded, pretending she had every bit of confidence in her soldiers.

A sudden flutter caught our attention as Killian waved his hand and gave an unimpressed look to Ajax. Killian waited patiently, however, for Laerina's permission to speak.

"If the words that escape your mouth are not relevant to this conversation, I will personally escort you to your prison cell," Laerina promised, eyeing him with uncertainty. We all were.

"Now, now, no need to follow through on that palpable threat. The question you should have asked right away would have answered your initial question. *Why am I here?* If I may have your ears for a few minutes, so much will be made painstakingly clear," Killian insisted.

Without noticing, a laugh broke free from my throat. Everyone looked at me, not amused by the intense situation. I wriggled under their stares, Killian's especially, as he seemed very offended by my outburst.

"Is something funny, princess?" Killian asked me. *Yes, yes, there is.*

"Why you're here is obvious, which is *why* it wasn't a question in the first place," I snapped back.

"Enlighten me," he challenged, pressing his arms forward on his knees, not flinching as the movement caused Hassan and Marshal to get in a defensive position.

"To hurt someone. Anyone. Everyone." I didn't hold back my poor opinion of the man.

"Is that honestly what you think of me? That I'm just

some selfish, altruistic tyrant who celebrates in the destruction of others?" he asked, alarmed, falling back into his chair in surprise.

"Well, I only have so much to base your character off of." I gave him an irritated eye roll, reminding him of our not-so-great history.

"Quick judgments never did anyone proper justice, princess."

"I've known you long enough to say Allene is right," Aleron piped in, defending me. I probably should have felt irritated by his attempt to step in for me, but I didn't mind the extra support.

Killian smirked as he stared at the armrest of his chair. "Ah, yes, and I've known you long enough to say that what you're about to hear will make you cry like a blubbering idiot, brother," Killian stated, giving Aleron a harsh glare.

Aleron didn't move. I could feel everyone brace themselves for the dramatic news Killian seemed to be preempting. I almost held my breath but thought it would be a waste. It was probably nothing. *He is all talk.*

Killian took the silence as his permission to speak. "Allene is right. Not about me, of course, but about Charles. I happened to run into him on my way here. Hence my state of distress that you neglected to ask about." He tugged at the bloodstains on his coat, pointing out the obvious while trying to make it a lighthearted joke. No one was laughing.

"What happened?" Aleron asked eagerly, sitting up taller in his seat.

"He did things only a leader of the Red Crows would do," Killian said solemnly, his jaw buckling slightly as he seemed to be replaying the memory from earlier. Killian shifted uncomfortably, a reaction I hadn't expected to see from him.

"And what's that?" Aleron tried to rush Killian, wanting him to get to the point.

Killian hesitated, looking at me instead of Aleron. His eyes that were now somehow reflecting a darker shade of blue, seemed to be pleading — as if he wanted me, or anyone, to step in. I was surprised to see him struggling to speak, especially for someone who adored having all the attention. Aleron reached out and harshly shoved Killian's shoulder.

"Don't be quiet now. Out with it!" Aleron raised his voice in frustration.

"The soldiers we traveled with, they are all dead," Killian replied, shrugging his shoulders like it wasn't something to make a fuss about.

"We?" Aleron questioned.

"Once they took mother, they didn't leave any survivors. I barely got away," Killian explained, once again referencing the blood on his clothes.

"Mother was with you? And you let him *take* her?" Aleron stood up, his face red and distressed as he towered over Killian. No one stepped in to stop Aleron from intimidating Killian. It seemed Damien, Hassan, Marshal, and Ajax stepped back to give him more room.

"Don't judge me, brother. You don't think I tried to fight?" Killian's last word left a sound of anguish that I hadn't thought possible to escape his always collected tones.

"If you did, you didn't try hard enough!" Aleron growled.

"At least I was there," Killian shot back, his tone becoming defensive.

"Right, much good that did," Aleron spoke through gritted teeth, driven past the point of anger, holding back his rage.

"I won't waste time defending myself to you. There were too many soldiers, and there was little I could do. I knew my best chance of getting her back was having at least someone alive that could tell the tale. Luckily for you, that someone happens to be me," Killian opposed, still sitting down as Aleron bore over on him.

"*Lucky?* You bastard," Aleron scoffed, shaking his head.

"*Language.* We're in front of ladies, brother," Killian chimed self-righteously.

Aleron clenched his hands tightly into fists, doing his best to remain patient and collected. Ajax eventually stepped in, seeing the staring contest between Aleron and Killian was silently escalating.

Aleron and I may not be on the best terms, but I didn't want to watch Killian run circles around him. A perilous man took his mother. What if that had been my mother? Laerina and I may not have seen eye to eye most of the time, but she was still my mother. Eveline may not have stopped Aleron's banishment and the fate of being a captive in Valteria. However, I knew he cared for her more than any other member of his family. I knew he understood the challenging position she had been in. I remembered her overall kindness towards me, despite King Vincent's obvious disapproval. She was a gentlewoman. She didn't deserve any of this.

I can't imagine the fear she is going through. What Nycolas has done, what he is doing — none of it is right.

"Why did you come in the first place?" Aleron asked quietly, taking a somber seat in his chair, unable to look at Killian any longer.

Killian sighed, looking at me once again as he spoke vexatiously. "Mother was attempting to negotiate the terms of your release. Father tried to stop her, but she insisted."

Aleron raised his head slowly, analyzing Killian for sincerity. I could see Aleron processing the information. *His mother was coming back for him.* She was going to right his father's wrong. He would have gotten back his title if he could have just held out hope a little longer.

Killian didn't appear to be lying. Aleron was biting his lip, trying to contain his emotions. For just a moment, I wished I could be by his side, holding his hand, comforting him. *Stop, Allene. That isn't who you are for him anymore.*

"Why did you come with her? I'm sure father was furious with you," Aleron assumed with a confused expression on his rugged face.

"Indeed he was. I'm certain even the residents of Lokali could hear his screams of disapproval." Killian laughed as he thought of the memory, humor in his eyes.

"But I couldn't let her go alone," Killian replied, shrugging.

Aleron's blue eyes seemed sympathetic as he gave a nod of gratitude to Killian. A word-free exchange, they both seemed calmer now.

It was hard to admit to myself that Killian had been right — I judged him too quickly. I assumed he came to Valteria under selfish pretenses. Yet, he disobeyed his father for his mother's sake to spare his little brother. *Not that having him around protected her.* But I couldn't disregard his good desires.

The conversation between Aleron and Killian had made the room feel heavy. Minutes of silence dragged on, people shifting glances between each other and the floor from the uncertainty of where to look. Laerina stood up, commanding all eyes to meet hers.

"Does anyone in this room have a reason to believe King Ulric is not the leader of the Red Crows?" she asked sincerely. Hassan and I exchanged a look of relief as she asked the question. *Laerina believed us. All this commotion, it would be worth it if she believed us.* No one replied.

"Very well. Differences aside, it seems both our kingdoms have been played as fools. Killian, you came to negotiate. Let's negotiate the terms for working together to defeat a common enemy."

CHAPTER 11

The positions of everyone in the room had changed. The extra guards had been dismissed. Ajax, Marshal, Hassan, and Damien had all pulled up chairs to sit down for the discussion. Hassan had pulled his chair next to mine, flashing a white smile as he relaxed in his seat. I could feel blue eyes staring at us; whether it was Aleron or Killian, I didn't care. I gave a shy smile back, not wanting to draw too much attention for fear of my mother noticing the interaction.

"Ajax, what do you think is Nycolas's next move?" Laerina asked.

Ajax stood to his feet, taking a position at the center of the room, his face determined and calm. "Your majesty, with this new information coming to light, it seems Nycolas's strategy is infiltrating kingdoms. Getting close to the royal families — gaining their trust so they will listen to his advice — and manipulating them to provide the destruction he seeks under their own name, and not his."

"He saw Aleron spying on him; that's why he fled. He realizes he's been caught. All the work he has done in Valteria and Praseria is now wasted," Hassan interjected.

Ajax nodded, seeming to be offended by Hassan's interruption. "Correct, which is why I assume his next targets will be the lesser kingdoms," Ajax declared.

"Like Lokali and Gree?" Risa questioned.

"Gelva, Veruje, and Cenan," Damien added.

"Cousin Lidia, she is the Queen of Veruje. We have to warn her about Nycolas," Risa replied loudly. She had become anxious, braiding her hair nervously.

"We have to warn them all. It's our only chance of surviving," Aleron spoke out, a look of determination in his endearing eyes.

"What do you mean?" Risa asked, tugging harder at her hair now.

"Praseria and Valteria are large kingdoms, but if you combine the forces of those five smaller kingdoms, we won't stand a chance. Nycolas — Charles, he knows that. He targeted Praseria and Valteria first; he wanted to see us fall. Now that he's lost the benefit of surprise, his only chance is forming alliances with smaller kingdoms — probably lying to them as he did with us. I assume he will scare them into fighting us, *for* him, by making Praseria and Valteria seem like a secret threat," Aleron observed sourly, his curly hair falling into his eyes as he put his head down in worry.

"Then we need to visit every kingdom and explain

what has happened in Praseria and Valteria. We need to beat them to it and get there first," Hassan jumped into the conversation, a confident expression on his handsome face.

I wanted to sink into my chair. The intense reality of Nycolas's probable plan seemed very likely, which left me frightened.

"Hassan, that's five kingdoms. We don't know which one is Nycolas's next target. How would we manage to speak to them all in time?" Risa queried.

The proposed task seemed impossible to achieve. Veruje was a day journey south of Valteria. Gelva was a four-day journey north. Praseria was a day journey east from Valteria. Lokali was a half-day journey northeast of Praseria. Gree was a half-day journey east of Praseria. Cenan was a three-day journey north of Praseria and a two-day journey east from Gelva. The terrain to Gelva and Cenan was hazardous through the snow-capped mountains. It would take much longer for anyone inexperienced with the landscape. We would have to reach every direction. Add it all up, and we would be traveling for at least 14 days if we hurried. Consider the additional time required to speak with the royal families in the kingdoms, negotiate alliances, and assuming nothing goes wrong in the process — it would be at least a month's journey, *if* we were lucky.

"We have to split up. Aleron and I will handle alliances with Veruje and Gelva," Killian encouraged.

"Ha! Please! I should entrust the two Praserian princes not to blindside me? Who's to say you won't go off and formulate your own plan for the benefit of Praseria?" Laerina laughed at the proposal.

"What do you think we will do, join forces with Nycolas?" Killian asked defensively.

"You easily could if it meant protecting yourselves. We may be working together, but it doesn't mean my prejudice for you or Praseria has magically gone away."

"Dear queen, do you have a better idea?" Killian pressured Laerina.

Despite his arrogance, my mother remained poised. She was handling everything so effortlessly. I studied her intently, taking notes for myself for future negotiations I may be forced to have.

"Of course I do. We split up, but we will have Praserians and Valterians in each group. I will personally see to your group, Killian, to give you my undivided supervision." Laerina gave Killian a twisted smile, satisfied with her idea.

I was nervous about speaking up, but I saw a flaw in her plan. *Be brave, Allene; you were right about all of this in the first place. You have to voice your thoughts, if not for yourself, at least for Valteria.*

"Mother, you shouldn't leave Valteria. Nycolas already took Queen Eveline. What type of leverage would he have if he took you too? If you go, you would need protection — the protection of our army. But if you do that, you leave Valteria vulnerable to attack. You need to stay."

"I need to be there to make proper negotiations," Laerina insisted. I knew she was right. To make a formal alliance, you had to speak royal to royal. I swallowed back the fear creeping into my throat as I knew what I had to say next. Something in my gut was screaming to hold my tongue, knowing my words would place me in an undesired circumstance.

"We have two princesses of Valteria and two princes of Praseria — representation from each kingdom. We split up into two groups. One group goes to Veruje and Gelva, the other goes to Lokali and Gree," I suggested.

Aleron held a deep look of concentration as he nodded slowly in reply. "It would give us the benefit of speed. Nycolas wouldn't expect us to work together. And even if he did, he would be surprised that we would split up," Aleron spoke with hope, supporting my idea.

Laerina observed me carefully, contemplating the plan. She almost seemed to hesitate, but she eventually bowed her head in reply.

"You have proven much to me today, Allene. If you and Risa feel you can handle this task, I will support you." Laerina spoke with proclivity, and my conviction superseded any doubts I may have had. Risa had reached over and took my hand, squeezing it gently, nodding in agreement as well. Killian interrupted the tender moment between mother and daughters, stealing his required spotlight.

"Splendid! We have a plan. I volunteer to go with the lovely Risa." Killian displayed a mischievous smile, leaning forward in his seat as he cocked his head to the side to study Risa more intently. It still made me shiver to see some of the similarities between Killian and Aleron.

However, the distinct difference was the uncompromising satisfaction Killian always seemed to hold in his eye, like he was always planning something devious.

Risa and I shuddered in unison. Killian had become one of my worst fears, literally the focus of my nightmares. I'd finally started to conquer the power he held over me. I was not about to let Risa fall prey to his numbing abilities.

"I will be going with Killian," I declared loudly, shooting Killian an unforgiving glare. Aleron and Hassan both exchanged worried glances. Hassan sat up taller, acting like he wanted to intervene, but decided to let me make my own decision. I knew he wouldn't like it, but I disliked the idea of Risa being with Killian even more. Aleron bit his cheek, also holding back an objection. Risa pulled me to the side, whispering in my ear.

"Allene, I can handle Killian. You do not need to protect me!" she hissed.

"What kind of big sister would I be if I didn't? I'm not doing this for you. I am doing it for me. I couldn't live with myself if I let you be alone with him, absolutely not." I gave her an imploring look, hoping she would give in for her own protection.

Killian chuckled softly, snapping our attention back to him as he winked at me. "Ladies, ladies, please — I know my devilish charms are greatly enticing, but I never meant for you to fight over me."

"Trust me, going with you is not a job they are yearning to claim," Damien interjected, trying to knock Killian's pride down a notch.

"That isn't how it seems from where I'm sitting, but sure, if you say so, Dallin."

"It's *Damien*," he said sharply.

"Of course." Killian held his hands up in defense.

I rolled my eyes; he really was incomparable in terms of his blatant pestering.

"Enough. I will assign the groups. Damien and Marshal, you will be accompanying Aleron and Risa," Laerina commanded. Marshal and Risa both perked up at the sound of their names being together. I caught Marshal holding back a smile, and Risa tried to conceal her excitement. Laerina continued. "Hassan, you will accompany Killian and Allene. Ajax will be staying here to oversee the kingdom's safety. He can spare another soldier to attend with you, Hassan."

"I won't need one. I can keep Prince Hadway in line," he said bluntly.

"Very well. Aleron and Risa will go to Veruje and Gelva. Allene and Killian will go to Lokali and Gree," Laerina announced the assignments.

Killian gave an ashamed smirk as he raised his hand innocently to speak. "Just a slight problem with that plan," Killian started to explain. *Of course there was.* "*I'm* not exactly what you consider, *well-liked* in Lokali," he admitted bashfully, obviously relishing in memories of his time there. I felt sick to my stomach.

"Or Gree," Aleron added, giving a disapproving stare at his brother.

"A handful of misunderstandings that never got

resolved between myself and some of the ladies there, nothing too scandalous," Killian said dismissively.

"That isn't the rumor I heard," Aleron huffed.

Why was I not surprised? I knew Killian was every form of trouble. However, at that moment, I was profoundly regretting being the brave volunteer to go with him.

"Anything else you'd like to mention?" I muttered.

"Don't be jealous, Allene. I have a bad history with Lokali and Gree, that's all."

"Do you have a bad history in Veruje or Gelva?" Laerina asked, holding her breath for his reply.

"Not yet," he shrugged, responding honestly.

"I trust you can manage to behave long enough to save both our kingdoms?" she asked dubiously.

"I will be on my most respectful behavior. Besides, I'm sure Allene will keep me in check." Killian grinned at Aleron, each word getting under Aleron's skin. I could see him struggling each time Killian spoke, but I admired his restraint. It was the only way to handle a man like Killian; you had to ignore his outbursts, lest you fuel his self-assurance.

"Hassan, Killian, and I can also go to Cenan," I volunteered, realizing we had forgotten the outskirt kingdom in our plan.

"No, you shouldn't go to Cenan." Aleron stood up eagerly, looking me over with deep concern. I raised an eyebrow, uncertain how to receive his opposition, considering how collected he had been with Killian's teasing.

"Cenan is notorious for being difficult to work with. We have a better chance if we are all there. As you know, strength in numbers," Killian explained, addressing Aleron's hesitation at my proposal.

Aleron is still trying to protect me. I felt a brief moment of gratitude. Part of me almost wished I was going with him — it almost felt wrong not to do this together.

I looked at Hassan, whose hulking posture oozed conviction, and Aleron's hold on me dissipated. *I have other people to protect me; I have more than Aleron.*

"I have been through those mountains before, and my father liked to hunt for elk in that area. I've seen the Cenan kingdom from afar; I can find the way from Lokali," Marshal had spoken for the first time during the conversation, lending helpful input.

"I know some men in Selvet who have been to Cenan. I can ask for their directions on the way to Gelva," Hassan declared.

Everyone was silent as we let the plan sink in. It sounded like our best option. We would cover much ground quickly, maybe giving us a chance to beat Nycolas. Our alliance would entice the smaller kingdoms when they saw that the two enemy kingdoms were working together for the same cause.

As much as I hated the idea of working with Killian to make these alliances, I knew it would give us a strong appeal to act as a united front. It would be a sacrifice of my sanity to interact with Killian. However, it was a necessary deed as princess of Valteria.

I observed Killian leaning back in his chair. His arms

spread out wide as he attempted to flirt with me, batting his eyes — his smile turning into the same crooked smile Aleron had. It was haunting seeing the smile of a man I had loved on the face of a man who made my skin crawl. This would be my next few weeks, somehow interacting with Killian while ignoring his persistent, chilling advances. *Heaven, please help me.*

CHAPTER 12

I was now glad Sonora had taken the next few days off; it was not a good time to be in the castle. Nycolas was dangerous. The kidnapping of Aleron's mother and the murder of all her soldiers was just one shred of evidence to support that. I was relieved we hadn't experienced something more tragic considering what he was capable of.

We had discussed the idea of adding more soldiers to our journey for protection, but we didn't want to stand out in our travels. The fewer people we had, the safer it would be. We wouldn't benefit from rumors spreading of Valterian and Praserian royalty with their soldiers wandering into different territories and kingdoms. Nycolas likely had spies everywhere, eager to please their leader with information that would be our downfall. We had to be as discreet as possible.

I placed my large leather satchel at the foot of my bed;

the reality of the journey starting tomorrow left me feeling nervous. The mountains would be easier traveled on foot in Cenan, so we would forgo bringing horses to ride. Luckily, we were only at the beginning of the fall season, so any precipitation would be light if we did encounter snow on our way to Gelva and Cenan.

I had never had to carry all my provisions on a journey before. I began to doubt if I was capable of what may be ahead — if I had the necessary strength for what we might face.

We would travel to Veruje first, then to Gelva, then meet up with the other group in Cenan.

Risa had stopped by my room earlier, beaming with excitement at the prospect of more quality time with Marshal away from the castle and mother. She was doing what she did best — finding positives in our unfortunate situation.

A quiet knock came at my door. I requested to have dinner in my room. I claimed I had no time due to the preparations needed for the journey — even though the actual reason was how unappealing socializing sounded at the moment. I wanted to be alone.

"Come in," I shouted, standing up tall by my desk to signal the placement of the incoming food.

Ruffled dark hair and blue eyes peeked around the door, accepting my invitation without delay. *Why does he keep showing up?* Surprised to be greeted by Aleron's presence, I hurried to the door, shoving him to the side as I shut it quickly behind him. I was afraid of the ramifications it would cause if servants caught sight of Aleron in my chambers at this hour. My dinner would arrive at any moment, and he wasn't supposed to be here — no man should — a lesson Hassan had most recently taught me.

"How do you manage to keep sneaking around the castle?" I asked.

Aleron's shoulder was touching mine as we both had our hands against the door. He hesitated at the question, shifting his lips back and forth as he considered whether or not he should answer. My only assumption was that Marshal had a hand in Aleron's ability to go about the castle undetected for a *second* time today.

I like Marshal, but if he keeps this up, he and I will be having a conversation. Realizing Aleron was not about to out his one friend here, I moved on.

"I am astonished you dare arrive to my chambers unannounced — or at all for that matter," I accused. I gave Aleron a stern glare as I turned my back to the door, ready to stop anyone else from entering.

The gruff of Aleron's beard caught strands of my long hair as he leaned into me for his reply, his forehead nearly touching mine. My knees felt dizzy as I smelled the clove scent of his skin, his nearness making me woozy. *This is exactly why I walked away last night — all it takes is being near Aleron for me to lose all sense of self.*

"I thought a proper conversation was in order before our departure," he pressed, our breath mingling from our proximity. I tried to cower away, but the door was preventing my attempted escape. I stared into his eyes, focusing on the specks of darker blue to distract me from his eyelashes that had a history of entrancing me.

"There is no conversation left to be had," I replied, uncertain of how much truth was actually in my reply. *Did I want to work this out with Aleron? Was there more to talk about? I subconsciously found my way to his room last night, but that could have been a coincidence.*

"Not about you and I, Allene — about Killian," he spoke innocently.

My teeth clenched, mortified that I had assumed he intended to discuss our relationship. *Had I wished that he had come to speak about us then? What did that mean? A disruptive and blood-hungry tyrant was on the loose, and I was more worried about my feelings for Aleron?* Maybe the separation of Aleron would be better for not only myself but for Valteria. Now was not the time for anything that diverted my attention from my primary purpose — finding and stopping Nycolas from causing any more damage.

Aleron placed his hand against the door, supporting himself as he tilted even closer to my face to allow himself to whisper. "You need to be careful around him. There is a lot more to Killian than meets the eye." Aleron's brows furrowed, agitation crossing his face at the thought.

"You mean there is even more to him than his obnoxious and tumultuous personality?" I asked in disbelief. I felt I had already seen the worst possible sides of Killian. This was the man that knocked me out to lock me away in a dungeon while he manipulated his kingdom to banish his younger brother. Could it get worse?

"He's sly, Allene. He is full of mischief and lacks

propriety. I don't want him thinking he has any supremacy over you."

I placed my hand on Aleron's shoulder, pushing him to the side as I walked past him to stand by my window. I was remotely offended at his medial faith in me when it came to dealing with his brother. I had conquered Killian today; I had overcome any doubt that I might not be able to handle his brazen comments. Yet here was Aleron, planting uncertainty into my mind.

"I am more than capable of handling the provocations of your brother," I announced, trying to gain back my confidence at the implication.

Aleron shifted from my reply, now guarding the door as he stared at me achingly. "I was afraid you would say that."

"Your faith in me is reassuring," I laced my tone with as much sarcasm as possible, shaking my head as I stared out the window at the dark sky that blanketed the pine trees that stretched on for miles. I was growing tired of being insulted. *It has been too long of a day.*

"I don't doubt your capabilities of managing Killian; I'm only expressing concern and words of warning to be on your guard around him. I don't want you getting hurt."

"It's too late for that." The words came out quickly; I had barely even realized I had said them out loud. Embarrassed by my outburst of honesty, I shuffled under the pressure of Aleron's renewed stare of longing and tried to salvage my mistake. "I'm aware of whom I'm dealing with. I'm sure Hassan and I will be able to keep Killian in line." I felt encouraged by the reminder of

Hassan's accompaniment. Aleron, however, instantly looked sick.

"Of course. Hassan and I may have had our differences in the past, but I should be grateful. At least I know someone will be looking out for you."

"I can look out for myself," I reiterated my independence, trying to force him to understand I was not an innocent girl who needed to be coddled. I was a strong princess, a future queen; all I needed was to stand behind my courage to get through the days ahead.

Aleron was smirking now, biting his lower lip as his eyes pried at mine with pure intrigue.

"Is there something amusing?" I asked. I folded my arms across my chest to form a barrier between him and my heart — my heart that was now pounding and my stomach in knots at the anticipation of his response.

"This new dynamic — you being angry and hot-headed towards me. . . it should make me upset, but I find it has quite the opposite effect. I was hopeful that if you hated me, it would make letting go easier for us both, but now as I try to find something to fault in you — in us — it just pulls me in more. It's a rather maddening process," he laughed at his epiphany.

I felt my mouth gape as I was left in shock by Aleron's comment. *Is he joking?* It was only yesterday that he insisted I let him go, that he insisted we shouldn't be together. Now he claimed my rage sparked a new standard of attraction? The interaction left me baffled beyond words.

"Why are you doing this to me? Why are you complicating everything?" I could feel my voice starting to raise as my fists clenched in frustration at my sides. His comment only added fuel to the fire already burning inside me — a fire that he ignited.

"I don't want to hold back what I'm thinking or how I feel when I am with you, no matter where we stand with one another. I thought you appreciated my forthrightness," Aleron shot back, his voice remaining in a levelheaded tone — which made me even angrier at the moment.

"Yesterday, you weren't honest; you were rash. You were hasty with your decision to push me away, and it isn't something I can easily look past and forgive. You shattered my trust, Aleron."

"You're right; I was rash, I was ignorant. We had an argument, Allene, and believe me, if I could change what was said yesterday, I would. I thought about everything I would say to you when I saw you again. I had been wrestling with my thoughts for weeks, and I was consumed with the idea of disappointing you. The news of my mother coming for me, to return with me to Praseria, has reignited my faith in my future. It gives me hope. I realize I shouldn't have given up." His attempt to smooth over our conversation had only magnified its intensity. I expected to feel some comfort from his words, considering he always knew what to say and when to say it. *What has changed? Him or me?*

"I was your hope. *We* were one another's hope. You allowed your identity as the future king of Praseria to have higher importance than a future with me." The words flew off my tongue like a raging river, unable to be held back.

"And I will carry that regret with me for the rest of my life," Aleron rushed forward, unfolding my fists to melt into his soft hands that now grasped mine urgently — his worried eyes searching mine for any sign of forgiveness as he continued his pleas. "I don't expect you to forgive me right away. I don't expect you to forgive me at all. All I can do is express how foolish I was. Trust breeds trust, and I full-heartedly give you *all of mine*. I will never hurt you again if you give me the chance to prove it to you."

Aleron's warm hands that typically left tingling in my palms now left my fingertips aching and cold. *How could one argument cause me to be so disheartened?* I had never experienced anything like this before, an unwavering contest between love and vexation — desire and uncertainty. What did it mean? *Is this what love feels like, or is this the sign to turn the other way?*

"Aleron, this has all been severely complicated, I —"

Aleron shook his head, stopping me. "Just because it's complicated doesn't mean it isn't right. I would be more suspicious if we weren't faced with some adversity. We are, after all, natural enemies," Aleron let out a quiet laugh. "I think that justifies a little bit of complexity in our lives. But it will make the victory of being with one another even greater if we can learn to overcome it."

My heart was in a tug-and-pull battle over how Aleron's words made me feel. The Allene of yesterday would throw herself into her emotions. She would push these arguments aside, and she would be led by her blind ability to hope and her feelings of love. But that wasn't the way for the new Allene. *Why couldn't he have said all of this yesterday when he had the chance to fix it? Why did he let it go as far as it did?*

My frustration and anger clouded my heart and my mind. I had other obligations and priorities to pour my attention into before I could give a thoughtful and logical response to Aleron. With my increased feelings for Hassan and the need to focus on saving Valteria from potential ruin, our conversation had to wait.

"I need time," I replied, shaking my hands away from his as I rubbed them together for comfort. Aleron's arms fell to his sides, letting out a quick breath to mask his offense to my gesture. He eventually nodded, indicating he understood my request.

"Take all the time you need. I couldn't bear the thought of you leaving without expressing how I feel and where I stand. Once we get through this, maybe you'll be ready to answer."

I let out a long sigh, communicating an unspoken thank you as we locked eyes, both of us fighting back the tears of frustration, and for myself, exhaustion. Each conversation today had been taxing and left me weary.

We would leave in the morning; I wouldn't be seeing Aleron for quite some time. I had great anticipation for the time away to possibly clear my thoughts, despite the reason for my departure being one that secretly terrified me.

"One last thing," Aleron began to speak, looking at me with a great amount of seriousness. "As we go to these other kingdoms, we need to be asking about Nycolas to see if we can find his whereabouts. The sooner we find him, the sooner we can stop his plotting, and the sooner we recover Queen Eveline," Aleron said her name softly at the end, in a form of reverence and respect.

Without my awareness, I glided to Aleron's side. The pain of his mother's kidnapping was evident, and my heart hurt for what he was suffering through.

Aleron turned toward me, hesitant at my movement. He was uncertain how to receive my gesture as I gazed deeply into his captivating eyes. For a moment, I felt like we were again one in the same person and mind.

Unapologetically, I placed my hand on his arm, grasping it lightly. I could feel Aleron shake slightly at my touch, his lips parting into a faint smile. I broke the silence in the room, parting with Aleron by giving him one last promise.

"We will find her, Aleron. We will bring her home."

CHAPTER 13

"I'll see you soon, Allene." Risa squeezed me tightly, now giving me a third hug — unable to part ways. I patted her shoulder, signaling so release me. Her long dandelion locks that had been buried into my face left a tickling sensation on my nose as she pulled away. Marshal was ready to take my place right away, escorting Risa and preparing to lead the way to Gree.

Damien had been standing next to me as he let out a long sigh. He hadn't stopped rubbing his head all morning, his straight hair replaced with a shaved, bald head. According to Damien, he lost in an arm wrestle last night with another one of the knights, and shaving his head was the cost of his loss. I only hoped it would grow back quickly. His new look aged him by a few years and made him more intimidating. I didn't want to tell Damien that. Otherwise, he would probably never grow it back.

"Watch over Risa for me," I demanded, pulling my best

friend into a rough embrace, wrapping my arms around his much bulkier body. Damien didn't feel younger than me anymore. It left me sad to realize we had both changed drastically in just a few short months.

"I won't let anything happen to her, but from the way Marshal hovers, I don't think I'm very needed — or noticed." Damien shrugged and gave a mocking nauseated look as he observed Risa batting her eyes at Marshal as he laughed at one of her jokes. *At least she's happy, and I know she's with people I trust.*

Aleron and Hassan approached us now, with Killian leisurely trailing behind as he quietly talked with my mother. Aleron had also undergone a haircut, but the main difference was the absence of his beard. His smooth skin was inviting; I could almost imagine his cheek pressed to mine, his clove scent making me dizzy. His tan skin still remained, even after being cooped up inside for weeks. I always assumed he was tan from his time in the sun on the beach. However, it seemed he had inherited his mother's olive skin, making him naturally and beautifully darker.

Hassan and Damien gave each other a firm, gripped arm shake, patting each other with force and rattling the large satchels on their backs.

"Be safe, brother," Hassan encouraged, giving Damien a faint smile.

"I will. Say hello to Pa, Ma, and Freira for me when you get to Selvet," Damien requested.

That was the one portion of the trip I was looking forward to. I enjoyed my short encounter with Freira, and it would be refreshing to see her again during the journey. I hadn't been to Selvet before, and I was excited to see the Valterian farming town firsthand.

Damien turned to Aleron, doing his best to be cordial as he attempted a weak smile.

"We should catch up with Risa and Marshal before they get too far ahead. I know Marshal thinks he knows the way, but he seems a little distracted by Risa at the moment, and I don't want us getting lost before our trip has even started." Damien politely nodded to invite Aleron to follow and turned to chase after them.

Hassan stood tall above Aleron and me, gazing down like an all-seeing authority figure. Aleron leaned back on his feet, patiently waiting to see if Hassan would dismiss himself to leave Aleron and me alone. Hassan didn't move.

Aleron gazed at me sheepishly, uncertain how to proceed. We had said our goodbyes last night, so not much was left to be said. Aleron waited for Killlian to leave Laerina's side, his lips curled into a devilish grin as he approached us. Aleron ignored his brother's pursuit for attention and exchanged a grim look between Hassan and Killian.

"Please, be careful." Aleron looked at me on the last word, giving me a half-hearted smile.

"Your concern for me is heartwarming, little brother. Don't run into father on the way — I would be deeply disappointed to miss *that* reunion." Killian waved at his brother and turned to walk away, then paused. "Oh, and tell the Tomsen twins I say hello when you get to Lokali. .

. and Elise and Lizbeth if you see them in Gree. Please express that I miss them *dearly*," Killian tilted his head with satisfaction in his eyes.

Aleron shuddered at Killian's suggestive comment — his body going stiff as Killian strode away with pride. Killian's shallow nature churned my stomach. This was a man I would be stuck listening to for the next few weeks, and this was only the start of a very long journey. I would probably learn *much* more about his improper scandals in all the kingdoms he had visited. *Lucky me.*

"I apologize for Killian; I don't know what else to say but that," Aleron extended an olive branch to Hassan and me. I didn't blame Aleron. It wasn't his fault Killian seemed to thrive on misconduct.

"I'm not afraid to give him a reminder punch or two if he misbehaves in front of Allene," Hassan shrugged, not intimidated at the challenge Killian posed to either of us.

"That brings me more joy to hear than it probably should," Aleron admitted and shook his head in disapproval of his brother.

Aleron huffed and turned to look at the sunrise, the break of dawn on our heels and ready for us to be on our way.

"Take care, and we will see you in Cenan," I spoke to Aleron, giving him a soft smile.

He nodded, holding his breath as if he debated on saying more. "Until then," Aleron gave me a respectful bow, not grabbing my hand to kiss my wrist like he usually did.

It bothered me knowing the dynamic between us had

changed. I missed the little things, the little surprises, and the thoughtfulness that brought me such joy. I couldn't help but wonder if we would ever have that again. And if we did, was it right? I had a lot to contemplate in the days ahead, and gratefully, I had plenty of time to consider all my options. All the directions my life could take, and with who it would be with.

Aleron jogged to catch up with Damien, Risa, and Marshal. After a few moments, we sawall four of them wave at us from afar.

Hassan stepped in front of my line of sight, displaying his happy smile. "Ready, Princess?"

Was I ready? Absolutely not — but did I have another choice? I nodded in reply. I was ready to undo the mess that Nycolas had unleashed, to diminish the tensions he caused between the kingdoms, and to bring Queen Eveline back to Praseria.

"You and Killian can go on ahead; I need to speak with my mother for a moment," I encouraged him. Hassan didn't hesitate at my request, respectfully walking away to follow behind Killian.

My mother gave me a hardened stare — concealing any emotions she might be feeling. The sun was higher in the sky, its rays pleasantly warming our faces. The light bounced off the wrinkles near my mother's eyes — wrinkles I hadn't noticed until now. Her face was beginning to show signs of aging as her cheeks had sunken in slightly. It was not easy to see unless you looked closely, but her hair now had strands of gray woven into her golden locks.

I was glad she was staying behind. She was a strong woman with a sharp personality that resulted in more arguments and awkwardness between us than I could count, but I still would always hold respect and love for my mother. No one was perfect, I was far from it, and I knew any of her displays of harshness towards me came from a place of caring. It was hard to grasp that someone who cares for me could be so hard on me as well. But I was beginning to understand it came from a place of concern and see her for what she was — a loving mother — even when she didn't openly show it.

"Thank you for trusting Risa and me. I know your support gave Risa the confidence she needed to manage all of this, and myself as well." I expressed my gratitude, sincere with what it meant to me to have her faith in the task ahead of negotiations with the other kingdoms.

Taking me by surprise, my mother reached out to grab my hands and held them tightly. She patted the back of my hand and gave a smile with only her lips.

"Allene, you have continually surprised me and caused me stresss — but I've come to realize that my anxiety for you resides from the resemblance you bear to your father."

I felt tears almost immediately swell at the mention of my father. "In what way?" I asked.

My mother's lips flickered into a smile. "In every way. In spirit, appearance, heart, and mind. His unorthodox perspective of life left me carrying heavy burdens, whereas other times, it left me full of ambition. When you proposed to take the negotiations yourself, I was initially apprehensive."

"Then what changed?" I inquired.

My mother let go of my hand, rolling her shoulders into a more proper posture as she stared towards the mountains in the east. Her appearance of being deep in thought only lingered for a moment.

"Your father. He was my balance. Without him here, I have feared my more *presiding* nature would override his desire to delegate the leadership of Valteria to you and Risa. Learning to give up things in my control is something I actively have to remind myself to do now that he has passed."

If only I were that self-aware. I hoped to one day channel that same thought process.

My heart that had been heavily burdened, suddenly felt light and lifted. "Hearing you speak about father makes it feel like he is here," I whispered, not wanting to disrupt the apparent change in the atmosphere I could feel.

Laerina nodded as she let out a long breath. "We all know your father's beliefs. If they are true, if we do have an existence after life, then we can be assured he is watching us right now and is with us always."

I had always hoped my father was right — about an afterlife, about a God who listened to our prayers, about unseen angels that came to our aid daily. It was a comforting thought and one I had more faith in as time went on. Or maybe it was hope — the hope that he was right. Hope or faith, I didn't know which to say I had —

perhaps a bit of both. I wanted to see him again and have faith that he was with me, that he was my angel, and that I didn't need to feel alone.

"Allene, Faris's aspiration for you and Risa was to grow to be strong, bold leaders, fit to be queens. He wanted you to lead Valteria with conviction and certain direction. When you proposed to go in my place, I realized that was an action I would have taken. You've grown exactly into the woman your father hoped you would be. Your attributes will make you a clever queen. As your mother, it is my duty to protect you, and it is my duty to understand when I need to let you go so you can truly become the greatest version of yourself."

I choked back the tears that still threatened to overcome me. I wasn't used to emotional interactions with my mother. I wasn't exactly sure how to react or respond to her complementary and heartfelt words.

"I appreciate the sentiment, mother. I strive every day to make father proud," I expressed a simple token of my gratitude.

"Allene, you are a princess; you have no need to fear. Fear is a restraint to your capabilities. The only person who can stand in your way is you. Those are the last words my mother said to me before she passed."

After all that had occurred in Praseria and the more cordial dynamic conversations usually held between my mother and me, her nostalgic moment was a breath of fresh air. Hearing Laerina speak of my deceased grandmother was a tender piece of my mother to share, something she hadn't done before.

I stepped forward, wrapping my arms lightly around my mother's frailing shoulders as her rigid stance slowly relaxed at my touch.

My mother and I rarely hugged. It wasn't part of her relationship with me or with anyone else. My mother kept people at a safe distance, maintaining her own designated space. But something between us had changed. Whether it was me, her, or both of us, I was beginning to feel a sense of solace in my mother — a feeling that I generally found in my father. It was the feeling of home that I needed, and I was overjoyed to be feeling that in Valteria.

"Thank you, mother," I whispered in her ear and pulled away, catching a glimpse of tears in her eyes. Laerina sighed and offered a smile, creating a way to hide her vulnerabilities as the evidence of tears dissipated. Laerina cleared her throat — her voice showing no signs of being shaken.

"Be careful. Don't be discouraged in the days ahead. Valteria will get through this. *We* will get through this. I will be anxiously awaiting the return of you and your sister. Safe travels, my daughter."

"See you soon." I looked toward Hassan and Killian. Killian was impatiently far ahead as Hassan turned around to watch my progress — waiting for me to catch up to him. I smiled and waved to my mother as I jogged away — doing my best to avoid tripping on my dress as I clutched at its hem.

The rising sun that kissed my skin sent a new wave of energy through me. The motivation to bring safety to

Valteria washed over me with unprecedented exhilaration and excitement. Running away from the castle and leaving Valteria to embrace the uncertain journey ahead was liberating. The time I unexpectedly spent in Praseria had been a turning point for me. I had discovered a drastic amount about myself and my capabilities while I was there.

Although the experience had its share of positives and negatives, it still left me with new experiences. The prospect of seeing so many kingdoms and towns in such a short amount of time was exciting. I had an undeniable and deep desire to explore what other kingdoms had to offer. Praseria had only given me a taste of the world around me that I'd never before seen. I could hardly imagine what I would learn in Selvet, Veruje, Gelva, and Cenan.

With that thought in my mind, any fear or anxiety for the task before me melted away — leaving in its place enthusiastic anticipation for what could be next.

CHAPTER 14

I cupped the wild berries in my hand, plopping them one at a time in my mouth — savoring each explosive bite. The flavor of the berries was intense and sour, making me squint each time a berry hit my tongue. The violet juice contained inside the berries had seeped into my skin, staining my hands a hue of dark blue.

Aspen trees towered at least twenty feet above us, shading the small dirt path we had cut through as the smell of dirt filled our noses. The pebbled road to Veruje took longer to walk, as the trail had been made for horses. Since we were on foot, Hassan insisted on a detour path through the mountains to arrive at Veruje before nightfall. The trail had the occasional steep hill or loose ground covering, resulting in a few slips and unco-ordinated falls on my part — leaving the bottom of my dress covered in blades of grass and dead, crunchy leaves.

Hassan was always nearby, catching me a few times when he could anticipate uneven terrain.

The day of walking had been pleasant; there was nothing rigorous to cross; however, it did take a more significant amount of concentration to stay on the small off-beaten path. After a few hours, the trail seemed to blur into the thick piles of grass on the sides of us, almost consuming the way before us. If I didn't pay close attention, it would start to mesmerize me as I walked, leaving me slightly disoriented.

We had kept conversations to a minimum. None of us knew what to say. Or maybe Hassan and Killian were secretly as out of breath as I was and hadn't spoken to avoid showing how labored their breathing would be. *Unlikely, Allene. These men are trained to be soldiers. They are probably only sparing you embarrassment, noticing how unfit you are for this amount of physical exertion.*

I tried to focus more on taking deep breaths through my nose and exhaling out of my mouth — on doing my best to slow down my heart rate and keep up with the pace that Hassan had set. *Was I the only one who felt like he was running and not walking?* I was ashamed to admit how difficult it was to keep up. How many miles had we walked? We had taken a handful of breaks, but Hassan and Killian didn't take long to recover before they were ready to keep moving. *This is nothing, Allene; this is only the first day. You better get some more stamina and perseverance if you want to make it to the other kingdoms in good time.*

I focused on my shoes to distract myself from the

tight feeling in my chest. Eventually, the constriction dissipated and left a burning sensation in its place.

We had to be close. Veruje was only a day's journey, and the air was starting to feel cool on my skin. The evening was upon us, and my stomach quietly growled at the reminder of it being nearly time for dinner.

Killian had trailed behind Hassan and me, keeping his distance as he took a more leisurely pace. I realized he was probably staring at me as I walked, adding to the pressure of being poised and collected that much more necessary. It didn't last long.

The heel of my right boot caught on a hidden underground branch. Staring at my feet, I saw what would happen, but I hadn't been fast enough to react. My arms instinctively went stiff as I braced for a fall. My left foot had landed firmly on the ground, allowing me to catch my balance enough to not tumble to the ground but tumble into an aspen tree instead. My shoulder hit the tree, slowing me down enough to stop in my tracks. I was fine, but I was not fond of the feeling of falling. That moment of uncertainty pushed my body into a mode of adrenaline, requiring me to take time to stabilize my breathing before confidently continuing.

Hassan had turned the corner up ahead, not taking notice of the incident. On the other hand, Killian saw the entire spectacle — his wicked smirk mocking me as he approached.

"That was quite the dramatization, princess. At least save the show for when Hassan can see you. That is unless it was intended for me. If so, then you are doing a splendid job," he chided as he passed me by, leaving me to follow behind him.

My mouth gaped in surprise and vexation. I pushed off the tree to gain on Killian, furrowing my eyebrows as I scowled at him — his height casting a shadow over me as we moved.

"Are you implying that I was pretending to fall?" I asked in disbelief.

"You're saying it wasn't intentional?" His tone was full of doubt.

"Of course it wasn't!" I exclaimed.

"All of your near falls today had to be an act; it's the only explanation for how clumsy you are," he insisted skeptically — his wavy hair flowing as he walked.

"Haven't you heard of being flat-footed?" I questioned him. Damien had mentioned once that he thought I was flat-footed. Although I didn't honestly know if my feet fell into that category, it was worth saying to escape Killian's misconstrued assumption.

Although Killian's pink lips remained relaxed, his glacier eyes smiled at the corners. "Now you're just making excuses to distract from your exposed intentions."

"I am not. Flat feet prove quite the challenge to achieve true elegance while walking in uneven terrain, and I just so happen to be flat-footed."

"You're in heels."

I rolled my eyes. "That isn't what flat-footed means. It has nothing to do with someone's choice in footwear."

"I'm aware of its meaning — I just find you such a joy to pester." Killian gave a genuine smile of pleasure. "You spiral with your words when you get defensive. I like it." His blue eyes sunk into mine as if he was ready for the prospect of arguing with me. I wasn't going to give him that satisfaction.

"How charming," I said sarcastically, but Killian seemed oblivious to the notion.

"Indeed I am. It's so keen of you to notice." Killian puffed out his chest and rolled back his shoulders, attempting to show off his fit physique like it was supposed to take my breath away. I shook my head, irritated at his smug sense of self.

I wondered if I would ever uncover a hidden side to Killian; a more vulnerable state of being. A part of me wanted to find some redeeming qualities regarding his character, and the other didn't see it as worth my time or effort. But I couldn't ignore the glimpse I caught yesterday of a deeper side to Killian's seemingly one-dimensional personality.

Killian's face seemed soft, almost penetrable when he discussed the kidnapping of his mother. I could have been imagining it, but he seemed defensive and wounded as Aleron interrogated him — as if he feared the acknowledgment of his failure.

It scared me to admit how that small, short moment of pain and anguish I witnessed from Killian yesterday had planted a seed of hope and curiosity that there may have been more to him than his obnoxious, egotistical self.

"Not everyone is putting on a show, Killian," I snapped back.

Killian laughed, his posture precise and proper as he walked. "Then you haven't met enough people. Everyone puts on a show, in one way or another. Especially women — usually as a feat for the attention of a suitor."

"Making such an all-inclusive claim on women is degrading. And to pretend I am falling for the sake of attention is an absurd assumption — I'm not undignified."

"Then you are the most uncoordinated person and princess I have ever come across."

"Anything else you'd like to add to that?"

Killian paused, stepping back as he scrutinized the sincerity of my question. I shouldn't have challenged Killian. I should have expected him to accept the prospect of saying more.

"You are also a hypocrite," he declared.

"Excuse me?" Killian had already gone too far with his previous comments; I had had enough. "What gives you the right to say such things to me?"

Killian shrugged, almost implying that I should already know the answer to my question. "You say not everyone is putting on a show, and you even defend yourself by saying you weren't but did you not put on an act for my brother in Valteria, *Amelia?*" He exaggerated the last word as much as he could.

Amelia. It kept ringing in my head. I did my best not to cringe at his point. I should have seen that coming. I had asked for it — no chance of ending this conversation now.

"It wasn't an act," I quipped back.

"Maybe not all of it, but most of it." Killian started walking again, trying to dismiss my comment and leave it in the dust.

"It was survival," I exclaimed.

Killian shook his head as he chuckled to himself. "It was an *act* of survival. Don't get me wrong; I admire you for it. You are a clever girl, Allene. It takes quite the talent of manipulation and deceit to achieve what you did." My stomach dropped from his delusive comment.

How was it possible that Killian made me feel like the villain? Like I had done something devious and corrupt?

"There was no manipulation; there was no act. I was more myself in Praseria than I ever was in Valteria," I defended myself honestly.

"Ah — so there were just the lies then? You're right, *hardly* an act."

I stopped walking; my lips were twisted to the side as I tried to regain my composure. I expected to have disagreements, arguments, and irritation from Killian, and I had hoped to be better than him — to maintain control over my emotions — to maintain control over *him*. Killian's comments left me feeling humiliated and ashamed. Something I hadn't felt since my true identity had been exposed to Aleron.

Maybe Killian was right; maybe it was all lies. The dishonesty was all my fault. What if I wasn't as estimable as I thought? Did it take someone as blunt as Killian to show me that?

Killian noticed I was behind him now. He turned

around to stare at me, his eyes searching my face for answers to my sudden halt to the conversation. "Oh, come now, don't pout and give me the silent treatment. You can't abhor a man for being honest."

I could feel the hardness in my expression as I looked back to him; not a word escaped my lips as I pondered how much I detested the man.

Killian shifted to the side and leaned against a nearby aspen tree — patiently waiting to see if I would break under the pressure of his stare. I didn't.

"Truly, Allene, you cannot be angry with me for speaking plainly. I assumed it would be refreshing for you."

"Why would you possibly think I find your frankness to be refreshing?"

"We are royalty; people constantly tip-toe around our feelings. Your whimsy of being a princess does not allure me as it would others; therefore, I have no hesitation to be candid when I speak to you," he explained.

Killian's comment reminded me of Aleron. The relationship he and I had revolved around my bluntness towards him and his forthrightness with me. Aleron, Hassan and Killian, all spoke plainly to me, but each of them did so differently. However, I had learned you could be blunt while still being courteous, something Killian didn't seem to understand.

"I approve of candidness, but you try to appear praise-worthy by calling your actions honest, whereas, in reality, you're just *rude*."

Killian's dark eyes seemed to sparkle as his lips

slightly parted at my reply. His expression softened as he curiously strode to stand in front of me. His unconventional approach left me feeling uneasy. Killian had proven to be unpredictable, and his sudden closeness took me off guard. He was staring down at me now, his hands clasped behind his back. The position pushed his jacket open to show the deeply plunging neckline of his white linen shirt — exposing quite a bit of his chest.

"You keep surprising me, little princess; you are proving to be quite outspoken. If you continue as you have, I may have to retract what I said before."

"And what statement would that be? I would consider everything you have said in this conversation as worthy of being retracted." I had to stop myself from rolling my eyes.

Killian flashed his bright smile. "Your ability to allure me. I may not be able to stand by those words for much longer."

I laughed. Killian seemed offended by my reaction, his lips turning down at the corners in disappointment. He couldn't be serious; it had to be another sick joke.

"I assure you, you won't need to worry about that. If being direct with you makes me alluring, then I will be sure to stop."

Killian scoffed, obviously displeased with my reply. "Would you truly find it such a shame if I found you favorable?" he asked.

"Perhaps not, but then you may think I am behaving that way to — how did you phrase it? Oh, yes, to gain your attention, and I would hate to mislead you."

Killian took a step back now, studying the trees intently. *I think I won this argument.*

Killian looked at me again, seeming less puzzled. "Tell me, is it natural for you, being direct with me?"

"Mind-numbingly so," I confirmed.

"Well, then there is no way around it. If you go against your natural inclination of being frank and are pleasant towards me, then I know it's an act. And as we discussed earlier, an act is also a sign of attention. And if you continue being forward, I will also find that as a sign of your attention. Either scenario seems to leave you finding me favorable. How vexing, isn't it?"

"I suppose I will just have to find another way to dissuade you."

Killian had stepped forward now. "I'll be eager to see you try."

Whether he was trying to be charming or intimidating, I didn't care. I stood my ground and ignored his persistent stare. He wouldn't shake me.

"Allene!" We both looked in the direction of my name being yelled — finding Hassan jogging his way towards us.

"Your knight, to the rescue," Killian jeered under his breath and took a step back to provide distance between us as Hassan approached. Hassan was perspiring along his hairline, the droplets of sweat reflecting off his light brown locks.

"I thought I had lost you. Was I walking too fast?" Hassan inquired.

"No," I replied quickly, looking down at the ground

now. I wish Hassan hadn't noticed our absence, but I suppose it wouldn't make him a very great soldier if he hadn't.

Hassan could sense the displeasure in my reply and immediately turned to Killian.

"What did you do?" he accused.

Killian's eyes widened to immediate shock. "Nothing at all, just some idle chit-chat with the princess. You missed it; she took a *hard* fall," he spoke dramatically.

"Are you all right?" Hassan asked, turning all his attention to my well-being as he grasped my arms lightly and looked me over.

"See, *just* the reaction you aimed for," Killian muttered as he started sauntering off in the direction of Veruje, leaving me with the attentive Hassan.

"What is he talking about?" Hassan replied, confused by Killian's comment.

I shook my head back and forth, unsurprised by Killian's brash reply to Hassan's tenderness and care. I waved my hand in the air, wanting to move on from the conversation with Killian and continue the journey.

"I'm fine, Hassan. Ignore him, please. Have we almost arrived?"

Hassan came behind me now and placed his hands on my shoulders as he gently turned my body to face the hill to the south. The sun was almost out of sight as it cascaded behind it, ready to be replaced by the moon.

"Over that hill — that is Veruje. We don't have much farther to go."

"Good, I'm starving."

"I wouldn't have thought so, considering the berry stains on your lips," he chuckled and turned me towards him as he reached out to wipe his thumb slowly across my bottom lip.

My cheeks became warm from his touch. I felt like a child — utterly oblivious to the mess I was. I felt silly for not noticing earlier. I didn't want to be embarrassed, but I had an intense conversation with Killian while displaying berry residue all over my mouth. *How intimidating I must've been.*

Hassan held his hand out for me to see the purple marks that had transferred from my lip, giving me a playful smile. His enticing olive eyes locked on mine made my stomach flutter. Hassan was the best at seeing *me*. I was incredibly grateful he was here.

"They must've been pretty delicious," he mocked, snapping me out of my daze. I softly elbowed his firm stomach as I covered my mouth with my hand and attempted to wipe away any further remains of my earlier snack. He laughed again and offered his arm for me to hold. "Let's go hungry girl, and we might be able to arrive in time for dinner."

CHAPTER 15

The castle at Veruje made me crave sweets. The splendor of pastels overwhelmed my senses — I felt dizzy from the blending of colors in each room. The fair pinks, bright whites, soft greens, light purples, and baby yellows reminded me of peppermint candies I would eat around the winter holidays. *I really am hungry.*

The castle was adorned in crystals. Large chandeliers seemed to slowly spin in the halls and dazzle my eyes with each turn they made. Delicate glass sculptures were proudly displayed in every corner, and there was a substantial amount of potent, fresh flowers in each room. The number of whimsical accents made it all feel child-like. The castle in Veruje felt like it had come straight out of a dream — a dream of a very wealthy and imaginative little girl — or in this case, the imagination of cousin Lidia.

My mother visited her cousin, Lidia, on occasion. I

vaguely remember visiting the castle; however, that was before cousin Lidia's extensive renovations. The castle in Veruje hadn't been anything memorable when I had visited. My mother mentioned that Lidia had taken a little bit of creative liberty to change the overall appearance of Veruje. *A little bit — that was understated.*

Lidia was always passionate about doing things her way and to her preference. She was an eccentric woman, and my mother always referred to her as a free-spirited visionary. She had to have been, considering how extravagant and distinctive she had made the castle.

In addition to the unique design and decor of the castle, the people had a curious type of taste. The gowns the women wore were vast, and their dress skirts were perfectly round in shape. The effect of the perfect skirts made the ladies appear like hovering illusions as they walked. If the skirts weren't distracting enough, their hair was.

The men and women all had hair that seemed to be reaching for the clouds. I was uncertain what invention allowed their hair to stand so tall and plump, but whatever it was, it did not seem to have any issues defying gravity. It almost gave me a headache; their hair looked heavy.

I felt out of place. I appeared dull between my darker green dress and my flat, black hair lying against my back. Neither myself, Killian, nor Hassan, blended in, and it was noted by each person we passed.

Hassan seemed overwhelmed by our surroundings. He gawked and stared at everything that shined. The problem was, *everything* shined. I constantly had to turn his way to remind him to keep up. Killian, on the other hand, seemed repulsed by the sweet show. His lips were twisted, and his eyebrows furrowed at each new room we passed through. I didn't know how I felt about it. Was it too much? Or was it enticing — the level of splendor the display captured? I would wait to decide. There was still much more to see.

We had come to a set of grand golden doors. The watchmen that stood by the doors wore crisp white uniforms that were accented with light blue buttons.

Killian and I patiently waited for the doors to open. Hassan — still distracted — snagged the corner of my dress as he heedlessly kept walking. I caught Hassan's arm, pulling him back while simultaneously retrieving my dress underneath his moving feet. Hassan seemed embarrassed as he realized his absent-mindedness had gotten the better of him.

"My apologies," he said as he held back laughing at himself.

I returned his apology with a smile. Killian quietly mumbled under his breath — likely a snide remark — but I wasn't interested enough to try and discern his words.

I held onto Hassan's arm now, prepared to keep each other focused and attentive. In unison, the men who stood guard opened the doors to escort us into the dining room, where cousin Lidia awaited our arrival.

The room could easily be mistaken as a ballroom if they hadn't filled a table with food at its center. The table was placed directly underneath the largest chandelier. More servants lined the walls in their white uniforms, standing entirely still like soldiers in a perfect line.

Lidia sat at the head of the table, her hands folded in her lap and her back as straight as it could be. Her blonde hair curled up into the shape of a beehive that stood proudly on top of her delicate head. Gems were pinned into the nest of her hair, and lavender ribbons were braided into the calculated chaos. Her lips, cheeks, and eyelids were all the same shade of dark pink.

Cousin Lidia, similar in age to my mother, appeared even younger than me. Lidia was radiant — literally *shining.* It appeared she had drenched her skin in a special shimmering cosmetic that glistened from the shine of the chandelier above.

Lidia stood from her chair and reached out her long arms, extending them in our direction.

"Tell me my eyes do not deceive me! Allene, my dear cousin, how long it has been!"

Lidia swiftly met us halfway — breaking my link to Hassan as she pulled me in for a hug. Her dress made crunching sounds as she embraced me more tightly, but she didn't seem to mind. *I have never heard fabric crunch before.*

"I could hardly believe it when they told me it was you! What an absolutely splendid surprise!" Lidia chirped with pure excitement. She gave a glance to Hassan and beamed even more as her eyes became coquettish at the sight of him. Hassan respectfully bowed to Lidia, oblivious to her intense staring.

"Your majesty, it is a pleasure to meet you," Hassan spoke reverently.

Lidia turned to me now, shifting her glance back and forth between Hassan and me.

"Who is this handsome gentleman that you have brought for me, cousin?"

I held back a smirk as I saw Hassan stiffen at her comment. "This is one of our most trusted soldiers, and my friend, Hassan Durand," I gave the formal introduction she was looking for.

Lidia crossed her arms now, her elbows balancing on her large baby pink skirt.

"Yes, I assumed you were a soldier, with arms and shoulders like those . . ." Lidia stared intently at Hassan now — flashing her shining smile as she continued to express her thoughts unapologetically.

I tried to hold back a giggle at Lidia's forward personality. She was twice Hassan's age, but something told me she was used to getting anything, and any man, that she desired.

Killian made a low, audible cough. *Always needing to be in the spotlight.*

Lidia, unimpressed by his interruption, gave a stagnant glare as Killian gave a slight bow. Hassan became less rigid, realizing Lidia's attention had been diverted for a moment. Lidia's eyes immediately observed Killian's black hair, and she shot me a hesitant look. Her face became grim, and her lips pursed as if her flirtatiousness was ruined at the sight of Killian.

"I understand bringing this dashing soldier with you,

cousin, but I am struggling to comprehend why you brought a Praserian to my home?"

Killian didn't falter at her jab. His motivation only increased from her disapproval. He shrugged his shoulders back and clasped his hands in front of his body to display a relaxed stance as he spoke to Lidia. "She needed someone to contribute undeniable charm and wit in negotiations. Naturally, I was the chosen party, *your majesty*," he embellished at the end.

"Negotiations?" she asked in alarm, once again turning to me to explain.

"We have a lot to talk about, Lidia. This is Killian Hadway, Prince of Praseria," I introduced them.

"Killian . . . I've heard of you," she stated with a tone of distrust.

"Of course you have. I am a popular topic of conversation for kingdom gossip," Killian replied smugly.

"Yes, popular indeed. The rumors are quite indecorous. My friend Penelope Covett had a lot to say about you last time I spoke with her," Lidia mentioned with scrutiny.

"Well, there are two sides to every story," Killian defended.

"From my understanding, you weren't considered a prince when she last saw you."

"Yes, Penelope— she and I met during my rebellious phase. I've recently reclaimed my throne. I am practically the epitome of responsibility now. I suppose that rumor hasn't spread much yet. It looks like you will have some new gossip to share with your friends."

Lidia looked oddly satisfied at his point — her eyebrow raised as she sincerely considered his statement. *Tempting gossip.* Killian had picked up very quickly on Lidia's social tendencies and gave her something that would satisfy her enough to stop her harassment. He was cunning and observant, that was certain. As much as I didn't prefer his methods, I couldn't deny that they worked.

Killian stood tall and patient — behaving like Lidia's earlier words were the opposite of an insult. *How did he do that? How could he act like he had no reason to be shaken?*

Lidia brushed out her dress with her delicate hands and weaved her arm through Hassan's — leaning into him and placing her hand on his shoulder like she needed his support.

"We will have plenty of time to talk about politics once we have full stomachs. Discussing politics when I am hungry just makes me irritable. Take a seat; Chef Lynyl has made one of my favorites. Who likes duck?" she chimed as she pulled Hassan towards the table — ready to claim him as her choice of nearby dinner company.

We all made our way to her large table. I took a seat next to Lidia. Hassan was across from me and on Lidia's other side. Killian chose to sit next to me.

Immediately after sitting, the servants rushed to push our chairs in and cover our laps with napkins. Others gathered the different dishes displayed on the table and made their rounds to come and offer the assortment of foods to each of us. The acidic smell of oranges flooded my senses. I clenched my stomach in an attempt to hush my hunger pangs.

I didn't shoo away any of the food offered. It all looked delectable. I didn't realize how hungry a single day of travel would make me. *I hope that subsides over time.*

I was happy with Lidia's proposition to eat before diving into the reasons for my visit. It had been an exhausting day, and the energy food would provide was what I needed to get through the rest of the evening. I tried to pace myself as I picked at my plate.

The duck had a sharp tang from the orange sauce that it had been drenched in. Freshly whipped butter melted on the steaming hot bread, seeping into the bread and finding its way into my now greasy hands. I reached for my napkin, trying to delicately brush off the evidence of oily butter on my skin. I picked at a variety of vegetables next, particularly seeking out the green beans that had been cooked to perfection. *If this was a meal Lidia had prepared for dinner on any ordinary night, I can't imagine what Chef Lynyl made for special occasions.*

Lidia's silverware caught the light of the large chandelier — sending piercing glares into my eyes. I kept assuming she would notice, but in-between each bite of food, she would pause to make hushed chit-chat with Hassan. Hassan mainly stared at his plate, nodding consistently and keeping his mouth full to avoid having to give many responses to Lidia.

In an effort to escape the burning side effects of Lidia's overly polished silverware, I made the mistake of turning to Killian. He was smiling at me. A wicked, misbehaving smile. How long had he been staring at me? Had I been so distracted by the food that I had lost my ability to sense prying eyes?

I looked down, noticing he had hardly touched his food. "You're not hungry?" I assumed, nodding to his plate of food.

"I'm hungry. I'm just saving room for the best part."

"Dessert?"

"No, something much *sweeter* than dessert."

I felt my mouth go dry. Killian was a man of loose morals. His comments and reputation were enough to prove that. *Sweeter than dessert.* Was he insinuating what I thought he was? I held back from cringing, but Killian noticed quickly how pale his comment had made me. Why had I tried to make conversation with the *worst* conversationalist?

He chuckled and leaned forward to push his plate away. A servant reacted immediately, sweeping up the half-eaten plate of food from Killian's side. "Oh, you didn't think I was implying anything scandalous, did you?" he reacted in surprise.

Killian did this on purpose. He was crafty with his words. He cherished being able to manipulate what people thought by how he phrased things.

"I have made no assumptions. Especially when it comes to you," I assured him.

Blinded or not from the silverware, I turned back to focus on my food, trying to dismiss Killian's comment. I chose to pick apart a grouping of grapes.

"I meant the after-party, princess," Killian clarified.

"Isn't that right, Lidia?" He spoke up now to catch her attention.

"Hmm?" She turned to face us, her head resting in her hand from inclining as close as she could to Hassan.

"I also heard a few things from Penelope. Particularly about the after-parties in Veruje. They are infamous."

It was clear that Lidia enjoyed being flattered, a characteristic that Killian would prey on to get what he wanted out of the conversation. *Again.*

Lidia shifted in her seat now, her face beaming from the recognition. Any hesitation or contempt she had displayed towards him had disappeared. Killian knew he was saying just the right things to get on her good side.

"Enlighten me, your majesty; what is your secret to throwing such memorable parties?" Killian beckoned.

"Spare no expense," Lidia practically whispered her response, pretending like it was a well-kept secret.

"Money? Spending money is the necessary component to putting together a great party?" I asked in shock at her reply.

"Of course, cousin, you can't dazzle without it." She acted like I should have known that from the start. I couldn't recall cousin Lidia being so materialistic.

"I have never heard of, or been invited to one of your parties . . ." I mentioned.

Lidia exaggeratingly laughed, throwing her hands in the air so she would have an excuse to place one hand on Hassan's bulky shoulder. *She was not one for subtlety.*

"Oh, my dear, of course not! If Laerina ever found out, she would lecture me on being reckless and wasteful. I love your mother, truly I do, but she is more uptight than your average queen. She doesn't know how to have a good time."

Killian shook his head back and forth, making tsk sounds. "What a shame. Lidia, I think it would be a disservice to let Allene leave Veruje without showing her a proper party, wouldn't you agree?"

"Yes! Yes, it would! What do you say, cousin? As long as you promise not to tell your mother. It has been a few weeks since my last party; it is splendid timing to have another." Lidia had reached out to touch my arm now, her glittered hand leaving a sparkling residue on my dark sleeve.

I shook my head, glaring at Killian. "We can't afford to spare the time for a party, right Hassan?" If anyone could tell Lidia no without making her upset, it had to be him.

"We are short on time," he confirmed my objection. Hassan looked at Lidia, who was displaying a marvelous pout. She wouldn't get under his skin — or so I thought. "How quickly could you put a party together?" Hassan inquired. *He can't be serious.*

"I can have the word out by tomorrow morning and have the party in the evening," she replied with a grin.

"That's less than a day's notice," I stated, confused.

"I have thrown large parties with only a few hour's notice, cousin. Less than a day is no obstacle for me," Lidia proclaimed.

"See! Just one day, Allene. You can spare that much," Killian pressured me.

I looked at Hassan and tried not to be disappointed. I

expected to feel disappointment from Killian, but not from Hassan. Why wouldn't he have supported me when I needed it? Time was running out to find Nycolas and stop whatever he was plotting. Stopping before we had even started did not seem like a good idea. How could they not see that? I had been cornered, and I had no feasible way of saying no now. I felt like the governing parental figure, despite being the youngest of them all. It was three against one. I had lost.

I sighed — giving into my defeat. "The matter we have come here for needs to be discussed first. If we can do that, then I will agree to stay for a party," I countered, setting my expectations.

"Sweet cousin, look at the amount of pressure you are putting on yourself! It lends even more reason to have a good time. We can chat about politics later this evening," Lidia promised.

Killian made a loud clap with his hands, making me jump in my seat.

"It's settled. You are going to learn the meaning of *fun*, princess," he said cheerfully, which made his words sound satirical.

Hassan's expression immediately communicated regret; Lidia's was full of excitement, and Killian's was vexatious. It's *just one party, Allene. It's just one day.* Killian's words echoed in my head. *You can spare one day.*

"*P*enelope, my friend from Lokali, has mentioned the Red Crows on occasion or two. I never thought their mission would amount to much from the way she spoke of them."

Lidia and I were now sitting alone in the dining room. The first course had been carried away and replaced with decadent desserts. An assortment of spiced cakes had been served and devoured almost as quickly as they had arrived.

After a long day and full stomachs, Hassan was ready to retire for the night. He asked to excuse himself for the evening, despite Lidia's numerous and plodding objections. Killian, surprisingly, excused himself as well. Lidia's servants escorted them to their rooms for the night, leaving Lidia and me to discuss the reason for my unannounced visit. With Hassan now out of sight, I had Lidia's undivided attention. I had soon noted how she was much more severe when men weren't around.

"I hadn't even heard of them until a few days ago. They seem rather cunning, Lidia. Their leader, Nycolas, he doesn't seem like the kind of person to give up without a fight."

"Men never do. Why do you think I have stayed single for so long? I never wanted to be in a battle for dominance. Being a single queen, I get the best of both worlds. Men — *lots* of men — and my kingdom ran my way. If this Nycolas had come to Veruje, even pretending to be someone else, I would have noticed. I don't take orders or suggestions for ruling my kingdom. Anyone aware of my approach to politics would know that. If he does come here, it won't take long for him to be apprehended," she insisted.

I smiled. I hadn't seen Lidia in so long, and I had almost forgotten how feisty she was. I wanted to be more like her. She didn't care what others thought of her outspoken personality, and people respected it.

"Your independence is inspiring, Lidia," I commended her.

"Mention that to your mother, would you? Every other letter I receive from her, she is haggling me to find a man to marry," she explained while rolling her eyes in frustration.

"She worries about you. After seeing Nycolas kidnap Queen Eveline when she was away from King Vincent —"

"I don't need a husband to protect me. I have an army of ten thousand men to do that," Lidia stated superiorly.

"Yes, that is true. Valteria has a large army as well, but that lends little comfort in times of uncertainty. I believe my mother feels vulnerable right now. She's been different since the loss of my father."

The mood in the large room had promptly shifted at the mention of my father. Lidia's body had tensed, and we both stared down at the empty table in front of us.

I wondered if there would ever come a time when talking about my father wouldn't damper the surrounding atmosphere. I had such fond memories of him. Shouldn't it bring joy and happiness when I reminisced in the memory of him? Death would always be sad, but if a person passed, did their memory have to remain sad forever? I wondered how long was long enough to feel the weight of his passing be lifted. But if it did, would that mean I no longer missed him? Or would I be giving him the respect and honor that should come at the mention of his name?

Lidia's lips became a hard line, and I could see the corner of her eyes had formed deep creases in her skin as she held back her emotions. "I apologized unceasingly through letters to your mother for not attending the funeral. I wanted to support all of you. But when it comes to funerals— I would have been more of a burden than a light at the time, and I know you all deserved better than that," she whispered.

I could see the guilt Lidia was harboring from her decision not to attend the funeral. I reached across the table to squeeze her hand.

"Lidia, you don't need to apologize. If there is anything I have learned from my father's passing, it's that there isn't a right or wrong way to handle death."

Lidia nodded, acknowledging my attempt to comfort her with a faint smile. "Well, Allene, you are as wise as your father and as brave as your mother."

"I wouldn't consider myself wise or brave."

"Not yet, but you'll eventually see what I see. You're young, Allene. You have much to learn. From what you explained to me, these visits you will be making to more kingdoms will bring challenging and new experiences. With each of those challenges, you will get to know your-self a little better."

"Thank you, Lidia. I am grateful you were our first stop on our trip."

"As am I. You have started with success! No Nycolas in sight, and if Valteria needs any additional support from Veruje to put a stop to the Red Crows, I will send my resources to your aid," Lidia promised.

"And Praseria's?" I asked.

I did not enjoy clarifying her support to us both; after all, Praseria was supposed to be Valteria's enemy kingdom. It felt silly even to ask, but if we stood a chance against the Red Crows, we would need Praseria's support. To get Praseria's help meant getting Veruje to support them too. A united front was the most important thing at the moment.

"Ah, yes, I almost forgot about the prince. I am honestly curious, how did this come to be?"

"What?" I wasn't sure what part she was referring to.

"Killian. I heard rumors that my cousin had been hiding in Praseria and that she had become love-struck for the prince. I didn't imagine the prince would be Killian."

"It wasn't. It isn't," I quickly interjected before Lidia could invent any other ideas.

"So nothing is going on between you two?" she questioned me.

"Absolutely not," I confirmed.

"And Killian knows that?" She raised her eyebrows in suspicion, clearly making her assumptions.

"Killian doesn't know me at all," I uttered under my breath.

"Then why bring him with you?" Lidia's eyes were full of curiosity. Each answer seemed to be piquing her interest rather than toning it down.

"To keep an eye on him. I didn't trust him with Risa," I explained.

"So Risa is with . . . ?"

"Damien, my best friend, Hassan's brother actually. And Aleron, the other prince of Praseria."

Lidia's eyes practically glowed when she heard my last sentence.

"Oh. My. You fell for his brother, didn't you?" Lidia was absorbing all of the gossip. I needed to be careful; I didn't need more rumors spreading, even if they would hopefully correct any misunderstandings.

I hesitated to reply this time, hoping my silence would be enough to stop her from pursuing more questions. She stopped asking questions, but it didn't stop her from making statements.

"If Aleron loves you, I'm surprised he trusted you with Killian."

"Why is that?" I realized too late that responding was my way of walking into her perfectly set trap.

"Because of the way Killian looks at you."

"You mean the way Killian looks at every woman?" I laughed.

"I have known a lot of men in my life, Allene. I have met every kind of man that there is to meet. Killian may have a past, but I know the look of a man who desires one woman and one woman only. That is the look he has when he watches you."

"You've barely met him. I don't think that one dinner together is enough to judge his intentions."

"It is entirely enough! He was incredibly obvious; I can't believe you didn't notice yourself."

"I noticed. I noticed him and all his gloating, self-obsessive nature. Killian only looks at me to irritate me. As you said, he has a history, a reputation, one that I don't think he is ready to let go of, and it's one I certainly would never look past."

Lidia nodded slowly as she processed my reply. "I see, so that is why Aleron trusted you."

"I wasn't looking for Aleron's trust; it all came down to my sister's safety. Aleron and I, we aren't on good terms at the moment."

"And the story deepens!" Lidia was clapping her hands now, ignoring how offensive her enthusiastic nature for my sad love life was. "So if it isn't Aleron, and it isn't Killian, is there someone else? Don't tell me it's Hassan. If you say it's Hassan, you will have officially ruined my entire night." Lidia gave me a stern glare, waiting for me to respond.

"It's not *anyone*. My life, and more specifically, my love life, Lidia, is complicated."

Lidia huffed. "Take some advice from my personal experience over the years, cousin. Complicated is just that — complicated. You're doing the right thing, not giving anyone time or thought. It's the only way you will gain clarity."

"Agreed," I gave a short reply to change the conversation, but Lidia wasn't ready to move forward.

"While I am already giving you advice, might I offer one more suggestion?" Lidia asked.

I paused to look at Lidia, who had a serious expression. I nodded for her to continue.

"Killian. I know you say his reputation has deterred you from being enticed by his good looks and devilish humor, but as a warning, even if you feel repulsed by him now, it only takes a moment to let your guard down. Sometimes, Allene, it's easier to fall for the bad ones."

"I can't imagine why that would be easier," I scoffed.

Lidia's face became consequential. She gave a long pause — seriously contemplating what she wanted to say. She leaned closer to me as she quietly whispered in hushed tones to avoid the ears of her nearby servants.

"They make you feel alive. *Limitless.* That's a powerful motivator to be around someone. And once you notice it, it can be difficult to let go. Especially if you are the person to actually change them into a better man. . ." Lidia trailed off in her words — taking a moment before she went on. "Just don't lose who *you* are to satisfy your longing for a man. Ever. No matter how good, or bad, they are. Promise?"

"I promise. Thank you for the advice and the support, Lidia. I will rest easy tonight."

"As will I. Since Hassan is not claimed, this will be the best party I have had in a while! I can't wait to see the look on my friend's faces when they see my new toy soldier." Lidia's eyes were sparkling as she daydreamed about her proposal.

"I wasn't referring to the party. Lidia, I don't think Hassan —"

"Oh, Allene, just let me have a little bit of fun? I know I'm harassing Hassan, but he is too polite to say so. I won't pester him for the *entire* party," she exasperated as she tried to defend her reasoning.

I considered her proposal. Hassan had left me to my own defenses tonight regarding the party — should I come to his defense when he hadn't come to mine? It would be playful, hilarious revenge to see Lidia fawn over him for one more night.

"All right, as long as it's not the *entire* time, then he is all yours. Goodnight, Lidia. Thank you for your hospitality."

A servant escorted me to my room. The fluffy, feather-down bed looked like an inviting, plush cloud, ready to devour me whole. I didn't make it wait.

Tossing off my shoes to the side, I jumped onto the mattress, sinking deeply into its soft fabric that soothingly embraced me. I was hoping the amount of sugar pulsing through my veins from dessert would somehow fight off my recurring nightmares of Killian.

I got my wish. I was surprised to have, for the first time in a long time, a *dream*. A dream that made me feel alive, that made me feel free, and that made me feel exhilarated. A dream filled with Killian.

CHAPTER 16

I woke up sweating. I realized I slept even more restlessly when I was dreaming of Killian than when I had nightmares of him.

For the first time since leaving Praseria, I actually yearned for the nightmares — they felt easier to escape. When I was having nightmares of Killian, I wanted to wake up — to do anything to rid him from my mind.

Last night, dreaming of Killian — I had no desire to wake; I didn't want the dream to end. I hated even to admit it. *I can't admit it. I am only dreaming of Killian because he has obnoxiously been by my side for an entire day. It's just Lidia's words getting into my head; it doesn't hold any significance. I still feel the same way I did yesterday. This doesn't mean anything.*

Killian was trouble. He was manipulative. He was far from what I would ever want. I was sure tonight I would be dreaming of Hassan or even Aleron. Anyone but

Killian, as long as Lidia didn't plant more thoughts into my subconscious.

I hadn't given much attention to my guest room yet, considering it was late when I had turned in for the evening. I couldn't tell if the room was overwhelmingly bright from the late morning peak of the sun or whether the all-white color scheme amplified the effects of its light. Turning to my side, I stared out the large glass windows that captured the oak trees that blocked any view of the mountains.

I noticed a flickering light but couldn't narrow down where it was coming from. I rubbed my eyes and found a glitter flake in my hand as I pulled them away from my eyes. I squinted and more closely observed the sheets I had been sleeping in. *Lidia.*

Specks of gold glitter covered the sheets and pillow, which now clung to my bare arms and face.

I arose from the bed and fiercely began dusting off as much of the shiny substance as I could. My efforts were futile. The gold flakes were like magnets. No matter how aggressively I brushed them off, they would somehow relocate to another part of my body. After noticing an increase of gold now in my hair, I eventually realized I was only making the situation worse. I would need a hard scrub and water to rid myself of Lidia's unique fashion trend and a change of clothes.

Sighing in frustration, I searched the room for my bag. If it was in the room, it wasn't visible. None of the four chairs, two tables, or ottoman had any items to display. The room was large and seemed to contain more wardrobe space in that single room than Valteria's entire castle. I searched through each wardrobe, moving the excess linens and bulky clothing out of the way as I sought out my lone, brown satchel bag.

I huffed as I shoved an oversized fur coat to the side in the second to last wardrobe. Deep in the corner, as if intentionally hidden, was my bag. I tugged it out from underneath the clothing that had cloaked it from sight and placed it on the ottoman. I now understood why it was hidden. All of the bag's contents had been removed, and a note lay in the bottom. The letter, in perfect penmanship, was addressed to me.

Allene,

Your items are being laundered until your departure. My designers have placed some custom options for you to wear in the wardrobe. Enjoy!

Lidia

Laundered? They hadn't even been worn. But Lidia knew that. It was her excuse to get me to indulge in her fashion fantasies.

Crumpling up the letter in my hands, I glared at the wardrobe in front of me — the one that hadn't yet been opened.

As much as I was hoping to be surprised by what I would find inside, the wardrobe met my expectations. Just like the rest of the castle, all the options I could see were pastels. Half of the closet involved large round hoops to go under the skirts, leaving only about five actual dress choices. I settled on the light green option — the most understated of them all. Tugging on the heavy dress, I pulled it toward me and saw the secret design I had missed.

The base of the skirt had crocheted pink, yellow, and purple flowers sewn into clusters to give the illusion of a bouquet. The bodice had been covered in a white floral lace that the green barely peeked through. A handful of the small crocheted flowers had been sporadically sewn into the lace to match the skirt. The sleeves were short, and the lace draped over the edge of the sleeves, which made it appear as if I was wearing a shawl. It looked like a dress I would have put on a play doll, not a living human.

Comprehending the grandeur of the dress, I expected it would require assistance to put on. However, the skirt, as heavy and firm as it seemed, stood by itself. I stepped into it and found the large buttons easy to do up on my own. I know Lidia would want me to place a hoop under the skirt, but I already felt as wide as a dining room table — I was not about to add to the volume of the dress.

As nauseatingly sweet as my new dress was, it at least helped rid me of some of the gold glitter. Until I could properly bathe, I decided to wear one of the hats in the wardrobe to cover my hair. I tucked as much of my long hair into the hat as I could. I didn't dare look at my reflection. I only needed to wear the outfit for a moment, just long enough to track down Lidia, kindly ask for the return of my clothes, and be pointed in the direction of a bath.

I ventured out of my room and into the hall, following the same corridors I had taken last night to find my way back to the main hall and dining room. Servants were waiting at the doors, and without a word, had opened them in the perfect timing of my arrival.

The dining room windows and doors had been opened, leaving crisp air all around me. I shivered from the change in temperature but also from the spectacle I had caused.

Lidia was in the far corner of the room, shining the same way she had yesterday, her hair taller than before. Lidia was having a conversation with Hassan, who had somehow also been coaxed into wearing an outfit that did not belong to him.

He wore a light blue jacket and dark blue vest with white trousers begging to be stained. Lidia had her arm wrapped around Hassan, wholly engaged with her toy.

Killian was sitting alone in a chair placed on the lush green lawn near a set of open doors. He wore a brown leather coat with black trousers and boots — a drastic contrast to Lidia's color scheme. I wondered if she had tried to dress him up too, or if he declined, or if she didn't care enough to try and bend his will. Either way, I didn't feel like I stood out much more than anyone else.

I noticed sandwiches and treats set up on the dining room table. *Odd breakfast choices, but this could be another unique trend in Veruje.*

Hassan gave a soft smile as he stared at me, giving me a long look and an encouraging eyebrow raise. I withheld the urge to turn away in embarrassment at the dress-up Lidia had managed to place me in, trying to act confidently in the unusual clothes. All my courage was quickly shattered as I heard Killian's muffled laugh.

I hesitated by the doors, contemplating if I should turn around and go back, but I was too late. Lidia's eyes went wide when she saw me, rushing to my side before I could disappear.

"Cousin, dear! Outstanding choice from the wardrobe; you have more fashion sense than I thought." Lidia's hands grasped my arms and held them out wide, inspecting me closely.

Killian was standing now, his insulting grin gleaming.

"I apologize that my servants weren't there to tend to you when you awoke. They waited as long as they could, but they had other obligations to prepare for the party. You understand how short-staffed it can be when parties are rushed like this," Lidia hurriedly explained. It was sweet of her to think I would understand that, but Valteria rarely put on large parties like Lidia's. I nodded, pretending to sympathize.

"They were waiting for me?" I asked. *Was it already the afternoon?*

"You overslept and missed breakfast, but we all agreed to wait for you to join us for lunch," Hassan chimed in from afar. The room was large enough that even with Hassan being so far away, his voice carried across the room as if he was standing right next to us.

"Or a tea party, from the looks of it," Killian chortled.

Hassan glared at Killian's comment, and Lidia waved a hand in the air.

"That is enough remarks from you today, Killian. Keep it up, and you will be dismissed before the game of Lockett."

"That would be a pity."

"It would. Sit," Lidia commanded, treating him like a disobedient puppy who would lose the opportunity of a good bone from his bad behavior. Killian and Hassan both took a seat and patiently waited for Lidia and me.

"Lidia, I was hoping to freshen up before engaging in any other social activities. Would you mind showing me to the bathing facilities and my clothes?" I eyed her with annoyance, but she didn't allow that to shake her persistence.

"There is no need to change or rush! I will be sure you have plenty of time to freshen up again before the party."

"And my clothes?" I addressed again.

"I'm not sure they will be quite ready. Remember, understaffed and such?" She created another excuse.

"Of course. Maybe I will just wear my dress from yesterday instead if they won't be done in time." I let the statement sink in. Lidia didn't approve of my clothes, but I knew she would disapprove even more of wearing my filthy dress from traveling.

"Come to think of it, I have some pieces in my collection from a few seasons ago that may be more to your liking," Lidia countered.

I grinned. "Fantastic. What time is the party?"

"Seven o'clock sharp; giving you just enough time to eat, enjoy a game of Lockett, and freshen up," Lidia assured me. She had our entire schedule planned out, practically down to the minute.

We all sat at the table to eat. The lunch seemed to drag on. Lidia's constant talking with Hassan once again left

Killian and me quiet for the duration of the meal. Once Lidia's servants cleared the food away, both Killian and I swiftly got up — ready to move on with the game of Lockett.

Lockett was a simple game, but that didn't mean it was easy. Lockett required precision. Each player would start in the same spot, on the first marker, with a wooden stick. The game's objective was to knock a marble ball past the second dedicated marker. Each player had up to three attempts to hit the ball. After three attempts, whoever's ball was the closest to the marker would win. The game required players to understand trajectory, their own strength, and pristine concentration.

Lidia had some servants set up the game outside the west doors. I was anxious to have a bath, and this game was the only thing standing in my way of soap and a scrub brush — I was ready to play and move on to the next items on Lidia's agenda. Lidia, however, was not in any hurry. She took her time explaining the rules to Hassan and Killian, giving a mock display of how to play.

"Seems straightforward enough," Hassan replied.

"I wouldn't say that until you've played," I said.

Hassan exchanged a grin as his eyebrows furrowed in anticipation. "Why don't you start us off then, Allene?"

Everyone took a step back as a servant handed me a heavy stick. They had placed a red ball on the ground in front of me. I studied the area for a moment. It had been some time since I had played Lockett, the last time being with Risa over a year ago. I was out of practice.

I placed my feet in a parallel position, perpendicular

to the ball. I took in a deep breath and clenched my arms as I swung back the stick and pulled back on its urge to smack the ball as hard as it could. The end of the stick met almost perfectly with the center of the ball and sent it halfway between the markers. It was a decent first play, and it would be a good setup for my next turn.

"Marvelous first hit, dear," Lidia said encouragingly.

I gave a small smile as I stepped to the side to watch Lidia play next. The servants issued her a purple ball and her personalized pink stick, adorned in jewels. She struggled to keep her dress skirt out of the way, tipping forward as far as she could to lean over the ball to get a good view of it. She held her breath — displaying her effort through squinted concentration. She tapped the ball, and it managed to travel a mere few feet, settling significantly farther back than mine. She let out a huff and twisted her lips in disappointment.

"Your turn, Hassan," she said, turning away to stand by me.

Hassan was given an orange ball and a long stick for his bulkier stature. He took a moment to consider his positioning and attempted a few mock swings to feel its weight better. Looking down at the ground, then back up at me with a sly grin, he hit the ball quickly, catapulting it a little past my own.

Lidia began clapping excitedly at Hassan's success. "Hassan, you're a natural!"

He gave a short laugh in reply and came to stand by me. Hassan's shoulder lightly brushed up against my own, the warmth of his skin making me shiver from the contrast of the outside breeze.

"Don't flatter him too much, Lidia. We haven't even finished the first round," I reminded her.

"I don't mind the flattery, actually," Hassan softly nudged his elbow into my shoulder, his olive eyes twinkling and his hair following the direction of the afternoon breeze.

"I do. I think you should withhold your awe until my turn is complete." Killian stepped forward, took the green ball directly from the servant's hand, and placed it on the ground.

Killian didn't spend much time preparing for his move. I watched him closely, somehow convinced he would find a way to cheat. He shrugged his shoulders and swiftly swung the stick — making perfect contact with the ball. I watched the ball as it leisurely carried its way across the dense grass and landed just inches behind my own.

Killian's move left me in a vulnerable position. When another player got behind you, they could potentially knock your ball out of its placement. Killian was aware of the consequences of his move, and he gave a proud smirk to declare it.

"It appears I've caught up to you, Allene."

I felt my body tense up at his words. Who was he to behave like he had the upper hand? Killian had transformed a pointless game into an ignited vendetta, and I wanted to be sure he would sorely lose.

I gripped my stick tightly and placed myself in front

of my ball. Killian stayed where he was, amused by my irritation.

I outlined two different courses of action and debated which one to take. Killian had obviously played Lockett before, so he would know all the rules. I wondered if he remembered that you could hit the ball in *any* direction. Although unconventional, I would do anything to see him defeated, even if that meant me losing in the process.

I placed the stick in front of the ball and sent it in the opposite direction of the marker. The trajectory was perfect. The move hit Killian's ball spot on, allowing my ball to absorb some of his impact to slow down its speed while sending Killian's even further from where it had started.

I looked up at Hassan and Lidia, who were both shocked at my choice. Lidia gave a loud laugh, and Hassan beamed with wonderment. Killian now had his elbow propped up on his stick, leaning against it and trying to seem relaxed despite everyone else's reaction. As much as he tried, his nonchalant attitude barely covered up the disdain behind his eyes.

Lidia didn't let the moment of victory last for long as she took back her position of being everyone's focus. She gave another pitiful attempt to hit the ball correctly — still barely getting it a few inches. Hassan gave his second play, smoothly landing about a stride length behind the finish marker. If I had to place bets based on the current positions of all the players, Hassan would win.

Killian was still leaning on his stick, his stare burning into me. He hadn't paid much attention to the rest of the game since I put him behind everyone else, but he was paying close attention to me.

"I pass," Killian declared.

"Is that allowed?" Hassan questioned, turning to me to verify Killian's move.

"It is," I confirmed — confused and curious behind Killian's choice.

"Are you forfeiting?" Hassan asked.

"No, I am simply passing this turn," Killian clarified.

"That will only give you one more play," Lidia added for extra clarity.

"I know," Killian replied.

What is his end goal here? Killian and I were now in a locked staring contest — his square jaw locked tight. I broke away from his eyes — the absorbing eyes that were nearly devoid of color.

I studied the position of all the players once again. We were all silent as everyone courteously let me concentrate and consider my final play. I noticed that Lidia was to the right of me, not much ahead. Hassan's ball was directly in front of mine, not much farther ahead and slightly to the left. Killian was behind mine and also to the left. *The left.*

I tried to hold back a smile as I silently observed the reason behind Killian's move. He knew Hassan would likely hit the marker spot on his next move; he was only a few inches away from it. Hassan would only lose if someone knocked him out of position — just as I had to Killian. The only player who could move Hassan's marker *was* Killian. Hassan would play his turn, hit the marker, and lose since Killian was the last player to make his move. Killian would win.

Killian was used to winning, getting what he wanted, and feeling in control. A feeling and comfort he relied on that I wanted to be stripped away.

I didn't hesitate as I hit the ball in the proper direction of the marker. However, this time, rather than hitting it straight on, I hit it at an angle — an angle that collided with Hassan's ball, giving it enough force to land his ball precisely on the marker. Lidia gaped as she looked to see Killian's reaction. Hassan didn't give any of his focus to Killian — instead, he shook his head back and forth at me as he ran his fingers through his hair.

"Whoops, that was clumsy of me." I shrugged, pretending it was a mistake. I walked over to stand by Hassan again, ignoring whatever new glare Killian was likely sending my way.

"Well, I'm not oblivious to see there is little hope for me now, but I don't give up," Lidia declared, gliding to her ball and giving it one last, uncoordinated shot as it flew right past the marker and into a nearby tree stump. "Hassan, I'm anxious to see your move." Lidia encouraged.

"I pass, isn't that right, Allene?" Hassan asked me. *He was observant.* I appreciated how keen he had been to understand my purpose of putting him on the marker.

I nodded, confirming his choice. "He passes."

"That leaves the last move to you, Killian," Lidia proclaimed.

Killian slowly nodded, holding a straight face, his

curls falling forward to cover the intentions behind his eyes.

"From my perspective, it seems I have two choices. I can forfeit to Hassan, or . . ." Killian stepped forward now, hitting the ball with a quick tap. His ball hit mine, nudging Hassan's out of the way. My ball was now on half the marker, while Killians was on the other half. "I can tie Allene."

I was expecting to see Killian fume, to see him get angry, to see him enraged as a result of my earlier decision. I ruined his plan — or so I had thought. But Killian always seemed to find a way to win. Now I realized the anger would be mine, but I would not let him see that.

"Someone remind me, what are the rules in the event of a tie?" Killian asked.

Lidia was quiet in reaction to the immediate tension, and Hassan didn't know the rules. The only person who could answer was me.

"The two players go back to the starting point and hit their ball at the same time. Whoever lands closest to the marker wins," I replied with vexation — knowing he already knew the answer to his question.

"Ah, that's right. You better take your place, Allene," Killian encouraged.

I felt Hassan put his hand on my shoulder, trying to calm me down. He could sense my frustration, and the visible shaking from my anger also didn't help. *Why did Killian, no matter the circumstances, always find a way to get on my nerves? I had beat him, hadn't I? So why was I angry?*

"It would be a shame to leave the game unfinished," I spit out the words that seemed to catch in my throat.

In truth, I wanted to walk away. I didn't like feeling preyed upon by Killian, but I knew the result of forfeiting would only prove what he wanted. He wanted my defeat, my surrender. Thankfully, my pride was stronger than my irritation or fear.

We took our places, patiently waiting for the countdown to be initiated. We all looked to Lidia, expecting her to start. For the first time since our arrival, Lidia was silent. She could sense the shift of tension and cowered behind Hassan, pretending to be distracted by something the servants were doing in the field for the party. Hassan didn't wait for her to mediate. He knew how much I wanted this to be over, so he took charge.

"On the count of three. One." I breathed out, focusing all my attention on the marker. "Two." Hassan paused, nodding to me with a smile. "Three!"

My ball traveled at a slower speed than Killian's, trailing behind his. Killian's came to a halt about a foot past the marker. My ball was still moving, approaching the marker at a crawling pace. Losing momentum, it achieved a few more rolls and stopped a few inches behind the marker. It didn't matter if the ball was behind or past the marker; it all came down to who was closer.

Hassan grinned, and Lidia had turned to peek at the results, trying to still shy behind Hassan when she realized the outcome.

I won.

I thought Killian would be smug from his half victory

or enraged from his half loss, but his face was unusual — it was almost soft, venerate.

"That's the game," Hassan announced.

"I'm impressed, cousin. You need to tutor me on Lockett before you go! My friends would be amazed if I won a game for once, and you might be my chance," Lidia stared up into the sky, daydreaming about a possible victory. She didn't daydream for long — finding a way to move on to other things right away.

"Allene, you can go get cleaned up now. I will be sure another dress is ready for you. Hassan, be a dear and escort me back to my quarters?" Lidia beamed, doing her very best to persuade him by manipulation. It worked.

"Yes, your majesty. I will see you tonight," Hassan confirmed, looking at me sweetly as he locked arms with Lidia. *She is relentless.*

I chuckled as they walked away. Lidia leaned her head against Hassan's shoulder, and Hassan's neck seemed to extend uncomfortably high to avoid touching her — trying not to give Lidia the wrong impression.

I handed my stick to a nearby servant and followed distantly behind Lidia and Hassan. I was too distracted by Lidia's uncompromising efforts for Hassan's attention to notice the presence that was walking beside me. *Either that or I just got very good at ignoring it.*

Killian mimicked my strides as I walked across the dining hall. I caught him staring at me with a look of concern flashing across his face. I didn't care to ask what his expression was about, but he would choose to tell me anyway.

"Helping Hassan almost win — sacrificing your position to try and see me lose — you've been holding back on me, Allene," Killian accused.

I shook my head at his ridiculous statement. "You were seeking out a reaction."

"I was; I just didn't expect the one you gave." Killian barely blinked as his ice-blue eyes seemed to search mine for a reason behind my decision-making.

"What did you think I would do?" I questioned him. I was baffled that he even cared.

Killian contemplated the question for a moment and gave a gentle reply — the gentle tone deceiving the offensive nature of his following words. "I'm not sure . . . throw an entitled princess tantrum or something of those sorts."

My eyebrows furrowed, and my lips puckered from his insulting assumptions. "I'm sorry I didn't stoop to your low expectations," I spat.

Killian approached the doors at the end of the room. He stopped my strides as he placed himself in front of my only way of escape. He held his hands behind his back in a relaxed posture. His curly hair was shielding his bright and troublesome eyes.

"I'm not." His reply was merely a whisper, the low tone in his voice leaving chills up my spine. I was stunned into silence as Killian seemed to stare through me — his eyes prying for any additional surprises I may be hiding.

The silence seemed to satisfy his curiosity as the intensity in his face seemed to dwindle.

"Enjoy your bath, princess." He swiftly turned on his

heels to exit from the room, leaving me to watch his figure disappear as the doors shut once again.

Killian's words left me feeling exposed. I wish I could say those feelings were tied to his lewd comment, but my instincts told me to hide myself for another reason — another cause for feeling bare. He understood something about myself that I couldn't see, a part of myself I had *forbidden* to see. He saw a part of me that was wrong; that brought me shame, and that left me exhilarated and terrified at the unknown.

CHAPTER 17

The interaction with Killian had left me in a daze. As much as I wanted to savor the revitalizing sensation of clean skin and fresh clothes, I was stuck with the same feeling I had when I left the dining room: a permanent sense of unease.

Why was it that no matter what kind of discussions I had with Killian, they all left me feeling the same way? Whether he was mocking me with compliments, spewing with fallacious bantering, or self-conceited praises, I was always left feeling strange. Different.

Killian made me feel intrigued and petrified, and it was the intrigue portion that frightened me. How could a man like him subconsciously be intriguing to me? Was it his relation to Aleron and how different they were that left me feeling fascinated? My fascination couldn't have been for Killian himself — I knew he was trouble, so where was the draw coming from?

The evening was approaching, and I had unmindfully gotten dressed for the party. I had barely even noticed the replacement dress that Lidia had sent up for me.

I rubbed the fabric against my palms, the black feathers attached to the dress were lightweight and delicate to the touch. They fluttered back from even the slightest contact. The dress was composed primarily of feathers that left me feeling comfortable and free — a transformative difference from Lidia's previous dress choices that were heavy and rigid.

Lidia had created a large transformation in her style preferences if this dress was popular a few seasons ago. The dress was all black. Even her accents of glitter around the seam lines were black. The fabric hugged my skin softly as the train landed directly at my heels. The neckline formed a sharp square that enveloped my shoulders and stopped. Additional feathers were pinned to the fabric at my shoulders to give a fanning effect that cascaded to my elbows. The dress held a subtle essence of purity behind its powerful, dark appearance.

Being in an unfamiliar kingdom, embracing new, strange styles, a dress hand picked for an unexpected party — the similarities made me think of Praseria.

The thought quickly entered my mind and the heartache along with it. The dress made me think of Noni, which led my thoughts of Ezra. I worried about them. I wondered how they were doing, what they were feeling, and what they were thinking. They had to be aware of Eveline and Killian's departure. They had to have felt the disruption of Praseria with Aleron's absence.

How were they handling everything? Were they still at the castle? Did they miss me as much as I missed them? *Would I ever see them again?*

It was a thought I often had and one I was not particularly eager to dwell on. I had to see them again; it wasn't an option.

I tried to focus again on getting ready, pushing the tears flowing to my eyes back into the deep corners of my heart.

It felt odd without Sonora's help braiding my hair, but I reminded myself that I had functioned my entire life without a handmaid. I could survive a few weeks without assistance.

I twisted the braid and pinned it high on my head so my hair wouldn't rest on the feathers at my shoulders. The feathers framed my pale face, and my hair sat like a crown. Combining my white skin and black hair with my black dress made my eyes seem bluer than before.

I hadn't been fond of Lidia's overbearing designs, but this dress was bold in its beauty. If I didn't have so far to travel, it was a dress I would have even requested to keep.

I stared at the gray moon that was backlit as the sun disappeared behind the mountains. The party would begin soon. Lidia had ordered us to skip dinner and save our appetites for some specialty hors d'oeuvres that would be served at the party.

This would be the last night in a kingdom I had a connection to — a kingdom that I knew I was safe. Our remaining travels would take place in new territories, with new faces and, likely new challenges.

As much as I wanted to be irritated by our delay of the party, part of me was hoping we'd find another reason to stall and stay, to avoid having to venture from comfort. *Comfort . . . look at what you are wearing, Allene. If you can wear the dresses Lidia throws at you, then you can handle more discomforting situations.*

Lidia had sent for a servant to escort me to the party. The young lady had knocked on my door, her eyes going wide as she observed my dress. I couldn't discern if her reaction was a good or bad sign. I realized the black was highly in contrast with Lidia's current pastel dream, but I didn't think my dress was alarming. Or so I hoped.

I could hear the music as soon as I left my room. The high-pitched wind instruments were playing in a staccato rhythm. The music gave enough indication of what my eyes would see as I turned the corner into the ballroom.

The ballroom had a similar setup as the dining room. Grand doors had been propped open to lead to the outside garden and pond. Lanterns hung throughout the green space to create enough lighting outside for guests to mingle and enjoy the cool evening air. A band was centered at the back of the room while servants in white maneuvered around guests to offer refreshments as they danced.

The party was distinctly disorganized. Everyone danced when and how they pleased. Some people could be found chatting and laughing in groups while others danced around them. Younger men were hunched over tall tables as they observed competitive card games. Young ladies were viciously flirting with men off the dance floor, on the dance floor, outside, or even with the band members. It was loud. It was distracting. It was not like any event I had ever attended.

The ballroom displayed sweeping floral strands that hung from corner to corner. The intensity of some of the dancing shook the garlands, making loose petals drift to the marble ground to be trampled over by rambunctious guests.

No one paid attention to my entrance, and I wasn't announced like I was at most parties. I was overwhelmed by the variety and style of dress choices and colors. The tall, exaggerated hairstyles made me feel lowly in comparison. I didn't just blend in with the crowd; I was overshadowed. Me, an outsider princess, the imitation of a Praserian, wearing all black, *didn't* stand out. Veruje was an oddity I would never find again. There were no judgments, no vicious scrutiny because everything was acceptable.

The sea of people and mayhem hindered my ability to focus. I stayed at the entrance to achieve the greatest view of the room to pinpoint Hassan or Lidia. Before I could successfully locate them myself, an observing voice ended my search.

"Far-left corner, by the stinky man with a horrendous mustache."

My eyes immediately followed the guidance to see Lidia in a bright yellow gown, embellished with fresh sunflowers, loudly laughing to her friend as she tightly clung to Hassan's arm. I don't know how I missed her. I would have never guessed that Lidia would be hard to distinguish in a crowd, but bright yellow seemed to be a popular color choice tonight as I was looking around the room.

I turned to the voice that had answered my unspoken question. Killian's hair was styled with the sticky product of Lidia's — allowing his hair to remain out of his face and fall to the back of his neck, his curls tighter than usual brushed against his jacket collar. His dark green coat looked waxed and firm, seeming impossible to crinkle. His outfit choice was also clearly instituted by Lidia. His leather boots had black stones that lined his ankle. She loved to add natural elements to her designs, it seemed. It felt more like a costume ball than a party.

"And I thought I had achieved going unnoticed," I replied, turning my head away after a glance at Killian. I could hear him shifting his weight, leaning closer to me. I didn't have to look up to know that he was staring at me. The chills up my back were indication enough.

"Maybe to the bystanders that weren't seeking you out," he boldly insinuated.

I felt my mouth go dry. *Did I hear that correctly? No, I didn't.* That tone, that phrase — it was probably one he had used a hundred times before. Killian isn't genuine; he's rehearsed. He always has a motive, and I would pay no heed to it.

I turned towards him, crossing my arms in exasperation at his pointless attempts to lure me as prey. He cocked his head to the side, his sharp features accentuated, patiently waiting to listen.

"We aren't doing this," I affirmed.

"Doing what?" Killian had shrugged his shoulders, his roguish gaze burning into me.

I shook my head and clenched my fists to channel the frustration I was already battling against. "Whatever twisted and exhausting exchange you have invented in your head, I don't have the time for it."

"Because you are eager to get to Hassan," he replied sedately.

My eyes went wide from his curt statement. I held back a blush. "I didn't say that."

"Then clarify. What other pressing matter would need your time and attention right now? Please don't say Lidia; she's plenty preoccupied with parading Hassan tonight. If it isn't Lidia, and if it isn't Hassan, then that would give the impression that you don't have time for me, and that would be *quite* offensive," he declared.

He was right; I didn't have the time for him. He wasn't worth expending the energy going back and forth as he both complimented and irritated me. What does it matter if I wanted to see Hassan or Lidia? Or anyone else that wasn't Killian?

I stepped backward, giving additional space between us. "There is an innumerable amount of women here that I am sure would drool over your company, Killian. Why don't you go and find one?" I encouraged him — not hesitating to hear his response as I made my way to meet Hassan and Lidia.

I tried to get to them before they moved on to another location in the room. I was consumed by the large dresses and tall people that left me feeling small, engulfed, and imperceptive. I did my best to focus on my feet, hoping that if I were at least traveling in a straight line, I would likely arrive in the near vicinity of Hassan and Lidia.

My eyes noticed a familiar set of brown boots. I looked up to see Hassan in an ivory coat and grey pants, entirely understated for Lidia's guest of honor.

Hassan's hair was intentionally rustled, and his face was bright as he smiled and nodded at Lidia's friend. I immediately noticed a stench of something putrid. Moldy food, maybe? Fish? Onions? I turned to see if a servant was near me with a display of hors d'oeuvres, but there was no food in sight.

I crinkled my nose to retreat from the horrid smell as I stepped in closer to get their attention. The smell hit me more intensely now than before. *By the stinky man with the horrendous mustache.* Killian's words repeated in my head as I noted the presence of the man Lidia and Hassan had been talking to. *He did stink.*

"Allene!" Hassan seemed relieved as he noticed my arrival. "You're finally here," he said, trying to hide the urgency in his voice.

"It took me a moment to find you. There are many people in attendance. Lidia, you weren't exaggerating about how quickly you can put together a party."

Being closer to Lidia now, I noticed that her hair had been spun and twisted to resemble a beehive that stood tall on her head, adorned with additional flowers. Her brown lip color was the most distracting of all — enhancing her already full lips.

"I never lie about my capabilities, Allene. If anything, I exceed them! Isn't that right, Saltz?"

The man with the broadly curled brown mustache, with food crumbs attached to the hairs near his lips, nodded excitedly.

"No reputation like that of your cousin, Lidia," he confirmed.

Lidia was now giggling. "Saltz, you *flatter* me."

Hassan and I exchanged glances, both of us trying to hold back our discomfort. Hassan cleared his throat as he tried to loosen his arm from Lidia to be closer to me, but Lidia's firm grip was not one to easily let him go. Poor Hassan. Who would have said being too polite was a hindrance? I would need to remind her to let him go for some of the night, she had promised after all. Saltz spoke again, his decaying, warm breath clouding my other senses.

"Lidia informed me of your business here in Veruje. I was quite surprised to hear the Red Crows are back, and with an agenda from the sound of it."

I did a double-take as I looked between Lidia and Hassan for answers to why a stranger knew the reason we were visiting. Hassan responded before I could get ahead of myself.

"Saltz is a close friend of Lidia's; he led her battle training for years," Hassan explained.

"He's an excellent resource. I don't know a man with greater militant knowledge than Saltz."

Saltz beamed at the compliment while hiding his blushing behind his patchy beard hair.

I tried to hold back the anger I could feel building up inside. But why was I angry? Lidia said she trusted him, and he was her friend. *But Nycolas seemed to be our friend too at first.*

The knowledge of the Red Crows plan was not to be taken lightly. Lives and kingdoms were at stake. We had to be cautious of whom we told to keep our position a surprise. I didn't know what Nycolas would do if he knew we had joined forces in an attempt to ruin his scheme. The fewer people that we informed about it, the better. At least for now.

I swallowed back the temptation to reprimand Lidia, realizing that it wouldn't matter what I said; she would tell whomever she wanted to tell.

I forced a smile on my face as I turned to Hassan.

"We aren't here to speak of politics any longer, are we? If you wouldn't mind giving me a moment, I'm famished. Hassan, would you show me some of the fine assortments of refreshments that Lidia has told us so much about?"

Hassan's eyes grew wide, realizing I was allowing him to leave Lidia's side. Lidia's eyes also grew wide at my suggestion, the contempt she had for the idea of Hassan being swept away from her evident to us all. I placed my hand on Lidia's arm, slowly prying it away to replace her grip on Hassan with my own.

"I will bring him back shortly, Lidia," I assured her, trying to make her less abrasive to my proposal.

"Yes, don't be gone long. Hassan was looking forward to meeting my friend Lux before she left for the evening," Lidia insisted — scrambling to find a reason for his commitment to her side. I could feel Hassan wince at her demand.

"Of course, I won't miss the opportunity," he promised her.

Lidia relaxed now, giving a small smile in reply.

Hassan placed his warm hand on mine as he restrained from walking away too quickly. We walked to the buffet table, trying to get far enough away from Lidia that she wouldn't be able to hear our conversation.

"I just hope for your sake that Lux smells better than Saltz," I whispered to Hassan as we stood now by the doors. Hassan was grinning at my comment, and I was holding back a laugh as I realized their names made me think of soap.

Hassan grabbed a plate of pre-selected food and held it out for us to share. He chose a dessert coated heavily in sugar while I picked a lighter option of flavored bread.

"Lux. . . Saltz. . . where does Lidia meet such interesting people?" Hassan wondered out loud between bites.

"Do we sincerely want to know?" I questioned.

Hassan's food caught in his throat as he chuckled. He coughed for a brief second, trying to regain his composure. He smoothly returned the plate to the table, now removing his interest from the pastries.

"No, I suppose we don't. Thank you for freeing me from Lidia's literal hold." Hassan emphasized by rubbing his arm and shaking it out.

"I apologize it wasn't sooner." I had no idea how long Lidia had forced him to be her date tonight.

"I can handle Lidia for a little longer," Hassan spoke

with his heavenly gift of patience, leaning his broad back on the wall for support as he looked in Lidia's direction. She had obsessively been darting glances our way to make sure we didn't leave her sight.

"I wouldn't speak so soon; the evening is likely still young in her eyes."

"Don't say that," Hassan rebuked, his shoulders slumping as he turned his back to Lidia so that he was leaning closer to me now.

"I don't want you getting your hopes up," I whispered from his closeness. "If it helps, we will be gone by morning," I reminded him.

"That makes me anxious, actually," he admitted.

"Anxious? What for?" I asked.

What was I missing? If one of the bravest people I knew was worried, then I would likely feel terrified. I held my breath, waiting for his response to pierce me with fear.

"We will be passing through Selvet," he stated the not-so-intimidating reason behind his anxiety.

I exhaled, the nervousness gone. "Why would that make you anxious?" I inquired, trying to understand his concerns.

Hassan turned his head to the side, confirming that no one could hear his answer before he proceeded. He inclined his forehead to be only a few inches from mine.

"While I have been enduring considerably tortuous conversations with your cousin, it will seem mild compared to the obnoxious nature of Freira."

"Freira is far from what I would classify as obnoxious. She is sweet," I defended.

"And chatty," he added.

I scowled at him now. "Friendly, Hassan; she's considered friendly."

"You sound like my mother," he admitted, smiling to the side.

"Did you just compare me to your mother?" I shook my head back and forth, not offended by his comment but rather amused he would make such a statement. *He really was Damien's brother.*

"My mother — another individual you'll be meeting. Can you see why I'm anxious?" His olive eyes peered into mine, begging me for sympathy.

I placed my hand on Hassan's shoulder, staring back at him. I adored how he looked at me. Hassan and I, we were comfortable. We were safe, he was kind, and in addition to his full and giving heart, he was truly beautiful.

"Don't be. I look forward to finally meeting the entire Durand family."

Hassan reached up to squeeze my hand, the satisfaction of my reply beaming in his eyes. "Just remember that when the time comes," he warned.

I smiled at Hassan, relieved to be having a conversation with a man that I found myself caring about more and more as each day went by. For the first time since we had met, we had no distractions. If there was anything to discover about my relationship with Hassan, about our potential, now was our opportunity to receive those answers — to gain clarity.

This evening was what I needed to distract myself from thoughts of Aleron and to give Hassan my focus.

I tugged on his hand that was holding mine, trying to pull him away to dance. Hassan politely followed, tenderly staring at me as we approached the large group of dancing guests. Before Hassan could take my other hand, the obstacle of tonight was there to stop us — my demanding, gorgeous cousin.

Lidia stepped in front of me, furiously staring down at Hassan. She obviously thought my time had run out. Clearing her throat, with her arms crossed sternly, she remained poised as she fought to get Hassan back.

"Lux can't stay much longer, and I know she is looking forward to meeting you. Shall we, Hassan?" Lidia requested, batting her eyelashes at Hassan.

Hassan retained his composure, communicating with a firm squeeze of my hands that he wanted to stay. Before he even gave me the chance to stand up to cousin Lidia, Hassan had smoothly replied.

"Of course. Allene, won't you join us?" Hassan didn't hesitate at his invitation. Lidia initially seemed flustered by his proposal, but she still managed to find an objection quickly.

"I'm sure Allene would much rather be dancing than be part of some boring conversations," Lidia replied, nervously chuckling.

Hassan was just as fast as Lidia with replying. "You're entirely right; Allene would much rather be dancing. In fact, she promised to be my exclusive dance partner the rest of the evening," Hassan tugged on my hand to be sure I understood.

I played along, nodding with him and holding back the urge to smile. I didn't want to offend Lidia, but I was flattered by his statement. He stood up for me — for us — something I wished Aleron would have done.

"I am sure Lidia will be prompt with our introduction. I won't leave you alone for too long," Hassan assured me, trying to hint a proper response out of Lidia.

Lidia's eyes went cold at Hassan's attempt to corner her. She knew she had to give a kind reply; she didn't have any other options.

Plastering on a hard smile, she managed to say a few words. "Yes, not too long."

We all went silent. Hassan exchanged a soft smile to Lidia, hiding the joy of his accomplishment as he winked at me.

"I'll meet you outside shortly," he confirmed. Hassan extended his arm to Lidia with a genuine smile on his face this time. "After you, your majesty."

The hardness in her eyes softened at his gesture. She held her chin up high as Hassan escorted her to a large group of women that giggled as Lidia and Hassan approached. They parted to make room for Lidia to speak with a woman in the center of the circle, dressed in a vibrant blue gown. Lidia, and whom I assumed was Lux, embraced dramatically — exchanging air kisses. Lux pulled back and began relentlessly fanning her red face that glistened with sweat as she stared in awe at Hassan.

Looking at the exasperated woman brought my attention to the suffocating side effects of the large party. Hassan's suggestion to meet outside and escape the hot air sounded lovely.

I brushed against shoulders and dresses as I shoved my way outside. There was still a large crowd by the entrance to the ballroom. Peering over the exhausted but dedicated guests, I spotted a pond reflecting in the moonlight. I turned back, trying to spot Hassan. He was nowhere in sight, just another guest in the crowd.

To the right of me, I could hear the obnoxious laughter of a group of women. I caught the eye of one of the ladies who seemed to be staring at me. I turned away, trying not to gain any attention.

"Oh! Isn't that Lidia's cousin from Valteria?" the woman spoke loudly.

"The princess?" a soft voice asked.

"We should go talk to her. Look at the poor girl, all by herself," another added.

I felt the heels of my shoes begin to sink into the soft grass as my feet instinctively began to walk towards the pond. I didn't look behind me — too afraid that if I did, I would be trapped into a conversation of prying nature, and I was not one for gossip.

The women made a weak attempt to call out to me, but I was already far enough away to be justified in pretending that I couldn't hear them. They didn't care enough to follow me, which was exactly what I hoped for.

The cool breeze immediately hit my face as I came to the edge of the pond. The cold touch of the wind made my skin sticky. Everything was quiet. The party's lights were absorbed by the pond's water, letting the moon and stars reflect brightly off the surface.

I took in a deep breath of air to replace the musty scent of sweat and food from the party. I closed my eyes and enjoyed the moment of tranquility. *The fleeting moment of tranquility.* Looking up at the moon, I couldn't help but think of Aleron and the many nights I would stare out my window, wishing he was by my side, hoping I could talk to him.

Aleron was likely in Lokali by now, and the separation didn't hurt as much as I expected it to. I knew, deep down, that I still felt attached to what Aleron and I had. I clung to a small amount of hope that things could go back to how they were, that I could regain that perfect love. But I couldn't ignore that something had changed since that day I went to see him.

It could be anger or frustration that was clouding my feelings. It could be temporary. Part of me prayed it was only temporary because I couldn't imagine my life without Aleron in it a few months ago. Was this just a disconnect needing to be resolved between us, or was it a sign that I still had more to learn? More to pursue, more to understand.

Did things happen too soon with Aleron? Were they too good? I knew relationships weren't meant to be perfect, and I could still see that possibility of Aleron and me. I could imagine choosing him just as fiercely as I did a few months ago. But if Aleron was my choice, I needed to know it completely. I couldn't have any regrets or any questions. The last few weeks, Hassan had been a question in my mind, and I couldn't move forward without receiving some answers.

Hassan and Aleron, my feelings for them were entirely different. That scared me. If they were that different, how could I have feelings for them both? Was one right and one just infatuation? It terrified me to admit that I didn't know.

I didn't want to feel like I was betraying Aleron, betraying us. But he was the one who wanted me to let go, so why hold myself back? If I got my answers — if I knew without a doubt that Aleron was my forever — I would fight tirelessly for him and our future. I could be confident again.

After our conversation, I felt powerless, confused, and unprepared. Those feelings should allow me to put myself first. With this time of separation from Aleron, I felt justified to have a moment of selfishness and a search for answers. I owed myself that much, *didn't I?*

My internal conflict seemed to answer for me, a response to my question ringing through my head.

"I wouldn't have left you alone — not even for Queen Lidia." Aleron's voice rang through my head so loudly that it was almost like he was next to me.

I shook my head in frustration at myself, trying to ignore the voice. I was going crazy. He was making me crazy.

I looked up at the moon again, folding my arms as I shook from the wind.

"But you did leave me," I whispered, trying to hold back the urge to cry.

"Only because you pushed me away," Aleron's voice replied.

Have I pushed him away? Not only was Aleron making me crazy, but he was also making me feel responsible for all of this. I could almost feel Aleron smirking at me, touching my shoulder. My stomach dropped as my mouth quickly shut. I felt myself shiver, but not from the cold. *Something is touching my shoulder.*

I hesitated to turn around. What would I say to Hassan to explain talking to myself? I braced myself to see his confused face and to hear his understanding, concerned voice.

I turned my head to the side to try and catch a glimpse of his golden hair, but I found it blended into the surroundings of the nightfall as if he was hiding in the shadows. It was not Hassan.

I pulled away, stumbling backward to create distance between us — *too* much distance. The edge of the water was closer than it seemed — my right boot sunk into the shallow water, leaving me more frazzled than I was before.

The man reached out and gripped my forearm as he pulled me towards him and away from the water. The man's touch was comforting and familiar, but I knew it shouldn't be. I nervously shoved him away; his warm touch still felt like it was lingering on my cold skin. The water was sloshing in my boot as I made my way up the small bank.

"Aren't you going to say thank you?" Killian chimed mockingly.

I turned around, staring up at him. The moon was now shining on his light skin, his eyes almost translucent as he stared back at me. I hoped the darkness was hiding how red my face was, red from embarrassment and irritation.

"*Thank you?* You startled me! Don't you know it is indecent to sneak up on a woman?" I questioned. It was *Killian; I don't know why I am surprised.* "Was my encouragement earlier for you to find other women to converse with not clear enough?"

"It was entirely clear," he assured me.

"Then what are you doing?" I asked, still confused why he was following me.

"Women rarely say what they truly mean. Your demands were simply a defense so you wouldn't have to face me," Killian shrugged, implying I should've already known the answer to the question.

"Stop comparing me to other women. I am nothing like any of the women you have met. I'm not afraid to face you, Killian," I hissed under my breath, trying not to cause a spectacle for the other guests.

Killian raised his eyebrows in surprise, stepping forward at my reply. I stood my ground as he approached me. "Precisely why I am here," he replied in a hushed tone — a tone that seemed sincere enough to leave me feeling nauseated.

I placed my hand on my stomach, trying to stabilize my nerves. "Killian, I have tried to be blunt with you. I simply didn't want to be burdened and bothered at the first party I have attended in months, yet here we are. I am not going to engage any longer in your games," I sighed the words in defeat.

Killian still didn't seem fazed by my expression or words. His eyebrows knit together, forming a V in the center of his forehead as he took a few moments to respond. Killian looked up at me, his eyes full of sympathy.

"I know I bother you," he said.

I felt my body relax, the tensing of my stomach melting away, and my anxiety with it. I almost felt sorry for being as harsh as I had been, but Killian was persistent; I didn't know another way to communicate with his stubborn personality.

"I'm glad you understand," I murmured.

Killian nodded slowly, a smirk starting to form. His wicked, full grin was now showing as he stepped even closer, closing any gap between us.

"I do. If you aren't convinced, then I will have to use the power of persuasion," Killian said.

He really doesn't know how to surrender. I laughed, realizing it didn't matter what I said; there was no possibility of getting through to Killian.

Killian cocked his head to the side at the sound of my laughter — patiently waiting for me to respond. He wouldn't like what I had to say, but I was sure he would find another way to object.

"By all means, use your power of persuasion — just use it on someone else," I replied.

"Okay, if not persuasion, how about negotiation?" he quickly countered, his perfect posture somehow straightening even more as he exuded regalness and poise.

"I will not negotiate with you," I said firmly.

"Two dances." Killian's voice was like velvet — smooth and enticing as he tried to convince me. I took a deep breath, attempting to stabilize my conviction.

"No," I replied shortly.

"One dance."

"No!" I exclaimed. I quickly regretted it. What if Hassan was nearby or another guest? What type of gossip might circulate if they saw me arguing with Killian? I needed to leave.

I turned away, ready to stop entertaining Killian's resolve. He caught my arm and spun me back around, placing both his hands securely on my wrists to pull me closer to him.

He stood a head taller than me, his neck directly in front of my eyes. I focused on the movement of his neck as he exhaled, too afraid to look elsewhere. His olive skin looked delicate, pale, and smooth in the moonlight.

We were both quiet, and my nerves immediately returned amidst the silence. Could he hear how loud my heart was beating? I didn't move; I didn't know what Killian might do.

I knew I should pull away, but being near him was intoxicating. The collar of his coat was underneath my nose, the smell of leather leaving me dazed. Killian sighed, his head now inclining down to look at me. He was so close. *Allene, you need to pull away.* I couldn't tell if the voice in my head was my own, Aleron's, Hassan's, or all three. What was I doing? Killian spoke before I could break my trance.

"One dance and I promise I will not say another word to you for the rest of the night," he softly promised.

I felt enough freedom to finally look to the side, leaving Killian's lips near my ear and his sharp jaw grazing my cheekbone. Part of me wished I hadn't moved at all, that maybe this was worse.

I swallowed and cleared my throat to finally speak. "One dance, and you will not say another word to me for an entire week," I replied, my voice shaky.

"Two days," he returned, his breath warm against my neck.

"Four," I said, less shaky this time.

I could hear Killian smile. "Agreed. I just hope you won't regret it."

"Agreeing to dance or the terms of our negotiation?" I questioned.

"Oh, you won't regret the dance, but asking for an entire four days, free of me — *that* you will regret," he whispered the last few words.

"I won't," I assured him, the angst I felt for him returning, snapping me out of whatever trance I had fallen into.

I pulled away now, looking around me to see if Hassan was anywhere in sight. The last thing I wanted was Hassan to see me with Killian. I didn't want to explain my surrender to Killian in exchange for his commitment to four days of peace. I didn't want to know what Hassan's reaction would be, and I planned on not having to find out.

Very few guests remained outside, the nightfall making the temperature drop significantly and moving the party entirely indoors. I looked around, trying to spot a secluded area to meet Killian's demands. I noticed the pond was surrounded by a walking path that led to a deep forest of trees. *Perfect.*

I didn't turn around for Killian's permission as I started walking down the path that surrounded the pond, leading into the deep forest trees. Killian followed behind, raising no objection.

The water in my boot drained with each step I took, finally leaving my foot damp with water instead of submerged. The only light available was that of the moon. The lack of light was in my favor, as I did my best to stay hidden from onlookers as Killian and I disappeared behind a thick set of pine trees.

The clearing was small, only a few feet around us in each direction, but it would do. I crossed my arms now, waiting for Killian as he slowly came around one of the trees.

The moon reflected off his shiny hair and absorbed into the dark tones of his clothes. My black dress merged with my surroundings, very little of me being caught by the moon's subservient rays. If there were any people capable of hiding, it was two Praserian's, dressed in dark clothing, in the dead of night.

"You promised me one dance." Killian's voice seemed quiet as it was being absorbed into the trees.

"Yes," I replied plainly.

Killian turned back around, looking in the direction of the castle. "We are too far away from the music," he objected.

I folded my arms tightly, trying to conceal the urge to shiver from the cold. "You don't need music to dance," I scowled, my teeth slightly chattering at the end.

"Very well then." Killian accepted my response as he smoothly approached me.

He stopped in front of me, leaving a distance between us as he offered his hand this time and patiently waited for me to take it. I unfolded my arms, a gust of wind making me shake.

Killian retreated his hand, staring at me with concern. "You're cold."

I shook my head in denial.

Killian gave me a disapproving look, his jaw clenched. "It is much warmer inside the castle," he pressed.

"I'm fine," I assured him.

Killian scoffed at me as he started removing his jacket.

"What are you doing?" I asked hesitantly.

"I'm not going to let you freeze." Killian held up his jacket, offering it to me.

The thick coat was inviting, taunting me with its promise of warmth. The only thought that held me back was simple: what if someone saw me wearing it?

Killian could sense my uncertainty. He sighed as he shook out the coat and swung it over my shoulders, too impatient to wait for my decision. I gripped the collar of the coat before it could slide off my shoulders — the smell of leather intensifying.

I gently placed my arms through the sleeves. The oversize of the coat I found comforting, like a blanket.

My shivering stopped as the wind was now unable to touch my skin. Killian's black undershirt hung loosely around his body; the hem half tucked in his right side. His chiseled features and masculine build made Killian resemble a statue more than a man. A flawless, awing statue. His charm, his overpowering and ideal figure, I couldn't deny. It was not easy to look away from him.

Killian stared at me now, standing eerily still. I could feel his eyes shifting up and down as he looked at me. His undivided attention made me uneasy.

Killian cautiously reached out to take my right hand. His touch was delicate and light as he slowly pulled me to him. He stared at me again, more concentrated than before as he wrapped his other arm around my waist.

The quiet night and hushes of wind made the silence between us seem appropriate. I didn't want to speak for more than one reason. I didn't know what to say, and I didn't want to be distracted like I was moments earlier.

As difficult as it was to admit, Killian was starting to affect me. I could see his appeal, as I was drawn to him despite my reservations. But I wouldn't let his zeal and ability to seduce women be used on me. My objection, my refusal, only fueled his competitive nature. Whatever he was trying to accomplish by seeking me out was for his own selfish pretenses and desires.

With that thought firmly planted in my mind, I stared

back at Killian, ready to follow through on our agreement.

Killian's face remained rigid, almost stern, as he led our feet to move in a circular direction. Despite his stiff expression, his eyes seemed to be full of movement as they searched mine. I wondered what he was thinking, what he was hoping to gain from this moment.

I found myself questioning Killian's motives every time I was with him. I didn't trust him. He was unpredictable, just like Nycolas. When someone is unpredictable, they are dangerous, and I think they prefer being that way.

Right now, all I wanted in my life was certainty. I wanted to be certain we would stop the Red Crows. I wanted to be certain of Valteria's future. I wanted to be certain we would find Queen Eveline. I wanted to be certain I would find answers to my feelings for Aleron, for Hassan. I wanted to be certain that Risa would be safe, that she would be happy. I wanted to be certain I would make my father proud — that I could be the princess Valteria needed.

After a few moments of swaying silently, Killian spoke, distracting me from my thoughts.

"No music and no prying eyes. You're either embarrassed to be seen with me, princess, or you want to be completely alone with me." Killian was smiling at his suggestion, hoping to take me off guard from his comment.

I kept my eyes locked on his, not faltering in my reason. "I don't appreciate bad gossip," I retorted.

"What bad gossip could be created by being seen with me?"

"I'm assuming that's a rhetorical question," I chuckled slightly. Killian, however, was not amused. His expression seemed solemn as his dancing slowed, his feet coming to a standstill. His forehead creased with worry, his lips turning down at the corners. The quiet evening was once again in the air, hovering over us with tension as we stood motionless, our dancing coming to an end.

Killian rolled back his shoulders and let out a deep sigh, his hands running through his already slicked-back hair. Was he nervous? No — it's Killian — the man feeds off others' nerves, not his own. It must be a tactic to make me feel remorse for my words. I wouldn't give him my sympathy.

Killian vaguely whispered as he looked at me from behind his long eyelashes. "Would being with me make you feel ashamed?"

I felt my throat become dry upon hearing his question. It wasn't what I expected him to say. He seemed serious, and it was almost more intimidating to realize he was sincere.

Killian's coat that initially seemed comforting and warm immediately felt heavy and stifling. I felt trapped. Our conversations were traditionally tinged with vexation, not unfeigned. I didn't know how to respond to this unguarded version of Killian appropriately.

I rarely felt speechless, but I didn't know what to say. I tried to consider his question honestly. Would I feel ashamed to be with Killian? The gossip surrounding his name alone would be enough for people to gasp about. There was also the matter of him being a Praserian — a Praserian prince — the result of that choice being one I knew too well.

I had almost lost Damien with the decision I had made to be with Aleron. *There was another obstacle.*

Aleron and Hassan, they would never forgive me. Risa was kind, but even she had her limits. My mother, I didn't even want to consider her reaction.

I had already experienced the repercussions of my stay in Praseria. I couldn't imagine a more difficult situation than what I had already been through with Aleron; the strains it had on my friendships I thought were unmatched. But Killian, Killian would be an entirely new extent of unforgivable. The thought of being with Killian wasn't a matter of shame or being wrong; it was a matter of being completely impossible.

I could feel Killian studying my expression, looking to gain an unspoken answer to his question. Killian spoke again, insecure from the silence that was intolerable to us both.

"You've delivered on your promise of a dance; now I will deliver on mine. Four days, free of me." Killian abruptly stopped, giving a slight bow as he turned away from me.

I felt stunned by his terse reply, my reaction came slowly compared to his speedy departure. When I realized the expectation that he would turn back around and finish our conversation did not occur, I finally followed in pursuit. Killian's heavy coat weighed me down as I tried to catch up to his pace.

"Killian, wait!" I shouted behind him.

We were still hidden in the shadows, but I could see Killian's movement stop ahead of me. He kept his back to me as I approached him. He turned his head to the side as he heard my footsteps. I shrugged off the coat, dismissing the sudden cold, and held it out at arm's length for him to take.

"Keep it. It's Lidia's." Killian's tone was joyless as he started to take another step away from me.

I sighed in frustration as I pulled on his shirt sleeve in an attempt to hold him back, to force him to listen to me. I wasn't sure why I felt obliged to make things right with Killian, but the guilt I held for offending Killian was more substantial than the desire to let him walk away.

Killian stopped again in reply to my tugging, his eyes full of confusion as I stepped in front of him. I tucked my arms under one another, trying to avoid shaking — not from the cold but from my nerves.

"Killian, I apologize. Your question, it just took me by surprise."

"It was hypothetical," he claimed defensively.

"I don't know if I believe that, and I don't know what to say if it wasn't," I replied honestly.

Killian stared at me for a long time, his gaze making me almost as anxious as his silence. Killian wasn't used to being challenged, to being engaged. He led the direction of his conversations.

I should have given more thought to my reply. It was a

statement, not an answer. What did I even expect him to say? Why did I even care to stop him? I had been trying to get rid of him all night, and as soon as the opportunity arises that he leaves, I stand against it? What is wrong with me?

I couldn't think of a solution to salvage the conversation, but thankfully, it seemed I was having a stroke of luck. Killian was quicker than I to notice that in the distance, someone was calling my name.

"Hassan's searching for you. You better hurry before he sees us together; I would hate for him to receive the wrong impression," he huffed and stepped back to let me proceed ahead.

Hassan's voice wasn't far in the distance. If I didn't move, he would stumble upon us soon. Killian's words echoed in my head and ached in my heart. *You better hurry before he sees us together. I would hate for him to receive the wrong impression.*

The Killian I thought I knew would love the embarrassment it would bring me to be caught alone with him. If that was the Killian I expected, why would he make such a statement? Hearing Killian speak like that, he didn't seem as malicious as I presumed; it made him appear *broken*.

Before I could change my mind, I reached out for Killian's arm, pulling him forward to walk with me toward the party.

"Hassan!" I shouted for him to hear.

"What are you doing?" Killian asked in surprise at the draw of attention I had just caused.

I'm asking myself the same thing. "Answering your question," I replied candidly.

I let go of Killian's arm and walked ahead, searching the darkness to quickly find a bulky figure appearing around the southeast corner, not far from the party entrance.

Hassan's face was now illuminated from nearby lanterns, his creased eyebrows smoothing out as relief spread across his face.

"Allene! I was about to send out a search party for you," he exclaimed earnestly.

As I came closer, I noticed Hassan's relief had been replaced with perplexity. He stared at the coat draped over my arms, to then quickly stare at the man approaching behind me.

"I was just waiting outside, as you suggested," I explained.

Hassan's joy had been removed with skepticism. "And Killian found you?" he asked.

I was starting to regret my decision. *Why didn't I take Killian's offer and not unnecessarily alarm Hassan?* I sighed and held my head high, hoping to convince him it shouldn't be such a surprise. "He saw me fall into the pond and offered his coat," I said, trying to sound unfazed by my oversimplification of the truth.

Hassan glared at Killian and then back at me. His eyes softened, and his jaw clenched as he gave a gracious reply. "I see. How chivalrous of you, Killian."

Killian shrugged. "We have much too far to travel for her to gain a cold on our first nights away. It was just me being practical, for all our sakes." His dismissive nature had returned, his tough exterior displayed once again.

I could feel my lips purse at his casual reply. Wasn't *my reply just as casual? Why would I fault him when I started it?*

"Allene, you can use my coat," Hassan offered while reaching to take Killian's from my arm.

"Nonsense, I'm going to retire for the night anyway," Killian declared.

Hassan chuckled. "Bored already? Even with such a diverse selection of women here tonight, you haven't found one to keep you entertained?"

Killian's posture went stiff. "The one that caught my eye didn't share the same sense of endearment," he admitted.

My stomach lurched at Killian's comment while Hassan raised his eyebrows in shock.

"Hmm . . ." Hassan mumbled, biting his lip as he held back his words.

"Something you'd like to say?" Killian challenged, taking a step toward Hassan — placing me directly between them both.

Hassan shrugged, folding his arms. "You must always get what you want. Whoever refused you, it must be driving you mad," Hassan said smugly.

Killian coolly laughed. "Actually, I find the prospect of her to be quite fascinating," he pushed back.

"Her or the *idea* of her?" Hassan questioned.

Killian looked directly at me now, a small smile appearing on his lips. "Definitely her," Killian replied firmly.

"I hope her refusal won't leave you in a stupor," Hassan snapped back, oblivious to Killian's purpose for staring at me. I hoped Hassan didn't notice.

Killian looked at Hassan now, clasping his hands behind his back as he stepped around me to be parallel with Hassan's shoulders. "Let's not pretend it wouldn't bring you an immense amount of satisfaction if it did. But you have no reason to fear, Mr. Durand, I'm a patient man, and I believe I made a fair amount of progress tonight," Killian replied in hushed tones.

Hassan nodded his head and let out another low laugh. "What a shame we leave in the morning then."

Killian's lips twisted to the side, suppressing a smile. He looked at Hassan and then at me, one last time.

"Enjoy the rest of your evening," Killian said, not replying to Hassan's comment.

Killian walked away and disappeared into the crowd of people, leaving Hassan and me alone outside. Hassan was shaking his head in disapproval once Killian was officially out of sight.

"I leave you alone for not even a half-hour and look at the trouble that finds you," Hassan said teasingly.

Trouble. Killian is trouble, Allene, don't convince yourself otherwise.

I didn't reply, and Hassan didn't linger for a response.

"Now that I have found you and successfully detached Lidia from my arm —"

"I was hoping to have a moment to change my shoes," I abruptly interrupted him.

Hassan paused, taking the time to now look at the

faint wet mark on the hem of my dress and my shoe. He looked back up, his kindhearted character not questioning my request for even a moment.

"Of course. I'll be happy to escort you back to your room," Hassan insisted.

I shook my head. "I should only be a moment."

Hassan nodded, stepping aside so I could pass by. "I'll be waiting right here," he promised sweetly.

He was so polite and considerate, which would only make my subsequent actions feel even more unjust.

I walked through the crowds that were starting to dwindle and made my way back to my room. My head was spinning — my thoughts wholly displaced.

I spotted a servant outside my door, ready to greet me when I arrived.

"Your Majesty, are you turning in for the evening?" the small woman asked as I approached.

I swallowed, my stomach clenching with guilt. "Y-yes. Please tell Mr. Durand that I feel unwell and have gone to bed for the night. Express to him my apologies for my early departure." The words caught in my throat but still managed to slip out.

"Yes, your Majesty, right away."

The maid scurried away, leaving me alone outside the bedroom door.

I closed my eyes and sighed. I questioned my decision to avoid Hassan. Truly, what was my reason? We were having a delightful time. I had been looking forward to time alone with him, so why did I feel the subconscious urge to be left alone?

I looked in the direction of the maid, seeing her disappear down the long hall. I looked in the other direction, expecting to see that I was finally alone. The other side of the hall was a dead-end, at least six rooms separating it from mine. I quickly discovered I wasn't alone.

I spotted Killian out of the corner of my eye, paused outside his room — the last door at the end of the hall.

I don't know how long he had been standing there or if he had been waiting, but we both became still, silently staring at one another. I was grateful for the distance. I hoped he couldn't see the distress on my face — I hoped he couldn't see that the distress was from him.

I was scared to breathe. *What if Killian could hear my labored breaths from the end of the hall?*

Killian still didn't move, and he didn't speak. He didn't address that I had left the party only seconds after him. He didn't address his coat, which was still hanging from my arms — his scent of leather still perfectly present around me.

With his penetrating blue eyes, he stared, unperturbed from the drowning stillness between us. *What is he thinking? Why do I care to know?*

I hope you won't regret it. His words rang in my head.

Four days, no conversation, that is what he promised. I was certain four days wouldn't be enough, yet somehow, I was struggling holding back from saying the first word — from breaking our silence.

I couldn't give in, and I couldn't let him be right.

I took a deep breath and rushed inside my room, shutting the door quickly behind me. I shook out my arms and dropped Killian's coat, letting it fall to the floor. I found myself hoping that a decent night's sleep could shake away whatever feelings were taking place inside me.

Hope. All I could do was hope.

CHAPTER 18

I had breakfast that morning in my room — in solitude. The time had come quickly to leave for Selvet, the morning not dragging on as I had hoped. We had to wake before sunrise to arrive in Selvet by nightfall.

As I made my way down to meet everyone at the gates, I stepped around various litter scattered throughout the castle hallways — the cluttered leftovers of last night's party.

I was the first to arrive at the gates. Lidia was waiting there, bright and cheery despite the still-dark sky. Lidia hadn't slept yet — she was still wearing her dress from the party, and the glitter on her eyelids now smeared across her cheeks. She embraced me immediately, ready to get on with the goodbyes.

"What a joy it has been having you here. I hope your stay was memorable and that it won't be long before I see you again. Hug Risa for me when you see her and tell your mother she is past due to visit Veruje. Veruje is here for you all and whatever the future brings. I am confident this Red Crows business will be put to an end soon enough." Lidia paused as she heard the footsteps of Hassan and Killian approaching behind her. She lowered her voice. "Remember to be careful in the days ahead, cousin. Trust your instincts," she gave her final bit of advice.

Hassan cleared his throat, forewarning his approach. Hassan looked exhausted, his eyes surrounded by dark shadows. I couldn't hide the graveness of my face as Hassan seemed to look right through me. I couldn't discern if his passiveness were from lack of sleep or lack of interest.

I forced myself to look at Killian; I didn't want the entire journey to be full of awkward tension. Looking at Killian brought me no better comfort than looking at Hassan. Killian stared to the side, refusing to meet anyone's gaze, but more particularly, neither man would look at me. Were they angry with me?

I bit down on my lip from the thought and tried to remember I had experienced worse heartache than men not looking at me. *Stop thinking everything is about you, Allene; they're probably both tired. It was a long night.*

Lidia gave Hassan an exaggerated and emotional goodbye while giving no notice to Killian.

"Watch over my cousin, soldier. Be sure Selvet treats her well," Lidia demanded.

Hassan seemed pained as he forced a smile in reply.

"Thank you again for your hospitality." He bowed and began walking, not looking behind him to see if we would follow.

Killian ushered me in front of him, both of us lagging behind in silence, leaving Veruje in a more somber mood than when we had arrived.

~

We walked in silence, we stopped in silence, and we ate lunch in silence. No one exchanged a word or a glance. It made the journey to Selvet seem never-ending. If I wasn't watching the ground, noticing a buzzing insect or a slow drifting cloud, then I was staring at the backs of Hassan or Killian.

It wasn't just boring — it was painful. I knew the silence was my fault. I knew that both men were avoiding me, and I couldn't ignore it.

Hassan seemed to march with ferocity and frustration, while Killian appeared leisurely and contemplative throughout the journey. I had successfully gone from having the prime attention of both men to having none at all. What had I done? Should I attempt to make conversation with them? I couldn't talk to Killian, not after I promised to avoid speaking with him for four days.

I couldn't come up with anything to say, so the silence endured, uncomfortably shadowing us as we walked.

The terrain was beginning to change as we approached the early evening. The mountains gradually sunk into a valley that leveled out to be flat ground. The walk became easier the later it got. The path we followed had minimal obstacles to avoid. Wheatgrass stretched as far as my eyes could see. Some areas of the trail seemed to sink slightly, which I discovered were small collections of ponds after passing by. I could hear crickets surrounding us as we journeyed, their consistent melody giving me something to focus on.

I almost didn't notice Hassan's shift to a brisk pace. We were still in silence, and I didn't dare ask where the new sense of urgency was coming from. I followed, faster now, trying not to fall too far behind. Only a few moments later did I notice the reason for Hassan's shift in pace. Homes.

Rows and rows of straw-roofed homes were scattered in the distance. Many had smoke coming from their chimneys in preparation for nightfall. Each residence was divided by large corrals for animals. A river hugged a hill on the outskirts of the village, with nearby fields blooming with crops fed by the water. I tried counting all the homes and farms I could see. There had to be well over a hundred just from a first glance.

We were almost to Selvet. We probably only had another mile or two until we would come upon the first home. That meant I didn't have much time to make amends with Hassan before meeting the Durand family.

I took a deep breath, trying to let go of my stubbornness, and gain the courage to talk to him. I didn't want this distaste lasting any longer than it already had. He didn't deserve to be in a poor mood upon arriving home, and I knew I was responsible.

Before I could lose my tenacity, I marched past Killian to walk alongside Hassan. He glanced down at me, the corners of his mouth turning down. His lips now formed a hard line; his eyes fixated on Selvet. He sighed, shaking his head in defeat as he overcame our long-standing silence.

"I waited." He said only two words — two bone-chilling words that emphasized my culpability.

"I sent a servant to give you a message." As if that made it all right somehow.

"I got the message; no servant was necessary," he replied bleakly.

"I-Im sorry," I stammered over my words and immediately became frustrated that I was incapable of giving him a better apology. He clearly thought so, too; his eyes were still firmly set on Selvet, and his facial expression was stern.

"You could have told me," he avered.

My stomach sank. How did Hassan find out about Killian? It wasn't significant! I wasn't required to tell him anything. *Don't get defensive, Allene; see things from his perspective. What would you think? ust stay calm; overreacting will not help the situation.*

I took a deep, shaky breath. "Told you what?" I countered.

"That you didn't want to dance or spend time with me. You didn't have to lie about it," Hassan stated in a disapproving tone.

"I didn–"

"You did, and it hurt." Hassan almost growled in frustration — interrupting me before I could finish. "I'm sure it's hard for you to understand, as you've likely never experienced the rejection and embarrassment of being so freely abandoned." His chest boasted out, his breathing becoming labored. He closed his eyes and stopped walking. I was disappointed that my first instinct was to look at Killian — to see what he was making of our prominent spectacle.

Killian had stopped, too, standing far behind us, as if he was afraid to encroach on our space. His eyes hid behind his wavy hair, but his lips were also turned into a noticeable frown. I began to feel panicked, wishing that I hadn't approached Hassan at all. *What if I had just made everything worse?*

For the first time since I had met him, Hassan actually scared me. I knew he was strong, I knew he towered over me, and I knew he was now a well-trained soldier, but around me, he always showed a tender, softer side. I had seen him angry, and it never terrified me before, but in those instances, Hassan had never been angry at me. I was ashamed to admit that I knew I had pushed Hassan many times before, but he would still exercise such patience with me. This time was different. He had finally had enough. I brought him to his limit, and it was an awful reality.

I rubbed my palms together, trying to find the right words to say. I didn't want to continue arguing. I was tempted to say how much I did understand experiencing rejection. Did he forget my upbringing as a Valterian with the appearance of a Praserian? Did he not understand the pain of such a situation? But because I knew that feeling and how terrible it indeed was, I only felt empathy that I had caused him to feel that way. I wanted to be someone he could trust, someone that made him feel good — because Hassan deserved that. He was good. I had done him wrong, and I needed to validate him.

I reached out to take Hassan's clenched fists, holding them lightly. His posture slightly eased at the gesture, his eyes finally meeting mine.

"I don't like this feeling between us. Frustration, vice; I just want to make amends," I pleaded.

"As do I," Hassan confirmed, letting his fists unfold into my hands.

"I am sincerely, deeply, terribly sorry. Tell me what I can do to gain your forgiveness and put this in the past," I practically begged.

Hassan hesitated at my offer. I caught him exchanging a glance with Killian. Whatever softness that had returned during my apologies immediately melted away into stiffness once again. Hassan crossed his arms as he now stared down at me.

"Tell me the real reason you left last night," he said quietly.

It was apparent what he was implying. *So he does know.*

I wanted to tell him the truth, but it would sound wrong no matter how I phrased it. I didn't want him to have a false impression. I could still be honest without giving him every detail for my absence.

"There was no other reason than me being a coward," I admitted. It was true. Last night, I had been a complete coward in more than one aspect.

Hassan's eyes narrowed with deep concern. Silence crept in as he carefully considered his following words. "You're afraid of me?" he barely whispered.

My response offended him; *this is why I should be candid.*

"No, of course not! Not of you, I'm afraid of . . . disappointing you. Which is ironic considering my actions last night did just that," I rushed to clarify the misunderstanding.

Hassan's worry and self-accountability stayed firmly in place. "I pressured you too quickly," he said to himself.

I shook my head, squeezing his hands tightly for reassurance. "You did nothing wrong. Last night — that was my fault, not yours. Hassan, you are valiant beyond measure. It is reasonable for me to fear disappointing you, or worse, losing you, over some foolish decision I could make. And to jeopardize having no relationship with you at all, it terrifies me."

Hassan's hands urgently moved to grip my arms, dismissing the fact that Killian still stood just a short distance away from us, his tone shifting from fear to solemnity.

"Allene, the only way you can disappoint me is by not giving me a fair chance. I won't be disappointed, no matter the outcome, as long as I know, you truly tried to see what I see. When you can honestly tell me that, and then tell me your feelings for me, whatever they may be, then we can carry on how you feel is right."

Hassan. Dear, always good, forever understanding, compassionate, Hassan. I choked back the urge of tears, partially from his sentiment and partially from my sin of withholding the whole truth. When would I learn to be forthright with our discussions? Why did I feed him a facade to believe I deserved his goodness? Was I really selfish enough to care more about keeping his reasonable opinion of me than of telling him the truth?

"You're too kind to me," I croaked honestly.

He placed his finger lightly under my chin to tilt my gaze to his. "You're too hard on yourself," he replied sweetly.

Hassan remained still, letting us be close for a moment longer. He gave me a small smile, his cheery demeanor returning. He hesitated as he stepped away from me to look back at Killian, who had been watching us quietly.

"No reason to slow down now; we've almost arrived," Hassan announced for Killian to hear. Hassan began leading the way again; this time, he and I were walking side by side.

Hassan couldn't hide his beaming grin as we approached the outside boundary of the village. The smell of smoking meat filled the air and made my mouth water. We walked past homes with windows and doors wide open for us to see families cooking food together, each dinner smelling better than the last. Most families would pause to wave at us as we passed by, while some yelled from their windows.

"Welcome home, Hassan!"

"Ah, Durand! Good to see you, sir!"

Hassan greeted each person with a heartfelt hello. It warmed me to the core to see Hassan so elated. The smile on his face only grew as he saw more familiar faces. *Is this what going home was supposed to feel like? Was this just Selvet? Or did Hassan have a sterling reputation here that I was oblivious to?*

The reaction from everyone was friendly, excited, and sincere. My first impression of Selvet was how badly I wished my arrival home could cause such a stir of joy in the hearts of my people and neighbors.

I pulled up the hem of my skirt that had been dragged through a nearby puddle of mud and became more observant to where I was stepping — avoiding various animal droppings, compost piles, and bundles of straw.

The sun was beginning to set, leaving a beautiful orange hue painted across the sky with a deep blue hanging above it to create a blend of contrasting colors.

Hassan led us past the rows of houses to follow a trodden-down grass path. A small house was situated by itself at the end of the way, with rows of fields on each side of the home. The door to the home opened, and three figures stepped out. The silhouettes of a large man, a short girl, and a woman right in between the two in height and stature emerged. The most petite figure began violently waving at us.

"Hassan!" the voice squeaked in the distance.

Hassan increased his pace, running with arms wide open to scoop up Freira. Killian and I let him go ahead, slowly catching up. I watched from afar as Hassan grabbed Freira and his mother, lifting them quickly as he embraced them both.

"Hassan, you are crushing us!" Freira cried out. Hassan laughed and put them both down, and then he hugged Freira — much more delicately this time.

"Apologies, but it is not my fault you haven't gained any muscle or weight since I've been gone."

"Don't pester your sister; she is exactly as she should be," Hassan's mother scorned and swatted his shoulder in protest.

"Yes, Ma," he replied, giving her a hug and kiss on the cheek.

"Oh, stop that now. Go hug your father," she encouraged him, wiping away the start of her happy tears.

Hassan threw his arm around his father's shoulder, both men exchanging quiet grins.

"It's nice to see you, son," his father said simply.

"You too, Pa."

Hassan was getting emotional. The sight of his family and their evident love for one another even made me fight back a tear or two. Hassan took a deep breath and gestured for me to stand by him. Before I could, Freira had already thrown her arms around me.

"Amelia! You actually came!" she said excitedly, her energized personality shining through.

Hassan cleared his throat. "It's Princess Allene, Freira, remember? Not Amelia," he reprimanded.

Freira went red in the face as she unfolded her arms from around my neck and gave me a lopsided bow. "Your Majesty, I apologize for my outburst, I—"

"No, no, you do not get to treat me any differently than when we first met. We are friends, aren't we? In the Durand home, I would like to be treated as such. No princess talk, call me Allene," I stated.

Freira anxiously looked at Hassan to gather his approval of my statement. He looked at me and then back at Freira, who looked like she was about to burst.

"She's the princess; what she says goes," Hassan replied with support.

Freira let out a loud sigh and clapped her hands quickly. "Friends! Yes, yes, yes! We are absolutely friends!" Freira looped her arm with mine and dragged me to her mother's side.

"Allene, this is our mother, Margaret."

Margaret was taller than Freira and me. She and Freira wore matching linen dresses, white lace at the collar, and green aprons hanging on their hips. Flour and spices covered Margaret's apron. She clasped her hands in front of her, the strength of them apparent. Her hair was mostly grey, with a few wisps of dark brown throughout. She had it pulled back into a neat braid. Looking at her eyes was like looking at Hassan's, their olive color twinkling with kindness. The wrinkles around the corners of her eyes grew as she offered a smile.

"It is a pleasure to have you in our home. I have heard much about you from both our boys," Margaret admitted, raising an eyebrow as she looked at Hassan. Freira giggled.

Hassan rolled his eyes and shrugged his shoulders. "There is nothing either you or Freira can say to embarrass me," Hassan said.

"Don't speak too soon son, you haven't even been here an hour," his father chimed in.

Freira pulled me over now to stand in front of the towering man.

"This is our father, Loren. He isn't as intimidating as he looks," Freira whispered at the end.

Loren stood taller than all of us; clearly, he was where Hassan achieved his height and build. Loren had dark brown eyes and long white hair that flowed into his tangled beard. Underneath all his hair was leather-like skin, tan and crinkled from long days in the sun. His knuckles were large, and his fingers were round and callused — his work as a farmer evident. His back arched slightly, his shirt tight to his plump stomach. Loren wore the same dull colors as Margaret and Freira and had faded leather suspenders to hold up his trousers.

"Welcome to Selvet," he said in his deep voice.

Hassan was smiling, like the sight of me with his family was the most incredible thing he had ever seen. Any nerves or contention seemed to have disappeared between us. Hassan was genuinely happy, and it was a relief to see.

The excitement of the reunion had passed to give attention to Killian's presence, which was now everyone's focus.

Suspicious eyes stared at Killian. He avoided eye contact, choosing to gaze at the beautiful sunset that was fleeting behind us.

"Is there a prince in Valteria that I am unaware of?" Freira whispered to me, but it was still loud enough for all of us to hear. Freira looked behind her shoulder and back to me, obviously questioning the person lingering behind us.

"He's a Praserian," Loren stated to answer her question. He looked at Hassan, his lips twisting to the side in displeasure. They held each other's gaze, silently communicating between one another. Margaret didn't seem surprised to see Killian. Freira seemed briefly puzzled, her face brightening quickly as she made the connection.

"Prince Aleron?" she asked with curiosity.

I tried not to blush at her assumption. Had the gossip of my affairs spread this far, or had Hassan said something to them?

I subconsciously gripped Freira's arm tighter as I waited for Killian's offended reply to be compared to Aleron.

Killian turned around, flashing his charming smile, his mood entirely shifting from what it had been all day. "Aleron . . . do I seem that dull?" he inquired. He shook his head, laughing as he came closer. "No, my dear, you're in luck and better company than that of my little brother. I'm Killian," he proudly stated, giving a short bow.

Freira giggled, and Hassan immediately went red in the face as he shot her a glare of warning. She immediately composed herself, and the uncomfortable moment halted the conversation. Killian retained his smile through the lingering seconds of silence, patiently waiting for someone to speak.

Loren grunted as he eyed Killian. "Hassan, show your guests inside; Ma made dinner," he said, leading the way through the short framed door.

We all briefly waited to see who would be the first to follow. Margaret didn't linger, following promptly behind her husband. Freira was still trying to conceal her urge to gawk at Killian, who stood firm in his effort to charm her. Hassan ushered Freira inside the house and gestured for me to enter next.

As I approached the doorway, I hesitated to give Killian one last glance. His smile was gone now, his expression vague. Was it a talent? Killian's ability to drive me mad and obsessive with his constant disillusionment? I thought my second stare was subtle until I noticed Hassan's jaw tightened as he caught where my eyes had shifted. I plaintively acted as if I had been looking at the village below, moving right past Hassan's uncomfortable stare and into the house.

The wood slat walls left the room feeling cozy as the fire's light licked all corners of the home. A rug and cushions surrounded the crackling fireplace. A small table with four wooden chairs was placed near the entrance of the house. Two short doors separated the area for two bedrooms.

"I would have had a more proper meal if I had known we'd have company," Margaret explained.

I looked at the table, noticing the large roasted

chicken and potatoes she had made took up most of the dining space.

"It was short notice; we only just got your letter after dinner had been prepared," Freira added. Hassan sent a letter the day we left Valteria, hoping it would give enough warning to his family about his short visit.

"If this is your dinner on an ordinary night, I can't imagine the feast you provide on special occasions," I gave Margaret a small smile. I was grateful for any food — the exhaustion of the day had begun to catch up to me.

"Plates and cups are in the cupboard, the well is behind the house, and you can eat wherever you'd like — help yourselves," Loren encouraged, taking the first step to the cupboard to grab the largest plate in the cabinet.

Hassan seemed embarrassed as his mother and sister grabbed plates too and started dishing up food, not waiting for anyone — not even their princess. It was an entirely new experience, this relaxed treatment towards me, and I rather enjoyed it.

I placed my bag on the floor by the doorway and approached the cupboard, taking a plate and following Freira's lead. There was plenty of food; the portions we each took barely reduced the pile of potatoes and chicken.

Margaret, Loren, and Freira sat on the floor near the fire, eating with their hands as they watched the flames silently.

I took a seat at the small table, letting the plate balance slightly on my leg to provide more room for it to steady on. Hassan sat across from me, hardly pausing as he dove into the chicken.

"They do not make chicken like this in the castle," Hassan exasperated as he grinned between each consecutive bite.

"They better not; your grandmother would roll over in her grave if anyone else knew her recipe," Margaret chuckled.

"I think it's only fair if you share it with me. I miss your cooking when I'm away," Hasan protested.

"If I told you how to make it, then you'd never come home," Margaret retorted.

Hassan rolled his eyes and shook his head at his mother. "That's not true," he insisted.

Margaret shrugged. "It's not, but it's still one more excuse for you to visit us," she proclaimed. Margaret looked at Hassan, then at me, then back to her plate as her expression turned to be suggestive. "Besides, you know the recipe is passed down from woman to woman. Find me a daughter-in-law, and I will gladly share the recipe with her."

Freira giggled at Margaret's comment. The two women stared right at me, their message clear to everyone in the room. Hassan's chicken caught in his throat as he felt everyone's prying eyes. He glared back in his family's direction.

"I told you it was too early to say they couldn't embarrass you," Loren chortled in his deep, booming voice.

I did my best to hold back a laugh. I adored how Hassan's family teased one another. It wasn't malicious; it was out of love. I had the sense it probably caused a few fights between them now and again, but they seemed like the type of family that would be quick to forgive and forget. Family was too important to hold grudges or to take too seriously. Fun-loving was the best way to describe his family, and their energy was entertaining to be around.

Hassan blushed as he finally swallowed the piece of chicken and regained his composure. He was quick to take the spotlight off of himself and to the next easiest target, dismissing his family's comments entirely.

"For a man of many obnoxious words, you've had nothing to say today, Killian. Are you feeling all right?" Hassan piped up.

Killian didn't shift his glance to me, the true reason for his lack of conversation. He seemed content with eating his food, standing up in the corner of the room, and watching us all in silence.

"I'm fine," he replied sharply. Killian's harsh tone left an uneasy feeling in the room. Thankfully, Freira didn't allow silence to linger long before she had a new topic of conversation to focus on.

"Can I ask a question?" Freira spoke up, fiddling with her fork as she gnawed on a potato.

"Depends — who is the question for?" Hassan replied.

"All of you."

Hassan looked up at me to see if I had any objection. I didn't need him inquiring for silent permission; I wanted Freira and his family to ask and say whatever they wished

— they didn't need to tip-toe around us. It was the least I could do for their hospitality.

"What is your question?" I asked, turning away from my food to better engage in the new conversation.

Freira beamed at my reply. "What brings you to Selvet?"

Hassan sighed, interjecting before I could give a reply. "You know we can't answer that, Freira."

Freira pouted as she chewed on her chicken. "I know. . . but our princess and enemy prince, accompanied by a knight from the kingdom? You could see how it may breed concern."

She was correct; it was a spectacle that may raise some concern among the Valterians in Selvet. It wasn't every day, or really any day, that royalty visited their farming town, especially from two different kingdoms, not to mention enemy kingdoms.

"You don't need to be worried about anything, Freira, everything is alright," Hassan reassured her.

"Well, your arrival won't go unnoticed. There will be questions. What do you expect us to say?" Freira pushed again.

"I'm sure the Gossett's have already shared your unexpected visit to half the town," Loren huffed with displeasure.

Hassan's face became rigid as he processed his family's assumptions. "You can tell them we were just passing through." He was stern in his reply.

"But —" Freira protested.

"You heard your brother," Loren hushed Freira.

Freira rolled her eyes and crossed her arms, clearly offended by her father and brother's reply.

"How long are you planning on staying?" Margaret questioned.

"We will leave the day after tomorrow. I need to speak with Till."

Till must be Hassan's friend that knows the way to Gelva and Cenan. The only acquaintances of Hassan's that I knew were Damien and Freira. It was exciting to think tomorrow would allow a greater understanding of who Hassan was in the eyes of others that truly knew him. Tonight's dinner had been enlightening enough of the Durands family dynamic and a peek into Hassan's upbringing. By exploring and learning more about Selvet, I hoped it would show me even more.

"Is he still working at his father's shop?" Hassan inquired.

"He's running it. Thomas fell a few weeks ago, and he is in pretty bad shape. Till has been picking up the work-load," Loren shared the news of their friends.

"Do you mind taking a basket of bread to Shelley when you visit? I'm sure baking has been the last thing on her mind since taking care of Thomas," Margaret added.

"Of course," Hassan readily complied with the thoughtful request.

"Mrs. Durand, could you direct me to my sleeping arrangements for the evening?" Killian's velvety voice penetrated the air. Not drawing anyone's attention, he had snuck away from the corner to place his empty plate on the table. He was standing right next to me yet glanced over me as he spoke to Margaret.

Margaret stood up and reached out to collect Freira and Loren's plates. "There are two stuffed cots in the barn for Hassan and yourself. Allene can sleep in Hassan's room," she responded.

"The barn?" Killian repeated, his posture stiffening at the proposition.

"Too ignoble for your taste, Killian?" Hassan berated.

"Believe it or not, I've slept in worse places than a barn," he proudly replied.

So have I — like a prison, for instance. The defensive comment came too quickly to my mind. I didn't share the comment, refusing to break on day one of four of no conversations with Killian.

"I will see myself out," Killian declared and exited through the front door.

Margaret came to our table now to gather the remaining plates.

"What a delightful companion on your journey," Margaret said sarcastically.

Hassan scoffed. "Disagreeable is a more accurate description of the prince. It's all right; at least I have Allene to bear it with me." Hassan smiled at me, encouraging me to join the conversation.

I hadn't said much throughout dinner. It wasn't that I didn't want to talk; I didn't have much to add to the conversations.

"He might not be delightful, but he sure is handsome," Freira appended.

Hassan's teeth clenched, and his olive eyes almost seemed to darken at the praise Freira gave to Killian — praise Killian's self-obsessive nature didn't need any more of. The mood in the house shifted as it was visible to everyone how irritated Hassan became at Freira's compliment.

"Freira, that's enough comments for tonight," Margaret's glare spoke loud enough that she only had to whisper the words.

Freira seemed uncomfortable for the first time tonight, her eyes darting back and forth between her mother, Hassan, and myself as she tried to mend her statement.

"I didn't mean it like that, Ma; it's subjective. We are Valterian, but I can see his appeal if you're a Praserian, that's all." Freira realized too late the consequences of her statement.

Loren's eyes flickered to me — actually, all of their eyes flickered to me. Margaret, Freira, and Loren seemed to be holding their breaths as they waited to see my reaction to Freira's offhand comment. Hassan's lips twisted to the side as his stinging glare pierced Freira. Her face was now as red as the hair on her head.

"I'm going to help mother wash dishes — outside. Goodnight, everyone." Freira dismissed herself, rapidly grabbing the plates off the table and rushing them outside. Margaret sighed while Loren shook his head. Hassan seemed frozen in place, his eyes still staring at the door his sister had darted out of for refuge.

"Your Majesty, we apologize for Freira; she does her

best to control her thoughts, truly. She never means anything offensively," Margaret nervously twisted a dish-towel in her hands as she spoke.

I gave a weak smile as I stood up from my seat. "It's all right; you can't fault Freira for having opinions," I said.

"They aren't everyone's opinions," Hassan clarified.

I reached out, tempted to place a comforting hand on his shoulder. I pulled back to fold my hands in front of me, one over the other, but he caught the gesture and my intention.

"I know," I assured him quietly. I turned to Margaret. "There is no need to apologize for Freira being perfectly herself. I wish more people would speak their minds in my presence."

Margaret returned a small smile, and Loren groaned as he stood to his feet.

"Hassan, why don't you be sure Princess Allene has everything she needs before you turn in for the night," Loren moved along the conversation.

Hassan nodded and stood up, extending his left arm to point in the direction I should follow. He walked past his mother and opened the door nearest to the kitchen. It was only a few feet from the dining room table. Hassan held the door open as he waited for me to enter the room. I picked up my bag from the floor and looked at Hassan's parents one more time before retiring for the evening.

"Thank you for dinner, Mrs. Durand, and your fami-ly's hospitality to me and our unexpected traveling companion," I thanked her.

Hassan's parents smiled and continued working on cleaning up the rest of the meal.

I stepped into the small, wood-paneled room. A long bed was pushed into the corner, with a brown knit blanket laid over the sunken mattress. A barrel was next to the bed for use as a table. A tattered towel was folded neatly and placed on top of the barrel, along with a water pitcher and a stout glass.

Hassan rubbed his neck as he stood in the doorway — letting me take in my temporary home for the night. He kept the door open and his distance as he spoke in hushed tones.

"I know it's not Veruje or Valteria, but —"

I interrupted Hassan. "It is perfect. Besides, I'm exhausted from today — I could manage to sleep anywhere — even the barn," I chuckled.

Hassan's eyes seemed to light up for the first time since Freira's comment. He gave me a simple smile as he shoved his hands into the pockets of his trousers.

"Well, make yourself at home. We will have a chance to wash up tomorrow," he answered the question I had wanted to ask since seeing the towel and water.

"What else is planned for tomorrow? Will we leave for Gelva?"

"I will meet with Till in the morning, go to the market in town to restock our food, and then we can continue on our journey."

"Can I come with you?" I inquired. I was hoping to see more of Selvet while we were there, even if it was only briefly.

Hassan grinned. "You mean that wasn't already implied? Of course you're coming."

"What about Killian?" The question croaked out of my throat, not wanting to be said out loud.

"My father will keep an eye on him; we won't be gone long," Hassan assured me.

I couldn't think of a more authentic way to see Hassan's hometown. Time with just him and I — alone. I felt no anxiety at the prospect of having a good conversation with Hassan away from prying eyes, away from his family, and away from Killian.

CHAPTER 19

Selvet was already busy and moving, the dawn
barely breaking. The city was loud and
bustling as farmers drove through the muddy streets with
wagons full of fresh produce from their fields. Shutters
on every house were wide open, the sun illuminating
their modest homes as the wives and daughters labored
with smiles on their faces over the meals for the day.

With our stomachs full of Freira's cinnamon muffins,
Hassan and I traveled to the west side of town to find his
friend, Till. Hassan stopped at a few homes along the
way, exchanging short greetings with family friends.
Hassan was comfortable and cordial as he introduced me
to each individual he stopped to speak to. Hassan's trivi-
alized introduction of their princess left the people wary;
however, I was surprised how comfortable they became
after Hassan would lighten the mood again with a joke or

a story. The people in Selvet seemed to enjoy Hassan's company — his presence seemed to soothe them.

Hassan said we had made it to the west block as we turned down a dilapidated street. Not many people could be seen. The windows that I had observed throughout Selvet were usually open and inviting with various baked goods. This street was different. All the windows had been boarded up along the road — a clear indication they did not want visitors. The houses were in need of repair as splintered wood peeled away from the rusted nails that strained to hold them in place.

I felt uneasy and unsure as Hassan continued to travel further down the row of unseemly homes. Sensing my sudden hesitation and noticing the slowing of my pace, Hassan turned around. His eyebrows went up as he asked a question that made me feel haughty.

"Don't tell me the same woman who survived by herself in an enemy castle is afraid of the oldest neighborhood in her own kingdom?" Hassan laughed as the words came out.

I rubbed my arms wearily. How snobbish I must've seemed. *Who was I to judge? Hassan would never put me in danger, and honestly, what did I have to fear?* Just because the houses were unkempt did not mean the people would be disagreeable.

"It's the oldest?" I tried to spin the conversation with a question.

Hassan's eyes gleamed as he saw me loosen my posture and keep walking down the decaying street.

"It is. You see that house with the red door?" Hassan

pointed to his left at a faded door that resembled the color orange more than red.

"Yes?"

"My great, great, great grandfather built that house." Hassan beamed with pride as he waited to see my reaction.

"Was he a craftsman?" I inquired.

"He was whatever he needed to be. He was a craftsman, a hunter, a farmer, a blacksmith, a soldier, a teacher, the town joker, a religious man, a baker even! Grandfather Pizzy was a legend in Selvet. He left quite the legacy for us to live up to. My father always said he would die a happy man if he could learn even half the things Pizzy did."

"I've never heard a name like that before," I said, smiling at the picture Hassan painted in my mind of his famous grandfather.

"Pizzy wasn't his given name; it was a name he earned. There will never be another Pizzy."

"You are a farmer and a soldier," I pointed out. "And obviously a baker," I added with a wink.

Hassan almost belly laughed at my joke. "I can't bake, but I can cook," he corrected.

"Really? What other talents of yours do I have yet to uncover?" My interest was piqued.

"I'm a fisherman. Do you eat fish?" he asked casually.

"Depends on the fish. I don't like fishy, fish," I admitted.

"*Fishy* fish?" Hassan stifled a laugh as he raised his eyebrows in confusion.

"I don't like fish that are strong in flavor. Or under-cooked. Or rubbery in texture. Or too boney," I clarified.

Hassan took a moment to process my long list of objections to the source of meat. He chuckled. "So . . . you don't like fish."

"I don't like the *majority* of fish."

He nodded slowly, considering my statement before a smirk spread across his lips. "Perfect. I will show you two talents in one. I will catch you a fish and cook it — and I promise it will change your misconstrued opinion of eating fish forever."

"That is a bold promise," I warned him.

"I'm that confident," he confirmed.

I laughed. "I look forward to it then." Hassan displayed a broad smile, his happiness a relief to see. "So who lives in Pizzy's house now?" I inquired.

Hassan walked slower now, his hands clasped behind his back as he reflectively stared at the homes. "No one, these homes are vacant."

"Your family sold the home and farmland?"

"We didn't have a choice. A good majority of the farms in Selvet ran into issues with their crops after freezing temperatures in the spring a few years back. The crops severely suffered in producing quality produce. Everyone was desperate for money, and many farmers had to sell their properties to feed their families through the winter, my family included. That is when a wealthy trader purchased our property and the remaining homes on this street. He made an offer my father couldn't refuse."

My heart sank as Hassan elaborated on how his

family lost something so precious to them, and to hear it wasn't just the Durand's but multiple families that had to sell their homes? It was awful.

"What does the man plan to do with them?" I couldn't help but ask.

"Rumor was he plans to tear them down and build a grand estate. The only reason he hasn't yet is because of Till's family. They own the last piece of land on this block, and the man won't build until he owns it all."

"Has anyone tried to repurchase the land?" I asked.

Hassan rolled his shoulders back and sighed. "As soon as things got better the following year, yes, but it was too late — the man had already made up his mind."

"If Till's family can keep their portion, maybe, eventually, the man will give up on his plan and sell the properties back," I suggested with enthusiasm.

Hassan slowly nodded as he looked at each of the houses we passed. "I hope. Hearing the news about Till's father, I don't know how it may impact them if he can't get better soon. Doctor's bills are expensive for a family like theirs. They have enough for their needs, nothing more. I don't know how long they could hold onto the property considering the man's high offer to buy their land. Money seems to speak louder in times of distress."

My heart grieved at his reply. These families' livelihoods — their long-standing history and possessions, wiped out in a single season. I mourned their losses as we passed each home and imagined what they once used to be — and I hoped if I revisited one day, to see the homes returned to their proper families and proper glory.

We approached the end of the street now — the initial hesitation regarding the road fading away to be replaced by pity and sorrow.

Hassan moved faster as he spotted his destination — a small wood house at the end of the row. Flower boxes were placed by the windows — the tiny purple flowers placed in them starting to topple and wilt. Smoke escaped the stone chimney, and an additional pillar of smoke could be seen behind the house. Hassan avoided the front door entirely and walked around the side of the home, approaching a small shed behind it.

The door to the shed was cracked open. I could hear a voice with a slurring accent proudly singing a tune I wasn't familiar with. Hassan grinned at the sound as he pushed the door open.

"Keep it down, Till, the birds aren't even awake at this hour!" Hassan exclaimed.

Till's head flew up from his work that he was crouched over, intense spectacles rocking on his head. His auburn hair stuck straight up from the pressure of the spectacles band, and his brown eyes were enlarged from their magnification — or possibly his surprise to see Hassan standing in his doorway.

He dropped the gadgets he was tinkering with onto the table, wiped his hands on his dirty apron, and rushed to the door.

"Hassan?" he asked in disbelief as he got closer. "My, my, it's really you! What are you doing here, brother? Margaret didn't tell us you were coming to visit!" Till embraced Hassan immediately, a grin appearing on his oil-stained face.

"I love a good surprise," Hassan belly laughed as his much smaller friend tried to tackle him unsuccessfully.

"I'd say I'm surprised! Surprised you are here and even more surprised you are here with a girl," Till jabbed. He was now looking over Hassan's shoulder, observing me a few feet behind them.

Hassan grinned as he smugly replied to Till's comment. "Princess, actually."

"Ha! And I'm the Queen's secretary. What's your name, sweetheart?" Till pushed past Hassan to get a better look at me — removing his oversized glasses.

"Allene Amena," I replied with a smile.

"And what has compelled you to come along with this oaf?" Till snickered at his joke.

"He agreed to come with me — by my mother's orders," I respectfully replied.

"The Queen?" Till teased.

Hassan sighed as he approached his friend, clapping him on the shoulder. "Yes Till . . . the Queen," Hassan emphasized again — this time, each word slow and stern.

"The Queen. Amena. . . this is the princess," Till processed his thoughts out loud, gazing back and forth between Hassan and me. The reality of my appearance and name finally seemed to sink in, and his mistake was made evident. "Oh, heaven help me," he squeaked as he looked up to Hassan for an escape.

"Don't fret; she's rather forgiving — sometimes," Hassan mocked, holding back a laugh.

I shook my head. "Don't let Hassan scare you; I'm not easily offended," I replied.

Till was silent as he still processed the situation. He seemed hesitant to believe me, but I was being honest. After all the names I had been called and the gossip I had heard surrounding my heritage and appearance — for years and years — it took a great deal to offend me now.

"Allene. Damien's friend!" Till concluded with relief.

"Yes, Damien's friend," I concurred happily, thinking about my best friend, who I wished wasn't so far away at that moment. I wished he could've been in Selvet with me. I enjoyed seeing it from Hassan's point of view, but I am sure having Damien would've been an excellent addition to exploring their hometown.

"I bet your brother doesn't appreciate you stealing his friend, Hassan," Till raised his eyebrows.

"I don't think he's bothered by it much; he was the one to facilitate an introduction," Hassan recalled the memory while giving me a soft stare.

I felt my heart slightly jump as I thought back to that first day we met. I would never have imagined we would be here, together as — well, whatever we were — in Selvet.

"I heard about Thomas. How is he doing?" Hassan inquired.

"He's doing fine. Ma and Susana have picked up my chores so I can pick up his. We are making due."

"You always do. I'm sorry, my friend; I hope he has a quick recovery. It's not much, but this is a gift from Margaret to Shelley. Hopefully, it'll ease her baking duties for a little while." Hassan handed Till the basket of goods. Till's eyes widened as he peaked underneath the cloth. He took in a large breath, letting the scent of the leftover muffins sink in.

"Bless Margaret — and Freira's cinnamon muffins? She knows they are my favorite."

"We don't have to stand around out here; why don't you both come inside? Ma and Susana would love to see you," Till encouraged, placing the basket on a large stump by the door.

"Thank you, but we aren't able to stay. I had a question for you, and then Allene and I must be on our way,"

"I see. What can I help with?" Till asked, placing his hands on his hips.

"Gelva and Cenan. You've been before, haven't you?" Hassan inquired.

"Oh yes, several times. It is Pa's favorite for hunting," Till confirmed.

"I need you to give me detailed directions and navigation for both," Hassan instructed.

"For you?" Till questioned.

"Yes, but that information doesn't leave this room," Hassan warned in a low voice.

Till paused as he studied Hassan's expression. Their families were clearly close, and Till seemed to read Hassan better than most. He knew not to press with more questions.

"Hassan, Gelva is one thing, but you would need a guide if you don't want to risk getting lost in Cenan," Till objected.

Hassan shrugged and leaned against the wooden wall. "I don't need a guide — I have you. I'm sure with your detailed explanations and experience that we will be just fine."

"It's getting late in the season, my friend — there will likely be a bit of snowfall when you get higher up the mountain, and the weather can change overnight in those parts. It would be better if you went in a few months when the summer returns."

Hassan's eyes reflected the same urgency that was now in his voice. "I don't have months; I have days."

Till seemed displeased with Hassan's answer, the corners of his mouth turning down. "Then you need proper provisions, supplies, and clothes."

"Make me a list of everything we need, and I will be sure we don't leave without every item you suggest," Hassan promised.

Till sighed as he opened up a creaky drawer that shook his entire desk and pulled out a crumpled piece of parchment. He fumbled through the drawer and found a quill and his oil well, and started writing.

"I'm assuming you do not want Fen to know your whereabouts," Till added.

Fen — the man that approached Hassan about joining the Red Crows? I felt the nerves drop from my stomach to my feet as I shifted back and forth at the thought of encountering a known member of the organization that was a Valterian. It felt worse than even Nycolas, a more significant betrayal considering Fen was one of our people.

"If he asks, tell him I went back to Valteria, that I was

introducing the princess to some of her trade partners and stopped in Selvet on the way back," Hassan said quietly, his words smooth and composed.

Till nodded. "Understood."

Till began drawing what appeared to be a map with a list of items on the side. He blew on the paper to dry the ink and folded it up tightly. Till held out the paper, and Hassan snatched it away, shoving it deep into his jacket pocket.

"Stick to the main roads when they are there. When they aren't, follow the direction of the cliffs — if you do, you won't be able to miss the castles. Both kingdoms are gated, so you shouldn't come across many people as you travel. The terrain on the west side of the mountain is much worse than the terrain on the east. Watch your step as you get closer to the top; there are a few steep cliffs when you get to Cenan. Getting to Gelva is flatter, and it is at a lower altitude, but you should still pay careful attention to where you are walking. I've written down more details and landmarks for you to look for as well. The main thing to remember is that there is a fork in the trail. One side leads to Gelva, and the other leads to Cenan, so be sure to pay attention."

Hassan hugged his friend in reply. "Thank you, Till."

"Always, brother. You just better hope you can sneak past Ma. If she spots you, she will be angry you aren't staying for lunch," Till added.

"After all this is over, we will be back for a longer visit — Damien too," I chimed in this time.

Hassan's olive eyes seemed to shine underneath his

blond eyelashes after hearing my comment. Our visit to Selvet was short. I wanted to come back under different circumstances that would allow more introductions of friends and further understanding of the town Damien and Hassan call home.

Hassan pointed his thumbs in my direction. "You heard the princess; I will be back soon."

"Good. Stay out of trouble, Hassan," Till said, clapping Hassan's shoulder.

"You too," Hassan smiled.

Till gave a short bow of his head as he turned to me now. "It was a pleasure to meet you, your Majesty," Till said kindly.

"Thank you for your assistance and directions. I'm sure we will see each other again," I replied.

"Safe travels to you all." Till nodded and returned to his workbench, seamlessly transitioning to tinkering once again.

Hassan and I snuck around the side of the house; his pace somewhat hurried as he tried to reach the street.

"You weren't even going to alert Ma of your visit? I sure hope you haven't turned into a stranger since your move to the kingdom." A crisply, pure voice rang through the air. Hassan and I turned around.

A tall, young woman was standing at the corner of the house, her curly blonde hair blowing in the direction of the wind. Her green eyes were fixated on Hassan, her attention not turning to me once. Her freckled complexion teased her time in the garden, as well as the basket of freshly picked vegetables she swung by her side with ease. Given her apparent age and her reference to Ma, I assumed this was Susana.

Hassan cleared his throat, the sign of surprise evident on his face.

"Hardly — I'm just pressed for time," Hassan said firmly.

Susana's nose crinkled as she made a face of disgust. "Don't let me keep you." Susana's tone was cold, and she added an additional element of unease with her pervasive stare.

Hassan nodded while avoiding her gaze. He gently held my arm as he turned us both in the direction of the street. His touch, which generally felt comforting, left me itching to sprint away from them both. The tone and the mood of the short conversation were oddly hostile.

"And tell Freira thank you for the muffins," Susana shouted behind us.

Hassan's footsteps faltered. He turned his head for just a moment to study Susana.

"Is everything all right?" I asked quietly, uncertain if I should say anything at all.

Hassan focused again on the street and hurried his pace. I wasn't following the urgency of the situation that just occurred, but I knew something about Susana, and her comment was leaving Hassan concerned. He didn't reply right away — he waited until we were at the opposite end of the street and responded in the softest whisper that left chills down my neck.

"We don't have as much time as I hoped."

CHAPTER 20

*H*assan didn't speak another word for quite some time. He anxiously scouted out our surroundings as we made our way back to what I assumed was the village.

I was still perplexed by our brief encounter with Susana and how it so quickly shifted Hassan's attention and priorities.

I sighed and proceeded to break our silence. "What are we doing?" I got the courage to ask.

"I'm going to get the supplies, and you are going back to the house. You don't have long to pack and bathe, so I hope you'll be quick about it."

"Hassan, can you slow down for just a moment and explain what we are so urgent about?" I tried to hide the frustration in my tone brought on by his allusiveness.

He shook his head, clearly surprised I hadn't kept up. "Susana heard our conversation."

I was still confused. "Susana is your friend. Do we need to be worried?"

"Till is my friend, Susana is not," Hassan said matter-of-factly.

"What does that make Susana?"

"Estranged." Hassan huffed as he turned around and grasped my shoulders, his eyes filled with apology. "Allene, I don't mean to be eager, but we really do not have the time to discuss it, not now. The house is just up the hill. Tell Freira you need help packing for colder weather, she will be happy to lend you some clothes. She can show you the spring. I will be back within the hour — then we must be on our way to Gelva, all right?"

Hassan's earnestness left me little opportunity to object. I gave a small smile and nodded in reply. Hassan hadn't withheld anything from me in the past — especially if I asked. If he said we had little time, even without giving me a reason, I believed him — and I trusted a full explanation would be offered later.

~

"It's just a little farther, Allene!" Freira encouraged me.

We had been walking for quite some time, making our way around the wide hill that sat behind the Durand's house. Freira explained they had a private freshwater spring on their land where I could clean up and not be disturbed.

As we made the turn around the hill, I saw the

spring. It was larger than I expected. The creek was feeding the spring with water from one side while being dammed up by rocks on the other. The water was more transparent than most springs I had seen. The bottom of the body of water was primarily rocks, so sediment and soil were hardly circulating the pond.

Freira took in a deep breath as she placed the fresh clothes and towel down on the edge of the spring. "Do you hear that, Allene?" Freira closed her eyes and held very still as she listened intently.

I paused, straining to hear the sound she was referring to. I could hear the noise of the river trickling to the side, an occasional bird calling to another, and the crackling of leaves hitting against the branches of the trees that perfectly hugged the rocks near the spring.

"The stream?" I guessed.

Freira, eyes still closed, smiled wide. "Nature — I hear absolutely nothing but nature. It's the most beautiful thing, wouldn't you agree?" she related excitedly.

"It is quite peaceful," I concurred.

"It is one of my favorite places in the entire world." Freira paused as she took in her surroundings for a moment longer. She sighed as she patted her pockets and rocked on her heels. "Well, you should be all taken care of. I will go pack up more clothes for the rest of your journey."

"Thank you, Freira. I apologize for the rush."

"Not a problem at all, I hoped you could stay longer, but I know you have other priorities."

"I plan to come back with Hassan and Damien, and when I do, it will be for an extended visit."

Freira beamed. "That would just be the loveliest! Mama will be ecstatic at the news."

She skipped away now in genuine Freira glee, her cheeriness rubbing off onto me.

Just as Hassan requested, I didn't waste any time. As soon as Freira disappeared around the hill, I began preparing for a swim in the water.

I tugged off my dress and folded it neatly by my side. I kicked off my shoes and shook out the braid that had tied back my hair. Leaving on only my underdress, I braced myself for the cold spring.

Hesitantly dipping in one foot, I noted how tolerable the water was. I waded in further, slowly, paying close attention to the rocks that wobbled in varying directions underneath my feet.

The shallow water wasn't offered for very long. Only waist-deep, my next step was no longer met with another rock to stand on; the bottom of the spring drastically dipped.

The last time I swam was at a lake near the castle over a year ago. It wasn't very deep, but it was deep enough that I had learned to swim decently there. For Risa and me growing up, it was the only source of cooling off that we had in the hot summers.

Although that had been the last time I had swam, it wasn't the latest I had visited a body of water. The last significant body of water I had visited was the grandest I had seen — the ocean in Praseria.

The spring in front of me was a drastic contrast to that day at the ocean. Palm trees had been replaced by aspens, waves replaced by a gentle current, sand replaced by grass, the smell of salt replaced with the smell of sap, seagulls replaced by magpies, jagged rocks replaced with smooth stones, a man emerging from the water replaced with no one in sight.

I felt my heart sink as I recalled the memory of that day. The feelings of each moment came flooding over me: the distress, the embarrassment, the infatuation, the beauty, the curiosity — and Aleron had been entwined in it all.

I stared at the clear water in front of me and the visible dip that gradually continued in depth. My reflection in the water was staring back at me, displaying my wavy hair, half-dry slip, and a notable frown.

I had successfully avoided thoughts of Aleron since departing Valteria — for the most part anyway. Having to remove him from my thoughts actively left me frustrated, but at least I was aware of it.

This is time for you, Allene. This is time for you to learn who you are, just as Lidia said. This is time without mother, Risa, Damien, or Aleron influencing you. It is time for you to realize what you want, and more importantly, your role as future Queen of Valteria.

I let my hands fall by my side to graze the top of the water. Moving my hands back and forth, the water danced through my fingers, mesmerizing my thoughts. The water was simple, calm, and somehow reassuring as it found a way to cling to every part of me that touched it.

Feeling the smooth stones I had been balancing on shake, I felt a small amount of exhilaration as I wondered if the rocks would tip me over the edge. Catching a quick breath and holding it in, without much conscious thought, I let myself fall.

The water quickly greeted me as I steadily sank. The coolness filled my ears and blocked all sounds. The eeriness of silence left no room for my thoughts, only permitting its offered serenity to consume me.

My eyes were tightly closed, the midday sun barely penetrating through the water's surface to leave an orange tint behind my eyelids. The world seemed to slow down. The weight of the water began to disappear; any feeling of its moisture faded the deeper it pulled me. The peace only grew the further I descended, the weightlessness intriguing and the diversion of thought all-encompassing.

My body swayed as a ripple of movement shattered past me. The slow-moving sound of protesting waters made me shudder after the silence I had been focused on. The floating sensation seized as an unyielding grip took hold of my waist and snatched me towards the surface.

My eyes flew open, the water blurring my vision and hurting my eyes as my body was being rushed to the top. Hardly able to make out more than the fact I was being clutched against another body, I was able to catch the blue of my eyes being reflected, and before I could process much else, I broke the surface.

I gasped for air as my adrenaline surged into defense. I pushed against the strong hold that had secured itself around my waist. It only got tighter in reply. Hassan's urgency from earlier left me panicked. What if it was Fen? I tried not to let the thought cripple me in fear. If — *when* — I got away, Hassan would need a description.

"I command you to let me go at once!" I tried to yell through labored breath. I shoved against the man again, water splashing in our eyes, but I was ready to take on whoever had followed me. I was prepared to push, shove, kick, scream and shout as much as I needed to get away. Freira couldn't be far; maybe she would hear me. I was preparing to let out a scream until the man interrupted me.

"I will release you once I know you are safe!" he shouted over my thrashing.

Safe? Did my dive underwater seem like I needed saving? I supposed it could. I wasn't a fantastic swimmer, but I was decent at holding my breath for quite some time. I suppose from a bystander's perspective, it could appear a bit alarming.

The realization that this wasn't a kidnapping but rather a mistaken rescue attempt made everything more apparent. Pausing at the realization that there was no unfavorable intention, through watery eyes, mine settled on his, and my heart began racing — not from intimidation, not from fear, but from shock.

My arms that had been pushing against Killian gave out at the new knowledge of whom I was facing. Too tightly grasped to move them anywhere, they rested on Killian's bare chest. Killian was still holding onto my waist, despite my halting opposition. He nudged his head to the side to remove the wet hair that had caught in his eyelashes, the usual heavy waves of black replaced by tighter curls in reaction to the water.

I found myself staring at Killian, attempting to understand what he was thinking. His sharp features did an excellent job of masking his emotions, and I struggled to see beyond the perfect lines of his jaw and cheekbones. Although I couldn't read Killian's facial expression, his body language communicated more freely. His shoulders were relaxed yet firm as if he was apprehensive while also trying to appear regal. He wasn't frowning, and he wasn't smiling — he was indifferent.

We did not exchange words, only breaths, as we each waited to catch our own. As we both bobbed on the surface in silence, my instinct to lecture, scold, and shove him away seemed dormant. I didn't want to move. *Why don't I want to move?* Killian's ice-blue eyes were locked on mine — the water that had inhibited all of my sensations seemed unable to quench the tingling I felt on my skin that brushed against his.

The silence, which generally drove me mad, was driving me mad in a different way — it was calming. Why would silence, with someone whom I knew I shouldn't be comfortable with, be calming? Although Killian was difficult to read, his body language made one thing clear; he wasn't planning on moving as long as I wasn't.

I could see his eyes shifting as he studied my face. Each time his eyes would move, my skin would burn as if it yearned for him to look a little longer.

I was aware of the many ways Killian was unsuitable

company, but he was also many things I hadn't ever known. Many things I hadn't ever experienced or felt. Things that made me want his company.

Killian made me feel seen — he made me feel desired. He didn't make me feel like a princess or a girl — he made me feel like a woman. I hadn't realized there was a difference, especially a difference that would be so intoxicating.

I had to actively remind myself of all the other ways Killian also made me feel — all the bad that came with the good. He antagonized and embarrassed me. He was outspoken, frank, and harsh in his criticism of me. Or maybe it seemed harsh because he was the only man who had shown interest in me that dared to be so blunt — the only one to push me when I pushed him.

Killian's right hand left my side, his left still not releasing me. He swept his hand across my face to smooth a displaced strand of hair that I hadn't noticed had stuck to my cheek. He gently brushed it back, following it all the way down to ensure it lay with the rest of my hair, his hand now lingering at the nap of my back.

I still hadn't looked away from his face — his distracting, gorgeous face. The face that at one time reminded me of Aleron and had made me uneasy from the resemblance was starting to leave a different impression — showing a different person. This feeling, being close to Killian, was different.

Why haven't I broken the silence? Why am I letting this moment linger? Why aren't I angry? One of us needed to become uncomfortable and fast.

My mind was racing as I considered what I should say. Killian's pink lips had parted to show a faint glimmer of his perfect smile. What I should do and what I want to do at this moment are very different, and it's the *want* to do that is terrifying.

"What are you doing here?" I forced myself to whisper through the quiet stillness between us.

Killian's eyes narrowed as he continued to look at me. He took his time replying, patiently studying my every nervous twitch or movement, his blue eyes becoming darker with every second that passed. "That's all you have to say?" he chuckled softly.

"What were you expecting?" I asked, uncomfortable now with my question.

He cocked his head to the side, his brows furrowed in confusion. "Nothing actually, you promised to avoid me for four days, remember?" Killian smirked in satisfaction as we both realized I had broken our agreement. He didn't let the realization linger, and took full advantage of my mistake. "But if you were going to speak, I expected a reprimand for how inappropriate I am, a lecture on how you didn't need saving, or possibly gratitude for saving you. Anger for not letting you go when you asked — a slap to the face or two. About a hundred other things, aside from my reason for being here," he explained.

Killian's arm loosened around me, letting me go as he pushed off the rocks underneath us to swim into deeper water. His body was still facing me as he stayed afloat. "And to answer your question, I am here for a delightful afternoon swim." He plunged underneath the water to swim farther away. My eyes followed his movements, and his head broke through the surface a few moments later.

I stayed where I was, standing firmly on the bed of the spring. I gathered my wet hair and set it all to the right side, the wind tickling my neck. "I don't mean to dampen your mood, but your swim needs to be cut short. We have to leave for Gelva before nightfall," I announced the news.

"Ah . . . so your visit to the spring isn't for pleasure," he suggested in an evocative tone.

I could feel my eyes widen in embarrassment. I looked down as my hands rang out the water from my hair, the droplets that were released leaving small ripples of waves around me. I hoped the distance between Killian and I concealed my shock, but my inability to form a response was revealing enough.

"Follow me," he encouraged loudly, trying to grab my attention once again while dismissing the need for my response.

I wrapped my hair loosely into a bun, holding it at the base of my neck to keep it out of the water. I looked to Killian, expecting to see his mischievous smirk, but his eyes and lips were soft, his invitation unfeigned.

"Killian, we need to get back," I protested.

Killian easily remained bobbing in place, his large shoulders exposed at the surface, the water distorting the rest of his faultless torso.

"It will only take a few minutes. I promise you won't regret it," he refuted.

His tone and demeanor were beguiling. It left a

hunger, an appetite, for me to discover what he teased. Our eyes locked in a battle of two stubborn souls.

Killian was my perfect storm of conflict. He was a terrifying stranger, yet comfortingly familiar. He was a man that stupefied me and empowered me in the same moment. A man that encapsulated the very definition of arrogance yet shared small bits of affection. A man of apparent strength held back by his own fear. A man that was frustrating and exhilarating to feel anything for — but the temptation always seemed to outweigh the vexation, the danger never as strong as the curiosity.

My fear softened, and my abandonment mollified. Letting go, my hair fell once again into the water. Killian's face remained docile as he patiently waited for me to swim the distance between us.

I took a deep breath, for the air and my nerves, and made a second attempt of diving into the water. I propelled myself in Killian's direction. I caught sight of his feet moving back and forth as he started to swim again, leading ahead of me, not waiting to see if I would change my mind.

I could feel the movement of his strong swimming strokes that were left in my path. The clear water of the spring tempted me to open my eyes, despite the irritation it caused. I found myself staring at the bottom, the sun managing to light only a few feet, to then have the darkness consume whatever lay beneath us. The thought of it was the distraction I needed to ignore how ignorant I was for following him.

I came up for air a few times, briefly observing the

surroundings before diving back under. The last time I came up for air, Killian was also at the surface, waiting for me.

We had circled to the backside of the spring, the landscape and depth the same as the other side. Killian effortlessly remained in place as he spoke, not even slightly out of breath as he reached out to the rock face in the center of the spring to steady himself.

"You aren't claustrophobic, are you?" Killian asked quickly.

His question left me uneasy. "If I were to say I was?" I asked hesitantly.

His eyes became suddenly intense and intimidating as he looked at me. "Then you will have made it all this way to miss the best part," he pressured.

I could sense his seriousness. I didn't consider myself claustrophobic, but I couldn't recall many times where I was placed in a situation that experienced it. *I had indulged Killian this much; I might as well see it through.*

"Lead the way," I encouraged him.

Killian smiled. "Don't panic; it's not as terrifying as it seems." He sunk back into the water and expected me to follow after his chilling advice. I saw his body descend headfirst and disappear entirely.

My initial reaction was one of panic. I waited with labored breath as I watched for him to resurface. More than a minute had passed, and Killian's body was still gone. I held my breath as I dove into the water, my eyes frantically looking for a sign of him.

Directly underneath where Killian had been floating

was a dark hole in the rock face. Not much wider than four feet, I realized it was what Killian had disappeared into.

Swallowing any of my fear, I gripped the side of the rock and pushed myself down to wiggle into the hole. My hands could touch both sides of the eerie tunnel — clearly why Killian had asked if I was claustrophobic.

I grasped the rock surfaces on each side of me as I glided through. I did as Killian said to help calm my nerves: I counted. *One, two, three* . . . my fingertips pulled on the rocks to propel me faster. *Four, five, six* . . . I could see a change of color ahead, the transition from nearly black to a dark blue. *Seven, eight, nine* . . . my hands found the other end of the tunnel, and I pulled myself entirely through, my feet pushing off the opening to send me to the surface. *Ten.*

I gasped for air. My nerves left me shaking as I smoothed my hair out of my eyes and processed what I had just committed to.

The cave was dim, with hardly any light coming through. Small areas of erosion let the sun in, but the chasm managed to consume it almost entirely at the openings. It was cold, and the little bit of sun that did come through resembled stars. Echoes of water dripping filled my ears, leaving chills from the spectral atmosphere.

I could make out Killian's large frame with the faintest light as his back hugged the cave wall. His blue eyes were almost as bright as the exposed sun, their blue hue piercing as he looked at me.

"I said you wouldn't regret it," Killian whispered, but his voice boomed through the trim area. His eyes were now looking at the high pitch of the cave, his sense of awe clear.

"It is quite the marvel," I confirmed as my eyes slowly adjusted to the darkness. The rock surfaces became more apparent with each second that went by. I soon noted I was the only one swimming, Killian's arms noticeably folded.

"I thought the depth of this cave would be too deep to touch," I said, nodding in his motionless direction.

"You would be correct. I'm sitting on a rock ledge," he shortly explained, offering a quick smile.

Embarrassed by my comment, I bit my lip. Killian couldn't see it, but I was blushing as his smirk grew wider.

The cave was small, Killian only an arm's length away. Killian unexpectedly reached out and caught my arm lightly, effortlessly pulling me over to him. I didn't protest as my body pushed against the cold water. Killian's grip shifted to my hand, his touch numbing as he guided me to the ledge to sit beside him.

The ledge wasn't large, and it was hardly comfortable to sit on, but it was a welcome break from the effort of staying afloat. Killian's hand seemed to hesitate as he waited to let go of me until he was sure I was steady.

I shifted under his hand and grabbed his forearm as I used him for support to balance on the uneven ledge. His smooth, bare shoulder brushed against mine, releasing a rush of nerves that made me shake.

Misinterpreting the shaking, Killian slipped off the ledge and gently pushed me over, placing me right on the center of the ridge, with no more need to share and no more need to balance. Killian's hands held the corners of the ledge to support himself, his face now at even height with mine — our bodies parallel to one another. I dropped my hands into my lap, uncertain what to say. *Thank you is a common way to repay an act of kindness, Allene.* But the silence had grown comfortable.

"You trusted me," Killian stated the obvious. I remained quiet, ashamed to admit to my own mistake. "You shouldn't trust me, Allene," Killian added in an almost agitated tone, his face twisted in concern.

Was he honestly angry I trusted him? Killian's warning left me uneasy, and I could feel the pressure to respond.

"I don't trust you; I've just seen a different side of you — a side of you that gives me hope," I explained.

It was the truth. I didn't trust him, not yet. But a part of me saw a glimpse of what Killian could be, and it was enough for me to give him a second chance before solidifying my opinion of him. At that moment, my opinion of him was impossible to explain or understand. I could only hope more time and conversations would make up my thoughts and feelings about Killian Hadway.

"Speaking of trust, I have no idea how you convinced Loren to let you out of his sight," I quietly replied, trying to shift away from the heavy graveness of Killian's warning.

Killian hesitated, uncertain if he was ready to move

on. Pausing for a moment, his face turned flat as he shrugged. "That was easy; it took him less than a few hours to realize sending me away was the only way to tolerate me," he mumbled under his breath.

I could see Killian's jaw flex as he turned his face to the side, avoiding eye contact with me. The comment did not have the normal satisfied tone that Killian so commonly flaunted. It may have been dark, but his body language and tone exposed his insecurity.

"That's sad." I hardly even realized the words had escaped my thoughts. I was afraid of being harsh, but it was the truth.

Killian shifted his weight uncomfortably before giving his reply. "That's freedom."

"Forcing people to disdain your presence is what you classify as freedom?"

Killian looked directly at me now, his confidence returning. "Absolutely. I never worry about disappointing anyone. It doesn't matter what I do; it will either be expected or be a pleasant surprise." His velvet voice harnessed my attention more, allowing me to catch the decrease of fortitude in his tone.

Killian's sharp features caught my eyes once again as he held perfectly still, like a statue to admire. His perfectly toned shoulders and chest displaced the water that clung around him. His hair was slicked back against his neck, leaving his smooth skin reflecting in the darkness. I could smell his usual scent of leather, mixed with the mineral scent of the water, the combination of it all completely tantalizing. In that moment, surrounded and forced to acknowledge every piece of him, left me consumed. All I saw — all I could think about — was Killian.

"What a selfish perspective to have," I managed to unharness my honest thoughts once again.

My knees pushed up against Killian's chest as he leaned in closer to me after hearing my reply. I felt myself cling closer to the wall. His tight jaw relaxed, his piercing eyes filled with wonder.

"You shouldn't be surprised; you know how selfish I am." Killian's words were slow and precise, each one hanging in the air longer than they usually would.

"I do know that you're selfish. I also know you hide behind a carefree attitude to avoid feeling certain things; I just don't know what, and I don't know why," I admitted out loud.

Killian shook his head back and forth, brushing off the comment. "Allene Amena, the philosopher," he mocked.

I ignored his comment as well, pushing again for answers. "You're a better man than what you display for the world. I've seen glimpses of your kind heart. I just can't understand why you don't let people see the good in you." My last sentence held the slightest bit of frustration, and Killian sensed it. His primal instincts seemed ignited as he was almost amused by my question.

"When people see good, they expect good, and I know what it's like to hold someone in high esteem and respect to have it shattered with a single mistake." Killian's words rushed out, the answer to my question finally breaking through.

Killian was silent now. He looked away again, this time to his left side. The light caught the crevice of a small scar near his temple. My eyes followed the line that ended near the corner of his eye. It was such a faint scar, one I hadn't noticed before.

Looking away, I caught another change in his smooth skin. This time on his neck, the scar was larger, about three inches. I unapologetically followed the scar with my hand to his chest, noticing two more, one nearly blending with his skin, the other more prominent and curved. I tried to hold back the shock as I saw another on his bicep, jagged and uneven. As my fingers brushed over it, Killian winced, barely long enough for me to notice before his face returned to its solid-state.

I reached out to trace another hidden scar on his eyebrow. Killian's eyes shifted to watch me. He knew what I was seeing. My heart sank as I placed my hand over the scar on his neck.

"Your father?" I asked hesitantly.

I knew their strained relationship from my conversations with Aleron, but I hadn't learned many details.

Killian remained still, the absence of a reply indicating enough of his answer.

What unseen battles had Killian gone through? How much mental, emotional, and physical suffering did he hide? How misunderstood had he been by strangers, family, and friends? What type of defenses would a person build up in his unforetold circumstances? Arrogance, pushing people away, maybe it wasn't a choice, perhaps it was his way of survival.

I choked back the cries that wanted to escape my throat. I hesitated at the urge to speak, but the silence could no longer consume what I wanted to say.

"What happened?" I barely got the words out. I immediately regretted asking the question. I knew I had overstepped, and I was completely uncertain of what reaction it would rise out of Killian. I braced myself for his appalled response yet found myself appalled as he started to laugh.

Killian's eyes were disillusioned, his lips curved into a pained smile. "Allene, as flattered as I am that you are pretending to care, I do not want to be your pitiful distraction."

I was stunned, my mouth going dry at his insult. "Distraction?"

Killian seemed confused by my question. He nodded slowly and elaborated on his statement. "A tempting diversion to numb your complicated feelings for someone else. I have seen this scenario many times throughout my bachelorhood, and I am quite familiar with what it looks like." Killian stayed confidently close, his eyes almost smiling as I scowled back at him.

"Why would you think I view you as a distraction?" I tried to ask the question in a collected manner, but it came out as more of a moping complaint. Killian didn't seem to notice the tone.

"I am not heedless to your feelings for Hassan or to the recent falling out you had with my brother. Your love triangle is tortuous. Adding me to the mix — you'd be unleashing absolute chaos," he concluded.

Chaos? Does he think I crave for my life to be more complicated? Is he so bold to assume my feelings for him are complex in the sense of passion? Was it so difficult for him to think I am trying to be his friend when he has none?

This time, I was silent. What good would it do to continue arguing with Killian? Why did I even care to ask the question in the first place? *Maybe he was right; maybe he does know better than I do. Maybe this intoxicating feeling was exactly as he said — distracting.*

Killian clearly had made up his mind of what I thought of him. He had no interest in learning and asking for my own thoughts; he would instead assume and come to his own conclusions of what was going on in my mind. He wasn't willing to be open, and it was clear he didn't want to be. I couldn't force him to talk to me, and I doubted there was much I could say to change his mind.

Killian pulled back for a moment, looking at me with a patient, unfaltering stare.

"Do not be offended; I am saying this out of respect for you. A distraction is only a temporary release. Your feelings for Aleron, for Hassan, they won't truly disappear. It doesn't matter how angry, frustrated, and certain you are that you are ready to move on. I have never met a woman who ends up happy with her choice of distraction. If I was to be yours — as enticing as it is, I don't want you having additional ill feelings towards me, if I can help it," Killian's head fell to his chest as he now looked into the dark waters below him.

His last sentence rang in my head — a sentence that alluded to caring. *He won't open up, but it doesn't mean he doesn't want to; maybe he doesn't know how. Killian not answering me when I asked about his father, about his scars, his fear that I wouldn't want to be seen with him — what if all of his abrasiveness is rooted in fear? Fears of letting go of his control, of giving into something unknown — what if he's terrified to give his trust?*

The compassion I had felt minutes before came rushing back. The clarity of Killian likely being misunderstood by anyone that knew him deepened my desire to see who he truly was. I had to get through to him.

"You don't have to put up walls with me, Killian. You can let me in," I whispered the words, my forehead falling to his, grasping him tightly. I felt my stomach clench from nerves as I tried to convince him to be vulnerable.

I felt him shudder as he took a deep breath, the warm air burning my lips that were only inches from his. His eyes gazed into mine with a burning intensity, but I was uncertain if it was a good sign.

"I bother you, Allene," he simply stated.

His thought process surprised me. *First, he claims he's a distraction, and now Killian thinks he bothers me? He had — many, many times — but I was not bothered at that moment. Why does Killian try to ruin my efforts? Does he honestly not find me sincere?*

"You don't bother me, Killian," I confirmed, my tight grasp now loosening in disappointment at my additional failed attempt to build our trust.

His perfect shoulders flexed subconsciously in reply. "Yes, I do," he insisted.

I felt my lips purse in irritation now, seeing through his facade. He was pushing me away, and I didn't know how to stop him. I remained quiet, letting my arms fall to his shoulders that now relaxed at my touch.

He seemed to ponder before he spoke again. His firm grip on the ledge shifted as he wrapped an arm around my waist and swung me around. I only briefly felt the sense of weightlessness as he smoothly took his place back on the ledge and placed me securely on his lap, cradling me tightly to his bare chest.

"I bother you," he whispered again, his nose touching the top of my ear. "It's the type of bothering that gets underneath your perfect, porcelain skin," with his spare hand, his fingertips lightly brushed along my cheek. "That you can't understand or explain why it is so inebriating," his fingertips now traced down my neck. The sensation of his touch, the chill of the water, and the air left visible goosebumps for him to see. I could see a small smile appear on his lips.

"That has you questioning everything I say, everything I do, everything I'm thinking," his hand now moved to cup my jaw, pulling it in his direction. My body felt entirely on fire despite how cold I was. "That makes you realize what you have been missing when you didn't have any idea until you found it," his last words slipped off his silver tongue, and I felt my body subliminally try to get closer to his. "That even as imperfect as it is, you want it, but know you can't allow it to happen," Killian whispered, trying to give me a way of escape — but it only made me yearn for more.

My hands moved from his shoulders to the back of his neck, trying to hang on to the moment — a moment that no matter how much my mind said it was wrong, and even Killian telling me it was wrong, I refused to let go.

Our breath in sync, our bodies holding back no barriers, I felt myself slip into his mesmerizing touch. I was ready to give in.

Killian gripped my shoulders now as his chin fell to his chest, ripping away our proximity and our opportunity. I was frozen in place, the pain of his rejection numbing the burning I had just felt. What had I done wrong?

"I'm not expecting anything from you. It doesn't mean anything," I ridiculously said the words almost in the form of a pathetic plea.

Was I so desperate to explore these unbounded feelings for Killian that I, a princess, would almost beg for him to kiss me? Embarrassment washed over me. I shook my head, self-consciously trying to slink out of Killian's arms and bolt back outside the cave.

Before I could run away like a coward, Killian tightened his grip. "It doesn't have to mean anything, but it will," Killian confirmed urgently, trying to harness my fears.

I scoffed. "For the first time in your life, a kiss means something?" I couldn't hold back the question.

Why now, of all the times, does he decide to be chivalrous? The one time I throw away caution, the one time I take a chance to be foolheartedly stupid, I get put in my place by the most carefree man I've ever met?

"There have been plenty of firsts in my life the last few days, and they all seem to involve you," Killian accused. He sighed and offered a lighthearted smile as he seemed to hold back reaching for my face — putting his hand up for a brief moment, to place it back on my shoulder. "Allene, I'm trying to preserve you from your own folly," he added earnestly.

"I appreciate the sentiment, but it may be too late for that," I admitted.

Killian's eyes became severe and sincere, the depth of their blue hue leaving me dizzy. "Not if I can help it," he concluded quietly.

I tried not to be hurt; I wanted to remind myself how foolish I was for letting the conversation turn in such a way to spotlight my feelings — the feelings, as Killian mentioned, that were likely rash and from the rejection of Aleron. My feelings weren't justified, they weren't thought out, and they would likely lead to regret. I should have thanked him, recognizing he was probably right. I was grateful he didn't take me up on my offer, that he didn't allow me to embarrass myself further.

Killian's body tensed, drawing my attention to his concerned face. He immediately put a finger over his lips, hushing me before I could begin speaking. His eyes darted to the faint light above us — the sun that seeped through slightly flickering. It only took a moment to realize the flickering wasn't from passing clouds or a tree swaying in the wind — it was the cast shadow of legs walking past.

Killian looked at me, his eyes stern and clear, even without words. He fanned out his hand, motioning for me to stay where I was and to be still. I nodded and tried to pace my breaths, to keep them shallow despite my heart racing.

My mind instantly went to the three possible scenarios — either Hassan had come, strangers had found their way to their secret oasis, or the Red Crows had found us. Two of the three terrified me — and I was uncertain which one scared me more.

Killian took in a deep, silent breath and pushed himself back under the water. In a matter of a few seconds, he was gone, and I was alone.

Every sense seemed amplified as I waited, shaking, in the black cavern by myself. My hearing was extra sensitive, every drop of water making my heart skip a beat. I tried to focus on the light outside to see if any motion would pass by — nothing.

The water was beginning to feel painful, the cold temperature becoming more evident than before. I waited until I heard the sounds of shouting.

The shouting was from a man, not a voice I knew, and his message was clear with what type of scenario this was — matching one that I had concocted in my mind — and it wasn't a pleasant one. The man's shout was a warning — a warning of the "Praserian."

The light seeping through remained unchanged. The shouting turned into more shouting somewhere nearby

— the men's voices and Killian's grunts, echoing off the cavern walls at a magnified volume. *They aren't right outside, but what if Killian needs help?*

Uncertain what to do, I at least knew I couldn't sit and wait for whatever the outcome would be — I needed to try and get help.

Before I could change my mind, and ignoring Killian's clear direction to stay put, I plunged into the water and through the opening of the cave.

As I pulled myself through the narrow tunnel, I could feel myself straining as I pushed against the protesting water. It seemed to take more effort and breath than before, making the process seem drawn out and suffocating.

I impatiently waved my extended arms until I caught the edge of the entrance, and with all the remaining energy I could muster, I dragged my body out and ascended to the surface.

I swam slowly, despite how desperate my lungs felt for air. Whether I needed to attempt to get away or to surprise and distract our guests, I knew the need for furtiveness was vital.

I kept my mouth and body in the water, only allowing my eyes and nose to break the surface to gain a better understanding of my surroundings and give me a moment to catch my breath. I didn't dare move, afraid the possible motion and sound of the water would draw attention in my direction. My feet were firmly placed on a rock, holding me still and in place.

I didn't see any signs of Killian or the men he was

confronted with — all I could see were the beautiful fields in the distance. Worried my eyes alone would fail me, I steadied my breathing and listened, trying to catch any sign of where the men were. Silence.

I felt my anxiety begin to rise as the silence continued. Not more than a minute prior, I had heard Killian and another man actively fighting. If it was silent so quickly, and Killian was nowhere in sight, I couldn't imagine that was a good sign.

I held still, and I waited — no movement, no sounds until the silence was interrupted by a short scream escaping my lips.

A sudden, firm hand gripped the back of my neck as it shoved my head under the water. I fought against every instinct to panic, but in the end, instinct won. I tried to pry away the hand that held me, my hands slipping as I attempted to scratch and claw my way to freedom. The grip only tightened and managed to push me down further — water flooding my nose and ears.

I focused on my attacker, trying to distract myself from the pain that encapsulated every fiber of my body as my oxygen depleted. I was sure they would find a way to hide any evidence of a struggle and my body — and Killian's. No one would know what dreadful fate became of us. Two royals disappeared without a trace and leaving no closure for our kingdoms — for my mother, Hassan, Damien, Risa, or Aleron.

After surviving the loss of my father, wounds from attacks, being among enemy territory, and imprisoned, I die from drowning? With so much unsaid and to still fight for in every aspect of my life, this can't be how I die. When people are relying on me to deliver my kingdom — when I've been given a chance to prove my right and worth of being Valterian, this can't be how I go.

I could only think of the worst as every second passed by, and my air reserve with it. I was dizzy, my body felt cold, and the pressure of the water invading my sinuses managed to push its way backward and down my throat, silently choking me.

I tried to use the water to my advantage, allowing my body to float as I attempted to kick my attacker from behind. My efforts were futile; the one kick that managed to hit the attacker only irritated them as they moved out of the way of my flailing legs.

My thrashing hadn't drawn any attention of a savior. All I could hope for now was to have what few seconds I may have left be ones of peace. Peace didn't come — but release finally did.

I felt a small wave of water ripple towards me. The pushing force of my attacker came to a halt. I grasped the hands around my neck and pried them off without any resistance.

I rushed my head to the surface. My lungs inhaled as much air as they could in between the water that was being projected out of my mouth. The violent coughing continued as Killian rushed and grabbed my arm and pulled me into shallow water as I caught my breath. He urgently pushed away the hair that veiled my eyes. His hands cupped my cheeks as he searched my face.

My vision blurred as I focused on the blood running

down the side of Killian's chin. Still disorientated, I looked past Killian to the man — my attacker — who lay face down in the water with a pool of blood slowly swarming around his head.

My body began to shake. I gripped Killian's bare arms as I tried to manage the sobs that were trying to escape my exasperated chest. The blood running down Killian's face now dripped into the water, one droplet at a time — reminding me of his injury I so quickly moved on from before.

I stared into Killian's blue eyes — their untamed nature seeming wilder than before. *Killian is alive! I am alive! What had just happened? Can't you say something, Allene? Anything? Can you move?*

I soon realized the last question wasn't coming from my head. Killian was holding my shoulders tightly as he asked the question again, this time with less patience.

"Allene! Can you move?" Killian shook my shoulders now.

"Y-y-yes," I croaked.

"We have to go. Now," Killian commanded. He hurriedly swung my arm around his neck, dragged me up to standing, and began walking as fast as he could. My feet shuffled and fumbled as I tried to keep up with his pace.

Leaving our belongings, we bypassed the shore and headed straight for the path back to the Durand's. I tried to displace the horror of the floating body of my attacker and focus on something else, like the fact I had just nearly drowned or that I should've listened to Killian — but the image was haunting my thoughts.

The blood — so much blood. The distracting thought left me dizzy once again, and if it hadn't been for Killian's firm hold, I would have slunk to the ground.

"We are almost there, Allene. You have to push through a little longer," Killian's voice encouraged as my feet began to drag.

I didn't reply; I didn't have the energy or the voice to — but I did try to give all the effort I could as I caught sight of the house.

Loren spotted us first. Running out to meet us, he grasped my other arm, releasing some of my weight from Killian as they approached the porch.

"Marg! Freira!" Loren shouted.

Margaret and Freira responded immediately, scurrying to the back porch. Their jaws dropped as they both frantically tried to understand the catastrophe in front of them.

"Allene! Oh goodness, Allene!" Freira cried out as she ran to my side.

Margaret followed behind her daughter, pulling her away as she looked over me.

"Freira, go fetch fresh linens, clothes, hot water, honey, and bandages." Freira was stunned in place — the order from her mother being ignored as she was now staring at Killian's half-naked body smothered in blood. "Hurry, child," Margaret pushed Freira out of the way, forcing her to obey her requests without further delay.

Margaret turned to look over Killian now, her

composed demeanor effectively soothing my troubled thoughts.

"Come inside," she instructed, ushering us in first as she shut and locked the door.

Loren placed me in a chair at the dining room table while Killian, shaking, took a seat opposite me.

My vision was beginning to steady. My breath had started to even. Feeling more collected but still slightly trembling from the shock of it all, I looked to Killian.

Killian's face was set in a stern grimace. I spotted the small, clean cut on his chin. The blood had trailed down his bare chest like dripping paint on a canvas. His hair was already almost dry, his curls messy and disheveled. His eyes were heavy as he stared back at me. From what I could tell, the only injury he had incurred was the cut to his chin.

I was at a loss for words, and I didn't know where to start. Killian, however, didn't skip a beat, his eyes now shifting to Loren and Margaret, their sharpness returning.

"Mrs. Durand, we need supplies made up right away; we must leave immediately."

"Not until I see to it that you are both okay," Margaret insisted.

"My cut will heal; Allene is in shock. We will be fine, but only if we leave before word gets back to their leader."

"Who's leader?" Loren inquired, his arms firmly crossing across his chest.

"The leader of the three dead men at your spring," Killian replied.

Loren's face turned tomato red. "For all that is mighty, what happened?!" Loren's deep voice in such an angry tone was almost more spine-chilling than the attack. Margaret turned her attention to her husband immediately following his outburst.

"Loren! This is our home, and we have two injured royals sitting in our living room. You will not interrogate them," she cautioned.

"I don't care who they are! We have three unexplained dead bodies on our property, Margaret!" Loren argued back.

"Hold your tongue! They are friends of our sons and guests in our home, and you will do good to remember that with whatever you are inclined to say next," she warned.

Despite Loren's fuming stare, he managed to remain silent as he stared at Killian.

Running into the tension, Freira rushed back in with the requested supplies as she tried to compose her alarmed face when she observed more closely the blood on Killian's chest. Margaret watched Freira's wide-eyed stare and her skin, which now looked white as the clouds. Placing a firm hand on Freira's shoulder, Margaret turned her daughter around to pull her attention away from the sight of the blood.

"Thank you, child. Now go find your brother in the city," Margaret encouraged Freira out the door quickly, her attempt to remove her from the situation a success as Freira ran out the door without any hesitation.

Margaret spoke to Loren now as she began to clean Killian's wound — the sight of blood not one to make her queasy. "Loren, the men at the spring —," she started.

"Don't say another word," Loren interrupted. "I will take care of it — but by the time I'm back, I want them both gone — royalty or not. It was a mistake to have them here in the first place," Loren spat.

Loren's words made me shudder — whether from fear or sadness, I was uncertain. *Is this what shock feels like? Like any ounce of control over my emotions is unraveling?*

Margaret sighed as Loren exited the backdoor. She looked at me with concerned eyes as she moved to dress Killian's wound.

"I apologize for Loren; I can assure you he doesn't mean his harsh words. He is irrational when he speaks out of anger," she reluctantly defended him.

"I understand. I'd consider myself pretty angry about the situation too, considering someone attempted to murder us and all," Killian scoffed, shaking his head as he winced when Margaret put pressure on his cut.

Margaret shuffled uncomfortably. "I knew having you here, even for a short time, would draw attention. However, I underestimated the impact such attention would have," she confessed.

"I'd say. Hassan never mentioned the distaste his small, innocent hometown had against Praserians. That would have been valuable information to know before making a leisurely detour," Killian retorted.

"It's not Praserians — it's royalty in general. There are ignorant people here that assume they know what is best for everyone," she tried to defend.

"Funny, their behavior sounds like the actions of royalty to me," Killian replied.

"They are hypocrites," Margaret shook her head.

"Do you think this attempt on our lives was the Red Crows?" I finally got the urge to speak up in the conversation, but the question only managed to come out as a whisper.

"I don't think that is even a question, Allene," Killian confirmed.

"It doesn't make sense; it went from absolutely nothing to nearly successful attempts of assassination? They have never been this dangerous," I processed my thoughts out loud.

"Or you have just never been this close to them before," Margaret suggested.

"Which is why we have to leave right away; we need to create as much distance from the Red Crows and us if we want any chance of getting to Gelva first," Killian said.

I felt awful for putting her family — Damien and Hassan's *family* — in danger. While they were showing us hospitality, we were threatening their lives. "Margaret, if I would have known the trouble it would cause you all by having us here, I wouldn't have allowed us to pass through."

"The Red Crows and their chaos are too well known here to be seen as trouble anymore, the deaths on our property . . . it will draw less attention than you think," she assured us.

"I can't imagine they would just let something like this pass by without making someone suffer consequences. We have already caused enough trouble for your family. If anything happened to any of you. . ." I shuddered. "I don't even want to imagine it. I will send guards to protect your home — I will not allow them to seek revenge on your family," I assured her.

"I am the one that killed them, and we are the ones that got away. They'll seek us, Allene, not them," Killian imposed, as always, never dodging the unpleasant truth.

Margaret nodded. "The Red Crows are very deliberate in their attacks. I'm not worried about us. I'm worried about the two of you," Margaret admitted solemnly.

I could feel my face flush white. I already felt rushed and anxious on the journey. Now that the Red Crows were so close to us, so close to *killing* us, we wouldn't only be running to warn other kingdoms — we would be running for our lives.

"What is it, princess? You're acting as if you've never been in danger before," Killian mocked.

"I've been in danger, but I've never been hunted," I exasperated. *Was this really not a surprise to Killian?*

"We are royals, Allene. If it didn't happen now, it would have happened at some point. Just be glad you have me by your side — I've outrun many upset parties in the past. The Red Crows won't have the advantage for long — I know how to disappear."

Disappear? I know Killian was trying to offer some

comfort as he observed the terror in my eyes, but he only added to the disheartenment.

Margaret sighed. "The fact you are forced to face a situation like this — it's not right."

"It keeps life interesting," Killian shrugged Margaret's sympathies as he patted dry the remainder of his cut and stood up to approach me.

How was he so collected? If I hadn't seen it with my own eyes, I wouldn't have believed that he had just killed three assassins. He gave me a short glance and offered his hand.

"You need to change your clothes," he informed me.

"You both do. Allene, you can borrow a dress from Freira. Killian, I'll gather an old outfit of Hassan's for you," Margaret proposed.

"I'm sure Hassan would be thrilled to know you offered his wardrobe to the likes of me," Killian laughed as he now boldly reached for my arm to help me stand. I took a deep breath and stood firmly, shaking his hand away.

"It would be best if you blended in; he knows that," Margaret assured him.

"I know he does, but it doesn't mean he will hate it any less," Killian declared with a smirk — the motion making his cut ooze again.

"I will finish packing your supplies. It would be best if you kept a topical on your wound to keep it sealed and to avoid infection," Margaret educated Killian.

Killian shrugged. "I've never died from a cut before Mrs. Durand, and I have had my fair share of them."

Killian's acknowledgement of his scars shocked me. Only for what seemed like moments before, Killian had evaded any conversation of his scars. *He wouldn't share much about them in an intimate moment, so why would he acknowledge them now?*

Margaret tried not to flicker her eyes to the scars that were even more apparent in the light of day than they were in the cave. To avoid the awkwardness altogether, she quietly nodded and left the room. Killian knew how to manipulate a discussion to its end.

I knew Killian was crafty, I knew he was calculated, but within an hour, I had learned more about Killian than I had in days. He knew a lot more than I thought he did. He had been through more than I thought he had. There was a lot more to him than what he exhibited on the surface.

Killian walked towards Hassan's room now, his toned back arching as he gripped the frame. He turned his head to look at me one more time. His curls had deflated to waves, and strands of hair brushed past his nose. His blue eyes pierced through the curtain of hair as he gave me a pondering stare.

"I'm glad you're all right," Killian whispered tenderly.

Odd, I was thinking the same thing about you — something I never imagined I would even care to think.

I took a few steps toward him. Killian immediately responded by turning his head, opening the door, and deflecting once again as he composed his posture and replied with urgency.

"You only have a few minutes until Hassan arrives,

and we carry on our way." Killian shut the door to Hassan's room, leaving me alone and speechless at his abrupt shift of conversation.

Before my thoughts could turn back to the new level of horror ahead of us that Killian attempted to distract me with, my mind slipped into a burning realization.

I had hoped this feeling of curiosity and intrigue for Killian would be alleviated with time — but the more time I spent near him, the more I discovered about him — it only escalated the condemning temptation that was Killian Hadway.

CHAPTER 21

"**N**o good — heinous vermin of the earth!" Hassan continued to spew hatred for the Red Crows with each word as he led us out of Selvet through an offbeat path to avoid the main road. The news of the attack had left him flustered, angry, and apologetic. Hassan had concluded that the attack was his fault. He blamed himself for taking me to meet Till and was convinced that the encounter with his sister was likely how the news got to the Red Crows as quickly as it had.

Hassan's urgency to leave Selvet was evident upon his return to the house. He ignored Killian's wound and the borrowed outfit that hung loosely on Killian's slender frame. He dismissed my disheveled appearance and the oversized dress of Freira's that draped my body. Hassan focused on loading up his bags with the supplies he managed to get in town before Freira delivered the news of our attack. He exchanged hurried goodbyes with Freira and his mother, not even waiting for Loren's return. Hardly able to express my thank you's and apologies, Hassan had us practically sprinting out the door. We had been nearly jogging behind Hassan ever since we left.

Hassan had led us further and further away — the small town of Selvet seeming even smaller since we had created a significant amount of distance.

Hassan told us his plan right away — insisting we travel as quickly as we could before nightfall, and even then, carrying on to throw off any possibility of the Red Crows catching up to us. Killian seemed composed and collected as he observantly scouted our surroundings ahead and behind us.

Hassan, on the other hand, seemed to be operating with tunnel vision. He had only one thing on his mind — outrunning the Red Crows.

I had been doing well at keeping with Hassan's pace, but he failed to consider that Killian and I had just endured quite the physical toll, and his fast speed was becoming more challenging to meet. I hesitated to slow him down, but my lungs could hardly conjure another breath. My jog began to shuffle into a walk.

With Hassan still treading on ahead, Killian approached me from behind.

"Are you all right?" he inquired as he placed his hand at the base of my back to lend me support.

I ignored the chills that his touch seemed to pulse through me. "Oh, just perfectly fresh — aren't you?" I snapped with sarcasm, finding the sweet gesture almost annoying since I assumed my exhaustion was obvious.

Killian didn't laugh at my attempted humor. "Durand, we need to stop!" Killian shouted.

Hassan halted on his heels and whipped back around. His expression was frantic as he approached us, waving his arms. "Are you trying to draw them to us?" Hassan hissed.

"We aren't being followed," Killian spoke at an average volume again.

"You don't know that," Hassan shot back.

"Yes, actually I do," Killian smirked. "I have been followed plenty of times, and I know what to look for. No one is following us."

"Right now, your *majesty*, I need you to keep your mouth closed and your feet moving," Hassan commanded.

"You do realize I have been on the run for years?" Killian queried.

Killian's comment only added to Hassan's impatience. "Do you realize I have no reason to trust you?"

"I saved Allene's life. I would say that earns me a bit of trust," Killian argued.

"Stop talking," Hassan said through clenched teeth and fists.

Killian tightly folded his arms, not ready to listen to Hassan's request. His face remained collected, his unwavering patience an emotional weapon in high-intensity situations. "You made an oath to protect Allene. You are running her into the ground, Durand. She needs rest," Killian replied.

Killian's comment made Hassan fume, and what little patience he was holding onto had dissolved, his hands gripping his head in frustration. "Don't remind me of my oath! Only months ago, you imprisoned us!" Hassan stepped forward now, shoving his way into Killian's face. "You saving Allene's life *one time*; does not add any credit to all the terrible things you have done." Hassan was intense as he addressed Killian's actions, his tone of anger turning to sizzling hatred. "I am only enduring the burden of being with you for the sake of defeating the Red Crows, to protect not just Allene, not just Valteria, but all the kingdoms! Including yours! You have no right to preach to me about anything, Killian." Hassan turned his back to Killian as he began to catch his breath.

Hassan's words didn't seem to impact Killian, his body not moving a muscle, but Hassan's arguments had gotten to me.

Hassan was justified in his anger. Killian had done all those things. How could I have so quickly forgotten? How could I put Hassan, innocent, admirable Hassan, through this journey?

I approached Hassan from behind, placing my hand on his firm shoulder, uncertain what to say to either of them. Hassan became still almost immediately, his breathing returning to normal. He turned back around, his eyes full of earnestness as he looked at me.

"We are going to defeat the Red Crows, we will stop every secret operation they have, and we *are* going to keep moving." Hassan made his final demand and promise as he waited for my reply.

"We will, but not with you, Hassan," I whispered.

"What?" Killian and Hassan asked in unison while their tones were opposite — excited and bewildered.

"I won't put your life in danger when the Red Crows want our lives, not yours," I explained.

Hassan shook his head. "The only reason you were in any danger in the first place was because of my stupidity."

"Even more of a reason to leave you behind then," Killian chimed.

Hassan ignored Killian's comment, although I could see Hassan's guilt returning.

"Allene, I am incredibly sorry for putting you in harm's way, but I promise that will not happen again." Hassan had his hands instinctively on my shoulders, forcing me to see the sincerity in his olive eyes.

I knew he meant it, and I knew it wasn't his fault either. But it would be my fault if something happened to him. It would be my fault if Damien's brother didn't return. It would be my fault if the Durand family were now a target for the Red Crows. It would be my fault if he defended my battles. He had already put his life at risk for me once. A soldier of Valteria or not, he was someone I cared for, and I wouldn't ask him to do it again.

"I don't blame you for any of this, Hassan," I replied.

"I do, I absolutely do. Where is my reverent apology?" Killian inserted.

Hassan ignored Killian again, his tender eyes searching mine for a breakthrough. "I am the only one who knows the way to Gelva and Cenan. You need me. We've already acknowledged my first mistake. My second mistake was leaving your side — that also won't happen again," Hassan vowed.

"And your apology just keeps getting better . . ." Killian mocked.

"Your family needs you, Hassan. I saw your father's reaction to the bodies. I don't want to cause any more trouble. I will sign a royal pardon and —"

Hassan interrupted with a fit of firm anger in his voice that left me still. "Allene, this is a waste of time. I am not going anywhere that you aren't."

I was waiting to hear Killian's insulting response to Hassan's passionate notion, but Killian remained quiet. We all remained quiet. Hassan seemed sure in his words, and although I didn't want to place him in harm's way, I also didn't want to take away his agency. If being here was where he wanted to be, I would support him, as he so often did for me.

I nodded my head in agreement. "Then let's keep moving," I encouraged.

Hassan sighed with relief, seeing that I wasn't going to argue further. A soft smile appeared on his lips, his more cheery demeanor replacing one of worry. "We will find a place to stay for the night, off the main road. Then you can get some rest, and we can start fresh tomorrow."

*H*assan set us up in a large grove of pine trees. Their heavy branches weighed against the ground, their thick needles camouflaging anything that might be underneath them. To my surprise, this was Hassan's reason for picking this spot — he intended for us to sleep underneath the tree.

Hassan had lifted one of the branches. I expected to find a network of more branches and needles, but instead, we saw a perfect canopy. The base of the branches were a few feet tall, leaving quite a bit of room to sit up and to sleep. The flaring out of the branches hid us well while also letting us see our surroundings. It was an unlikely choice to camp underneath a random pine tree, and I hoped it would be as unobvious to the Red Crows as it had been to me. It seemed to surprise Killian as well, which made me more confident we would have a restful night's sleep.

We had all been silent on our way to find shelter and spoke very little since settling in. We ate some of the food Margaret had packed us for and made do without a fire. We were too nervous about drawing attention with the light. Thankfully, the night was unusually warm considering the upcoming cold season, and layering my clothing seemed to provide the extra bit of insulation I needed for my first night sleeping in the elements. The tree branches offered a decent amount of protection, lending a feeling of safety in the unfamiliar setting.

As the night sky took over, Hassan had offered to take the first watch. Killian didn't object, immediately using

Hassan's words as an invitation to sleep. Although Killian hadn't said anything, I could tell the day had been draining for him. He and I — I knew we had a lot to talk about, but we both knew now wasn't the time.

Pushing the thought aside, I settled my bag on the ground and laid my head on top of it. The light of the moon hardly gave off any light. The combination of quiet and darkness made my eyelids heavy. The burning I had felt in my throat and chest from our earlier attack was now the only thing left on my mind, and even that faded quickly.

In times like this, I often found myself reflecting, questioning, and agonizing over the many things that would typically go through my head. I was unsure of the reason for the change in my usual evening routine of anxiety and memories. Tonight I didn't labor over or replay my earlier discussions, my bad decisions, or any poor use of words. I didn't debate if my father would be proud, I didn't fret about what trouble Aleron, Damien, or Risa might have encountered, and my mind didn't wander long enough to consider the danger of our enemies.

Tonight, I was exhausted. Tonight, I was content with not worrying. Tonight — the first night I could recall ever feeling such a way — I was satisfied with silence. Mind-numbing silence.

"Good morning."

My eyes opened to Hassan crouched above me, his voice a sweet whisper. The rising sun peeked through the branches and settled on Hassan's smiling face. A pleasant start to what I hoped would be a better day.

"Good morning," I replied, propping myself on my elbow as I tucked my hair to my right side — my fingers running through it to detangle the mess that it had become in the night.

"How are you feeling?" Hassan inquired.

I paused and took a moment to focus on my throat and my chest. The burning sensation that had pulsated yesterday wasn't as apparent anymore.

"Better," I concluded.

"Good." Hassan grinned as he looked at me — a *cheeky* grin.

My eyes narrowed in suspicion. "What are you so glee about?"

Hassan shrugged as he casually swept his hand through my hair. "I was just thinking if you showed up to Veruje looking like you do right now, you might start a new fashion trend among Lidia's friends." Hassan held his hand in front of me to display the sticky green pine needles that had clumped together in my hair.

I sat up and ran my fingers through my hair, catching a few remaining clusters that had managed to attach during the night. I let them fall again to the dry ground.

"A new fashion trend or a new joke? I can't imagine

anyone in Veruje approving of my well-traveled appearance." I sheepishly wiped my sappy fingers on my already dirty dress.

Hassan's olive eyes settled on my back as he removed another stray needle.

"I like wild, Allene," he assured me softly, his eyes flickering back to meet mine. "Then again, I haven't met a version of Allene that I don't like," Hassan added, showcasing a sly smile.

"I appreciate the reassurance," I replied, following a short laugh to stop the awkward direction I could feel the conversation turning towards. *Awkward? It was sweet, Allene. Why can't you just let him be sweet? Why do you stop yourself from the conversations progressing with Hassan?*

Before I could try again to match his complimentary response, I had already lost my chance. Hassan nodded, sensing my few moments of hesitation. He was more aware of my emotions than even I was, and he always catered to them. "I'll give you a few moments to pack up before we head out." Hassan began to shuffle out from underneath the branches to give me space. *Hassan —never too eager, but always there — but how long would his patience actually last?*

I didn't have much left to pack. Once Hassan was out of sight, I took off one layer of undergarments and placed it in my bag. I brushed out my hair and braided it tightly to my head, trying to hide any sap that may have remained.

The grove of trees mixed with the morning dew left a captivating smell. In between hot and cold, the air perfectly energized my body and mind to take on the day ahead. For a brief moment, it made me think of my father.

I remembered my father inviting Risa and me out to the cotton groves where he would go once a month at the break of dawn. Regrettably, I had only accepted his invitation a handful of times. He would wake early and hike to the secluded grove when the only light to lead him there was that of the moon. Once in the grove, he would wait for the sun to rise and stay until the late morning. He would kneel in a patch of grass and stare at the trees, the clouds — all the nature that surrounded him. It was his time of rejuvenation and self-reflection.

I felt myself smile as I thought of him. I instinctively reached for my ruby ring, rubbing it softly as I took in a deep breath of the fresh air and gave a thought of short prayer. *Please be with me, father, as I head into unfamiliar territory, as I try to protect our country. Lend me your wisdom and your strength.*

I focused now on Hassan, who was finishing packing up his belongings. He had changed into a clean half sleeve shirt and brown trousers, the fabric gripping tightly to his body. His new outfit made me question the choice of wearing yesterday's travel dress.

The loose-fitting tan dress that Freira had lent me seemed dirty from the moment I put it on, but the fabric was thicker than the dresses I had packed and gave an extra amount of warmth that I needed as we traveled into the colder territory. She was gracious enough to lend me undergarments as well for the frigid evenings that we

would now be frequenting. *We are traveling and camping —
I shouldn't expect or care to look as I traditionally would. Wild
Allene, as Hassan said. It wasn't a bad thing.*

I smiled as Hassan stared back at me, his stunning smile giving me additional confidence.

I looked around and spotted Killian on the other side of the clearing. Killian's back was towards us, his bag on a nearby rock, along with the dressing supplies to care for his wound.

Hassan's lent clothes made Killian seem casual and less intimidating, but with his sharp and bold features, he still somehow managed to look regal. Killian wore one of Hassan's grey linen shirts that Margaret had packed for him, a much different look than his usual dark color palette. The shirt was much longer on Killian — the fabric nearly meeting his knees. He wore patchworked trousers, which contrasted with his black leather boots. It was a sight I hadn't expected to see.

Hassan walked into my view, interrupting my focus.

"Hungry?" Hassan extended his hand, offering me a small loaf of bread. I happily accepted the loaf, my stomach finally feeling well enough to eat.

"Thank you," I replied, ripping off a small piece to chew on.

"I'm going to scout out the area before we start moving. Are you okay to stay behind?" Hassan hesitated as he looked in Killian's direction.

I appreciated him making sure I was comfortable. I nodded.

"I'll be right back. If you need anything, I'm just a

shout away," Hassan assured me. He stalled a few seconds more before turning to tread away.

I picked at another piece of bread as the silence of the clearing took a turn to the uncomfortable. Killian knew I was there, I was sure my chewing could be heard past the clearing, yet he acted like he was alone. I self-consciously placed the remainder of the loaf of bread in my bag. *Was Killian's plan to sit in silence? Hadn't we had enough of that on the walk yesterday?*

I swallowed my fear of uncomfortable conversation and approached him. Killian didn't pause at the sound of my nearing footsteps, but he did finally speak.

"Loverboy won't find anything — it doesn't matter how many times I tell him we aren't being followed, he won't believe it."

I stopped a few feet behind him, trying to make sense of his choice of first words.

"It's nothing personal; Hassan's not easily trusting of people," I explained.

I heard Killian let out a small laugh under his breath. He turned his head to the side to glance at me, his ice-blue eyes filled with skepticism. "So you're saying it doesn't have anything to do with clumping him over the head with my sword, throwing him in prison, and he's never forgiven me for it? That is considered *not* personal?"

I couldn't help but laugh at Killian's point. "Well, that could be a contributing factor," I agreed.

I didn't say out loud how there might be the hope of Hassan forgiving Killian, of moving on from the past —

eventually. After all, Killian subjected me to the same treatment. I never thought I would be standing here — trusting him, forgiving him, wanting to be close to him, or much less concerned for him. If I could somehow overcome every logical reason for loathing Killian, surely Hassan, and others, could conquer their prejudices against him.

Killian let out another short laugh and turned back to organizing the supplies for dressing his wound.

I approached the supplies, noting the small amount of ointment Margaret had packed for him.

"Do you need help with that?" I asked, realizing he had no way of seeing his cut. I attempted to reach out my hand to cup the other side of his face, trying to get a better view of the wound.

Killian's hand defensively caught mine, holding it at the level of his chest. I felt my body freeze in place, stunned from the rejection, while Killian was shocked by my gesture. His grip softened as he matched me with a subduing stare.

"I apologize; I didn't mean to frighten you," he quickly said.

"You didn't," I lied.

Killian replied with a short smile, a dimple appearing at the top of his right cheekbone. "You just took me by surprise," he explained while swiftly placing my hand on his cheek so I could continue my inspection.

He let his hand fall away and patiently waited for me to carry on. With the clarity of his invitation, I gently pushed his head to the side and tilted it slightly upward to see the entire length of his cut.

The skin around the gash was less swollen than before, and the blood had begun clotting to form a scab. I may not have known much about medicine, but I did know common signs of infection. Killian's cut was absent of warmth and redness. If he continued applying ointment, I imagined it would heal quickly.

I let go of his face and reached for the supplies. The ointment was sticky but malleable. I scooped a small amount onto my fingertip and lightly dabbed it onto the wound.

Killian stood still, his eyes fixated on my face as I worked. I tried not to squirm under his stare. I tried to focus on other things, but my mind kept returning to Killian. I kept thinking of things I wanted to say or things I wished he would say to me.

My mind raced as I remembered yesterday — Killian's touch — tantalizing yet shocking. *There have been a lot of firsts in my life the last few days, and they all seem to involve you.*

I held my tongue and tried to gain control over my unnerving thoughts, but Killian's piercing, calm face, was not helping — or his soft, pink lips that nearly brushed my fingertips as I worked.

I'm trying to preserve you from your own folly. The words echoed as a warning in my head, cautioning me to stop. *Why can't I stop?*

"Are you feeling all right?" Killian's voice was smooth and penetrating. I felt my cheeks flush.

Did I not seem all right? I thought I had been doing a decent job hiding my emotions, but maybe I was wrong. *What did he see that I wasn't outwardly showing?*

I blamed myself for being in a vulnerable situation. Hassan asked if I would be okay, and I urged him to go. *Killian had been silent; I could have stayed on the other side of the clearing, so why did I do this to myself?* What was the draw for self-torment?

I nodded, avoiding eye contact, afraid it would only give away more evidence of my panic from the question.

"Am I bothering you again?" he mocked and creased his lips together.

I paused, this time daring to look up at him, focusing all my attention on composing my face for the lie I was about to tell. "Not particularly, no."

"Hmm, I suppose I will have to put forth more effort then." Killian's mischievous smirk and response only added to my confusion.

Yesterday he warned me, practically pushed me away, yet today he was trying to capture my attention? How was I supposed to understand what he wanted? Or maybe all of it was as I feared — just a game, and I was the prize for winning.

I felt myself grow resentful at the thought. I removed my hand and reached for a small towel that Killian had laid out. The smell of oregano penetrated the air around us as I mixed the remaining ointment on my hands with water and began scrubbing it away, the mixture making my skin slightly burn.

"Your volatility is hard to keep up with," I murmured

as I scrubbed with more force now, trying to distract myself from the new stinging sensation.

Killian quietly observed my frustration. He reached down and gathered a handful of dirt. He reached out for my hands and began massaging the pasty mud mixture into my skin without hesitation. With no explanation for his quick and odd behavior, my initial reaction was confused and disgusted — until the cooling effect began.

Killian continued to rub my hands until the mud had almost dried. The stinging sensation had subsided, the soil drawing out whatever oils had seeped into my skin.

Grasping my hands, he pulled on the hem of his over-sized shirt and brushed away the dirt with the fabric — ignoring the stain it was leaving behind.

"You trapped the ointment in the towel when you mixed it with the water," he explained softly. *The only thing he had explained so far while successfully ignoring my comment.* Or so I thought.

Killian sighed, his grip on my hands tightening. "I apologize for my fluctuating moods. You're challenging my every natural instinct, and sometimes I'm not strong enough to stop it," he defended.

I took a short breath, completely taken off guard that he acknowledged my comment and even more surprised that he was apologizing.

"What are you trying to stop?" I asked.

Killian paused and began sincerely pondering my question. He kept his head down as he stared at my hands, his thumb slowly caressing mine. His lips parted while a brief chuckle escaped, followed by an answer that astonished the both of us.

"The subjugation of my free will." His blue eyes briefly flickered to mine, attempting to read my reaction.

"I'm not trying to change you, Killian," I told him honestly.

"You haven't been trying? That almost makes me more afraid," Killian's face became rigid. His body language seemed uncomfortable as he loosened his grip on my hands — neither of us fully letting go.

Killian shook his head, his curls falling forward to shield his face. "I've never experienced the desire to satisfy someone else more than myself before." Killian's words were barely a whisper as if they were difficult for him to say. He entangled our fingers to clasp our hands more closely, and he pulled them to our sides, our shoulders now nearly touching. Killian took a deep breath and let his chin fall to his chest as he exhaled. His breath was warm against my face, taunting me to lean in closer.

I didn't draw nearer to him, but I also didn't pull back, even though every particle of my being was telling me to walk away before it was too late.

Killian locked his eyes with mine once again, his eyelashes no longer a curtain to his emotions. I felt I could easily see through him for the first time — that he was consciously letting me in.

"Allene, I fear you will be the best and worst thing to ever happen to me." Killian's tone fluctuated from intrigue to solemnity, making my stomach turn into knots as I pondered over his meaning.

"It sounds as if it isn't my folly you need to worry about preventing after all," I disparaged.

Killian shook his head and pulled back to look at me straight on, his eyes full of sincerity and concern. "It absolutely is. You speak as though you would be my undoing when the opposite is true. You'd be my *redemption*, Allene, and I would be your downfall in the process."

Killian's words left a sinking feeling in my chest. I fought between being offended and flattered by his assumptions. *How could he so readily assume the worst? Was it thoughtful or selfish for him to save me before I needed to be saved? My agency, my actions, my outcomes — good or bad — should be mine to make.*

A part of me saw what he saw and could envision the ruin he was foretelling. I knew any relationship with Killian, no matter its extent, would be drastically different from any path my life could have been heading. I knew others wouldn't understand my decision. I knew I didn't understand it either, but I couldn't ignore the driving compulsion to see the outcome for myself — if he would just let me.

My thoughts left me at a loss for words. I was upset, frustrated, offended, and felt we had come to a standstill. I wasn't ready to see things Killian's way, and it seemed futile to try and convince him to see mine.

I took a deep breath and focused on my frustration. The emotion was strong enough to pull me out of the stunned state Killian had placed me in. I stretched out my hands, breaking our connection, and settled on making a decision.

I needed to separate myself and decide if these conversations were worth what felt like wasted breaths.

I looked up at Killian's face, a flicker of sorrow flashing in his crystal eyes. As difficult as it was, as much as I wanted to grasp his hands again to argue and convince him to break down his barriers, I chose what felt like the harder decision. At that moment, I chose myself.

I chose to walk away.

CHAPTER 22

"When is your birthday?" Hassan smoothly hopped over a small flowing creek and patiently waited for me to mimic his elegance. I successfully made it over the stream, but not without needing to catch my balance at the end.

Since leaving the camp and realizing we hadn't been followed, Hassan had been in one mood and one mood only: chatty. *Hassan is beginning to remind me of Damien more and more.*

Killian remained quiet and elusive, lingering behind Hassan and me to create as much distance as possible.

"October 22nd," I replied.

"That's soon. And you'll be twenty?"

"Yes, I will have officially made it two decades — somehow." I couldn't help but smirk, beating Hassan to the joke I assumed he had already thought of.

Hassan grinned. "That's a reason to celebrate. We will throw a party!" he exclaimed.

It was odd discussing life a month from now, assuming everything would work out, assuming we would be back in Valteria, assuming we would all be there together. Part of me wanted to have the same hopeful outlook for the future as Hassan, while another part worried I would be tempting fate if I thought that far ahead and in such a positive way.

"My mother is not fond of parties. If she were, I wouldn't have had to sneak out to the Gala festival, remember? Besides, I am not much of an event planner," I protested.

"I'm sure Lidia would love to help organize a party if I asked," Hassan teased, his arm nudging my shoulder as he began walking right alongside me.

Multiple party scenarios flashed through my head, the possibilities of Lidia's creativity absolutely endless and equally terrifying. *To leave her to her own devices for my birthday party might not be the wisest choice.*

"I'm sure she would, but you would need to supervise her decision-making," I explained.

Hassan smirked. "Now, where is the fun in that?"

I shook my head, smiling back. "Why don't you have her put together a birthday party for *you*, and depending on how that goes, then we can approach the topic of her coordinating *my* birthday party."

Hassan held his hands behind his back now, his face in deep consideration of my proposal. He let out a long sigh and nodded his head. "That's fair," he concluded.

"When is your birthday?"

"April 17th."

"And how old are you?" I asked him the same questions he had asked me, realizing they had never come up before.

"Twenty-three."

Damien was two years younger than me. "So there is a five-year age difference between you and Damien?"

He nodded. "And seven between myself and Freira."

"Did you and Damien get along growing up?"

"He left when he was so young; we didn't have a lot to argue about when we got together because we never saw each other. I'm sure you two argued more than he and I ever have," Hassan winked.

"He is like a brother to me." I smiled, thinking of sweet, pestering Damien. I missed him, and I missed Risa. The reminder of Damien and Risa made me anxious to see them — to ensure they were safe. "Do you think they're okay?" I asked.

"I do, and in a few days, you'll see I am right," Hassan promised.

Hassan's confidence was a relief, but it still didn't entirely erase my fears.

I gave a half-hearted smile. "I can only hope their travels have been less life-threatening than our own."

"I don't think we need to be worried; trouble doesn't seem to be drawn to them the same way it seems to be drawn to you." Hassan intended his comment as humor, but I couldn't stop myself from faltering in my footsteps.

"What do you mean by that?"

Hassan's strides halted as well, his forehead creasing as he hurriedly tried to get back to our original mood. "I don't mean to offend you, Allene, and I don't mind it either. It's just. . . ever since I've met you, the number of deadly situations you and I have found ourselves in is more than most people likely ever experience." Hassan tried to laugh at the end to lighten the tension.

My eyebrows raised, and my head slowly nodded as I absorbed his stark observation. Hassan was right. Since his arrival in my life, Hassan had been a personal witness to three life-threatening situations. Each had been centered on me, and they all had occurred in less than a year. Not to mention the unfortunate death of my father right before he met me. *I really do attract misfortune. Was it just bad luck, or was it a result of poor decisions on my part? Or possibly both?*

I felt my feet continue in stride with Hassan's, but the silence remained as I pondered his statement a little longer.

"So I am a walking storm of destruction," I stated, accepting the conclusion of my bad luck and circumstances.

Hassan nervously chuckled. "Not a storm. . . more like an occasional flurry."

Our conversation dissipated after that, all three of us in thought and concentration as we continued our journey to Gelva.

~

*I*t didn't take long for the terrain to change. The mountains we had been approaching didn't seem very large until we arrived at the mouth of the canyon. The mountain had a steep slope, with a dirt and pine needle trail leading to a rockier terrain further up the mountain. I tried to see how far the path led, to see if there was any sign of the kingdom of Gelva, but the trees were thick, and the path blended into the landscape. The walk would now be a climb, the leisurely part of our journey clearly at its end.

Hassan paused and took out the sheet of paper that had Till's directions. He turned in circles as he continued to look up from the paper and back down to confirm what he was seeing. He nodded and mumbled a few times, Killian and I waiting for the go-ahead.

"This is it. Till said the trail to Gelva is relatively unchallenging. Keep a watchful eye for the fork in the trail. Till's instructions say we shouldn't come to it for about a day, but I would hate to miss it. Ready?" Hassan looked at Killian and me for approval to continue.

"Lead the way, soldier," I encouraged with as much enthusiasm as I could, trying not to let the towering mountain seem like a daunting, dreadful task.

Hassan smirked. "Yes, your majesty."

"You know not to call me that." I glared in his direction as he started walking on the new trail.

Hassan chuckled. "You started it by calling me soldier," he shot back.

I was asking for it.

We were quiet for a while, following the same formation as we had all the other days of travel. Hassan led the way, I followed behind, and Killian stayed at the back, ensuring we weren't being followed.

The trail had a slight incline, but nothing exhausting yet. I could see that as we progressed, the route would likely get narrower and take more time to navigate. I enjoyed the leisurely pace the current smooth path offered, falling behind Hassan a ways as I attempted to enjoy the thick forest scenery, smells, and sounds.

The leaves rustled loudly in movement as the wind whistled through the branches. Hawks soared above, proudly seeking attention with their calls.

"What's wrong with 'your majesty'?" Killian had caught up to me, his voice merely a whisper against the strength of the rushing wind.

I felt my brow furrow in suspicion of his question. Now he wants to talk?

My initial reaction left me wanting to make a snarky comment, but I couldn't manage to get out the words. I kept my eyes straight ahead, not trying to seem bothered by his sudden attempt to strike up a conversation — no matter how much it irritated me.

"I'm not fond of titles," I replied shortly.

Killian followed closer, the edge of his sleeve catching the palm of my hand as he brushed by to stand side by side. With wonderment in his eyes, he pressed further.

"Why not?"

I caught my breath as his stare continued to burn through me. I debated if I would reply with another short answer, but Killian's beguiling eyes forced a genuine reply.

"I suppose it felt like more of an insult than an honor. The way people treated me, looking the way I do. . . they were obligated to say it, but it was apparent how much they loathed me as their princess."

"So you do not like being referred to as princess or majesty?"

"Not by my true friends."

"And Hassan is a true friend?"

"Yes," I replied earnestly. Hassan and Damien were some of the most genuine friends I had been fortunate enough to find.

"Just a friend?" he interrogated.

I slowed down my pace, scoffing at his childish attempt to ask me about my relationship with Hassan.

"Yes," I said dryly, not feeding into his attempts of making something of it.

"Hmm," Killian mumbled, considering my reply. He was quiet for a few moments before continuing his thought. "Don't tell him I said this, but Hassan is a good man. He's loyal, nauseatingly kind, handsome, an honorable soldier, rooted in a wholesome family, and decently intelligent." Killian smirked at his compliments laced with condescension before getting to his point. "By description, he is the perfect option for any woman, and the man has his sights set on you. So why is he just your friend?"

Killian was sincere in his question. I looked onward to Hassan, who mercilessly carried on, intently focused on any obstacles ahead and leading us safely to Gelva — oblivious to the conversation unfolding behind him.

Killian was right, and he was right about every single attribute that Hassan possessed. His question brought forth the clarity I had been searching for. The same question I had battled with again and again, finally finding its answer. I finally understood why I could never feel the way I thought I should feel for Hassan.

"Perfection doesn't necessarily equate to joy," I quietly gave my answer.

"That's not the opinion of most people," Killian countered.

"And it's a shame it isn't. My life has hardly been the definition of perfection, but it has had its moments of immeasurable joy in some of its messiest moments. That's enough to convince me I don't need perfection to be happy or fulfilled."

Killian chuckled. "You are teaching me new things every day, princess."

I scoffed, wholly flabbergasted that he had deliberately chosen to ignore me once again. "Princess. . ." I said the word sharply, allowing my displeasure to cut through.

Killian's arm swung in front of me, holding me back, his fervor clear as his eyes nearly pleaded for me to listen to him. "An exceptional woman deserves to be referred to by her most respected title. Being called princess doesn't hold resentment or offense when said by others — it holds an element of power and respect that you are only barely learning to yield. Once you have it mastered, you may even have me bowing at the knee." His last sentence was a whisper, and the admiration I could feel as his eyes locked with mine left me feeling weak.

His arm fell back to his side, and he patiently waited for me to find the ability to continue walking, his gesture indicating he wasn't expecting a response. But I did want to respond — I wanted to scream. I wanted to demand an answer for the antagonizing back and forth compliments that left me feeling admired and incomplete as I tried to process what he was trying to achieve.

I found the desire not to seem stunned enough to force my legs to move and keep myself quiet.

I focused on Hassan, nearly a shadow ahead of us. I focused on the rhythmic sounds of all of our footsteps, letting them fill the void of silence as we journeyed on. I found myself wishing I would've kept up with Hassan's fast pace, that I wouldn't have allowed opportunities for Killian to approach me in the first place. Part of me wished I would have given him the cold shoulder, while another part of me knew it was imprudent to want for something I couldn't have stopped.

Leaving Valteria, I had been frustrated and confused enough by my conflicting feelings for Aleron and Hassan. I told myself I would give Hassan an equal chance. I had prayed for clarity, and I had gotten an answer, yet it was anything but straightforward. I should've been happy. I wasn't confused anymore. I knew Killian was truly who I wanted to take a chance on — but it was terrifying.

I was intimidated by the changes that had taken place in just a few short days. I was liberated by knowing where my heart was being pulled, and I was horrified of the backlash I would receive, of the stupidity it would be considered of me if I let myself admit it to anyone else.

Was I ready for more harsh judgment? Was I prepared to have the people I respected most likely assume me to be insane? Was I ready to stand firm in my choices and live with the consequences — the good and the bad? Was I willing to risk so much for just a chance there really was something between Killian and me? Or was I satisfying a curiosity?

It was difficult for me to understand. With Aleron, everything, from the very start, was romantic and beautiful. With Hassan, everything was genuine and simple. My feelings towards Aleron and Hassan were reliable; they had been consistent.

With Killian, my feelings towards him transcended from vexatious to enticing, from loathful to tender, and the waves of different and opposite emotions only seemed to get more drastic and substantial with time. It was a dangerously taunting trap to be caught in because as more time went on, the less likely I'd be able to escape it.

I wished I had a confidant I could talk to. I yearned to see Ezra, Noni, or Sonora. People that cared about me but also people that were open-minded and honest with me. I didn't know what I needed; advice, support, or possibly a lecture.

I stroked the ruby ring on my finger, gripping it tightly as I held back tears. *I need my father. He would know what to say, and he would know what I should do.* My heart had ached every day since his passing, but in that moment, it felt like his funeral all over again. It left the deepest, agonizing feeling in the pit of my stomach.

Why did you have to leave me? Why couldn't you have held on a little longer? Valteria needs you — I need you. No one understood me better than you — except maybe one person.

Killian saw parts of me I kept hidden from even myself. He forced me to see things and feel things differently than I ever had before.

What does that mean? Does it even matter? Valteria should be my focus. My first priority is my kingdom and its safety, not some complicated feelings for an egocentric enemy prince. So why isn't that my focus? Why can't I get Killian, Hassan, Aleron — all of them, out of my head?

I had a lot of feelings and thoughts to sort out. Thankfully, although our traveling didn't allow me to talk to anyone that could help me, it did at least give me time, and silence, to try and figure them out. *Father — God — anyone. Help me.*

CHAPTER 23

Morning came too soon. The frigid air made for restless sleep, and my eyelids fought to stay closed as the sun began to rise.

After a long, tiring day, we had taken shelter underneath another grove of pine trees — their abundance proving to be an excellent resource for temporary camps.

Hassan tried to start more random conversations as we walked yesterday, but he quickly caught on to my heavy mood. He was respectful and comfortable giving me space, and he soon realized chit-chat wasn't the best choice, which led to a remarkably silent day.

Killian had also given me space, staying even further behind than usual. I needed a day like yesterday, a day to self-reflect, but it had been emotionally exhausting.

I took in a deep breath, letting the scent of the pine pierce my aching lungs. After breathing in cold air all night, walking more than I had ever walked, and nearly drowning days prior, the air left a deep burning sensation in my chest.

I stretched out my arms, trying to release the rigidity in my back muscles. With my body aching, my hair flat and ratted, my head pounding from the previous long day, my clothes striped with dirt, the two nights of sleeping on the forest floor were evident.

I could hear Hassan humming, his mood much cheerier than mine. I groaned in reply, my body not ready to move and my mind not prepared to think. I could hear Hassan laugh.

"Rise and shine, sleepyhead!" he exclaimed. *Someone must've slept well.*

I rubbed my eyes and stretched some more — listening to Hassan's humming a little longer. My stomach soon reminded me I was hungry, and the motivation to move finally came with it.

Shaking out my shoulders and my sluggish mood, I sat up and grabbed three peaches at the bottom of my bag. I stepped out from under the tree to face a grinning and still humming Hassan. I couldn't help but smile back, my mood immediately shifting.

"I have peaches," I offered, waving one in my hand and tossing it at Hassan.

"My favorite," he replied, smoothly catching the ripe peach and immediately taking a bite.

I looked around the rest of the clearing, ready to deliver the second peach to Killian and to set aside the tensions of yesterday, but there was no sign of anyone else.

"Where is Killian?" I asked.

Hassan hesitated to reply to me, his humming coming to a halt. I crossed my arms, trying not to jump to conclusions while I waited for an answer. "Hassan, where is Killian?" This time, my question was more of a demand for information, and Hassan finally complied, but not without wrinkling his nose in dissatisfaction first.

"He's gone," he said shortly.

"Where did he go?" I asked the question with the assumption Hassan would have the answer, but I was quickly disappointed.

"I don't know how long he's been gone or where he went. He was keeping the second watch, and he wasn't here when I woke up."

I tried not to show my worry and frustration. *Hassan doesn't seem concerned, and I'm sure he has a plan.*

"What do we do?" I implored.

"We continue to Gelva," Hassan replied so matter-of-factly that I felt I shouldn't even question his decision — but a stronger part of my concern pushed through.

"What if he comes back?" I protested.

"What if he does?" Hassan derided as he took another casual bite of his peach.

"We can't leave him, Hassan; what if something happened and he needs our help?"

"Like he would wait and help us? No, Allene, he left without waking either of us. If he wanted us to know where he was going, he would have said so," Hassan said firmly.

"He wouldn't leave; there has to be an explanation," I argued.

"What has you so convinced?" Hassan seemed irritated now as he gripped the soft peach in his strong hand, bruising the skin.

"We have an agreement," I reminded him.

"I don't believe an agreement with your mother is enough to keep Killian loyal," Hassan scoffed.

"Maybe not, but we need Killian as much as he needs us."

"Are you truly surprised he would leave? He prefers doing things on his own."

My mind felt flustered as I tried to counter with a solid argument. "If he wanted to leave, he had far better opportunities than in the middle of nowhere on the way to Gelva," I contended.

"You mean at the spring . . ." Hassan's words trailed off as he caught on to my meaning right away. He shook his head. "I wasn't going to ask, seeing as you were pretty upset yesterday, but since you brought it up, what happened at the spring? Did Killian follow you?"

I could sense Hassan's defensiveness as he drew his conclusions of the other day's events, assuming my troubled mood yesterday was tied to my experience at the spring. *I wish it had been tied to that.*

I shook my head, wanting to dissipate any preconceived notions he had. "I went to wash up, and Killian was already in the water —"

Hassan threw his hands up, his body almost immediately shaking. "Wait — you were *washing*, he *knew* you were there, and he *approached* you?" Hassan practically growled as his following words rushed from his lips. "I already loathed the man, but now you have truly given me no reason to wait for him or show him even an ounce of civility! What indecent person preys on an unsuspecting woman like that?" Hassan questioned.

"It didn't happen like that; it was an accident," I insisted, trying to calm him down.

"How are you so sure?" he shot back, his face turning a light shade of red.

"The same way I was sure that when Aleron found you lying in my bed, that your intentions behind the scene weren't ill-intended," I proclaimed.

Hassan's shoulders stiffened, my reply clearly hitting a nerve. He took another large bite out of his peach, swiftly cleaning it to the pit and tossing the remains into the dirt.

I swung my bag around and placed the two peaches back in the bag. I took a few steps towards Hassan, trying to bridge the growing gap between us, hoping he would believe me. I chose my next words cautiously.

"If Killian hadn't been at the spring, I wouldn't have made it back alive, and we *both* know that," I softly said as I approached, stopping a few strides away to give him space.

Hassan was unwavering as he silently accepted the facts. He folded his arms and stood firm. I could feel his discontent, and I was uncertain of how to make it better. Even if I was right, it didn't mean he had to accept it.

I sighed. "You don't have to stay, Hassan. I already told you this isn't your battle to fight."

Hassan's eyebrows furrowed, his forehead creasing as he stared at me with hopeless eyes, his anger slipping away into frustration. "I want to be here; I want to help, but I can only protect you if you are willing to listen to me, Allene. I found it ridiculous enough that I had to lecture you about Aleron. I never, in my most untethered imagination, thought I would have to lecture you about Killian."

Hassan's words stung. The exact scenarios I feared and fretted over yesterday were unfolding, and they were just as awful as I thought they would be. The more I defended Killian, the more credibility I was losing with those I cared about and the more I was losing their trust.

The reminder of our previous conversations — or lectures as Hassan referred to them — left me voiceless. The feeling of embarrassment from my time in the Praserian prison, with Hassan, committed at my side, filled my heart with shame. The reminder pained me with conflicting thought processes.

As much as I knew Hassan's opinions held merit, I found myself fighting with the thought that they may have been rooted in jealousy. Or maybe I told myself that to justify disregarding Hassan's advice, again.

Was I such a horrible judge of character that I had to be warned against my own thoughts and feelings? Or were my ideas of others, specifically Praserian's, not as radical as my Valterian friends and family tried to claim? Was I too trusting? Too willing to give others the benefit of the doubt? Did I senselessly search for ways to connect with others — even people that I should never attempt to connect with? People like Aleron; people like Killian.

On the other hand, did I just have a different point of view? My Praserian blood — my upbringing in a kingdom full of people that loathed what my appearance represented — did it bring an empathy inside of me that I wouldn't have otherwise had? Did my experience growing up in Valteria, looking like a Prasesrian, change how I regarded others?

Valterians, even those of my dearest friends, seemed to view everything in black and white. *Once an enemy, always an enemy.* I've had Valterian's *and* Praserian's attempt to take my life. It was only two days ago one of my people tried to kill me, and it was only two days ago more of my people helped me. It was only months ago I was in a Praserian prison from the actions of Killian, and it was only yesterday I could sympathize with who he was. Things change. Good and bad people exist in every kingdom. How could we so easily place labels of one kingdom being good and one being evil?

When I reflected on Praseria, I thought of friends. When I thought of Valteria, I thought of family. Both kingdoms held a positive place in my heart. Maybe that was why I felt so confused.

Each kingdom, each people, as fond as I was for both — they each wanted me to choose between them. They wanted me to see things in black and white. However, my entire life had been grey, every bit of it, and the grey only became worse when my father passed.

If finding my identity, desires, aspirations, opinions, and values can only be achieved by seeing things in two colors, I fear I will never know myself.

"Are you talking about me behind my back, Durand?" Killian's voice traveled through the trees, exposing his hiding place a few feet behind Hassan. Killian's entrance grabbed back my attention, the weight of our conversation still hanging in the air.

Killian's tunic was untucked, and his velvet jacket was open and loose. His curls clung tightly to his head. As disgruntled as his appearance may have seemed, there was no trace of dirt and sap to be found on his olive-colored face.

Hassan's hands were clenched into fists at the sight of Killian, his rage swiftly returning at Killian's smug entrance. "Where were you?" Hassan interrogated right away, holding himself back as he allowed Killian to explain.

Killian obstructed a smile, his eyebrows raised at Hassan's reaction. "I didn't realize I had to report to you my every move," Killian contested.

"You do if you don't want to get left behind," Hassan confirmed.

Killian stood at the edge of the clearing, rocking back and forth on his heels as he considered Hassan's warning. "Well, I'd thank you for waiting, but I think it should be you thanking me. If you had left before my return, you would have missed some precious information regarding our travels," Killian teased.

"You tend always to have valuable information at the most convenient times, Killian," Hassan hissed, his patience growing thin as he seemed to debate just how much longer he would allow Killian to speak before punching him.

Killian made eye contact with me and hid from Hassan the wink he sent my way. "I'm resourceful," he stated simply.

Hassan began to charge Killian, the pestering bending his patience. "You're a shady, deceitful —" I reached out and grabbed Hassan's left hand, pulling him back as best I could.

"Hassan, please! Fighting isn't going to get us anywhere. Let him speak," I spoke up this time, attempting to end their continuous back and forth. Hassan's lips pursued together as if hearing my request left an awful taste in his mouth.

Killian paused, inviting Hassan to act against my plea. Hassan remained quiet, his lips shifting into a hardline as he turned his face away from both Killian and me, his eyes set on the forest.

"You have five seconds to get to your point," Hassan warned.

Killian gave me a pleased stare. I was uncertain if it was pleasure from Hassan's reaction, delight in sharing his news, or both. "You can't go to Gelva," Killian said in his most composed manner, likely with the intent of not alarming Hassan or me.

"I should have known you would say something completely useless. We were assigned to go to Gelva, so we are going to Gelva," Hassan insisted, turning around to face Killian.

"I should have been more clear. I'm going to Gelva —
you and Allene are going straight to Cenan," Killian
stated.

"Splitting up defeats the purpose of the plan to have
both a Praserian and Valterian royal present for validation," Hassan replied.

"Aleron will be in Cenan; you'll have him to represent
Praseria," Killian countered.

I shook my head, just as confused and irritated as
Hassan now. "I don't understand. You said you had valuable information, but it sounds more like you've just
made an executive decision to leave," I pointed out. "What
aren't you telling us?" I pressed.

Killian paused. I could sense his hesitation as he
looked between Hassan and me. His expression was difficult to read, leaving my stomach in knots.

"I left this morning to see if anyone had followed us. I
came across another camp about two miles from here;
the fire had just been put out. I assumed it was from the
Red Crows in Selvet until I caught sight of the same
group of men that attacked me on my way to Valteria,"
Killian announced.

My stomach became sick. "You saw them?" I asked.

Killian nodded. "In the distance — they were headed
in the direction of Gelva."

"How do you know it was the same group of men?"
Hassan queried.

"Trust me, their faces are seared into my memory,"
Killian assured him.

"Either way, they aren't with us, and I am not going to

take a chance that they are working with the Red Crows. If they are headed in the direction of Gelva, they could ambush us on the way." Hassan voiced his thoughts out loud, working through the possible scenarios, Killian not being his primary focus anymore at the news of the Red Crows so close by.

"To keep Allene safe, you both need to go straight to Cenan," Killian confirmed.

I was angry as Killian excluded me from the chance to discuss our choices, even if his commands had come from a place of concern. "If it's not safe for me to go to Gelva, then why is it any safer for you?" I asked, attempting to hide the concern in my voice.

"I never said it was safe for me to go."

"So you plan to go off alone and follow them? Do I need to remind you that you barely got away the first time?" I challenged him and hoped he would see my point of view.

"I will have the element of surprise on my side; they won't beat me again," Killian said confidently.

"Or they will, and you won't have anyone to help you," I countered.

Killian's face hardened with sadness as he looked back at me, disregarding Hassan completely.

"Those men took my mother, Allene. I left her once, and I *won't* do it again."

My heart was pounding as I sympathized with his pain. There was a chance that Queen Eveline could still be alive, but things could also have taken a turn for the worst. I never thought I would see things this way, but at least I knew what was coming when my father had passed; at least I had some time to process it. The thought of not knowing what had happened to my father or not realizing our last moment when it had happened would be crushing.

I understood why he was doing what he was doing, but it didn't make it hurt any less.

This time, the roles were reversed. Killian turned his back to us, choosing not to indulge in any further conversation.

This time, he walked away.

CHAPTER 24

"Allene, if the Red Crows are that close, we have to move," Hassan's words were soft as if he didn't want to frighten me. I remained still, Killian's exit leaving me quiet as I processed my thoughts.

Hassan placed his hand on my shoulder, trying to get me to turn towards him, but my feet were firmly planted to the ground, my eyes still set on the trees Killian had passed through before disappearing out of sight.

My heart was heavy, my mind was spinning, and I knew what I had to do. I couldn't let Killian walk away.

I squeezed Hassan's hand that rested on my shoulder and turned to him with the same desperate expression I had given him in Praseria. He knew it right away, and his lips turned down at the corners.

"Don't say it," he pleaded.

"I need to talk to him. I can't let him make a martyr of himself," I exclaimed.

Hassan shook his head and took in a deep breath before responding.

"A stubborn personality like Killian's won't have his mind changed, not by anyone. Trust me, Allene, I have had enough experience trying to change your headstrong decisions to know how this will go."

"But even knowing the outcome, does it stop you from trying?" I asked. I didn't take offense to Hassan's comment, I knew I was strong-willed, and I also knew I was running out of time.

Hassan's shoulders sank slightly, his face expressionless. He let out a long sigh as he walked over to a nearby rock and sat down. He placed his hands on his knees and let his head fall towards his chest. He looked up at me, his lips in a hard line and his eyes filled with defeat.

"Not yet, but I don't know if I can say that for much longer," Hassan whispered.

His confession left its usual accompanying guilt in my heart. I understood his abandonment for hope, and I knew how difficult I had been — difficult for him to follow, understand, and stand by. I hated hurting him, but as much as it pained me to see the despair in his eyes, I realized it may have been what we needed to achieve what we should've been all along. I couldn't bring myself to love Hassan, but I could be his devoted, unwavering friend, and hope it would be enough to keep him in my life.

"I will wait here, but remember every minute you spend talking to him is a minute the Red Crows have a chance to find us," Hassan warned.

"I understand," I whispered. *My gratitude for Hassan's understanding and patience is nearly incomparable.*

With Hassan's warning and passive permission, I turned in Killian's direction and ran.

I tried to stay soft on my feet and avoid rustling branches as I caught up to Killian. I focused on the ground, navigating quickly over rocks or tree limbs that threatened my uninterrupted speed. I wasn't sure what I would say or how I would convince Killian to stay, but I couldn't let him go to Gelva without a fight.

I took a brief second to look up from the ground to see my surroundings, just in time to spot Killian in the distance.

"Killian!" I barely whispered, but the forest was quiet and still, a whisper being loud enough to notice.

"Allene?" Killian turned in surprise, followed by alarm. Killian came rushing towards me, getting to me faster than I anticipated. Without another word, he gripped my arm and pulled me off the trail.

Killian was rushing, his pace nearly making me trip over the large stumps that had fallen on the forest floor. I slightly protested with a huff, and Killian immediately shushed me, grasping me tighter as he tried to help me move faster. *He is angry I followed him. Hassan was right; I shouldn't have thought I could change his mind.*

If Killian hadn't wanted me to follow, there was no reason for me to stay any longer. This time, I used my other hand to remove my arm from his grip. Killian stopped, shocked as I turned back.

Insistent, Killian grabbed my wrist immediately and

pulled me to the side, placing us in front of a large oak tree, the trunk of the tree enough to hide us both from the path. His closeness trapped me against the tree, his breathing shallow as he quietly looked around us, waiting to catch sight of movement or sounds that didn't come.

"Are you trying to get yourself killed?" Killian hissed under narrowed eyes.

I shook my wrist free from his hand and failed at containing my annoyance. "I'm trying to stop *you* from getting killed, you narcissistic fool!" I shoved against Killian's chest, trying to move him out of my way. This time Killian caught both my hands in his and pinned them to my sides.

"Will you please stop trying to run," Killian huffed.

I growled in frustration. "You clearly didn't want me to follow you or to hear my opinion, so why won't you let me go?"

Killian finally released me. He took a few steps back, the worry on his face clear to me now. "That isn't true. I value your opinion, but I value your safety and the safety of my mother more."

Killian's explanation showed his fear and his uncertainty. He wanted to fix everything, but he knew as well as I that this wasn't the right way.

"Killian, we will help retrieve your mother, but you cannot do it alone."

Killian shook his head. "I have more of a chance on my own. The more people with me, the more people I have to worry about, and the more likely we will get caught. I can't have any distractions."

"Hassan is a trained soldier — he's an asset, not a burden," I argued.

Killian was quiet, his arms folded as he looked at me with sorrowful eyes, allowing his silence to answer for him.

"I see. . . you are referring to me. *I'm* the distraction," I whispered.

"It's nothing personal," Killian assured me.

"Of course it isn't — if it were, you wouldn't go," I spat back.

"You're right. I wouldn't."

Killian's reply stunned me. My acute response didn't shake him; his reply was instant and showed a desire to stay, which was enough for me not to give in to his persistence. I decided to try another argument.

"The smart decision is to wait. I will send for members of the Valterian army, and they will extract your mother. There is a reason we have been working together; defeating the Red Crows isn't a one-person job," I explained.

Killian shook his head again in disagreement. "If I wait, I may not ever find those men again. This may be my only chance to mend things with my family — to fix my mistakes." Killian's words were fast and passionate, his objective clear.

"And that is honorable, but you will be no help to your family if you are dead." It felt harsh to say, but I had never held back my genuine opinions from Killian before, and I wasn't going to start now.

Killian laughed, his mood shifting as he stared back at

me. "You really do have such little confidence in me, don't you? I did kill three grown men and defended you, remember? While shirtless, I might add."

"I do; you're a walking reminder of it." I pointed to the cut on his chin that was only barely starting to heal, undermining his arrogant comment.

Killian scoffed, my reaction not what he was hoping for, but I wasn't going to agree that he got the better of them. There was no reason to tempt fate by putting himself in that situation again deliberately, but Killiam still didn't seem convinced.

Killian stepped closer to me, his pale blue eyes locked on mine. "Allene, for once in my life, I am attempting to do the selfless thing."

"No, you are doing the *reckless* thing," I countered back, resisting his attempt to intimidate me into submission.

"Is that such a surprise to you?" Killian threw his arms out in frustration. "Being reckless is part of who I am, Allene!" Killian's eyes were like fire as he held himself back from saying more, his rigid and serrated features adding to the intimidation he was trying to convey.

Killian's outburst left me stunned. I wasn't afraid of Killian — I was afraid of what assumptions he had made about what I wanted from him. *After all our conversations, did he truly assume I thought the worst of him?*

Killian's eyes were tightly closed, his fists clenched. The ease of his ability to captivate was one to envy. Even in pain and frustration, his distinct, sharp features were enticing. I found myself struggling against the distractions Killian was leaving in my thoughts. It was nearly impossible to look away from him. *I need to remain focused.*

I knew I was running out of time and that Hassan was waiting for us — I couldn't continue with back and forth conversation. There had to be a way to soften Killian's determination, a way to break through his hard exterior.

My mind raced as I thought about the last few days and the moments Killian had let me in. Dancing, dressing his wound, the spring. . . they all had one thing in common. Touch. All those moments, Killian let me touch him. I had seen him become defensive when I touched his scars, when I first attempted to help with his wound, and then a barrier broke as he let me *feel* him. Those were the moments I got through.

Going against every muscle in my body that was yelling how terrible of an idea it was, I swallowed my hesitation, moved forward, and placed my right hand on Killian's warm cheek. I was ready to give him one last chance to see things my way.

Killian's eyes opened, his hands finally soft at his sides. He placed his hand on top of mine.

I was ready for the rejection, prepared for him to peel my hand away, but instead, Killian pressed his hand firmly into mine, his cheek even closer to my hand than before. A short smile came to his pink lips, his perfect teeth gleaming as he shared aloud his thoughts.

"Have you ever thought how things may have been different if you had met me first?" Killian asked the question quietly, his voice deep and soothing, as if our previous conversation had never happened, but I wasn't going to oppose the shift in our conversation.

"Different in what way?" I dared to ask.

Killian's smile faded, his doubt settling in. He released my hand and stepped away, the gesture leaving me anxious. Killian turned his back to me, unable to look at me as he spoke.

"I apologize; I shouldn't have asked such a question." Killian went quiet, his body rigid.

"I see you changing the subject, pushing me away to deflect from what you're feeling. Killian, I only have the strength to ask you this one more time. *Why won't you let me in?*" My breathing became shallow as my pleading words hung in the air, waiting for his reply. I couldn't ignore the door he had just opened.

Killian didn't move; his body still turned away from me. Killian ran his fingers through his loose curls, his face turned to the side, his hands holding his neck, almost to stop himself from completely turning around to face me, creating a barrier between us.

"I can't let you in until I know you want from me the same thing I want from you — and I don't think that can ever be." Killian's tone was different from any conversation we had — he spoke like we had missed an opportunity that had never even been offered. Yet, his words left me desperate to understand.

"We won't know unless you tell me what you want — until we actually have that conversation," I pressed for him to say more.

Killian expressed what had been holding him back,

but there were still words left unsaid. I didn't think my words would make an impact, they hadn't before, but to my shock, Killian finally gave in.

Killian's hand released from his neck as he turned around to face me, accepting my invitation for him to say what he wanted to say.

Killian slowly walked in my direction, his steely eyes fixated on mine. As he approached me, I found myself creating distance, stepping back until I hit the tree. I felt my hands grip the trunk, uncertain what to expect and even more uncertain of why, for the first time in days, I was now afraid to be near him.

I found myself holding my breath as he got closer, trying to block his enticing scent. His eyes were amorous as if he saw right through my unease. He stopped inches away from me, his relaxed hands clasped behind his back as he watched me shift under his fervent stare.

"You, Allene. I want *you*." Killian's voice was a bold whisper, sending chills up my neck. The fear I had felt was immediately replaced with anxiety. I was hardly able to process his words. Killian's eyes filled with distress, his voice now filled with dejection as he continued. "Now you have your answer, but what was the point of me admitting that? You won't ever be ready to fully give in to me."

Was he right? Was there no point in all of this? Was it just a way to distract my heart, as Killian had claimed before? A curiosity? Was this me being careless and tempted by something I shouldn't have? Did I want this? To open my heart and life to one that nearly destroyed it?

I knew it didn't make sense. I knew I thought what I had experienced with Aleron was love. What I was feeling with Killian was entirely different.

What if love was more complex than I thought? How would I ever know if I didn't allow myself to learn from my own experience? Would I be able to live with the question of what could have been?

Giving in to Killian could be a disaster, but I also knew it could be glorious, and that was a risk — a possibility — that I was willing to take.

Killian valued independence more than anyone. The hypocrisy of him placing words into my mouth, claiming I wouldn't ever be ready, was infuriating.

I stared back at the vast blue eyes that waited for my reply, that waited for me to walk away. My hands still gripped the tree, my arms leaning against it for support as I stayed firmly in place.

"I am capable of making my own decisions. I thought out of everyone you would support that," I rebutted.

Killian sighed, my response taking him a few steps back. "I do — for every aspect of your life I do — except when it comes to me."

I wasn't going to let him keep pushing me away. I removed myself from the comfort of the tree, closing the distance between us once again. Killian cautiously stared back at me, his eyes fierce and his jaw slack.

"In Veruje, you asked me if I would feel ashamed to be with you. I didn't have an answer for you then."

"I don't expect you to have an answer now."

"But I do. I feel a lot of different emotions when I

think about being with you, but being ashamed is not one of them."

Killian's eyes shut tightly, his face turning to the side as his jaw clenched. "Don't you see I can barely control myself when I am with you? You saying these things, you are only making it worse. I'm *trying* to protect you," he insisted.

"From what?"

"From *me*."

"You don't need to hold back with me."

Killian's expression was stern and certain. "Yes, I do."

"Why?" I exclaimed in frustration.

"Because I'm not Aleron!"

"I never asked you to be," I reminded him.

"You didn't have to. You fell in love with him." Killian's tone was bitter, like the words were hard for him to say out loud, but they were even more challenging for me to hear.

I felt my face go pale, and my lips set into a stubborn frown as he turned the focus of our conversation on Aleron once again. However, as hard it was, I reflected on Killian's insecurities.

"What if there is more than one type of love?" I asked, hoping Killian would give me the validation I needed to identify my conflicting feelings and thoughts.

Killian seemed distant as he studied my question. He knew what I was implying. I didn't deny the love I had for Aleron, but I didn't see another way to articulate that my feelings for Killian, although radically different, were also real.

Killian let out a short laugh, but his face was solemn. "I know you could feel a different love for Aleron than you would for me — that's not what I fear. I fear which one is more powerful than the other — I fear which one you will find everlasting. Aleron and I, we are complete opposites, Allene." Killian's voice was low and despondent. His words made me feel like I had become more of a risk to him in this scenario than he would become to me.

"I know that," I assured him, trying to shake the feeling of criminality that had washed over me.

Killian's eyebrows furrowed, his lips parted in exasperation, and his lashes nearly hid his eyes. "I don't think you do. How could you love Aleron — *perfect* Aleron — and have even a fraction of love for me? Do you know how different I am?" Killian's voice was full of doubt.

"I do," I replied quickly and with more certainty in my voice than I expected.

"Then you know how terrible of an idea this is." This time, there was a slight edge in Killian's voice as if he was afraid to hear my answer.

"I do, but I don't care," I assured him once again.

"How could you say you don't care? I care, Allene — for the first time in a long time, I care! I care about doing right by you. I will not ruin you! I can't have that on my conscience."

Killian paused and looked at me, waiting for my counterargument. I remained silent, choosing not to fuel the conversation in the direction he was trying to go. He wasn't going to change my mind, even if he was trying to play the chivalry card.

Killian sighed, folding his arms across his chest. "I can assure you that I won't meet your expectations." Killian's eyes narrowed, waiting for me to falter in my persistence from his threat. I didn't.

"I'm not expecting anything," I said firmly.

Killian stepped forward, his figure towering over me as he tried to take control.

"I won't change for you, Allene," he promised in a deep whisper, his tone trying to frighten me.

"I don't want you to change."

Killian's eyes narrowed, his determination to dissuade me from my opinion growing stronger. "Do I actually have to *list* the reasons why I am entirely wrong for you? I'm impetuous; I'm outspoken, I'm arrogant, I'm offensive, I'm selfish, I'm rude, I have a terrible reputation —"

"You're unfriendly, you're an antagonist, you hold back your feelings, you lash out, and you drive me insane most of the time, including right now!" I spoke loudly over him, putting an end to his rant.

Killian's eyes shifted, now looking at the ground in uncomfortable silence. I had given him what he wanted, recognition of his flaws, but he didn't seem to understand that my choice was being made *because* of who he was and *how* he made me feel.

I reached out to grasp his hand, interlocking our fingers. I could feel his eyes trying to avoid catching mine. Instead, he studied our hands, confusion sweeping across his sharp, beautiful face.

I patiently waited in silence, procrastinating speaking until he would look at me. Killian shifted, his lips pursed together as he met my eyes. I tried not to let him distract me as I found the words I needed to say.

"I know who you are, Killian, and I know what I'm getting into. Despite the long list of things you *think* should deter me, I know that there is a longer list that keeps me here. I care for you, Killian," I swallowed, trying to gain the courage to continue as I now displaced my eyes to study the ground, too afraid to see the reaction on his face.

I felt myself trembling as I gained the strength to meet Killian's eyes that stared down at me with suspicious awe. I took in a deep breath, composing my next words. "I know we both feel this draw towards one another, and I know the thought of leaving these feelings between us untouched — undiscovered — will drive me absolutely mad." I bite my lip, my body slightly shaking as I let out a deep sigh, my confession now out in the open.

Killian looked through me, his face reflecting his apprehension. I felt humiliated and nervous as I desperately waited for Killian's reaction.

Killian placed his other hand under my chin, his finger brushing my bottom lip as he forced me to look up at him. I felt my heart racing as he stroked my chin, his fierce eyes fixated on intently studying my face. I felt my stomach twisting as I prepared for the worst.

"Well, since we both have made quite a long list of all the reasons I am abundantly wrong for you, I feel I should disclose one more character flaw of mine that you neglected to mention," Killian's voice was deep and taunting. His stare and warm touch made me uneasy, but I didn't want to move, and neither did Killian. He patiently waited for me to take the bait.

"It doesn't matter what you add; it won't change my mind," I declared with determination in my voice.

Killian smiled. "I wasn't planning on it."

"What is it?" I hesitated to say the words, terrified to hear his answer.

Killian's face shone with radical satisfaction, his eyes fastened to mine as he leaned in closer, his velvet-smooth voice answering in a penetrating whisper. "I'm not a gentleman."

Killian pressed his warm lips to mine, his eagerness clear as he cupped my face in both his hands, his intensity still managing to be soft as he kissed me again and again.

A weightless sensation traveled through my body. My head was spinning; the only thing keeping me standing was Killian's firm hold that had now traveled to my neck, his grip pulling me closer to him as his lips moved so effortlessly with mine.

My mind was telling me to stop — to not fully give in to him too soon, but the yearning I had suppressed for Killian was begging to be released — his earnestness inviting me to let go. I tried to control myself, to hold back, but the euphoria Killian had placed me in was intoxicating.

I managed to separate our lips long enough to catch a breath — Killian's scent only adding to his compulsive hold over me. The short pause didn't faze Killian, his lips flashing a brief smile as he placed his hands on my rib cage and used it as an opportunity to press me against the tree. I could hardly process his movements as he continued to kiss me, his lips moving faster and fiercer with every second. I gasped as his hands clenched tighter around my torso — as if he was restraining himself from moving them any further.

My hands were flat against his chest, the openness of his shirt revealing his hot skin underneath that tingled against my fingertips. Killian seemed to be calculating what I would do next, but he was always one step ahead of me — surprising me as I tried to keep up with his intensity.

Whatever passion Killian had stirred in me was more uninhibiting than I could've imagined. It was penetrating, all-encompassing, and magnificently dangerous.

This was a moment of compromise that I had desired and longed for but hadn't foreseen. Killian had let me in, and I had given in.

Killian wasn't holding back, his touch, his lips, not ready to let me go. Without much thought, I twisted Killian's shirt in my hands and pulled him closer to me — this time, surprising both of us. Killian let out a low growl as his teeth tugged at my bottom lip, clearly delighted at the surprise. My hands released the fabric of his shirt, slipping underneath the opening of his neckline, my fingertips digging into his smooth skin.

Killian smiled underneath my lips, his hands moving to the nap of my back and squeezing me close. His near-ness made me fear he could hear how fast my heart was beating or sense my skin that felt like it was on fire. His focus was solely on me, but thankfully he didn't seem to notice the nerves and emotions he was stirring inside of me. For a moment, it felt cruel that Killian could have such control over my sanity, yet it made me feel alive in a way I had never felt before.

My desire to be as close to him as possible left my hands twisting into his soft curls, forcing his face even closer to mine. Killian released my rib cage, allowing his hands to trace up my arms, his hands finding mine and entangling our fingers. That moment, with our bodies intertwined, sent me into oblivion, all my nerves shedding away.

Killian pinned my arms to my sides, pressing both our bodies against the tree as his lips followed the line of my jaw. I felt my body shiver as Killian's lips found their way to my neck, my labored breathing a stark comparison to how collected Killian was, and he quickly noticed.

Killian paused, a smile parting his lips that still rested on my neck. I tried to focus on my breathing, but I knew it would take more than a brief pause to recover.

Killian's lips hovered lightly on my skin, chills erupting wherever they touched. Following the length of my neck, Killian slowly kissed me, each one fainter than the one before. Killian stopped when he came to the top of my jaw, his lips now brushing against my ear, his hair tickling my neck.

Killian's velvet voice was a quiet whisper, but his words were tumultuous to my soul.

"Allene, I am giving you an escape clause. Say the

word and this between us — all of it — can stop, right now."

At that moment, I felt many things. I felt afraid. I felt alive. I felt daring. I felt foolish. I felt exhilarated. I felt free. I felt untethered. I felt consumed. *I felt new.*

I felt the strongest, addictive emotions when I was with Killian, and although I recognized it, I didn't know how to stop it. The battle of my conscience versus my heart raged on at Killian's words.

I should have listened to my conscience earlier when I had the chance. It was trying to spare me from the road of complicated hardship and pain that was beginning to unfold before me.

Deep down, I knew it was too late. My heart had won.

There was no turning back from the raging, enslaving fire that was Killian Hadway.

END OF BOOK TWO

PRONUNCIATION GUIDE

Allene Amena – Uh-leen   Uh-men-ah

Risa Amena – Rih-zuh Uh-men-ah

Laerina Davore (Amena) – La-ray-na Du-vor

Praseria – Pra-sehr-e-ah

Praserian – Pra-sehr-e-ahn

Valteria – Val-tare-e-ah

Valterian – Val-tear-e-ahn

Veruje - Ver-uje

Cenan - Ken-ahn

Gelva - Gel-va

Lokali - Low-cu-lie

Gree - Guh-ree

Hassan Durand – Haa-sihn Der-and

Damien Durand – Day-me-en Der-and

Freira Durand – Fur-ear-uh Der-and

Aleron Hadway – Al-eh-ron Had-way

Vincent Hadway – Vin-cent Had-way

Killian Hadway – Kill-e-en Had-way

Eveline Demese (Hadway) – Ev-e-lin De-mese

Nycolas - Ny-kol-s

Ezra – Ez-ruh

Noni – Non-ee

Ajax – Ay-jax

❀ Created with Vellum

ACKNOWLEDGMENTS

I want to thank Chasen Tolbert and Kendra Thomas for being major influencers for this book. They each significantly contributed by helping me work out my thought process and were both supporters when I needed it most.

I want to thank my beta readers who helped finesse my thoughts and lent me the confidence to continue this path as a self-published author.

Thank you to everyone who has supported me to this point in my author journey.

Kaydrie grew up in Mapleton, Utah and currently lives in Utah with her husband and little boy. She loves baking, traveling, all things Disney, and spending time with family and friends. She has had a love for literature since she was a little girl. Some of her fondest memories are bonding over books with her father and mother. She has been writing since she was 12 years old. Her books are creations of what she wanted to read as a teenager. These books that were once exclusively hers to enjoy are now available for the teen and young adults across the nation.